BEYOND DARKNESS

THE PERIPHERALS: BOOK FOUR

MARK ALDRICH

Wallace Street Press • Kill Devil Hills, NC

Cover Design: Chris Sorensen
Proofreading: Gretchen Douglas
Formatting: Chris Sorensen
Editing: Amy Gillespie
Author Photograph: Justin Patterson Photography

ISBN#: 979-8-9871069-3-8

Published by:

Wallace Street Press
P.O. Box 211
Kill Devil Hills, NC 27948

For the Oldsies (original and honorary), my own real-life Grumbles. For so many years, you have inspired, amused, and encouraged me. To say you play a part in these books is no exaggeration. Brady, Kristie, Kevin, Nick, Sharkey, and Stuart.
I am forever grateful.

Yes, even you, Brady.

I still think our multi-year text thread should be donated to the Smithsonian someday.

CHAPTER I

Brandy Johns glanced at the speedometer and hit the gas harder. She felt a trickle of sweat slide down the back of her neck and couldn't escape the sense of dread seeping up from the rear of the Ford Bronco as she pushed the old truck to its limit. She knew she risked being stopped by the police at this speed, but it was after midnight and Route 91 lay empty here, south of Hartford. They had been on the road over four hours already, having left Lancaster, Pennsylvania, and the Fulton Theatre just after dinner. The thinking had been that traffic would be lighter overnight. They were all theatre people, which meant they were night owls. Overnighters didn't scare them.

But as they had driven, Sullivan Nichols's condition had started to deteriorate. He'd injured his arm early in December. What had seemed a serious but straightforward gash had stubbornly refused to heal. None of the remedies they'd tried had been effective, so when their run of *A Christmas Carol* at the Fulton Theatre had come to its end, they decided to try something different.

Marcello Pettirosso, the Artistic Director of the theatre and a vastly powerful Fae, had suggested a visit to an island off the coast of

Maine. An island renowned for its healing properties. An island known as a haven for artists. And a center of Otherworldly activity. All of those things seemed to fit the bill for what they needed.

While Nick had insisted he could go alone, Brandy had shut that down quickly. In fact, all of their friends had promptly agreed with her. If Nick ran into any problems, someone should be there to lend a hand. Brandy had been the first of the group to step up. The group was known as "The Grumbles." Middle-aged character actors who found themselves regularly playing secondary roles on Broadway and stages across the country. Many of those characters were cranky, vaguely bad people. Fans had taken note and thus dubbed them "The Grumbles." They enjoyed the small amount of attention it brought them. And they were the fastest of friends.

Dan Trout, the gangly, mustachioed Montanan had insisted they take his Bronco on the trip. A very generous offer that Brandy had grudgingly accepted. He was right. The space to stretch out had seemed like a good idea given the long night ahead.

At the mention of an artists' island, their friend Jasten "Noodle" Roberts, a fine actor who had also become the preeminent Broadway illustrator and painter, jumped at the chance to ride shotgun. Extra eyes and hands were a good thing, and his curiosity was piqued by the rumor of an island that attracted artists from around the world. And so, Noodle joined the trek.

Next to jump into the Bronco had been their friend Bayard. Bayard was not a Grumble. He was, in fact, what they called a Peripheral. The Peripherals were creatures from another plane. In Celtic lands they would be called the Tuatha De Danaan. However, the Grumbles quickly found that Peripherals were found in cultures and lands across the globe and came with their own unique powers and politics. Bayard had become a friend over the last few months. He was compact, wiry, with long chestnut hair. Standing barely five and a half feet, his appearance belied his great strength and agility. His greatest gift, though, was the ability to communicate with all creatures of the world. He often would choose the company of animals over humans. Until he had met the Grumbles. And where Bayard went, his faithful companion, Cinder, went. Cinder was a highly endangered red wolf, whom they had encountered on one of their adventures. This time in the Outer Banks of North Carolina. She was one of only a handful of red wolves in the wild, so had not taken to the road lightly. But she had found a heart-friend in Bayard and now never left his side. Bayard argued, successfully, that they would need a Peripheral with them to help ease the entry into the mystical side of the island. He was right, and the friends all admitted it.

The last occupant of the Bronco was, incredibly, perhaps the most unique. Next to Nick, in the back of the Bronco with the seats folded down, lay an enormous unconscious Scotsman. Tim McCloud. They knew little of McCloud. He was a Peripheral, and had come to help them, at the behest of Pettirosso. McCloud was a powerful and rare Peripheral, a Timestrider, gifted with the ability to move through time as easily as others moved through the world. But McCloud had been felled by a curse from Hide-Behinds, some of the decidedly evil Peripherals they had encountered. He had lain unconscious for weeks, and as he was the only one of his kind, they had been at a loss as to how to heal him. The island to the north could be his best and only hope. And so, into the Bronco he went.

They had learned, much to their dismay, that the Otherworld, the Faerie Realm, whatever anyone chose to label it, had begun to splinter. Their friend and fellow Grumble, Sean Curley turned out to possess great powers, and the ability to unlock them in those around him. Power that came from their art. Their singing, writing, painting, creating. It harkened back to a time long ago, before mankind had drifted from the natural world around it. When storytelling, and the mystery of music, carried more weight and strength than technology and equations. Together the Grumbles had become formidable with their newfound strength. And that made them a threat to any Peripherals who harbored ill will for humankind.

The remaining two Grumbles had not been at the Fulton with them. Stewart Garland had remained in New York while the others performed in Lancaster. Garland had become a star on the ascent in the Big Apple, and his blend of gentle optimism and goodwill, had begun a trend toward goodness and decency that the Grumbles all agreed had been sorely lacking recently. Garland was on his way to becoming a superstar.

The final Grumble was the most problematic. Ken O'Carroll had found himself on the wrong side of a number of their recent encounters with the Otherworld. He'd been possessed and manipulated, in the process alienating his friends and sending his own career tumbling. That had all changed when he selflessly chose to remain trapped in the past when they had gone to retrieve Sean from the 1960s where he had been stashed for his own protection. With Ken lost in the past, McCloud was the only hope to bring Ken home to the present. The McCloud that lay cursed and unconscious next to Nick.

The Bronco thundered though the night, Bayard perched in the back tending to Nick as best he could. Cinder curled on the floor at his feet, whimpering and nudging Nick's motionless foot. Brandy drove, often recklessly, sensing the creeping infection in Nick as if it were pursuing her from the rear of the truck. With each moan from Nick, Brandy tried to coax more out of the old Bronco. Noodle sat in the passenger seat, his normally jovial mien creased with concern as he monitored the GPS for any changes in traffic that could slow them down.

Things were complicated. And perilous. And getting worse.

"So," Noodle said, half turning to Brandy, "Eight and a half hours all told, according to the GPS. You sure you're good to do the whole thing? I'm happy to drive."

"Look," Brandy answered, "I appreciate it. Really. But Nick is one of my closest friends and I feel helpless right now. If driving is the only thing I can do to help, let me. Trust me, you do not want me in the passenger seat right now. I'd drive you nuts."

"Okay, if you say so. I'll check in again when we stop to gas up, just to be sure."

Brandy shot him a brief smile. "Right. Thanks."

The Bronco rumbled on toward Hartford. They'd been on the move for a few hours and the sense of urgency continued to build. Brandy tried to even her breathing. Still a long way to go. She brushed a stray hair out her eyes and focused her attention on the road stretching out in front of them.

"Just over six hours to go," Brandy announced loud enough for Bayard to hear all the way in back. "We can do this. Hang in there, Nick. You, too, McCloud!"

"I wonder if he can hear us," Noodle mused.

"No clue," Brandy said. "But, hey. Can't hurt. You know, I think we're going to be okay. The highway is mostly empty this time of night. We should be there by six in the morning."

"Yup," Noodle agreed. "We've got this."

Bayard called from the back, "I have faith!"

At that moment, the January sky decided to throw a snow squall of whiteout conditions at them. Brandy cursed, gripped the steering wheel tighter, settled herself deeper into the luxury seat, and leaned forward to get a better line of sight. In the rearview mirror, she saw a tractor trailer shimmy slightly in its lane before starting a slow slide that left it traveling sideways along the interstate before disappearing down an embankment.

"No, no, no," Brandy chanted. "No time for this." She redoubled her focus, and the big Bronco carved a path through the flying snow as Bayard peered out the rear window and said a quiet prayer for the driver of the truck.

Sean Curley and Dan Trout had seen the others off in Dan's Bronco before loading their things into Sean's Subaru Crosstrek. It all fit. Barely. They had chosen to make a stop in New York to unload and decide what came next.

Two of their Peripheral friends were in peril. Kallan, a Scottish Fae and fierce warrior, had been captured by the Otherworld denizens who had arrayed themselves against Sean, the Grumbles, and mankind as a whole. Not all Peripherals had made that choice. Some had chosen to ally themselves with humans after avoiding them for eons. Kallan had been one of those they considered friendly. Despite his considerable prowess, he had been captured, while on a parlay, by Balor, the leader of the opposing forces and a godlike being long thought dead. But he was certainly not dead when he appeared on Prince Street in front of the Fulton Theatre, surrounded by his minions. And one of those minions had been dragging a catatonic Kallan along behind the horde.

It was the second Peripheral that posed a more problematic, and emotional, predicament. Breena had been carried into the fray along with Kallan, but her situation was less clear. She came from a royal Fae family and had been caught in a power struggle where her hand in marriage had been promised to another powerful family in the Otherworld. This, despite it being known that she and Sean had developed feelings for each other. Or perhaps *because* of those feelings. She had appeared lucid when Balor presented her. And this raised the question of whether she was being held against her will or if she had somehow fallen in with the enemies of the human she had professed to love. She had been conspicuously missing from the entire series of events at the Fulton. In fact, the only time "she" had been seen was when a Naga shapeshifter had taken her form and tried to change the course of events.

So, which was it? Was Breena friend or foe? Sean, naturally, refused to accept that she could have turned against him and planned to travel to the Otherworld to rescue her. That plan hit a snag when Nick's wound refused to heal, and what had been a full group effort found the Grumbles going in two different directions. At least for now.

Trout folded his considerably lengthy frame into the front passenger seat of the car and turned to Sean.

"I dig the new ride," he drawled, his enormous drooping moustache twitching with each syllable. "I'm used to being a little higher off the ground, but I like this. Feels solid."

Sean turned to Trout, and despite his words, he was unable to hide the concern in his eyes. "Dan, I appreciate it. All of this. Loaning your Bronco. Sticking with me. I know you have things that are important to you, too. Eleanor is still waiting in North Carolina. You're a real one, Trout. Thank you doesn't even begin to cover it."

Trout, at the mention of Eleanor's name, turned to look out the windshield. "Yeah, I need to get there to see her. Never thought it would be this long before I got back to the Outer Banks. But at least I know she's safe there. Let's take care of this business and then I can relax. Last thing I want to do is drag all this mess down to her doorstep where she's trapped."

Eleanor was none other than Eleanor Dare, one of the first European settlers in North America who had been adopted by a Native tribe centuries ago and became one of their powerful conjurors, shapeshifters and holders of tribal wisdom and history. But she had been cursed to remain forever in the Outer Banks or lose her claim to immortality and the powers she had acquired throughout the years.

To say true love did not run smoothly for Sean and Trout was an understatement. But nothing in their lives had been smooth since the day, only months earlier, when they had first discovered that Sean possessed great power. Power that his friends shared to some extent. Power that threatened the balance between the Otherworld and this one. An Otherworld they had been blissfully ignorant of until recent events. Despite Sean's attempts to simply disappear, his very existence was a threat to too many. They had pursued him, and he finally came to accept that there was no going back to his old life. He would confront those who hated him. Because they feared him. He had no choice.

"Right," Trout said quietly. "What's the play? Find one of the portals we've seen and drop into the Fae world? Do we even know how to do that? Or where to go?"

Sean paused a moment as he pulled out of the parking garage and turned left onto Prince Street and the road home.

"I don't think the regular portals are going to work this time. Too many of the Others will be watching. That portal back in the Fulton's basement is under more guard now than Fort Knox. We'll have to find another way."

"What about the portal we found in the woods at the ghost town? Buffalo City in North Carolina?" Trout asked, a tinge of excitement creeping into his voice. Eleanor was there. Near that portal.

Sean turned a sympathetic glance to Trout. "I'm sorry," he said, gently shaking his head, his ginger hair sweeping low over his eyes. He still had a longish Victorian-style haircut from the just-completed show. "I know that would solve a lot of issues, but I just don't think the portals are safe. The one in Buffalo City was discovered by the Others even before Bayard stumbled onto it."

"You're right," Trout acceded. "I know you are. Worth a try, though. So, what's it to be?"

"That's a very good question," Sean answered. "Wish Bayard were here with us. We need someone who knows their way around the other side."

"It would help," Trout agreed, "but he needed to be with Nick. They'll need the help of a Peripheral. You know, I still feel like maybe we should have gone with them. Take care of Nick and then tackle this next bit together, you know?"

Sean's blue eyes almost seemed to grow colder as he peered out the window. "No," he said, with no room for misunderstanding. "Nick needs help now. But so does Breena. And Kallan, of course. The longer we wait, the more time that Balor guy has to prepare. We have to do this as soon as possible."

"You're probably right," Trout said quietly. "I'll jump on my phone and see if I can dig anything up. Would be great if we could go north for this. Maybe check in on Nick and the others on our way."

"That would be fine, but it's not our priority," Sean declared. "We go where we need to go. And I doubt we'll find what we need in an online search."

The Crosstrek was pulling out of Lancaster and headed into farm country and Trout turned awkwardly in his seat to glance back and bid the city farewell. A lot had happened there. Too much.

Next to him, Sean sent out a quiet call to any Peripherals nearby. As his powers had grown, he found himself more in tune with them. Able to sense them more easily. Communicate with them. But his call went unanswered, and the car continued on its way, the two men lost in their own, very different, thoughts.

Brandy had been white-knuckling the drive since the snow began falling. It stuck with them through the rest of Connecticut and into Massachusetts. The snow began to taper off as they passed Sturbridge and took Route 495 around Boston and toward New Hampshire. Even late at night, the highway was busy, and even with the weather improving, Brandy remained tense.

Just before they passed Haverhill, Bayard called quietly to Brandy and Noodle in the front seat. "Friends, I think something is happening with McCloud."

Noodle turned to look toward the rear of the Bronco and was surprised to see the massive Scotsman trying to sit up. His eyes were still closed, and he didn't speak, but he was most definitely struggling to sit.

"Holy cripes," Noodle said. "He's right. McCloud is trying to sit up! This is the first sign of life from him since we found him laid out back at the theatre."

Brandy, glancing at the rearview mirror, saw the large man's head rising into her field of view. "Oh wow," she muttered. "Okay, good news/bad news situation. Good news? Glad he's showing signs of coming around. Bad news? There's not enough room for him to sit up back there. *And* he's blocking my view out the back and I really kind of need to see what's happening back there."

"Understood," Bayard replied, as he quietly coaxed McCloud back down. "He's already sliding back into whatever state he's been in. Not sure what just happened."

"Yeah, me either," Brandy said. "I'm going to take it as a good sign. It's been a while since we've had one of those. Hey, any change with Nick?"

Bayard turned to their other fallen friend and took his measure.

"Sadly, no," Bayard reported. "If anything, he seems more feverish. Agitated. Even more than he has been."

"I knew it was too much to ask for," Brandy said, with a shake of her head.

"Hey," Noodle said, staring out his window, "we just passed Salem. I didn't think we were near there. Maybe some of the witch folk there can help us?"

"Wrong Salem," Brandy answered. "That was Salem, New Hampshire. The one in Massachusetts is southeast of here. Near the coast. We'd have to pass through 'Lynn, Lynn, the city of sin' to get there."

"My sister's middle name is Lynn," Noodle mused, still looking out the window.

"I'm more inclined to follow the advice we got from Pettirosso anyway," Brandy noted. "He says we should go to this island. We should go."

"Yeah, you're right," Noodle agreed. "Did not know there were two Salems. Learn something new every day."

In the back seat, Bayard noticed that McCloud had settled back into his previous senseless state and Nick's angry fever seemed to slack off just a bit. He glanced out the rear window and watched the sign for the Salem exit slip away and out of sight, his gaze lingering on it and a curious look crossed his face, unseen by the others.

Brandy finally began to relax as they merged onto the interstate north and entered New Hampshire. The traffic eased. The towns began growing farther apart. The sky cleared.

"Glad to be clear of all that mess back there," she said to no one on particular.

"We're about three hours out of New Harbor," Noodle announced, his face lit by the glow of his cellphone's screen. "My offer to drive still stands." He shot a look to Brandy.

"Nah, I'm good, buddy," she said. "I've come this far, might as well push through. I will have to stop for gas, though." She glanced at the gauge. "Oh, yeah. Definitely will."

"Map says there's a rest stop just into Maine. Can we make it that far?" Noodle asked.

"We can and we will," Brandy said.

Bayard, still lost in thought in the back seat, noticed movement just ahead of the truck on the shoulder of the highway.

"Is that—?" he started.

Brandy and Noodle followed his eyes and both gasped when they saw what had caught his attention.

"Is that a dog?" Noodle asked, eyes fixed on a large grey canine standing perfectly still and seeming to stare directly into the Bronco and at them as they passed.

"That is definitely not a dog," Brandy said confidently. "Coyote. Gotta be. Big one, though. I'd say wolf, but I know for a fact there are none in this neck of the woods. What say you, Bayard? You're the expert."

Bayard remained silent and tracked the canine as they passed, and he noted that it slipped silently into the trees by the road after they were clear of it. Cinder had gotten to her feet and had seen, also. She pressed her nose into Bayard's hand and let out a tentative whuff.

"I know, girl," he said quietly. "I'm thinking the same thing."

Twenty minutes later, they cruised past Portsmouth as the city was beginning to rouse itself, and then crossed the bridge into Maine.

"That snow slowed us down a bit," Noodle noted. "Our revised

ETA for New Harbor is eight a.m. Let's call it eight thirty with a gas and comfort stop."

"Comfort stop?" Brandy scoffed. "When did Miss Manners get in the truck? Gas up and hit the head, is that what you mean?"

Noodle laughed. "Yes, fine. Bathroom break. Potty time. Whatever you want."

"That's more like it," Brandy chuckled, as they passed a sign declaring "Maine. The Way Life Should Be."

"Good God, I hope so," Brandy said, touching a hand to the ceiling for good luck. "I really hope so."

Sean and Trout had been on the road for less than an hour. They had been silent nearly the entire time. Sean seemed entirely focused on getting back to New York. To their apartments to regroup and plan the next moves. Trout sat awkwardly in the passenger seat. Not just because he was tall and barely fit. He felt awkward because Sean seemed...different, somehow. For the first time, conversation didn't flow easily, and silence seemed the wiser option. At least for now.

Trout had been staring at his phone's screen for the entire drive. Hoping to find something that would offer some hope and maybe lighten the burden Sean was carrying. He leaned closer to the iPhone, squinting. He huffed a "huh" into the cabin and sat up straighter in the seat. No easy feat. For his part, Sean made no sign that he noticed Trout's exclamation.

"So, listen, Sean," Trout said, tentatively. "You said no go for the portals, and that makes total sense to me. We need something different. So, I might have found something?"

"Okay, great," Sean replied, never taking his eyes from the road. "Don't keep it to yourself. What is it?"

"Well, it's two things actually. There's an area called the Bridgewater Triangle in Massachusetts. Lots of weird activity. Ghosts,

UFOs, Bigfoot sightings. Goes back a long time, too. Just sounded a little like Camp Hero and Montauk to me. Maybe something near there?"

"I don't know, Trout," Sean said, still focused on the highway ahead of them. "That's all pretty vague. I mean, maybe? But it would take a lot of research. I don't mean to shoot you down, but I think it's going to take something more precise. Does that make sense?"

"Yeah, it does," Trout answered. "It was just a thought. Grasping at straws here."

"What's the other thing? You said there were two."

"The other one...I don't know," Trout stammered. "It's probably even less likely than the first. There's a place I found called 'America's Stonehenge.' Also in Massachusetts. But from what I can find it seems to be a tourist attraction. An older one, at that. I mean, I have friends that are Massholes, and no one's ever said anything about it."

"Did you just call the state's population assholes?"

"No, no, no," Trout insisted. "Massholes. Just a funny thing they call themselves."

"Okaaaay," Sean said, but his attention diverted from the road ahead for just a moment. "We'll come back to that later. Unimportant. Tell me more about this Stonehenge place."

"Well, not a lot to tell. It's over four thousand years old. That much is certain. No one seems to know who built it. Indigenous peoples or European migrants. Stone chambers, meeting places. Huh. Wild. It's actually an accurate astronomical calendar. You can even predict solar and lunar events with it. It used to be called Mystery Hill Caves. Didn't the Tuatha retreat underground? Might be something to that. Oh, wow. They've found inscriptions throughout. Phoenician. Ogham! That's nuts. Isn't that the ancient Irish language? Drawn symbols?"

"It sure is," Sean said, his voice rising with the first sign of excitement since they'd started out. "I'm pulling into this Turkey Hill. We could use some gas, and I want to read up on this place."

"And they have delicious iced tea," Trout noted.

Sean actually laughed. "They do have delicious iced tea," he agreed. "I'll get the gas; you grab some drinks, and I'll pull up out front to meet you. Deal?"

"Deal," Trout agreed. He climbed out of the Subaru as Sean started to pump the gas. The entire feel of the trip had shifted when Trout had brought up the archaeological site. His steps were lighter as he entered the store.

Five minutes later, Trout climbed back into the car to find Sean engrossed in his phone screen.

"Trout," Sean said, turning a brilliant smile toward his passenger. "You may be a genius. This could be exactly the place we're looking for. I can't explain it, but something feels...right about this. Would you mind horribly if we skipped New York and went straight there? Everything just feels—I don't know—urgent."

"Hell, no," the Montanan answered. "I'm already packed. No need to go back, unpack, repack, and lose a few days. Let's do it."

"Thanks. Really."

"Hey, don't get all shmoopy on me," Trout chuckled. "This gets us closer to Nick and McCloud. I'm worried about them. And I can't help thinking that big Highlander still has a part to play in this. Plus, you know, I wouldn't mind getting my truck back."

"I hear you, Dan," Sean said. "I do. Let's take it one step at a time, though. Yeah? First, let's see if this is the back door into the Otherworld we need."

"Fine," Trout agreed. Something on his phone caught his attention. "Don't go declaring me a genius just yet. I was wrong. It's not in Massachusetts. It's just over the border in New Hampshire."

"Whatever," Sean said. "Just tell me what to put in the GPS."

"Right. Should take about five and a half hours from here. We'll get there in the middle of the night."

Sean nodded. "True, but maybe that's for the best. Fewer people around."

"Okay then. We're going to Salem. New Hampshire. Not the more famous one in Massachusetts."

Sean entered the town into the maps app and backed out of the parking space.

"Salem, here we come," he announced.

Unknown to either of them, they began to trace nearly the same path as the others had taken not long before.

CHAPTER 2

After a stop at the first rest area in Maine, Brandy had driven through the night without another stop. The roads were empty, and the bitter cold of early January mercifully remained free of snow. The big truck roared up Route 95, the only witnesses seeming to be the odd families of deer scouring the shoulders of the roadway for anything edible that wasn't frozen solid. Their heads raised as the Bronco cruised past, but quickly returned to their foraging, satisfied that there was no threat.

While Brandy hunched forward in the driver's seat, pinching herself on the neck from time to time if she felt the slightest bit groggy, Noodle kept his face pressed to the frigid window on his side. He cupped his hands around his eyes to block the cabin lights and his breath fogged the glass in front of him. His eyes were pointed toward the sky, and every few moments he would let loose a small cry of wonder. Finally, Brandy couldn't contain her irritation.

"Hey, Noodle," she barked, "what gives? I'm trying to concentrate over here."

Noodle turned to her, his eyes wide. "Whoops," he said, "I didn't realize I was making sounds. I just haven't seen a sky like this for so long. It's breathtaking. Reminds me of my home back in Oregon. I'll try to keep it to myself."

Brandy took a breath and shot a quick glance to the passenger seat. "Nah," she answered, "don't hold it in. It's nice. I'm just wired tight right now and a little tired. It's good you're noticing it. I shouldn't be so cranky."

From the back seat, Bayard leaned forward putting his face between the front seats. "You know," he said, "Noodle did offer to drive. And, frankly, I don't understand how you people live in that massive concrete monstrosity of a city. New York. You have no idea what it cost all of our kind to walk those streets with you. The noise. The dirt. Entirely devoid of natural connection. It baffles us. Let Noodle have his joy."

"Hey, I just admitted I was wrong," Brandy protested, "and you're absolutely right. We give up a lot to live there. It's good to be reminded of that sometimes. If for no other reason than to make sure our reasons are good. Please, have at it, Noods. Stargaze all you want."

"Thanks," Noodle said, "I'll try not to annoy." He cupped his hands to the window again and stared skyward. "But maybe we can come up with a better nickname than that?"

After a moment's reflection, Brandy erupted in a true belly laugh. "I see your point," she chortled. "We'll just stick with 'Noodle' for now."

From the back seat Bayard could be heard trying to hold back his laughter. Even Cinder, let out a light chuff in response.

"Yeah, yeah," Brandy feigned outrage while grinning. "Enough piling on the driver. ETA to New Harbor is now eight thirty. If it's like other working waterfronts I've been around, they should be in full swing. We'll need to find someone to take us out to the island. Someone who won't ask too many questions about us having a couple of unconscious passengers. Any thoughts on that are greatly appreciated."

Noodle nodded his head and dragged his eyes from the skyscape above.

"On it," he replied, pulling his phone out of the center console. Before tapping the screen awake, he was distracted by the sight of a massive globe rotating in the glass lobby of a building just off the highway. He punched quickly onto his phone's keyboard. "I guess we're in Yarmouth. That's Eartha. The world's largest revolving globe. Cool. Okay, will find us a boat to charter now." His eyes reluctantly left the globe and slid back to his screen.

"Maybe we can stop and see it on the way back down," Brandy said. "If you're a good boy. And we all survive."

"I'd like that," Noodle answered, scrolling on his phone. "Especially the surviving part."

The sun broke over the horizon minutes later and Noodle sat up higher in his seat, mouth open at the stark beauty around him. So different from the mid-Atlantic topography of Lancaster. Even in the deep recesses of the January winter, with the trees a skeletal shade of their summertime verdancy, the landscape seemed beautiful in its austerity. The sky seemed bluer, largely free of the air pollution that blanketed the lower coast, so thick in the air that most who lived there had long since ceased to notice the unnatural haze that hovered over them. The shoulders of the highway showed the remains of a recent snowfall, but the pavement was clear, and the dawn seemed to give Brandy a renewed energy and she, too, sat taller in her seat. Even Bayard and Cinder took note, the red wolf pressing her nose to the cold window glass and allowing her tongue to loll sideways in a smile.

They traveled north through the town of Brunswick, through Cook's Corner, then Bath, and eventually into the village of Wiscasset, with a welcome sign proclaiming it "The Prettiest Village in Maine."

As the road narrowed and the speed limit dropped to twenty-five, the Bronco slowed to a crawl as it snaked through the hamlet.

Brandy noted a small red shack to their left as they approached the bridge out of town.

"Red's Eats," she said. "Even I've heard of that place. Supposed to be the best lobster rolls in Maine."

"That's a pretty big statement," Noodle replied. "Where'd you hear that?"

"Don't even remember. Probably the Travel Channel. Something like that."

"I hate to be a downer," Noodle said, craning his neck to watch the red shack slip past them. "If it's on national TV, it's almost certainly not the best. Gotta ask a local. They know the real spots to hit."

"Well, we don't have time for that," Brandy pointed out. "Add it to the list for the trip home."

Bayard poked his head between the front seats again. "Is this lobster roll as good as pizza?"

"Pizza?" Noodle turned to face the Peripheral.

"Yeah," Brandy said. "He's got a thing for pizza. Hate to tell you, pal, but you won't find good pizza in Maine. Just not their thing up here. Tell you what, when we have a chance, I'll set you up with a lobster roll and you can decide for yourself. Deal?"

"Deal!" Bayard agreed, enthusiastically. "Although I have to say, my people don't generally think to eat lobster. Bottom dweller, after all."

"Necessity is the mother of invention," Brandy said. "Early settlers here felt the same way, but when food is scarce, you make do. So—lobster it was."

"Fair enough," Bayard answered. "Terribly disappointing about the pizza, though. I thought you could get it everywhere."

"Oh, you can," Noodle said. "But *good* pizza is a different ballgame."

"You just got lucky trying it for the first time in New York," Brandy chimed in. "That's about as good as it gets."

"Probably need to get ourselves focused," Noodle said. "A half hour to New Harbor. I couldn't pin down a boat for us, but I'm thinking we'll be able to hire someone at the docks."

"I took the liberty of sending a text when we stopped for gas," Brandy admitted. "I know one guy down south who charters sometimes. He should be awake by now. Can you check my phone to see if he responded? I would but—safe driving and all that, you know."

Noodle retrieved Brandy's phone from the center console and swiped open the home screen.

"You really should have a passcode or something," Noodle noted. "Anyone can get into your info this way."

"Eh. Nothing all that interesting in there. And definitely nothing worth stealing. This way I can have friends lend a hand. Like when I need them to see if I have a text." She raised her eyebrows to Noodle.

"Message received. But with all the fancy stuff in the Bronco, you should just sync your phone to the sound system. Okay, off my soapbox," Noodle said with a chuckle as he checked the phone messages. "And yes, you do have something. From someone named Grier?"

"That's the one," Brandy said, tapping her hands on the steering wheel. "Give it to me. Can he help?

Noodle paused, reading the text message. "As a matter of fact, he can. He knows someone in Pemaquid, which is apparently not too far, and has arranged for him to meet us. Said to look for a boat called the *Acheron*."

"The *Acheron*?" Bayard appeared between the seats again. "That is a sign. Must be. Acheron was a River God before being transformed into the river leading to the Underworld."

"The Underworld?" Noodle squeaked in response. "That doesn't sound good at all."

"Not necessarily," Bayard said, pausing for a moment. "It's Sean, not us, that's seeking a way to the Otherworld. Tir Na Nog. Faerie Realm. Underworld. Call it what you will. This is different, but certainly significant. The Acheron is not a dire place. In fact, many consider it to be a river of cleansing and healing and wiping away of past wrongs. Given that, I choose to think of it as a good omen for us."

"Well, when you put it that way"—Brandy sighed—"I'll take it as good sign, too."

"Wise to call on Grier," Bayard said, squeezing Brandy's shoulder from the back seat.

"Who's this Grier?" Noodle asked. "Don't think I've heard you mention him."

"One of the best guys you could ever meet," Brandy replied. "World traveler. Waterman. Solid as a rock. Someone you never have to doubt. Lives down south now. Outer Banks. But he's been everywhere."

"Great," said Noodle. "I'll take your word for it."

"How are our patients doing?" Brandy shot back to Bayard.

Bayard scanned the bed in the rear of the truck. "No change," he replied. "McCloud is just kinda there. Nick looks the worse for wear, but he's calmed down from that fever."

"Okay, friends," Brandy said, flipping a switch on the dashboard. "Time to turn off this seat massager, wake up, and get these two some help."

"Hold on"—Noodle shot a dagger of a look at Brandy—"there are seat massagers?"

"Oh, yeah," Brandy said with a grimace. "Did I not tell you that? Well, just think how amazing the drive back south is going to be."

"Yeah, yeah," Noodle grumbled. "Whatever. This Grier says to park by Shaw's seafood restaurant. He called ahead and cleared it with the folks there. His pal with the *Acheron* should be nearby."

Twenty minutes later, the Bronco slowed and signaled a right turn into a parking lot.

"Got it. That's Shaw's there, so here we go," Brandy said, turning right into a parking lot and bringing the Bronco to a stop as close to the docks as she could.

The harbor in front of them was a hive of activity. Docks were crowded with lobster traps, piled high on top of each other. Working boats crisscrossed the waters in front of them. A sign announcing Hardy's Boat Tours sat just to the left of the restaurant, seeming to indicate some relationship between the two.

Brandy stretched her arms and hopped down out of the truck.

"Bayard, want to come on down with me and find this boat? Noodle, do you mind hanging here just for a sec? Don't want to leave those two alone in the back, know what I mean?"

"Not a problem," Noodle agreed. "If you leave the engine running, we can keep the heat on. Keep them comfy."

"And you can check out the seat massager, right?" Brandy smirked at Noodle.

"Perish the thought," Noodle protested. "Although, now that you mention it, it would probably be in everyone's best interest if I were relaxed and ready to go, yeah?"

Brandy shook her head. "Whatever, *Noods*. Just don't fall asleep. We'll be right back."

Brandy and Bayard headed down dockside. New Harbor stretched in front of them, and it was so picturesque that it looked like a Hollywood soundstage version of a Maine fishing village. To the right, Brandy saw a hand painted sign declaring that particular dock for "Commercial Fishermen Only." She turned left away from that dock and immediately saw an attractive boat docked and idling. A green hull below with white above and painted in black on the stern, the name *Acheron*.

Sitting aft and considering them was a compact but athletic-looking man with dark blond hair, tousled by the breeze, gleaming blue eyes that blazed with intelligence, and an open, friendly face that broke into a contagious grin as he rose and climbed onto the dock, walking toward them. He was dressed simply in faded jeans, a blue knit sweater underneath a warm and waterproof jacket.

Approaching, the man thrust a hand out as he neared Brandy.

"You must be Brandy?" he asked. "Pleasure to meet you. Glad Grier reached me. Happy to lend a hand. I'm Andy. Andy Plummer."

"Well, any friend of Grier's is a friend of ours," Brandy said, shaking the proffered hand. "Really appreciate you doing this. And this fella here is Bayard." She gestured to the Peripheral who had held back during the introductions.

"Bayard," Andy nodded and held his hand out again. "Pleasure is mine."

"I assure you it's mine," Bayard replied. "You may, quite literally, be a lifesaver."

"Just helping out a friend. And some new friends," Andy said, smiling. "Oh, I hope you don't mind. I do have one other passenger headed over to Monhegan. He's a semi-regular. Shows up a couple times a year. Nice guy. Quiet. Let me introduce you."

Andy turned and jumped nimbly aboard and headed toward the bow. Bayard followed him with nearly as much alacrity while Brandy made a valiant but futile effort to keep up before eventually tumbling onto the boat. She straightened up and tried to gather her dignity as she smoothed her coat.

They approached the bow where a figure was perched, watching the harbor traffic lattice its way across the water, the rising sun filling the air with glittering diamond shards. The figure stood ramrod straight. He was wearing deep brown heavy cotton pants beneath a flowing calf-length duster jacket. He had midnight black hair tied back in plaits that reached almost to his waist.

Brandy paused briefly. Something in the set of the shoulders, the confidant regal posture seemed familiar. Before she could think of who it reminded her of, the figure turned to reveal a deeply lined face full of wisdom and secrets. Brandy's breath caught and before she could find her voice, Bayard was off like a shot, almost diving into the arms of the man before them.

"Kelphit," Bayard said quietly, enveloping the ancient wise man in an embrace.

"Let's get the others on board," Brandy said. "We have a lot to tell you."

Trout was dozing in the passenger seat while Sean pushed the Crosstrek faster than was probably wise. His weather app had shown snow squalls earlier this evening along the route from Hartford through to Massachusetts and their ultimate destination, Salem, New Hampshire, but the clouds had cleared out now and they had clear roads through Worcester, Northborough, and onto the Mass Pike. It was well after two in the morning when they turned off the highway onto Haverhill Road.

Trout roused as the car slowed and gave his eyes a good rub while shaking the cobwebs out. He looked at the silent and decidedly suburban neighborhood slipping past and cast a skeptical glance toward Sean. Checking his phone, he took another look out the window.

"Seriously?" Trout asked, indicating a street sign for Cowbell Corner to the right. "Are you sure this is right? And if it's right, maybe this whole Stonehenge thing is just a gimmick. An amusement park for archeology nuts. 'Cuz this looks all wrong for what we need."

"Well," Sean said, never taking his eyes off the road. "If this thing was built four thousand years ago, that Dunkin' wasn't here. None of this was. Just wilderness back then. Can't blame those ancient builders for what we did after they were gone."

"I guess," Trout muttered. "Doesn't feel very Otherworldly to me. That's all I'm saying."

"Let's give it a chance. We're here. Might as well make sure one way or another. And—we're here."

Sean turned right at a simple brown sign. "Welcome to America's Stonehenge." The Subaru crunched its way through the gravel parking lot, the sound echoing off the surrounding trees. In the silence of the residential area, the tires might as well have been sonic booms to Sean's ears and he was sure someone must be hearing them in the closed lot, but no lights came on. No one appeared. He quickly parked close to the front door of the visitor center and cut the engine.

An overhead light glowed halfway across the lot throwing more shadows than illumination, making the trees seem sinister. Silent watchers as the two men climbed out of the car and made their way to the front door.

Trout kept throwing looks over his shoulder, expecting a police cruiser to appear. "I'm not liking this, Sean," he said. "I don't much think I'd enjoy spending the night in a Yankee jail cell. How are ya going to explain this if someone asks? 'Oh, sorry, officer, we're just looking for a back door to the Otherworld'? 'Cuz I don't see that going over well. Strike the jail cell part. They'd put us straight into a padded room."

"Would you shut it?" Sean turned quickly to Trout. "If you're that scared, just sit in the car and wait for me. Jeez."

"Nah," Trout retorted, "I just tend to avoid breaking the law when possible."

Sean stopped and held up a hand for Trout to be quiet.

"Do you feel that?" he asked, turning to Trout.

"What?" Trout asked. "I don't feel anything."

Approaching the chalet-like structure of the visitor center, Sean cupped his eyes against the glass pane in the door and tried to see inside. The interior was dimly lit by the emergency exit signs and he strained to make out what lay within.

"Nothing," he said. "Thought I picked up on some Peripheral energy, but I'm probably just jumpy. Not much to see in here. Just the usual. Gift shop. Ticket counter. A few displays. Looks like the entrance to the grounds is through the back and that doesn't help us."

Trout joined him at the doorway and peered into the darkened building, too.

"Hey cool," he said a touch too loudly. "They have alpacas. I love alpacas."

Sean hit him sharply on the arm. "First, keep it down. Second, focus, Dan. We're not here for the petting zoo."

"Fine," Trout huffed. "But if the entrance is through the back, what are we going to do? Why don't we just come back in the morning when they open?"

"And exactly how are we going to explain to the other visitors why we're singing to the stones and hopefully finding a hidden entrance to another plane?"

"Yeah, I guess," Trout agreed. "Doesn't mean I have to like this, though, Ginge."

"Trout, I don't like it either. But remember, this is to save Breena. We can't just leave her where she is."

"And Kallan, too, right?" Trout asked, turning pointedly to Sean. "And the whole save-the-world part factors in there, too, yeah?"

"Of course!" Sean said, hands up. "Yes. All of that. It's all part of it. Let's see if there's a fence around the side we can jump. And don't get all touchy on me. We're doing good work here. Let's get to it."

Trout held back a moment as Sean stalked off to the right, scanning the enclosure that surrounded the grounds and cast a searching look at his friend. For his part, Sean moved quietly along the fence line, hands running along the planks. He looked every bit the amateur cat burglar as he disappeared around a corner and into the darkness. Trout shook his head before loping after Sean.

Sean turned a corner and nearly collided with a lamppost, positioned just outside the enclosure and craning over the fence. It was clamped along its length to the fencing, and Sean grabbed onto it and tested his weight on it. It held.

"Trout!" he whisper-shouted back into the darkness. "I found our way in. Get up here."

Trout emerged from the gloom and cast a wary look on the lamppost. "That's our way in? I haven't been ten feet off the ground since I did that gorilla musical, and I had to swing from that fake palm tree. I don't like heights. You know that."

"Look," Sean protested, pointing at the clamps along the length of the pole. "It's practically a ladder. They're begging us to go in. Don't be a baby. Give me a hand."

With a none-too-gentle push up, Sean scampered up and over the fence, landing with a sizeable thud on the other side.

His voice came wafting up and over, sounding winded. "Yeah, that ladder on your side isn't over on this side, so you'll have to lower yourself. Hopefully a little more gently than I did."

"Great," Trout said to himself. "Just great. Well, here goes nothing."

The big mountain man heaved himself up and, with significant effort, over the fence. He looked nervously behind before he began to slowly lower himself into the grounds, but there was no sign that they had been detected.

Sean was standing to the side, orienting himself in the darkened enclosure.

"Whoa," Trout said, as he got his feet under him and stood next to Sean.

"What happened?" Sean asked. "You all right? Twist something?"

"I'm fine," Trout said. "It's just...don't you notice anything in here?"

"What do you mean?" Sean replied. "I'm just trying to find the center of it all. Figure we should start there."

"That's not what I mean," Trout said, his voice quieter now. "You must really be distracted for me to notice and not you. You were right. There is some sort of Peripheral energy and it's stronger in here."

"What?" Sean barked back. "I would pick up on that before you and I got nothin'."

"That's my point, Sean. Take a breath and focus." Trout peered intently into the dark, the shapes of the standing stones now coming into sharper focus and looming over them. "We're not alone."

<hr>

It had taken quite an effort to get the two patients safely aboard the boat, especially the big Scotsman, but with it finally accomplished, they were ready to begin the voyage.

With assistance from Bayard, Andy Plummer had maneuvered his twenty-eight-foot Cutwater trawler away from the dock, pulled the bumpers in, and set a course for Monhegan Island, ten miles out in the Gulf of Maine. The water was like a sheet of glass, perfectly calm and reflecting the billowy clouds that wafted across the brilliant blue winter sky. Plummer nodded to the handful of fishing boats they passed as the *Acheron* chugged out of the harbor.

Brandy sat in the starboard bench aft, half turned to her left to take in Kelphit, seated next to her. The ancient wise man and healer had first crossed paths with Brandy and the Grumbles months earlier when he had encountered them in the woods of Montauk. It had been early in their experiences with Peripherals. Sean's powers had only just been discovered, and Kelphit proved a gentle and sage mentor and protector as the group had encountered true evil for the first time. In fact, Kelphit had been almost singularly responsible for safeguarding and ultimately healing Ken O'Carroll when he had been stricken unconscious by their foes.

Kelphit was known to be peripatetic, following a seasonal travel path that allowed him to visit various locales, offering his brand of knowledge and healing to many people and creatures. However, that schedule was known only to the healer. While technically a Peripheral, being of the Otherworld that they inhabited, Kelphit was ancient even by their standards and the Peripherals who had been there treated him with great deference. Brandy and the Grumbles had taken a cue from that, and quickly realized that they were fortunate to be in his presence.

Brandy, the wind tousling her short hair as the boat picked up speed upon exiting the harbor, squinted into the morning sun, her eyes watering in the crisp, cold, clean air. It felt good, invigorating, after the anxious drive through the night. She let the silence linger as she took in Kelphit. He seemed somehow older, which was troubling to her because he had seemed so ageless before, so outside the grip of something as pedestrian as the passage of the years. Despite his small stature, he had seemed a titan. Unflappable. Resolute. All-knowing. But here, he seemed...not diminished, but weary. And therefore, more vulnerable than she had ever imagined.

Finally, the silence grew too much, and she brushed the hair from her eyes. "Kelphit, how did you end up here? Just when we need you. Again. And if you don't mind my asking, are you okay? You seem...tired."

Kelphit turned his face from the wind and stared out over the stern, watching New Harbor slowly slip away toward the horizon. He closed his eyes, the morning sun bathing his upturned face.

"Ah, Brandy," he said. "So many questions. I remember that from you. Questions." He raised his hand as she began to apologize. "That is not a criticism. Questions bring knowledge. And on very rare occasions, wisdom. Always ask the question." He sighed. "This island, Monhegan, is a sacred place. Even to me. Perhaps especially to me. I have always journeyed here with the coming of your new year. Much as you found me in Montauk on my annual time there. I come here for many of the same reasons. To help those in need. To heal those in distress. But this place is more than that. It fills me. Restores me. I see so much. So much that no one person should have to witness. But that has ever been my lot. Eventually, though, even I find myself in need of rest. Recovery. Who heals the healers when they find themselves in need? Often, it is incumbent upon me to do exactly that for myself. Monhegan allows that and enables me to go on."

Brandy sat silently for a moment. "I'm sorry I never really thought about that. You were just...you. Wise beyond anything I could imagine. Infallible. Our savior. Protector. I never considered what *you* go through and the toll it must take. Sorry about that. You Peripherals still seem like superheroes to me. I should have known better."

"And why should you have known better?" Kelphit asked. "Why should you, having just discovered that there are realms beyond your knowledge, that those realms contain beings of great power, some who wish to befriend you and some who wish to destroy you? Why should you, while experiencing all of that and finding yourself and your friends in dire peril, why should you be expected to rise above all of that and sense vulnerability and limitations in these new beings? No, once again, no apology."

"Well, whatever," she replied. "Still feel like a jerk for not picking up on any of that. So, what is it that can make someone like you wear down? Can I help?"

Kelphit turned his eyes to her and placed a surprisingly strong hand on her shoulder. "The simple act of asking that is a help in and of itself. You should allow your friends to see this side of you more often. But thank you. Your presence is a surprising balm." He turned back toward the receding mainland. "This world, your world, that I have chosen to travel for so long, is changing. Darkness is coming. Hastened by your friend Sean and what he means to the balance of things. I'm surprised it took this long. I suspect there were others like him through the centuries who never realized their potential. Or who were prevented from doing so. Removed. Yet here we are now. And there is so much pain. So much that needs healing. You are not wrong. I am weary as I haven't been in a long time. War is coming. For such as myself, that is a great burden. It's not my first. I do wonder if it may be my last, though. Even I will dwindle and pass someday. Many thought it would have happened long ago."

"Don't even talk like that," Brandy protested, now placing her hand on Kelphit's shoulder. "You just need some time on your island. Some R & R. Look, we need you. And a lot more besides us. You're Kelphit. You don't give up."

"Kind words," he answered. "But I will never give up. Not while there is work to do. However, it is possible that I will give out. But not today."

He slapped his thighs as he rose to his feet. Now in the open water of the Gulf, there was a gentle sway to the trawler, and Kelphit adjusted his stance, accordingly, clearly having spent time on the water.

Brandy squinted up at him and then realized that the boat having settled into its course, Bayard and Noodle were making their way back to them. She rose to acknowledge them and introduce Kelphit to Noodle, whose eyes were as big as saucers while he took the ancient's hand in his own.

Bayard, too, shone with delight in the presence of Kelphit. Clearly, the wise man's presence calmed him and gave him a sense of safety. The four moved back toward the cabin, where Andy was at the wheel and their patients were stretched out on berths.

"We should have you take a look at these two," Bayard said, as he walked. "Have you ever met a Timestrider? I imagine you've seen just about everything."

Kelphit placed an arm around Bayard's shoulder, and Brandy saw Noodle lag a step behind, with a sketch pad in his hand, pencil furiously moving about the page. All three stepped lightly along the deck, Kelphit seeming to pull a cloak of positivity around himself somehow.

But Brandy could not shake a feeling of impending danger. Kelphit's words refused to leave her. *Darkness is coming...there is so much pain.* And her footsteps were not as light as the others' as she followed them into the cabin.

CHAPTER 3

Sean stood silently beside the fence of America's Stonehenge. He closed his eyes and let his perceptions flow out and around him. The shadows of the many standing stones around them fell about the two intruders, shading them with seeming disapproval at their interruption of the peaceful night.

A gentle breeze caught the fallen leaves that lay dead at their feet. They had browned with age and seemed like so many husks of scarabs from long ago as they rattled and scuttled in the wind.

Sean shook his head. He tried his best to tune out the distractions around him, but he sensed nothing and was growing frustrated. He was the sensitive one. He had the special relationship with the Peripherals. Trout had never displayed anything close to his perception.

He opened his eyes. Frustration turning to anger as he still failed to notice anything. He scanned the grounds around them. Standing stones ringed the grounds, but as he peered further into the attraction, he saw stone structures of many shapes and sizes. Dolmens, stone chambers, walls, even large flat surfaces that looked to be tables or altars of some kind. It was far larger and more intricate than he had expected.

"What *is* this place?" he whispered. "It's huge. And old. So old. How can we not have heard of this before?"

"There are a lot of mysteries in the world," Trout answered. "As we've found out lately. But yeah, seems like more people should know about this. You picking up on anything yet?"

"No," Sean answered, his irritation clear in his voice. "It's just a lot of cold, dead stone. Age, yeah. But I'm not feeling anything in here with us—" He stopped suddenly, and raised his hands, signaling for Trout to be quiet. "Wait. Yeah. There it is. How could I miss it? Something from the Otherworld, but that's all I get. Not a Peripheral. At least not one of ours. Can't tell its intentions, but it's hiding. That doesn't sit right."

"Well," Trout whispered. "Whaddaya say? Stay or go? I wouldn't mind exiting stage left and trying something else."

"Hell no," Sean said, turning a look of disbelief to Trout. "This is the best idea we've had. And if one of them is here, there's got to be a reason. I thought Montanans didn't turn tail and run."

"Easy there," Trout growled. "We don't. But we also ain't stupid, and we don't know what we're dealing with here. It's the middle of the night. We're trespassing. And something from another world is waiting somewhere in this ancient, unexplained ceremonial setup. Think it over."

"Nothing to think over," Sean shot back. "You can take off if you want. I'm gonna find out what the deal is here." And with that, he pushed forward past the first rows of encircling

stones without giving Trout a chance to respond.

"With friends like him..." Trout muttered as he pushed off from the perimeter fence and followed. "Something feels wrong. But no. Don't listen to the guy who noticed it first. Damn tenors always think they know best."

"I heard that," Sean answered from the other side of the stones.

"Good, I wanted you to," Trout replied. "If I die here, I'm coming back to haunt you."

"You may have to wait in line for that," Sean said, poking his head around the side of a particularly tall stone. "Come on!" He gave Trout a quick grin. "Where's your sense of adventure?"

"Ah, bite me, Ginge," Trout answered, trying to hide his answering smirk. "After the last few months, the last thing I need is a sense of adventure. How about a sense of calm? Of peace? Okay. Let's get a move on. Dawn waits for no man."

Together they moved inward. Peering into chambers as they passed, creeping slowly toward the epicenter.

"It's getting stronger," Trout said quietly, after examining a small and pitch-black chamber.

"I noticed that," Sean agreed. "Anything else?"

Trout paused, listening. "Not really," he answered. "I don't hear a thing."

"Exactly," Sean replied. "The further in we get, the quieter it becomes. No birds. No planes. Not even the odd car passing on the road. Total silence."

"Now that you mention it," Trout said, "feels like we're in a world of our own."

"Remember what Pettirosso warned us about. The fabric between this world and the Other is fraying. Too much back and forth. Too much energy flowing in both directions."

Trout nodded and continued into the maze of stonework. "Yeah, that's exactly what I'm worried about."

They continued on for another hundred yards, Trout gently cursing when his boots continued to stir up the floor of dead leaves, the crisp crunch of them sounding like trees falling in the silence. Sean disappeared around the corner of a low wall, clearly ancient and crumbling. Trout approached a particularly massive standing stone, placing his hands on it and leaning his head wearily on the slab.

"This place is also an astronomical calendar, apparently," Trout said, his voice bouncing loudly off the stone in front of him. "How did these people, whoever they were, know all of that? I can't even find Orion, let alone build a calendar out of rocks. And what were the fire pits for? I almost broke my ankle in that one we just passed."

"Uh, yeah," Sean answered from deeper in the warren of chambers and caves. "But you need to take a look at this."

Something in Sean's voice made Trout stand up straight and look into the gloom where he'd disappeared. He turned and headed in that direction; the crunch of the leaves underfoot forgotten as the skin on his arms goose fleshed.

"Why do I not like the sound of this?" he muttered.

Rounding a corner, he was surprised to see the jumble of stones open into a clearing. A clearing where Sean stood next to a massive table made of a slab that had to be at least four tons.

"Take a look at this," Sean said, pointing out a groove in the edge of the table that ran around the circumference. "What do you think that could be?"

Trout approached and ran his fingers through the groove, feeling its surface, worn smooth through millennia of use. "I mean, could just be a simple table. Pressing fruit, making soap, preparing food. Day-to-day stuff. That makes the most sense to me."

"Really? *That* makes sense?" Sean answered, crouching slightly to look along the stone canal more closely. "Look around you, Dan. This place screams 'ceremonial site.' I don't think anyone did anything so commonplace as preparing food in the middle of this place."

"Okay. So, what's your thought on it, then?"

"I think they performed sacrifices on it," Sean said. "I think that groove there collected blood and channeled it to"—he followed the channel to a point where it disappeared below the edge of the table —"here, where it was gathered underneath. That's what I think."

"Lovely," Trout replied. "You've taken a pretty dark turn, Ginge. Now we're talking human sacrifice?"

"I didn't say it was necessarily *human*," Sean said. Then more quietly, "But it was probably human."

At that point, the silence of the open space was shattered by a deep and rumbling voice that seemed to come at them from every side, bouncing from stone to stone and impossible to pin down.

"You don't belong here!" the voice cried. "Get out! Should not be here." It paused. "And one among you is abomination! Go! Now! While I still allow it!"

Trout turned in a circle trying to find the speaker and seeing nothing. He turned to back out of the clearing, but Sean put a hand on his arm stopping him. When Trout turned a pleading look to him, Sean turned to him with determination in his eyes and slowly shook his head. This was exactly why they had come here.

As Brandy followed Kelphit and the others into the cabin, she noticed Andy looking pointedly at the horizon, a hand over his eyes to limit the glare of the sun. His hands flew across the controls, the boat seeming to be an extension of him. Where others, even Kelphit, seemed to adjust their feet to account for being at sea, Andy was as natural as if he had been crossing a street.

"Funny," Andy said, pulling his eyes away from the water and adjusting to the darker cabin. "I haven't seen the water this calm in —actually, maybe never. It's like glass out there. Odd, but I'll take it. Should make it easier on everyone, especially these two." He nodded toward Nick and McCloud. "So, what's the deal with them? The big guy hasn't moved an inch since you brought him aboard. And that other guy looks pretty rough."

"Good questions, friend," Kelphit answered, stepping to McCloud's side. "Let me take a look and perhaps we'll get some answers."

The wise man knelt by the bunk and examined the enormous Scot, small murmurings escaping him from time to time. He opened a small pouch at his belt and removed some dried herbs from it, crushed them, and scattered them above McCloud's head on the pillow. Next, he removed a few stones, some that seemed to glitter from within. These he placed along certain points of the patient, before sitting back on his haunches and hovering his hands just inches above the massive chest of the Timestrider. He closed his eyes, deep in concentration, and the cabin fell silent around him, the only sound the gentle lapping of water on the hull.

"To answer your earlier question," Kelphit said finally, opening his eyes and glancing to Brandy, "No. I have never met a Strider before. Very few have. There is, almost always, only one alive at a time. I daresay, though, he's never met anyone like me, either."

"I have no doubt about that," Bayard interjected.

"Sadly, he lies under a very powerful enchantment," Kelphit continued, turning back to McCloud. "An enchantment that has taken him far from this waking world. And beyond my limited abilities here."

"Well, if you can't handle it, I don't know who can," Brandy said.

"I did not say I couldn't. Just that I couldn't *here*," Kelphit said, his hands returning to the space just above McCloud's forehead. "There are resources on Monhegan that may help. Other healers who rival even my knowledge. And, possibly even more importantly, this man is filled with strength. He is far away now, but the light of life burns strongly. If we can show him the way back, he will emerge a formidable figure, as I suspect he was prior. It may take time, but this world has not lost its Timestrider. Not yet. Do you know who set the charm upon him?"

Bayard leaned in. "Pettirosso and I believed it to be a Naga. But that is a guess. Educated, but a guess."

"That would explain much," the healer replied. "Powerful. But not powerful enough to vanquish him entirely. Naga. Fascinating."

Kelphit now pivoted in the cabin to face the berth where Nick lay, covered in a sheen of sweat and his arm, gently propped on a pillow, an angry and unhealthy puce.

"And now for our dear Nick," he muttered as he repeated the process he had completed on McCloud. His eyes focused even more fiercely on Nick, and the muttered sounds were deeper and weightier than they had been with McCloud. "You were right to bring him here. I can slow what is happening to him, but only partially. We must get him to the island. Quickly. As you rightly suspected, this wound is not what it appears. There is an evil beyond what can be seen. Whatever caused this wound had been infected by a Barghest. Deadly creature, not seen in this part of the world, which inflicts wounds that never heal. Unless, of course, they are treated properly. Time is our enemy here. Andrew?" Kelphit looked to the helm.

"Understood," Andy replied, throttling up. "Hold on, gang. We've got about ten miles to go. Should be there in under an hour. Just watch yourselves. Luckily, there's not much chop." He looked again to the waters in front of the boat, before whispering only to himself, "Actually, this feels weird. Something's off." He raised his voice again. "Hang tight. And keep your eyes peeled for anything unusual. Something about today feels...different."

The *Acheron*'s bow rose slightly in the water and the sturdy boat muscled toward Monhegan. Andy reached for the stereo and turned on a Schooner Fare album and the boat filled with the sound of sea chanties as they powered ahead, the music echoing across the unnaturally still waters.

Trout, startled by the sudden shout, leaped back from the table and found himself backed up to a tall stone. His head swiveled from side to side, but in the darkness, he saw nothing and no one.

Sean remained where he was, neither startled nor alarmed. He continued his examination of the grooved canal on the table.

"Sean," Trout called, "what are you doing? Get out of there!"

Without missing a beat, Sean said, "Why would I do that? Whoever is here with us obviously doesn't have the strength to face us directly. They would have, if they did. Nah, someone's just trying to scare us off. And I'm tired of running scared. So—no. I'll stick where I am."

Trout shook his head. "This is a fine time to get all uppity."

Finally, Sean stepped away from the stone table and turned to Trout. "Dan, we sensed something. But faintly. It barely was a blip on my radar. There's nothing here that can hurt us. In fact, whoever it is might be of some use to us. If they're hiding out in an overgrown roadside oddity, they aren't exactly in the thick of this fight for control of the world."

"You can't know that, buddy," Trout pleaded. "If this is a forgotten portal, this could be a gatekeeper of some sort. They gave us a chance to hightail it. Let's take it."

"Not only am I not interested in hightailing it," Sean answered. "I think we should force the issue."

Sean climbed on top of the immense table and slowly turned in a full circle. The only light came from the emergency lamp they had used to scale the wall. It barely reached where Sean stood, and faintly caught him on the table, giving his hair a flame-like nimbus in the half-light. In that moment, he looked as if he himself belonged to the Otherworld, and Trout pressed himself harder into the stone at his back, his boots scrabbling for a hold in the gravel path.

"Hey!" Sean shouted. "Whoever you are, get yourself out here before I drag you out myself. Or just clear out. I don't care which it is but make it fast. We're here for a reason and you're slowing us down."

Sean stopped moving and extended his arms fully to each side, inviting a response. When none came, he cast a glance to Trout with an I-told-you-so implied.

"See?" Sean asked, about to jump down. "Some minor so-and-so hiding from both worlds here where no one would think to look. We don't back down anymore, Danny-boy. We're the chosen ones, remember?"

Trout gave a shake of his shoulders, trying to unclench as he walked back toward the table.

"Never seen you so cocky," Trout said, approaching, "but maybe you're right. They didn't even bother to—"

The night was split with a piercing shriek. Trout literally ducked where he stood and Sean, in the process of dismounting from the table, lost his footing and nearly tumbled to the ground.

"You *dare?*" boomed the earlier voice. "You will now feel the wrath from which there is no return. My family and I will shred you and scatter your mortal self to the corners of the world. You will writhe in agony, begging for mercy."

Sean steadied himself before turning to Trout and mouthing *blah, blah, blah* while gesturing the same with his hand.

"You asked for this," Sean said quietly, before beginning to hum.

Trout looked on, eyes wide, as Sean increased his volume. As he did, he began to emit a blue light. Faint, at first, and then brighter. Brighter. It flowed down his arms and pooled in his palms. Sean glanced down, seemingly taken aback himself at this result, before drawing his hands together and creating a pulsing, glowing orb of bright azure. He spun it in the air as if it were a ball.

"Last chance," Sean growled.

Suddenly, the booming voice began to screech. A high caterwauling that became piercing and panicked. Sean began to peer around the clearing, a grin spreading across his face. Suddenly, his head whipped back toward the table itself. He moved toward the far corner, maintaining his sound throughout. He stopped and drew his hand up, pointing toward the drain in the gutter. The blue sphere in his hand grew in intensity, and he lifted it high in the air as if to unleash it on the spot, when suddenly Trout jumped in front of him, hands raised.

"Wait!" Trout shouted as he ran to the drain in the canal and got on his knees to look below the table. "There's a tube of some sort. Give me a sec."

He followed the tube with his hand, sprawling on the ground to reach deeper below the table.

"It feeds into something down here," he said. "A chamber or

room. Let me just—" Before he finished his sentence, he lunged downward. He cried out as his hand encountered something, but his voice was soon drowned out by a high keening that came from below the table. Desperate fear filled the voice, which began to cry out in a language that neither Trout nor Sean recognized. Trout began to draw his hand out from below, pivoting to brace his feet against the base of the table, gaining leverage.

"Come on, whatever you are," Trout barked. "I'm the best friend you have right now. You almost bit it there, so—" And with a great cry and a massive heave, he fell backwards. "Get. Out. Here!"

Whatever had been resisting him gave way and a figure came tumbling out of the chamber below, landing squarely on Trout's chest and chattering in a squealing voice. Trout shouted in alarm, tossing the being aside and scrambling back, only to relax slightly when he saw a small man, no more than two feet in height, with long dark hair, a long nose, and piercing eyes that flashed fearfully around the open space where the table lay. He scrabbled in the dirt for a moment, before screeching again and gaining his feet, about to dash toward the nearest opening on the surrounding stones.

"I don't think so," Sean said quietly, rearing back to fling his power at the now exposed creature, but again Trout intervened.

"No!" Trout cried. "Look at him. He's pathetic. Harmless."

Sean turned a skeptical eye on Trout before giving an almost imperceptible nod. "Softie," he said, as he allowed the blue ball of power to slide from his hand and settle almost gently about the being, entrapping him. "Now let's all have a talk, shall we?" Sean said, jumping up to sit on the edge of the table. "I think you owe us an explanation."

Trout got to his feet and brushed his jeans off while crossing back to the stone he had been leaning against earlier, crossing his arms, and fixing the newcomer with a steady gaze.

"Can't argue with that, friend," Trout said to the little man. "Least you can do."

At Trout's use of the word "friend," the creature ceased its chattering and crying and turned to the big Montanan. It paused, before settling cross-legged onto the ground. And nodding.

The *Acheron* was making good progress. The calm seas had stayed with them, and they churned along through the Gulf of Maine. Andy stayed by the wheel, pushing the craft as far as he was comfortable doing.

Kelphit sat by Nick, monitoring his condition, which continued to deteriorate. Kelphit reached often into the pouch at his belt and refreshed the herbs and stones that he'd placed around Nick, but the others could see the concern in his eyes, and collectively they kept glancing forward, trying to will the island closer.

Bayard and Brandy remained in the cabin, near Andy and keeping their eyes on Kelphit and the patients. Cinder paced from the cabin to the stern, restless. With each pass through the cabin, she stopped by Bayard and nosed his hand, fixing him with her bright amber eyes. She was not made for small spaces, especially after the ride in the Bronco, and she let him know that he was the only reason she was willing to put up with it.

Noodle finally put his sketch pad down and, shaking his hand to ward off a threatening cramp, wandered to the stern, breathing deep and appreciating the clean, clear air over the water. He turned his face to the sun, closing his eyes, and basking in the sheer different-ness of the natural beauty, so very different from his usual home in New York City. The rocky coastline and massive pine trees reminded him of his family home back in the Pacific Northwest and he felt a pang of homesickness grab hold of him.

Suddenly, he felt a warm blast of air hit him in the face and he opened his eyes, which immediately stung in the tepid, moist breeze. A breeze that felt out of place. Wrong. He wiped his eyes with his fist and they began to water, and he tried in vain to clear them. He grabbed the cuff of his jacket and used that to clear his eyes.

While doing that, he felt something wet brush his other hand and he jerked it suddenly back, only to be greeted be a familiar woof. Shaking his head, he glanced down to see Cinder by his side. She put her paws up on the stern rail and faced back toward the harbor they had recently left. She woofed again, her hackles raising as she nosed Noodle's hand again, this time with a sense of urgency.

Noodle shot her a confused look. "What is it?" he asked, immediately feeling slightly silly for talking to a wolf. "Hey, Bayard!" he called, "I think there's something up with Cind..."

The words died on his lips as something to their aft caught his eye and he turned his full attention back toward the receding New Harbor. There was a commotion in the water. It was churning, frothing, and from the froth a wave was forming. As he watched, it grew larger and gained speed. Like the breeze he'd just felt, it gave off an unnatural feel. Nothing around it was behaving similarly, the rest of the Gulf lying still, interrupted only by this wall of water that turned in their direction, and though he knew it couldn't be true, the swell seemed to take aim for them and move in their direction.

"What was that?" Bayard asked, emerging from the cabin and stopping short when he saw what Noodle and Cinder were watching. "Brandy! Might want to get out here!"

Brandy followed onto the deck, a question in her eyes before she noticed the wave, which continued to grow and gain on them.

"Well, what the hell is this now?" she asked. "I knew this was too easy. No way the baddies want McCloud to wake up. Dammit."

"I think you may be right," Bayard agreed, stepping to the rail and placing a protective hand on Cinder's head and ruffling her ears. "I think—" He squinted his eyes into the sunlight. "Yeah. Kelpies. Many kelpies."

"Kelpies?" Brandy asked. "You mean those water-man-horse things we tangled with in New York Harbor? Great. Just great."

"Exactly right," Bayard answered, before turning toward the cabin. "Andy! We have company, so if this boat can pick up any speed, now would be the time for it."

Andy turned from the wheel at being called. His eyes widened in alarm when he saw the pursuing wave, which was now large enough to be seen easily.

"On it!" he called back to Bayard, before pushing the throttle even further.

Noodle turned to the others, fear and confusion plain on his face. "Kelpies? The mythological creatures? Uh, what can we do?"

"Well," Brandy answered, shooting a glance toward the bow. "That's Monhegan on the horizon, I'm guessing. So, all we need to do is get there before those kelpies get to us. Is that right, Andy?" she called to the captain.

"That's the plan!" Andy called back.

All faces turned back to the stern. The wave was still growing, now far taller than the boat. As it gained on them, figures could be seen flashing through the whitecaps of the pursuing wall of water. At times, one—or more—would launch itself into the air, crashing back into the wave with a powerful slap of its tail on the water, and each strike of a tail sent a sound loud as thunder across the water to the watchers.

"It's getting closer," Noodle said quietly. "We can't make it."

The others, gauging the distance between them and seeing it shrinking, saw that he was right.

Kelphit strode from the cabin, a larger pack in his hands. He stopped at the stern and thrust a hand into the bag, drawing out a smaller pouch filled with herbs. He reached in and drew a handful out, crushing them in his fists before cupping his hands, raising them to his face, and speaking quietly into them. When he finished, he scattered the crushed leaves across the water being churned by their engine. Where they landed in the water, a vibrant green streak appeared and snaked along the surface toward the pursuing wave.

Next, Kelphit drew a stone from his pocket, cupped it in his hands, also, and closed his eyes in concentration. He slapped the stone once. Twice. Three times. And then hurled it from the *Acheron* into the waters behind. It arced slowly through the air before plunging into the sea. When it touched the water, a brilliant blue light exploded just below the surface. A mystical depth charge, meant to slow the pursuers.

The wave weakened and the kelpies veered, avoiding both of Kelphit's spells. As they slowed, the water settled and lost momentum, before they tried to regroup and continue the chase.

"Holy crap, Kelphit," Brandy cried. "You are a handy guy to have around. I think that might have actually done it. Bought us the time we needed. Monhegan should be no problem now—" But her voice died as she turned back to where the island had appeared in front of them. "Aw hell, you have got to be kidding me."

The others turned to see what had caused her alarm, and there, where Monhegan had been just moments ago, a wall of thick grey fog had settled. The island was nowhere to be seen, and the *Acheron* felt smaller than ever as it steamed toward the enormous wall that now was the only thing visible to the fore. With a choice between the pursuing kelpies and the mysterious mist that blocked them going forward, Andy shot a resigned look to the others and powered ahead. In mere moments, the boat would be swallowed by the darkness.

"You sure about this?" Brandy called from the rear of the boat.

"I don't know what's in there"—he pointed to the mist—"but I can guarantee we won't like what's back there." He tossed his head in the direction of their pursuers. "So here goes nothin'."

"Everything was going so well," Noodle said softly, as he grabbed the rail and planted his feet firmly on the deck.

"All right," Trout said gently to the small man, shooting a warning glance toward Sean, "why don't you start from the beginning and fill us in. Why are you here and why did you try to scare us off?"

Now seen in the overhead emergency light, the little man looked pathetic. His hair was long and thick with grease, plastered to his oversized head. His nose was somehow both beaked and bulbous, making for a very unattractive sight. His ears curved around and up, ending in a point. His eyes were dark, and he looked most often at the ground between his feet. He wore a leather tunic and cap, with rough pants underneath. His skin was sallow, grey. He looked as if he had not seen the sun in a very long time. His nose was running, long strands of mucus sliding uncontrollably toward the ground. He tried, sometimes successfully, to catch them and, inexplicably, push them back up his nostrils. He shook uncontrollably, and when he tried to speak his voice either failed completely or emitted an indecipherable squeak. All in all, he was a pathetic sight. But despite all of that, there was obviously something "Other" about him, not even accounting for his small stature. He clearly had come from the Otherworld.

Trout placed a hand on the man's shoulder. He appeared enormous next to the little fellow, who jerked away from Trout at first. As he began to understand that Trout meant him no harm, he risked a look up into the Montanan's face and relaxed. A little.

"You won't...won't hurt?" he stammered. "No punish? No send away?"

"We don't even belong here ourselves," Trout said with a chuckle. "We can't send anyone anywhere. We didn't even know you were here until you spoke up."

"Stupid, stupid," the man cried. "Always wrong. Always stupid."

Sean stood up and moved toward the other two and the little man shrunk into Trout's side, eyeing Sean with naked fear.

"Okay, look," Sean said, holding his hands up in an attempt to settle the creature. "We didn't come here to cause harm. Certainly not to you. You're obviously from the Otherworld. All we want is to find a safe way to get there and we thought this place might hold a portal. Or a gate. Honestly, we don't even know exactly what we're looking for."

The man looked up at Sean, squinting. Calculating.

"Must not," he said. "Must not. Other side is angry. All is fighting. There is a way here. But not safe. Watched. They keep me out and"—he paused, and something more than the sniveling creature shone in his face—"I am far less a threat to them than you."

Sean tried to interrupt him, but the man stood suddenly and pointed at Sean.

"I don't know you," he said, "but I feel you. There is power in you. Power that should not be in man. I think you are why Others are angry. I think I should get far away from you."

The little man began to sit again by Trout and then suddenly leaped to his feet and made a mad dash toward the nearest chamber. It was a clumsy and ill-fated attempt, and Trout's massive hand grabbed him by his collar and held him off the ground. His legs pumped furiously for a moment as if his brain had not yet told them to give up, and then he went completely slack, a rag doll in Trout's grip.

"Sorry," Trout said, sounding genuinely apologetic. "We need some more info before you can hightail it. Let's all just get comfy and you can fill us in. Then, you go on your merry little way."

The limp form remained still, swaying slightly in Trout's grasp. "Nothing merry. No more merry. Not since them. I no fight. I tell you. Then you let me go?"

"Then we let you go," Trout assured him.

Sean shot Trout a dubious look, prompting the mountain man to double down. He looked squarely at Sean when he said, "I *promise* you'll be free to go."

Sean shook his head but returned to his perch on the stone table and gestured for the man to proceed. With a look toward Trout, who set the man back on the ground, the newcomer flopped to the ground and heaved a quivering sigh.

"Was never like this before," he began quietly. "I had a home. Had purpose. For long time. Before you ruined everything."

"I've never seen you before," Sean said. "I'm getting blamed for a lot of stuff lately, but I had nothing to do with this."

"Not *you* you," he replied, "*all* of you. Men."

"Take a deep breath," Trout said. "Start at the beginning."

The little man looked up at the stars and there were tears in his eyes. He drew a clay-colored hand across his face, sat up straighter, and took a less quivering breath.

"Been here—*there*—long time, so long. Was my place. Home. Not big. Small. Tiny even. But mine. I adopted it before any of you came here. Even the ones who were here first. The ones who belonged. At least they understood. Left me to myself. Me and my *fioruisce*. I was to watch it. Protect."

"Excuse me, I'm sorry," Trout interrupted. "I'm from Montana. I've got no idea what that is."

The man looked at the ground in front of him. His brow furrowed. "Thought you would know that. My folk would call it *kildevand*."

Seeing that Trout didn't recognize that word either, he thought some more, before shrugging.

"Don't know," he said. "Water. From below. Ground."

Sean leaned forward on the table. "Do you mean 'spring'? Water that comes up from underground."

The man's eyes filled again with tears, but a bittersweet smile broke on his face. "Yes! Yes. Spring. I had my spring. Was my place. *Mine.* Then pale people came. A few at first. Then more. And more. Everywhere. Took everything. And then they took my *kildevand*. Built home over it. Shut out the sky. The wind. The rain. But still I stayed. Tried to tell them, but they not listen. Then I tried to warn them. Scare them. But nothing. Finally, they brought pale person who had magic. Knew things. She found me. And banished me. Sent me away from *kildevand*. I begged to stay. Cried. Screamed. But no. Could tell women who lived there felt guilt, but not enough. They threw me away. Told me to be free. *Free!* I was free! I was home! They stole all of that. No place to go. No one to help. Felt the power here. Came here. Hid here. Hoping to go home. Portal is here. But I can't go to Other place where my kind live. Shame is too great. I failed my *kilde-vand*. I have no home. No purpose. They would shun me. Nowhere for me. I am alone."

"Okay," Trout said after a pause. "There's a lot to unpack there. Let's focus on you for now. You were—I don't know—stationed at a well? And someone moved in over top of it and you got yourself booted. Is that what I'm hearing?"

At last, the tears spilled from the little man's eyes and he nodded. Then dragged his clammy arm across his eyes and his now cascading nose.

"Got it," Trout said, then looked to Sean. "I have no idea how to respond to any of that."

"Yeah, me either," Sean replied as he pulled his phone from his pocket. "Where was this well? Do you happen to know the name?"

Shaking his head, the creature whimpered. "I don't know your names. Mean nothing to me. Something about seasons. What do I know of your seasons? Was just my home. Not far. Close enough for I to come here."

Trout walked over to Sean at the table. "Any idea what to do with him? Sounds like this portal isn't going to be much help to us. Not if it's watched. Seems like they're watching even the old ones."

"I agree," Sean replied. "But we did get some information out of this guy. I don't really know where to go next, though. Any ideas?"

"I mean, my first thought is we need to do something to help him," Trout said with a jerk of his head back toward the sniveling form on the ground behind him.

"Help him?" Sean asked. "Help him how? This guy is stuck here. We can't get his spring back for him. And my best guess is he's a troll. Fits the description. And, if that's the case, he's no friend of ours."

"Look at him!" Trout protested. "He probably hasn't spoken to anyone in years. We're better than that, aren't we? I thought we were the good guys."

"Dan, it's not that simple, and you know it. Things aren't black and white. Ever. We have to focus on what we're trying to do. Find Breena. Save her."

"And Kallan," Trout interjected. "You keep leaving him out."

"I'm not leaving him out," Sean barked. "I know Kallan needs us, too. Stop being overly sensitive."

Trout had taken his phone out of his pocket and was tapping the screen as Sean spoke.

"Hey, buddy, does the name Somerville mean anything to you?"

"Yes!" came the raspy reply, and another quivering breath followed. "Summer. Winter. All same to me. Yes, my *kildevand* was in place pale ones called Somerville. To me—just home."

Trout turned his screen to face Sean. "Not hard to find, actually. The Somerville Troll. Come on, Sean. We have a chance to do something good here. Not exactly the Wall Street Journal, but this website about cryptids and stuff has it right there. If it's true, this poor thing has been here since"—he turned the screen back to himself and scrolled—"the mid-eighties. He's been stuck here for forty years. Sean, we have to do something."

Behind Trout, the troll had now lifted its head and was watching them with interest. His whimpers had ceased, and his eyes seemed brighter than before.

"Like what?" Sean hissed to Trout. "It's a troll. What are we supposed to do? Go knock on doors in Somerville until we find his old house and ask them to take him back?"

"Of course not. Let's take him to Monhegan. He needs a place to call home and that's a place of healing where people should understand him. Plus, we really should find out how Nick is. And McCloud, for that matter." Trout placed his hands on Sean's shoulders, forcing him to look him in the face. "We don't know where to go anyway. Monhegan is the best option we have. Every time things have looked bad, the one thing that's gotten us through has been... what?"

"Me blasting things with my voice," Sean said flatly.

"Wrong answer!" Trout replied sharply. "Our friends have been what's gotten us through. You should be ashamed I have to remind you of that."

Sean did not seem ashamed. "Yeah, sure. We do well together.

But why Monhegan? Let's find something closer. We don't have time for this, Dan."

Another quick scroll and tap on his phone and Trout replied. "It's two and a half hours from here. You have any better magical ideas that are closer?"

"You know I don't," Sean said. "Fine. Monhegan. But no troll."

Trout turned to the troll who had now risen to his feet and watched with a pitifully hopeful expression.

"What's your name, little buddy?" Trout asked. "Need to know what to call you. Can't keep shouting 'hey you!' every time I talk to you."

A wary look flitted across the troll's face, quickly replaced by a docile, willing-to-please expression. "You can call me Jotunn. Thank you. *Buddy.*"

Trout turned to Sean and raised his eyebrows.

"You know, Trout," Sean said. "You seem like a simple man on the surface, but sometimes I think down below you are the most manipulative devious person I know."

Trout let loose a booming laugh that echoed through the surrounding stones. "Well, thanks, Sean. That's the closest I've ever come to being called smart. I think."

"That is definitely *not* what I said," Sean said. "And if we didn't already have to leave, we do now, you idiot. Everyone within five miles must have heard you. Let's get out of here."

Sean turned to retreat to the fence where they had climbed into the enclosure and Trout made to follow. After a few steps, he stopped and looked back to find Jotunn still rooted to where he stood.

"Jotunn!" Trout called. "You comin' or what? Let's get you out of here!"

Jotunn's eyes grew wide as dinner plates. He hesitated, doubting for a moment what he had heard. Then his eyes filled again as happiness flooded his face. He jumped in the air and shuffled his feet gleefully when he landed. It was awkward and unattractive and so purely joyful that Trout couldn't help but smile. He made sure the troll was following and then turned back toward the perimeter fence.

"Coming! Coming, Trout! Buddy!" Jotunn cried. Then, more quietly, "Found a new *kildevand*. New home. New friend. First friend."

Jotunn scampered after Trout and Sean, casting one last look at the compound with its stones and fences. As he turned, he let out a rude noise and laughed a deep rumbly laugh.

CHAPTER 4

The *Acheron* seemed to be shrinking the closer it got to the fog that now blocked out even the sun. They were still moments from entering the cloud, but its shadow had fallen over the deck and as it did, the temperature dropped quickly. The passengers were unsure where to look. The unknown ahead *seemed* the better option, especially when they focused toward the aft where the kelpies had regrouped and increased their speed yet again. The clap of their tail slaps increased in frequency, a terrible drumbeat that echoed across the deck of the boat and could be felt through their feet.

Andy, eyes locked on what lay ahead, called out to the others. "We're going in! Get into the cabin and grab onto something that's battened down!"

As the passengers crab-walked along the bucking afterdeck toward the relative shelter of the cabin, Brandy found herself bringing up the rear, unable to drag her gaze from the tumult chasing them. In the midst of the water horses galloping behind them, she suddenly saw another form emerge from the depths. An unearthly hum rose from below and a dark shape floated lazily toward the surface and as it did the kelpies veered out of its path.

The humming grew louder and, before the shadow broke the surface, stopped suddenly leaving a silence as unexpected as it was terrifying. Long nails emerged from the water, followed by thin, sinewy arms that glistened an unhealthy shade of green. Next a tangle of jet-black hair settled on the surface before sliding limply along the sides of a hideous face rising. The creature had the shape of a woman, at least what could be seen above the water.

The kelpies reacted in unison, tails slapping the water with new energy and anger as they redoubled their pursuit of the beleaguered *Acheron*.

"Bayard!" Brandy called to the Peripheral as he was about to enter the cabin.

He spun and stopped where he was, his brow creasing as he absorbed what he was seeing. He shook his head, and Cinder found her way quickly to his side. She pressed her nose into his thigh and her hackles rose as she, too, saw what had emerged behind them.

Bayard rushed to Brandy and grabbed her by the shoulder and pulled her, none too gently, into the cabin.

"Sit!" he shouted to her. "Grab hold!"

From the wheel, Andy, unaware of what approached the boat from behind, shouted, "This is it! We're going in!"

Brandy, now seated at the main table, twisted on the bench, craning her neck to witness whatever happened next. The ghastly woman was now above the water from her waist and cut through the water, leaving a strong wake behind her. She outpaced even the kelpies and was reaching a scaled arm toward the stern of the now small-seeming boat. Bayard flicked his wrists and two long, gleaming daggers slipped into his hands, and he stepped to the doorway to the deck. Cinder, ears flat along her head, stepped to his side, her teeth bared.

As the gruesome sea-witch grabbed the railing, many things happened at once. The great fog toward the fore reached the boat and it felt instantly as if a heavy blanket descended upon them.

Light, sound, even air to breathe, all felt as if they had been snatched away.

Brandy was in the midst of turning her attention toward the enveloping mist, when flashes of movement to the rear snapped her eyes back in that direction. A phalanx of massive seal shapes erupted through the water from the south. The kelpies, caught completely unaware, reared in the water before being battered from the side and swept aside.

As the kelpies fled, another mass of seal shapes rose from below the witch, throwing her high in the air, her angry, ragged nails clutching vainly at the air for something to slow her ascent. In the midst of the seals, a figure clutched the sea-witch in muscled, olive-hued arms, one of which carried a deadly-sharp blade. The blade flashed high above both figures, before the hilt crashed down on the sickly green head of the attacker. As the witch went limp and began to sink below the surface, the elegant, rugged defender turned briefly toward the passengers on the boat, smiled, and then flashed down and was gone.

"Was that—?" Brandy stammered.

"I have no idea who that was," Bayard said. "But our island hosts may."

"And we're in!" Andy shouted as the *Acheron* became blanketed in total darkness.

An hour and a half into their drive north into Maine, Jotunn had still not settled into his seat. He jumped from side to side in the back seat, pressing his still running nose to the windows leaving enormous slug-like trails behind. All the while, he muttered small sounds of wonder and surprise. At one point, the troll managed to crawl behind one of the seats into the hatch area of the Crosstrek. Passing motorists didn't seem to notice the small heavily wart-splotched face peering halfway over the rear window, until two children, riding in an SUV they passed, saw

Jotunn and began calling to their parents in the front seat. The parents clearly dismissed the children's claim of a bogeyman in the passing car.

Trout, from the front passenger seat couldn't stop chuckling, but for his part, Sean was decidedly less amused, gesturing for Trout to get the troll out of the hatch.

Trout shrugged at Sean, but eventually turned and called Jotunn back to the rear seat. Casting a last look out the rear window, the little creature climbed back into the seat. He sat still for exactly nine seconds, before his enthusiasm won out and he was back pacing from side to side. The steam from his breath was now combining with his nasal discharge to create a decidedly unpleasant gelatinous mess on the glass.

Sean, seeing this in a quick glance backwards, cast a very unhappy look toward Trout. "I know he won't clean that himself, so I expect you to do it. I feel like we adopted a puppy. A pale, disgusting, oozing puppy."

From the back seat, Jotunn harrumphed and finally sat back, crossing his arms.

"He can hear you, you know," Trout said, returning Sean's unhappy look. "He's just excited. You would be too, if you just got sprung from your self-imposed prison sentence. Cut him some slack. He could actually come in handy."

"I find that highly unlikely," Sean replied. "Let's just get to Maine, drop him at the island, and maybe someone there can give us some ideas on how to find a back door into the Otherworld."

"Should ask Jotunn," came a small voice from the rear seat. "Troll live underground. Cave. Caves often where veil is thin, and Otherworld comes close. Should ask Jotunn. Jotunn troll."

Sean cast a dubious look into the rearview mirror but couldn't help himself. "Okay," he said. "Jotunn, do you know a secret way into the Otherworld that we can use? Someplace quiet. Hidden."

"No, Jotunn no know that," the troll said with a shake of his head.

"Why did I even bother?" Sean barked, with a slap of the steering wheel. "Unbelievable."

"But I can find out," Jotunn said quietly, with an impish grin. "Will do it to help my *buddy.* Trout." And then more quietly, "No help mean one."

Trout laughed again. "I told you he'd come in handy! Might try easing up a bit on him, Sean. Maybe just ease up in general."

That earned Trout another angry glance from Sean, but he paused and took a breath. "You're right, Dan. I'm sorry, Jotunn. I'm not behaving very well. I apologize. It would be great if you could help."

"Hmm. Better," the troll said, leaning forward between the two front seats. "Will help! Need to talk to others. Will find them where we go. I know of this island. Monhegan."

"You do?" Trout asked. "How?"

"Famous place," Jotunn explained. "Much power. Good place. Peace."

"Excellent," Trout exclaimed, drumming on the dashboard in excitement. "Now we're talkin'."

"But first, Jotunn need to stop or will make mess in car," the troll said.

"No, no, no," Sean protested. "My new car is not going to become a troll crapper. I'm pulling off."

Trout grabbed his phone and began scrolling on the map. "You know, contrary to urban legend, Thomas Crapper didn't actually invent the flush toilet. He did, however, have a patent for an improved ballcock and U-bend. And you can still see his name on manhole covers in Westminster Abbey."

"Delightful," Sean shot back. "I'm not even going to ask why you know these things. I'm pulling off here."

"Aha!" Trout exclaimed. "I was stalling until I could find—yeah. Here we go. Take the exit and—Jotunn, what do you need? I assume we can't just take you to a Dunkin' restroom."

"What did you just say?" Jotunn whispered, creeping between the two front seats again. "What you call me?"

"I, uh…called you Jotunn. Isn't that what you said to call you?"

The troll seemed to unclench a bit. "Yes. Yes. You said Jotunn. Why you say dunker?"

"Sorry for the confusion, pal," Trout replied, turning halfway in his seat to check in with their passenger. "I said 'Dunkin'.' That's just the name of a coffee place. Bit of a religion up here, which I always thought was kinda odd, but there you have it. Sorry for any confusion."

"Coffee place," Jotunn muttered, leaning back.

"Okay, if you two are done, can you tell me where to go, Trout? I don't feel like having to get my upholstery shampooed."

"Hang onto yer pants, Ginge," Trout said. "A few lights up, take a left. I'll walk you through it. Old bridge on the left. I assume you'd be comfortable with an old bridge and a stretch of river, yeah, Jotunn?"

"Oh, yes," the troll answered, lighting up at the mention of an old bridge. "Old bridge just right." He wiped his still leaking nose with renewed enthusiasm.

"Where are we?" Sean asked, turning in his seat. "How do you know about this bridge?"

"Same way I knew about Mr. Crapper. Good ol' online search. Bada bing, bada boom. That, and I saw we were close to Brunswick. I did a summer season here at Maine State Music Theatre a stretch back. Probably know a few folks around here still. Theatre people are *our* people, so maybe a quick stop will do us good."

"Oh, man, yeah," Sean replied. "I did a couple shows here, too. Loved it. Hadn't even stopped to think that through. Sorry, Jotunn! We'll give you some privacy and be back in a little while. That work for you?"

"Work for me?" Jotunn asked, clearly not comprehending.

"He just means that we'll let you do your thing and come back in a bit to pick you up? Stretch your legs, bud. Probably your first time away from that basement and Stonehenge place for a long time."

As Sean turned where Trout indicated, a river came into view on the left and the troll's cavorting in the back seat seemed to become less frantic and more joyful.

"Beauty! Beauty!" Jotunn cried, pointing to the water sliding by beside them. A sign flew past declaring the Androscoggin Swinging Bridge to be just ahead. Sean made a quick turn into the small parking lot, and ahead of them they saw a charming old footbridge traversing the lazily flowing river and connecting to parkland on the far bank.

Trout jumped out of the Crosstrek and opened the rear door for Jotunn, who seemed to fly from the car and through some thick brush, disappearing into the undergrowth. The only sign of his presence was the periodic hoots of glee that drifted back to Trout and Sean, who had rolled down his window.

"Subtle, he is not," Sean said, relaxing his arms over the top pf the steering wheel. "I remember this place. I loved it here."

"Well, luckily, it's still early, so I don't think we traumatized any locals. But, yeah, we'll have to try to keep him under wraps," Trout said with a gentle laugh. "And I loved it here, too. Spent many afternoons over the other side on that beach."

"The theatre doesn't run during the winter months," Sean noted. "Will we be able to find anyone?"

"Hell yeah," Trout answered. "No mainstage shows, but they work themselves crazy in the offseason. We'll find 'em."

"It's just eight now," Sean said, glancing at the dashboard clock. "I remember Big Top Deli on Maine Street being pretty awesome. Hungry?"

"I'm always hungry," Trout answered, tapping on his phone's screen again. "Been a good while since I've been here, but—wouldja look at that. Big Top is still here and they...open at ten. Option B?"

"That's too bad. I'm guessing if we swing by the theatre offices at ten, someone should be there, so we should eat now. What was that other place? Other side of Maine Street?"

"Oh, yeah!" Trout exclaimed. "Wild Oats. Yeah, yeah. It is"—

more tapping on the screen—"still open! But moved. Out on the old naval base. But opened at half past seven."

"Yeah, let's do it," Sean said, entering the name into the GPS. "Seven minutes. Now that I'm thinking about it, I am tired. Was running on adrenaline. Really wanted that Stonehenge place to be the answer. I could use a sit down and a good meal."

"It's a plan," Trout said and leaned back into his seat. "Jotunn should be fine for a while. Eat and then swing by the office?"

"That works," Sean replied. "And honestly, if Jotunn decides to stay under that bridge, it wouldn't break my heart."

"No chance," Trout said with a shake of his head. "He wants to help us. And he *really* wants to see that island. I think it will be good for him. Take it easy on him, yeah? He's lost everything. Be the change you want to see in the world, and all that."

"I'll try," Sean answered. "Don't know what's gotten into me." He turned to face Trout. "I know I haven't been myself. I'm sorry."

"No, you haven't," Trout agreed. "But you've been dealing with a lot. We put up with Ken at his worst, this is nothing. But I would appreciate you watching the road. I don't think those new powers of yours include seeing out of your ear holes."

Sean whipped his head back to the road and steered the Subaru back into the center of the lane.

"Right," he said quietly. "Message received."

Two minutes down Maine Street, Sean turned left onto Bath Road and the morning light off the pine trees lifted their spirits in ways they didn't know they needed.

The crashing of water sounded strong enough to threaten the boat. Until it entered the cloak of dark fog. For a moment, the sound remained, but then suddenly faded. All fell silent. The water below them ceased moving. The stillness that grabbed them was so sudden it felt violent, as did the way the boat came to a gliding stop.

The *Acheron*'s engines died with the fog. Andy began to frantically work the controls, but nothing happened, and he finally resorted to grabbing an enormous Maglite that was stored by the wheel. Even this did little good. The beam was swallowed immediately when it reached beyond the cockpit, as if it was swept away into nothingness.

"This can't be good," Brandy said quietly, and even her voice seemed muffled by the void.

Kelphit stepped to Andy's side, his dark eyes trying in vain to pierce the black curtain surrounding them.

"I don't know," Kelphit said. "Whatever it is hasn't harmed us. In fact, it appears to have removed us from our pursuers."

"I'd feel a lot better if I could get any of our systems up," Andy replied. "We're dead in the water right now. We should have been close to Monhegan. So close. But we are completely vulnerable right now."

"This feels...familiar," Bayard said, stepping to the others. "Familiar but not for a very, very long time."

Brandy began to hum quietly. A rich alto note that floated into the nothingness. Suddenly her sound began to pulse and slowly assumed a faint green glow.

"I know we're down a few voices, and I'm not Sean, but this is worth a try. Care to join, Noodle? I think I could use some help."

"Me?" Noodle almost squeaked in response. "I haven't done any of that in a long time, but—"

Noodle found a crystal-clear tenor note that slid in perfectly with what Brandy had been singing. Brandy grinned in response and picked up where she had left off. Together, their sound drifted up on a cloud of verdant purity. Their light expanded and settled over the cockpit, then crept outward over the deck. Within moments, the *Acheron* was bathed in the light, and the water surrounding them began to reflect back at them.

Andy turned, slack-jawed, at the wheel.

"I was told to expect the unexpected, but this is way beyond that," he said.

For their parts, Kelphit and Bayard had turned their focus to the bow. The green radiance began to form a beam, a tunnel through the darkness. It stretched further and further until something at the very limit of its reach seemed to take shape. Shadows lurked at the edge of their perception.

As the light touched whatever was in the distance, it brightened. The tunnel strengthened. And faintly coming back to them over the water they heard an answering voice, harmonizing with Brandy and Noodle, the sound echoed along the still water and as it did, the boat began to move again. The engines remained still, but they moved silently forward toward what should be Monhegan Island.

"That voice sounds familiar," Bayard noted.

"It does, indeed," Kelphit agreed. "I had hoped—"

As they drew closer, they saw a pier ahead of them, figures standing at the edge, glowing green and surrounded by the dark cloak that still lay behind them.

Cinder whined and put her nose in Bayard's palm. The patients in their berths remained silent. Still. Deathly still.

"I know where I've seen this fog before," Bayard said suddenly.

"I have never seen it, but I know of it," Kelphit replied, wonder in his voice. "Even I can still be surprised."

"The mists of Hy-Brasil," Bayard said quietly. "It doesn't belong here, but I am grateful."

"I have no idea what you're talking about," Andy said, still staring at the green beam of light. "What does Brazil have to do with anything. Why are they singing? And why is it glowing?!"

"Hy-Brasil," Kelphit corrected him. "A mystical island off the coast of Eire that appears every seven years. The rest of the time it is shrouded in...this"—he gestured to the darkness around them— "and cannot be found by man or Fae. And here it is to save us."

"Okay, sure," Andy said. "That actually was the least of my concerns."

"Must be some strong magic on that island," Bayard said. "I've never heard of this appearing anywhere else."

The boat was cruising quickly now, pulled inexorably toward the pier and the watchers there. When the momentum was such that they were sure to land, Brandy stopped singing and gently touched Noodle's arm to let him know he could stop, too.

As the *Acheron* slid silently to a stop by the pier, they were greeted by three figures. Their features took shape as the *Acheron* settled by the dock. Two of the people were unknown to Brandy, but her breath caught as she glimpsed the third.

"As I had hoped," Kelphit said with a smile, before calling out. "Well met, Sandy Dale!"

—

As the Crosstrek headed out Bath Road toward Cook's Corner, both Sean and Trout nodded and smiled as they pointed at the Pickard Theater on the corner of the Bowdoin Campus. A column of glass enclosing a staircase recalling memories for them.

"Ah, wow," Sean said, grinning. "It's all coming back now. Running up and down those stairs between scenes. Costumes trailing behind as I tried to make a costume change. Funny." He paused, turning back to the road ahead before another quip from Trout. "I haven't thought about being here for a while, but I loved that summer. I really *loved it.*"

"Me, too, actually," Trout responded. "Just the pure joy of making theatre. That's what I remember. Fast, crazy, lots of hours, but everyone just here to make it happen."

"Yes!" Sean said a bit more loudly than he intended. "Exactly. Look, don't get me wrong, I love commercial theatre. I definitely love a Broadway paycheck. But—I don't know— there's something very pure about making theatre just because you love it. And love the people making theatre with you. But, watching the box office numbers every week. Checking how full the balcony is as soon as the curtain goes up. It takes a lot out of you."

"It takes a lot out of you and a lot out of the reasons we got into this all to start with," Trout said, his eyes lingering on the theatre building as it dwindled in the side-view mirror. "And so many people in that process who have different motivations. That's me being polite, by the way. Not all of them, but enough of them don't give a hoot about us as people, let alone as artists. They say we're all replaceable. I s'pose in a way that's true, but in a deeper sense, *none* of us are replaceable. Easy to lose sight of that when you're watching award nominations, and which theatre might become open soon. Hurts a lot more when you realize every show closing means a few hundred folks out of work."

"Absolutely," Sean said, nodding again. "And someone's lifelong dream just came to an end. Writer. Actor. *Someone*."

"It always steams my clams when people say, 'They'll be fine. They'll get another show and something more deserving will take the theatre.' People who say that have no idea how hard it is to land one of those jobs."

"Unless you're one of the lucky few."

"Damn straight," Trout agreed. "Unless you're one of the lucky few."

"Hey," Sean said, sitting up straighter in his seat, "maybe we should try to come back here next summer. Make some theatre because we love it."

"That's not a half-bad idea," Trout replied, turning to face Sean. "I mean, with everything going on, it feels like a lifetime away, but— hell yeah. Let's look into it."

"Not that it's that easy. I think I saw somewhere that they auditioned a few thousand people for one of the recent seasons. A few *thousand*."

Trout whistled long and low. "I tell you, Ginge, it's a miracle we survived as long as we have in this biz."

"I tell myself that a few dozen times a day."

Trout whipped his head out his window. "Hold the phone," he exclaimed. "Did you see that?"

"No idea what you're talking about," Sean said shaking his head.

"Black Pug Brewing? Just passed it. Since when did they have a brewery in town? It's a bit early right now, but if we're still here at lunchtime—"

"You're kidding, right?" Sean asked. "Every town has a brewery now. Or two. You must be tired after last night, because I assumed you saw the brewery we passed on Maine Street."

"What? Another one?"

Sean laughed. "Yeah. Moderation Brewing. Heard good things."

"Look, when we're done with all of this mess, how about a road trip? Grumbles only. See some pretty scenery, hit some breweries, eat some food that's bad for us. Whaddaya say?"

"I love it," Sean said, pursing his lips. "Hard to think that far ahead, but, when we get there? Yeah. Definitely." He stopped short and started to say something but held his tongue.

"What?" Trout asked. "I know you too well to let you skate on something like that. Just spit it out, bud. The Crosstrek is a safe space."

Sean sighed. "It will just feel...wrong without Ken. We haven't talked a lot about it, but I think I'm more upset about losing him than I've let on. I mean—he's gone, Dan. Probably long gone by now. It's just—I don't know. Wrong. The first one of us to...go."

"I know," Trout said, reaching over and putting a hand on Sean's shoulder. "I'm sorry I wasn't there. Maybe I could've made a difference. But from what you've told me, he had his mind made up. Look, he made a choice. A tough one, but a selfless one. I miss him. I miss him like hell. But I'll always respect him for sacrificing himself for the rest of us. In the end, he came back to us. More importantly, he came back to himself."

"I know," Sean agreed. "I know it. But it still hurts. I still miss him. And it still makes me mad. It's all my fault. All of it is."

"Yeah, you can stuff that 'my fault' crap in your back pocket and have a seat," Trout said, shaking his head. "You didn't go looking for any of this. Trouble came looking for you. If you hadn't been you, they would have gone harder for Ken, and that would have been a lot worse." He paused before continuing. "And I gotta tell ya, if ol' Ken can get that time visor thingy running again, he could still show up here again. I wouldn't put anything past him."

"I can't even let myself think like that," Sean muttered. "But you may be right."

Sean turned right at a sign for Brunswick Landing, and they cruised past a number of decommissioned airplanes now refurbished and on display by the roadside amongst the growing community of condominiums and shops. A few minutes later, Sean pointed ahead to the right toward a large blue building.

"That can't be it," Trout said before stopping short. "Holy—well, they've come a long way since their little spot downtown."

As Sean turned into the bustling parking lot and began hunting for a spot. He finally found one and as he settled into it, Trout began laughing far too loudly for the cabin.

"You have *got* to be kidding me. Wouldja look at that!" he exclaimed, pointing directly in front of them, in the lot opposite the bakery.

When Sean followed Trout's gesture, his eyes widened and he, too, started to laugh. Mere feet from them lay a large sign for Flight Deck Brewing.

"Another one!" Trout crowed. "I'm still retiring to Montana, but Brunswick is moving up the list of alternative possibilities!"

As they climbed out of the SUV and headed toward the bakery, Sean paused for a half stride and shook his head. "Stuff that crap in my back pocket and have a seat?"

"Yeah, you like that one? I made it up just now on the spot."

"Really?" Sean said. "I never would have guessed."

They followed their noses into the bakery, both realizing how hungry they were the closer they came to the source.

It took some wrangling to get the two patients, Nick and McCloud, off the *Acheron* and safely onto the pier. Once it had been accomplished, Andy climbed back aboard his boat and fired the engine again.

"Hey, you sure you should be headed back out there?" Brandy asked. "We barely made it through with more than a little outside help."

Checking his gauges and screens, Andy hesitated before answering.

"I should be good to go," he finally responded. "Everything looks clear. Whatever caused all that fuss, it wasn't me. I have a two o'clock charter. Gotta pay the bills."

Brandy dropped to her haunches next to where Andy stood by the wheel. "Could you do me a favor? Actually, me and someone else?"

"I will if I can," he answered. "What's up?"

"That Ford Bronco we came in is more than it looks like from the outside."

"Oh, cool. I noticed it when you pulled in. Classic," the Mainer said. "What does that mean exactly?"

"It means, first and most importantly, it's not mine," Brandy replied. "A friend very generously loaned it to us. Can you just keep an eye on it? Make sure it doesn't attract the wrong attention?"

"New Harbor isn't exactly New York," Andy said with a laugh, "but I'll make sure to check on it. Any idea when this friend will come by to pick it up?"

"I don't even think he *will*," she said. "It's more likely to be me getting it when we leave here. I just wanted to be careful. Speaking of which—" She reached into her coat pocket and took out the keys to the truck, tossing them over to Andy. "Just in case it needs to be moved or something. I noticed a lot of 'Do Not Park' signs."

"Yeah, don't worry. I know people. My crew comes on this afternoon, and they know even more people than I do. I'll let Emma and Alex know what's what."

"Thank you," Brandy sighed. "I just really want to make sure it's okay. You'll understand when you look inside."

One of the strangers on the pier crossed to the rail of the *Acheron*, hailing Andy as he approached. The man was small, wiry. He had fair hair, grey eyes, and was clothed in simple earth colors. His coat, boots, and hat were well-made. Made to withstand winters on this exposed island. If Brandy hadn't been attuned to things like this, she may never have noticed that he bore all the hallmarks of the Peripherals she had met. If she had doubted, that was over when she noted the quick, graceful gait that carried him to the boat. This was a Fae, and apparently living openly here on Monhegan.

"Fintan!" Andy shouted to the man. "How's it going? Just dropping off these visitors for you. Anything you need to go landward?"

"Thank you, Andrew," the man responded. "We have nothing to send with you other than our thanks." Fintan nodded out beyond the harbor, and everyone turned to see what he was acknowledging. Almost as one, they saw that the heavy fog had nearly disappeared, and the open waters beyond had stilled.

"I'll be damned," Brandy whispered.

"I believe you will be just fine, but if anything should arise, let us know," Fintan said to Andy. "We'll make sure you arrive back safely."

"I know you will, Finn," Andy shouted back, giving a salute and backing the boat away from the pier. "You've always got my back! And I've got yours! Hope your friends are okay, Brandy! That Bronco will be just fine!"

The *Acheron* had now turned to face out to the Gulf and chugged on its way, Andy waving his hand high in the air.

"He's a good guy," Brandy said to no one in particular.

It was Fintan who answered her. "One of the finest I know. He'll be safe on the crossing now that you are all here."

"Yeah, I feel bad about that," Brandy answered, her eyes lingering on the boat as it grew smaller and smaller, making its way back to New Harbor. "I thought we were just delivering some patients. Forgot we could still be targets."

Fintan paused to consider Brandy. "We have much to share with each other," he said. "Sulevia!" he called to the other stranger on the pier. "Ready things above and I will bring our guests along shortly."

The woman nodded and without a word began up the hill away from the hard dirt and gravel that made the pier and road. Like Fintan, she was slight. And like Fintan, she was dressed simply but well. Her hair, where it escaped the hood of her calf-length puffy coat, blazed a brilliant red in the now bright sunlight. Her movements were also distinct. She was graceful. So much so that she seemed to almost glide across the ground, and Brandy noted with surprise that she made no sound as she crossed the gravel surface. Unlike the rest of them, who crunched and clattered with each slight step.

Noodle and Bayard approached Brandy, who noted that Sandy was deep in conversation with Kelphit a few yards away by the community bulletin board at the end of the pier.

"I'm a little surprised you gave him the keys to the truck," Noodle said, nodding toward the rapidly disappearing *Acheron*.

"Desperate times," Brandy replied. "Besides, Grier Roleth recommended him. And any friend of Grier's is beyond trustworthy."

"So true," Bayard agreed, arriving by the other two. "We could use him here now. A handy person to have around. Resourceful. And great stories."

"Hopefully, we'll all see him again soon under much better circumstances," Brandy said, looking into the distance and seeming to see something the others did not. "He's making a difference wherever he is right now. I know that much." She pondered a cloud overhead, noting that it looked like a bird taking wing. She nodded. "But for now, I need to get a report from Sandy Dale!" She called the name full-voiced and started her trademark Brandy Johns march toward the bulletin board.

"What the hell are you doing here?" she said, fixing Sandy with a very stern look and entirely ignoring the conversation that she had been having with Kelphit.

Sandy shot a quick look and a shrug to Kelphit before turning to Brandy. "I had always heard of an island off of Maine where art and healing were the highest priority. Montauk is pretty empty in January, so it wasn't a tough choice to close the shop for a bit and head here to see if I could learn anything new." Another glance at Kelphit. "And I may have heard that there would be a need for extra hands around now."

Brandy shook her head. "I clearly need to have a real sit-down with you." Brandy turned to Fintan, who was settling McCloud and a very restless Nick into the back of a golf cart. "And you, Fintan! Can I call you Finn? You seem like more of a Finn to me."

"As you wish," Fintan answered with a smile.

"Love that movie," Brandy muttered. "What's your story? You're Fae, yes? A Peripheral."

The smile never left Fintan's face, but left his eyes and there was no mistaking the steel in his reply. "Not here. When we settle your friends, we will talk."

He turned and climbed into the golf cart and started up the hill, turning left at the first intersection.

"Okay, then," Brandy said. "Guess we're walking."

Kelphit was chuckling as he proceeded up the hill, Brandy noting that he, too, made no sound in the gravel roadway. "There is truly not another like you, Brandy."

"And don't you forget it," she huffed.

Bayard and Noodle followed behind, with Cinder bounding back and forth, soaking in an entire island of new smells and fresh air.

"I think it's going well, yeah?" Noodle said, turning a hopeful expression to Bayard.

"Oh, definitely," Bayard shot back, jumping after Cinder and frolicking with the wolf as they clambered up the hill. "No doubt who is in charge here. Fintan is going to give Brandy a run for her money. I like him!"

"Finn, a big guy in the water just saved us," Brandy said, walking next to the cart. "Dark hair braided down his back. Big. Really big. Any idea who that is?"

"Most likely an indigenous spirit named Gluskabe," Fintan answered. "But he is rarely seen here. I'll need to hear more."

Noodle trudged upward last, already reaching for his sketch pad as he began to notice the sturdy cottages that dotted the hillsides and the tall, powerful trees that surrounded the community. Despite everything that had brought them here, the island was wildly beautiful. And rugged. And remote. Even for Maine.

CHAPTER 5

Sean and Trout found themselves, ten minutes later, seated at a table with massive breakfast paninis in front of them. Huge, steaming mugs of coffee sat beside each plate and the two were silent while they tucked into their meals.

Finally coming up for air, Trout broke the silence. "This is the best breakfast I've ever had. And I'm not just saying that because I was possibly moments away from starving."

"Drama queen, much?" Sean said around a mouthful of egg and bacon. "But I get it. Didn't know how hungry I was 'til we walked in, and I smelled...everything."

"Should we get something for Jotunn?" Trout asked, his brow creasing. "I have no idea what a troll eats. You?"

"You are such a softie," Sean replied. "I'm sure the little thing is fine. He lived in that Stonehenge place alone for years. He can take care of himself."

"But that's exactly my point," Trout protested. "He's been stuck there all this time. Who knows how he survived? Wouldn't it be nice to get him a treat? I'm getting him a treat. Be right back."

"You're a pushover!" Sean called after the receding Trout, but he had a smile on his face.

Sean sat back in his chair. He'd been running on fumes for too long. The overnight drive, fence climbing, troll discovery, and early morning drive to Maine had finally caught up to him. He was done. He let his head loll backward and stared at the ceiling.

"Coffee," he muttered. "That will help." He reached for his cup and his shoulders sagged as he lifted it and realized it was empty. "Figures."

As he was mustering the energy to hoist himself up and go for another coffee, Trout came racewalking back to the table, casting repeated glances over his shoulder.

"No treat for the troll?" Sean asked.

"I ordered it," Trout answered, dropping into his seat and pulling the collar of his jacket up high onto his neck. "I just saw someone. Someone I know. From way back when."

"Okay," Sean replied, sitting forward in his chair and cradling his chin in his hands while fixing Trout with a stare. "Do go on. Because you're acting like you stole a loaf of bread and there's an inspector hot on your trail."

"Ha, ha, ha," Trout hissed at Sean. "This is serious. I didn't even think she would still be around here."

"Aha!" Sean crowed. "A she! This gets better and better. Did you break her heart? You cad."

"No!" Trout said a bit too loudly before lowering his volume. "No. It's not like that. I mean, she was amazing, but *everyone* had a crush on her. Including me. But she was way out of my league. Everyone's league really. She was a bartender at the pizza spot back then. Pizza was okay, but everyone went to hang out with her."

"Wait a sec," Sean said, leaning forward now. "You're not talking about Mal?"

"Yes!" Trout said in a very audible stage whisper. "Exactly! So, you know!"

"Mal is here!" Sean replied, and now it was his turn to be a little too loud. "Whoa. Mal…"

"Yeah," Trout said. "I froze. I felt like I was in seventh grade. I spotted her and ran away. I don't think she saw me."

Just then, across the dining room, they heard someone call, "Dan Trout? Hey, Dan!"

Terrified, Trout made eye contact with Sean. He looked like he was about to make a break for it, but before he could move a woman arrived beside their table. Both men looked up, their expressions like two teenagers who'd been caught trying to sneak a beer out of the refrigerator.

"Mal?" Trout asked, turning to the woman and doing some of the worst acting of his illustrious career. "Well, whaddaya know! Hi, Mal. Long time no see."

Mal smiled widely at Trout. She was average in height but was dwarfed by Trout as he rose to greet her. Her long, jet-black hair reached halfway down her back. Her complexion was fair, a trail of freckles across her nose and cheeks spoke of summer months past. Her almond-shaped eyes were bright, keenly intelligent, and seemed to change their color as the light shifted. Now hazel, now grey, now blue. But always alert. She was wearing comfortable jeans and a green and black plaid shirt under her heavy Maine winter coat. A tattoo peeked out from under her sleeve. Both Sean and Trout were instantly struck dumb as they remembered what had made Mal… Mal.

"And Sean Curley?" she cried, spying him at the table. "What are the two of you doing here? It's January in Maine? Are you nuts?" She laughed as she spoke, and the two men instantly felt at ease and remembered what made her such a good bartender. And friend. She genuinely listened to people and made them feel important. And it didn't seem put on. Mal was the real deal. Schoolboy crushes aside, they were just flat out happy to see her.

Trout shook his head, as much to knock himself out of his stupor as to acknowledge that she had a point. "Can you sit with us for a minute? We'll fill you in."

Mal pulled out a seat and settled into the table. "So good to see you two! Gets quiet around here this time of year. Hit me with it! What's new?"

Sean sighed loudly and looked at Trout. Where to start?

Ten minutes later, Sean and Trout leaned back in their seats having shared as much as they thought safe. That meant no talk of magic, the Otherworld, their troll passenger, or a comatose time traveler. What it *did* mean was a story about a friend who suffered a freak accident in Lancaster and a recommendation from the staff at the Fulton to seek help on Monhegan.

Sean shot a look to Trout, feeling quite proud of himself for threading the needle with a believable story that didn't give too much away. The last thing they wanted was to put Mal in danger. Or give her reason to doubt their sanity. Something in Trout's eyes gave Sean pause and he glanced back at Mal who seemed to be considering him very carefully before turning her eyes to the tabletop in front of her. She disappeared in thought for a moment, before nodding slightly to herself and returning her eyes to Sean and Trout.

"Sounds like a tricky situation," Mal began slowly. "Lots of good hospitals between here and Pennsylvania." She glanced out the window. "But sometimes hospitals aren't quite the right fit for certain ailments. Look, I know some folks on Monhegan. I love it there. Studied there some. What you two couldn't know is that I've spent a lot of time learning about...natural remedies, shall we say? I grow my own herbs. Raise goats. Stuff like that. I guess what I'm trying to say is...I may be able to help your friend. He's not here, though. Already on the island?"

"Yeah, he's up there now," Trout said. "We aren't trying to drag you into anything, Mal. We're good. Just wanted to explain. Right, Sean?"

"Oh, yeah, totally," Sean agreed. "We're all set, Mal. But amazing of you to even offer."

"Right," Mal said, giving them each a look. "Well, let me just say this, then. You both look like hell. The drive to New Harbor isn't bad, but it's slow. You've already missed the early boats and if your friend is being looked after, you should drop anchor here in Brunswick for the night. Stop by the Maine State office. They'd love to see you. Especially this time of year. Kath will be there, for sure. Bert—I'm less sure. He gets around a lot. Say hi over there. Then see what makes sense. I think you're going to find out that a lot has changed here. Some of it's even for the best. Some."

"Thanks, Mal," Sean answered. "We had thought about stopping over to the MSMT office, but I don't know about staying over. We both"—he glanced at Trout—"have some pretty pressing business to get back to."

"Your call," Mal said, rising from her seat. "If it's any incentive, I'm behind the bar at Bionic tonight. Should be quiet, so if you come by, we can have a real catch-up. But up to you!"

"Thanks," Trout replied, clearly more open to the idea of staying than Sean. "I'll shoot you a message if we hang around. Still on the socials?"

"I am!" she answered brightly.

And she picked up her bag of pastries and headed to the parking lot. The two watched her go silently.

Trout opened his mouth to speak, but Sean held up a hand to stop him.

"Trout, we have things to do. You wanted to check on Nick and McCloud. Let's get to it. I need to find a path to the Otherworld to Breena. And I thought you wanted to get back to the Outer Banks to see Eleanor. We can't do it all. And the last thing we want is to put Mal in a dangerous place. People who get caught up with us end up in bad situations. If we really like her, we should leave her out of it. Raising herbs in her garden isn't likely to equip her for battling Dullahans and the like."

Trout pursed his lips and absently stroked his impressive moustache.

"I know what you're saying makes sense," he said slowly. "I guess a normal night just sounded, I don't know, normal. Let's swing by the theatre office and then go from there. You think Jotunn is okay?"

"He's fine," Sean said. "Let's get back into town. Get things moving."

They gathered their things. Trout rushed back into the retail area to pick up some baked goods. "Never show up empty-handed! My mom taught me that!" he called over his shoulder. And he knew Kath over at the theatre would appreciate the gesture.

Back at the table, he and Sean shrugged into their coats and headed for the exit.

"She was right about me being tired," Trout said, his lanky legs dragging on the way to the Crosstrek. "My butt is in low gear."

"Same," said Sean. "But work to do."

As they walked outside, their breath misted in the air in front of them, and they felt the not unpleasant sting of the winter wind in their noses and throats. In their fog of exhaustion, neither noticed Mal three cars over in a black Jeep Wrangler. Her car was idling and sending out a plume of exhaust. She held her phone to her ear and smiled as she watched the two climb into the Crosstrek. The smile lingered as they pulled out of the parking lot, and she waited a few minutes before pulling out.

The group marched up the hill, past the houses nearest the harbor, and on. The island's lighthouse sat atop the steep incline, but they continued beyond that. The path grew thinner. The gravel gave way to mulch, and then finally simple dirt. Following Fintan and the golf cart with the patients loaded in back, they finally veered off the visible path entirely, crossing an open field ringed with incongruous electrical and cell towers. Maintenance equipment filled much of the open space and seemed at odds with the simplicity and purity they had seen on the island thus far.

Brandy shot a quizzical look toward Noodle as they continued on toward what looked like a solid wall of forest on the far side of the opening. Noodle, for his part, seemed to have his head on a swivel, soaking in every new sight.

As they neared the trees, Fintan slowed the golf cart, and Brandy was sure they would have to leave it behind if they were going to enter the woods. The cart slowed, but only for an instant, before Fintan turned quickly to the right and accelerated again. Brandy was about to shout out a warning, when she saw the cart glide into a break in the trees that had been disguised from their approach. The cart disappeared into the darkness beneath the canopy and the group plunged after it.

They were now moving toward the side of the island opposite the harbor and the hub of the community. Silence cocooned them, growing more isolating as they continued along the mysterious trail.

Brandy hustled to keep up. Her legs pumping in an effort to save face. Kelphit and Bayard, though they were smaller than she was, seemed to move effortlessly in the wake of the vehicle. Cinder was as animated as Brandy had ever seen her. The cool, clear air was working a different kind of magic on her, and she flashed back and forth, disappearing into the trees for minutes on end before erupting from them and sprinting in another direction. For his part, Noodle followed in a near daze. The island was already seeping into him and his sketch pad dangled loosely at his side, the constant inspiration finally overwhelming him and stilling his hand.

Curiously, as they followed the disguised trail, it began to widen. Brandy noticed that the packed dirt was eventually replaced by a heavy, loamy mulch that filled the air with the scent of rich earth. Someone had taken great care to maintain the path, and, though her legs were still working madly, and her cheeks were flushed with exertion despite the cool temperature, the way seemed to become easier. She relaxed a bit and fell into a gentler gait.

A few minutes later, the group emerged into a wide clearing in the trees. They were deep into the island, closer to the east side than the west where they had arrived. In the clearing, Brandy was surprised to see a cluster of houses. Cottages, really. Small, cozy, stone homes. Each with a chimney sending plumes of smoke skyward. Brandy felt instantly as if she had wandered onto the set for a *The Lord of the Rings* film, which was not an unpleasant sensation to her, at all.

Fintan steered the cart to the door of the largest building in the settlement. The low building was made of sturdy timber, rather than the stone of the others. It was long and squat, and rather than the chimneys of the other structures, featured stovepipes poking out of either end of the building. It seemed to be a gathering place, in contrast to the smaller homes surrounding it.

Fintan jumped from the cart and crossed quickly to the rear where he checked on both the patients. Kelphit and Sandy arrived just after, and helped prepare McCloud and Nick for a transfer inside. McCloud remained still, but Nick was jerking from side to side. At times, a guttural snarl emerged from him, and Sandy directed her attention entirely to calming him as much as possible.

The grey sky was growing darker, and a wind was building, threatening harsher weather. Brandy noted that the ground beneath her feet was frozen. Unforgiving, it refused to give at all at her steps and they became almost mechanical as she found it necessary to carefully place her feet.

The front door opened and the woman they had seen at the dock appeared. Her hair was a flaming red, her eyes emerald green. Unearthly, but gentle. She stepped out, rolling an antique-looking wheelchair to Fintan. Despite the chair's basic construction, it moved easily across the frozen earth and Fintan accepted it with a nod.

The healers worked together to shift the massive Timestrider into the chair where he lolled to one side. As he was wheeled in, Sandy remained by the cart, keeping an anxious eye on Nick.

Minutes later, with Brandy, Bayard, and Noodle still standing awkwardly in what seemed to be the town square, the door reopened and the healers, minus Kelphit, repeated the process with Nick. As Sandy shepherded the chair toward the front door, Fintan paused and, placing a hand lightly on the red-haired woman's shoulder, turned to Brandy and the others.

"I do apologize," he said. "My manners have been known to be lacking when there are patients nearby. Allow me to introduce Sulevia. My partner here."

The woman nodded to Fintan before turning to the others. "I'm named *after* the goddess of healing; I am not the goddess herself. Always important to make that known immediately." Her voice was startlingly low, a rumbling contralto completely at odds with her appearance. "Welcome. You've done well in bringing your friends here. But, please"—she gestured to the doorway—"come into the warm. You must be frozen. After you."

With a quick glance at the others, Brandy led the way into the building. Cinder came racing in from the surrounding trees to join Bayard just as he was entering. Noodle was close behind, eyes glazed, his expression one of wonder.

The interior was a welcome relief. There were two coal-burning stoves, one on either end, matching the stovepipes seen outside. Dark wood dominated the space, both the walls and the pillars that formed two rows along the floor. Plush rugs lay scattered across the floor. Blue and green, some bore symbols in a language that Brandy could not decipher. Next to either fireplace, wooden privacy screens had been placed, and as the group moved further into the space, she saw that Nick and McCloud had been placed on beds close to the heat. Large soft pillows cradled their heads, and fluffy comforters had been placed over them. McCloud lay as still as stone. If not for the rising and falling of his chest, he could easily have been mistaken as dead.

That was most definitely not the case with Nick, who struggled beneath the covers. His head shook side to side, and he pushed one of his pillows onto the floor. Sandy stood at his side, doing all she could to calm him and stop him from hurting himself. Kelphit was at the foot of his bed, his pack open by his feet and Sulevia rushed into an alcove to the left of the front door only to emerge with a leather case. It looked heavy, but she bore it with ease, and settled on the far side of Nick's bed, popping the clasp on her case and working feverishly with a collection of containers inside. Herbs, tinctures, stones, and parchments were examined and most discarded.

Fintan saw Brandy watching with concern and gently took her by the elbow and led her to the center of the room, where a collection of chairs and sofas created a meeting space.

"Sulevia is the most gifted healer I have ever known," he said to Brandy, easing her into one of the chairs. "And you know well how talented Kelphit is. Your friend Nick is the more urgent of the two patients, but the other, the Timestrider, may prove the more difficult. If they can be saved, this is the place for it."

"*If?*" Brandy responded. "We were told you could help."

"And so we will," Fintan reassured her. "Let them work. Let *us* work. But in the meantime, you must be exhausted. Can we get you some tea? Something to eat?"

Bayard appeared suddenly at Fintan's side, a hopeful look on his face.

"Yes, please," Bayard interjected. "It's been quite a trek."

Noodle also appeared and settled into another of the chairs. "Honestly, I could eat something."

Brandy glared at both of them. "I have no idea how you can think of eating with the two of them just...laying there. But whatever."

"It's settled," Fintan said, crouching by Brandy. "I think you will find all things seem better with a full stomach."

"I doubt that very much," she replied, leaning forward in the chair and cradling her head in her hands.

Outside, the wind was rising and could be heard whistling along the roof and past the stovepipes. The patter of sleet and rain could be heard, soft at first but quickly gaining in strength. The sturdy building held firm, but in almost no time it sounded as if the skies had declared war on the earth. Brandy lifted her face to the ceiling, where branches from the nearby trees tapped and scratched along the roof above her, like so many skeletal fingers probing for a way in. It felt as if they were in the only safe place left on earth.

"I really hope this wasn't a mistake," Brandy muttered, nervously scanning the ceiling and listening to the groan of the timber walls.

Sean pulled into the Hannaford parking lot next to the theatre office. His hands lingered on the steering wheel and his head dropped onto them. Exhaustion settling in after the big breakfast.

"We used to get passes to park here," Trout said. "Hope we don't get ticketed or—whatever a supermarket does to people in their lot."

"I'm sure we'll be fine," Sean answered, without lifting his head.

"Actually," Trout continued, "I forgot how much I love the Hannaford. New York grocery stores are all so cramped. This place is *huge*. I'll pop in when we finish at the office and hit the hot food bar. My buddy James Masterson taught me about it."

"Love that guy," Sean replied, his head still unmoving. "Shame we missed him at the Fulton by, like, a day. But I have no clue how you can even think about food right now."

"Trust me," Trout said, pursing his lips and nodding. "You'll see. Plus, we'll need munchies if we're hitting the road again."

"First things first," Sean mumbled from his steering wheel pillow. "Let's check in with Kath. With any luck, they'll have coffee on. I need something."

Both men climbed slowly, very slowly, out of the Crosstrek and crossed Elm Street to the theatre offices. The front door was locked which prompted a surprised look between the two. Trout spotted a buzzer off to the side and pushed it. Deep within the building, they heard a faint ringing.

"Don't remember the doors being locked when I was here," Trout noted. "Seems very out of character."

"It's a different world than a few years ago," Sean said. "Even the normal world has gotten harder."

"You saying I got hard?" came a call from the other side of the door just before it was flung open to reveal Kath in all her glory. Kath was of an indeterminate age. Neither young nor old. She just...was. Her curly auburn hair was piled high atop her head. She wore worn jeans and, despite the frigid temperatures outside, a tie-dyed Maine State Music Theatre t-shirt. She pushed her large red-framed glasses onto her forehead and laughed at the startled looks on both the men's faces.

"Okay, okay, settle down. I'm kidding with you!" she cried. "Get your butts in here. You two are a sight for sore eyes. Trout and Curley in Brunswick in the offseason? Yes, please!"

All three laughed together as she grabbed their arms and pulled them inside and into a three-person Maine-sized hug. She shuffled the group around and broke the hug to push them further into the building.

"I'm happy to see you, but you guys look like crap!" she continued. "Dip into the candy bowl outside my door and then pop a squat in my office. I have to run out back for just a sec and then you can tell me what the hell you're doing in Maine. In January. I always thought you two were smarter than that. Well, at least you, Sean. Trout?" She waggled her hand back and forth in a "could go either way" motion, before laughing again and nudging them toward her office door down the hall.

"Back in a jiff!" she called and disappeared down another hallway to the right.

Sean and Trout lingered in the hallway. The walls were filled with framed photos of past shows, and they wandered deeper into the building looking for the years that they would be featured.

"Ha!" Trout called. "Here I am! *Perfect Crime*, 2014. Man, I loved that show. Great costumes."

"Yo!" Sean replied. "Found me. *Bell*. It was about Alexander Graham Bell." Then, in a remarkably accurate Scottish accent, "Och, aye! That was great craic, but I was hoachin'."

Trout turned, laughing. "I have no clue what you just said, but it sure sounded good—"

They were interrupted by a crash from the hallway that Kath had taken, and both stopped, suddenly concerned and stepping toward the noise. The short hallway took them by a printing station. A massive commercial printer surrounded by shelves of supplies. Just past that, the space opened into the green room, the area where employees gathered on breaks or for a quick meal during work hours. Before they got into the green room, Kathleen came bustling out of a door on the opposite side of the room and held her hands up high.

"Nothing to see here!" she declared. "Just those jokers in the scene shop making a mess. How they were put in charge of power tools, I'll never understand. My office?"

Without waiting for an answer, she stretched her arms out and herded them back in the opposite direction.

"Find yourselves on the walls?" she asked. "I think there are a couple of good ones of you both down towards the board room. They go chronologically."

Kath settled them into chairs opposite her desk before sitting.

"So. Talk to me," she said. "What could possibly bring you here now? I don't even want to be here. Big snow coming this weekend."

Sean and Trout shared a glance and Sean started into the spiel he had given Mal not long before. Enough truth to keep things straight in their heads, but no mention of magic or myths or danger. Just a couple sick friends who had been referred to someone on Monhegan Island.

Kathleen was no fool and suffered them not at all, and it was clear that something about the story had stood out to her, but instead of saying anything, she sat back in her rolling office chair and steepled her fingers in front of her face.

"Monhegan, huh?" she asked. "Good place to get...some very specific kinds of care. Guess your buddies caught the early boat?"

"Yeah, they drove through the night," Trout answered. "We made a stop on the way. Originally, we didn't think we'd be headed up this way, but"—he glanced at Sean—"things changed a bit."

"Is Bert around?" Sean asked, steering the conversation toward a safer topic. "We'd love to see him. We're hoping to catch a later boat to the island, but we have a little while."

"Bert is...around, but has a lot going on," Kathleen answered, lowering her hands to the desktop. "I'll try to lasso him if I can. Um, do you guys have anything else you want to share? I know you just blew into town. Maine's a big state, but a small place, if you get my drift. If your friends are in trouble, I may know someone who can help."

"Thanks, Kath," Sean answered, putting an arm out to stop Trout from responding. "I appreciate that. That's the company manager in you coming out. Wanting to help two old buddies you haven't seen in years. It's why you're so good at your job. But I think we have things under control. Definitely don't want you getting caught up in our situation."

Now Kath leaned forward. "See, that makes me feel like you all are in some sort of trouble. All the more reason to offer to help."

"It's not trouble, really," Trout began. "Just some details to work out and we have to set our buddies right. We're looking out for them the way you're trying to look after us. Funny, huh?"

"I don't know, Dan," she replied. "Is it? Is it funny, or—"

Suddenly they were interrupted by another clattering explosion of noise from deeper in the building. This time, though, it didn't stop but grew louder. Kathleen stood quickly and made her way back into the hall.

Trout turned to Sean. "Yeah, those stagehands are noisy considering it's five months until they have a show here again."

"I was thinking the same thing," Sean said, turning in his seat and craning his neck to get a look out the door.

Suddenly a voice began to shout in the midst of the cacophony. It was just gibberish at first but seemed to be getting louder and finally some words came through. Well, one word.

"Trout! Trout! Trout! Trout!" it cried.

Dan was out of his chair in a heartbeat. "I know that voice."

"Me too," said Sean. "But that doesn't make sense. We left him—"

Before Sean could finish his thought, the little troll, Jotunn, came skittering around the corner from the other hallway.

"Trout!" Jotunn squealed, spotting the big Montanan. "I knew! I knew! Could smell you!"

Without a pause, the troll flew at Trout and wrapped his arms and legs around him like a toddler welcoming his dad home from a day at work, eventually working around to Trout's back and peering out cautiously at Kath.

"So happy!" Jotunn continued. "Trout here! Trout!"

"What in the hell is goin' on?" Trout exclaimed, turning to Sean, whose eyes had grown three times in size.

Kath came sliding around the corner before spotting the troll latched onto Trout. A fraction of a second later, Mal came rushing out behind.

"Oh, shit," Mal muttered.

"Yeah, well, there's a really good explanation for this," Kath said, turning from Mal to Trout and holding her hands up, palms out.

Sean squinted and shifted his gaze from Mal to Kath, and back.

"I hope so," he said quietly. "I really do. Should we take our seats again?"

Jotunn had burrowed his still leaking nose into Trout's neck and his frantic breathing had begun to settle. Trout gave Sean a nod, and began to waddle, troll-laden, back into the office. It would have been comical under most circumstances. But not these. Sean's face took on a stony disposition as he resumed his seat. Mal couldn't meet their eyes as she followed them in and perched on a windowsill by the doorway.

"No more BS," Sean said. "Not us. Not you. Given the current circumstance"—he glanced at the troll, awkwardly still clinging to Trout—"I think you should go first."

Kath sighed. Then nodded.

CHAPTER 6

The wind continued to pick up. Brandy stood and paced the length of the meeting hall, stopping by Nick's bed and then crossing the floor to stop by McCloud. There was little change in either. Actually, there was no change in McCloud, at all. Nick, however, seemed to have calmed somewhat. He was less flushed than earlier and had stopped sweating. His seizures had grown less frequent. The healers were clustered at his bed. Only Fintan tended to McCloud.

Pausing in her pacing, Brandy approached one of the shuttered windows, but a blast of wind shook both the shutters and Brandy, who jumped back from the edge of the room.

"We sure we're good here?" she called to no one in particular. "That wind is getting worse."

From across the room, Fintan turned to her. "We are safe here. The walls are not the only things keeping the weather at bay."

Sulevia rose, drying her hands on a cloth, and brushing a stray bright red strand of hair out of her eyes. "It does seem to be getting worse," she said to Fintan.

"This is no ordinary wind," Kelphit said, also rising. "No ordinary storm."

Noodle was still ensconced in his chair, rolling a pencil between his fingers, his sketch book forgotten on the floor at his feet. Bayard was seated next to him and looked up at the healers, giving a curt nod. Cinder had been mirroring Brandy, pacing the opposite direction around the room, but at Bayard's movement rushed to his side and curled up at his feet, a light whine barely audible.

"What does that mean?" Brandy demanded. "We came here to cure our friends. This was supposed to be the safest place. Now—what? Did someone send this storm? What's happening?"

Bayard rose from his seat, Cinder gaining her feet by him. "I think it would be a good idea to take a look out there. We'll be right back."

Fintan looked inclined to argue the point but thought better of it and returned his attention to the Timestrider on the bed. Sulevia simply bowed her head before dragging a forearm across her brow and setting back to work on Nick.

Kelphit detached himself from Nick's bedside and met Bayard at the entrance. Reaching into a pouch on his belt, he pressed a small stone into Bayard's hand.

"Fairy stone," he explained. "Some small protection and possibly even some warning as to what is happening."

"Thank you, friend," Bayard responded, clasping Kelphit's forearm in gratitude.

Before Bayard could open the door, it crashed open. Everyone started in alarm, but just as quickly a man entered, pushed along by the wind at his back. His dark hair was cropped short and plastered to his head by the drenching rain outside. He wore a heavy black and green plaid coat, buttoned high and with the collar up to protect his neck. His jeans were worn and broken in from what had clearly been hard work. He stamped his substantial boots on the floor, shaking excess water from them.

All of the newcomers looked up, surprised at the appearance of someone in the midst of the storm raging outside. Fintan and Sulevia, however, barely registered his arrival.

The man placed a large bag on the floor at his feet and used his hands to wipe the water from his eyes. He scanned the room, taking note of the new arrivals with deep brown eyes that were as intelligent as they were troubled.

Shaking his head to get rid of excess water from his hair, which raised a canine smile from Cinder, the man hoisted his bag.

"Right," he said. "Who ordered the food? And yes, I do expect a generous tip. Have you looked outside?"

"I'm afraid I'm to blame for that, Jay," Fintan said, stepping to the newcomer. "Our guests have had a long journey and no respite."

"Hey, Finn, no sweat. I'm just messin' with you," came the response. "Don't want to get anyone's hopes up, though. It's just some basics—cheese, meats, some fresh bread. You know, actually, yeah, get your hopes up. This charcuterie board would cost an arm and a leg in Portland. Who am I kidding? Anywhere between here and Boston."

"I knew he seemed like a Finn," Brandy muttered.

"Sounds perfect to me," Noodle said, rousing himself from his chair. "Thank you to both of you. And sorry to drag you out in the weather. Jay, is it?"

"Don't give it a second thought," Jay answered. "And yes. Jay. Pleased to meet ya. And I'm no saint. If that was full of Chicago Dogs, I'd have found a dry doorway and camped out with them."

"I have no idea what any of that means," Bayard said, joining the others by the door. "But I do know I'm famished. So, thank you."

An explosion of wind shook the building, and Fintan and Sulevia exchanged a look. Jay caught sight of it and laid a hand on Fintan's shoulder.

"That sounds pretty bad out there," Jay said quietly. "Should I help?"

Fintan smiled in response. "Thank you, Jay. I believe that Sulevia and I will be able to deal with this ourselves." He glanced at Sulevia, who nodded in response. "Why don't you stay with our new friends while we clear this up?"

"If you say so, Finn," Jay said. "You know where to find me if you need me."

Fintan turned to the group. "Jay was a patient here, at one point. Some of our guests end up staying even after they have been healed. Jay is one. And now we couldn't imagine not having him with us."

"Sure, you say that when I'm in the room," Jay replied, with a smirk. "It's what you say when I'm *not* in the room that worries me."

"I would never dream—" Fintan began.

"Relax, Finn," Jay said, with a slap on Fintan's back. "I'm kidding again. You"—he gestured at Bayard—"grab some food and sit by me. I'm going to explain to you the glory that is a Chicago Dog."

"Is it as good as pizza?" Bayard asked, eyes wide.

"Oh, you wanna talk pizza? Ever had Chicago deep-dish pizza?" Bayard shook his head.

"Ooh, boy. You are not prepared for what I'm about to lay on you. Come on!"

Jay grabbed his bundle of food and crossed to the seating area in the center of the room.

"So, um, can I get some, too?" Noodle asked, trailing behind.

"Sure, you can!" Jay cried. "You, too, miss!" he called to Brandy. "And you"—he gestured to Kelphit and Sandy, who were still tending to the patients—"look busy, so I'll bring some your way in just a sec."

"*Miss?*" Brandy grumbled, joining the others by the food. "Don't even know how you can eat with Nick and McCloud just lying there. And the sky falling down on us. But whatever."

Brandy paused, while the others helped themselves, and watched as Fintan and Sulevia climbed into their cold weather clothes again. They paused by the door and seemed to confer without saying a word before opening the door and, heads down against the wind, trudged out the door. As she turned back to the room, she heard Jay talking to Bayard as if he was a small child.

"Now, I'm not saying New York pizza is *bad*, I'm just saying Chicago pizza is something completely different. Picture this,,,"

Despite herself, she chuckled and crossed to grab some food for herself, while outside it sounded as if the heavens had unleashed their fury and aimed it at the little island.

Kath took a deep breath, ran her hands through her considerable curls, and looked at Trout and Sean.

"Look, I haven't been entirely up-front with you," she began.

"You think?" Sean replied. "Let's start with how you ended up holding our troll friend here hostage."

Jotunn lifted his head from Trout's neck to fix a stare on Sean. "Friend?" Jotunn said quietly. "Sean likes Jotunn?"

"Time and place, buddy," Trout said, patting the troll reassuringly on the back.

"Now, hold on," Kath protested. "He wasn't our *hostage*. It's... complicated, but it's not like that."

Mal leaned forward from her seat on the windowsill. "Sean. Dan. We know a bit about what's been going on with you. Not everything but"—she shot a look to Kath—"some."

Kath held up her hand and rose from her desk, crossing to the doorway. She opened the door, stuck her head into the hallway, scanning in both directions. Satisfied they were alone, she closed the door, closed the blinds, and slowly crossed back to her seat.

"Maine State, as you well know," Kath said, haltingly, "is a theatre. As such, we are home to a number of—how do I put this?—sensitive types. Folks who can *feel* the Others. The folks you call Peripherals." At Sean's look of surprise, she held up her hands again. "MSMT and the Fulton have a close relationship. Have for years. Even more so now. Marcello Pettirosso and our artistic director, Bert, have a relationship. I'll let them fill you in on that, but suffice to say, we all communicate often. We heard, after the fact, about what happened down there."

"I'm still not hearing a reason you were holding Jotunn against his will," Trout interjected.

"Completely separate from our connection to the Fulton, the sensitives here at MSMT made a decision a while back," Mal said, leaning back against the window. "There are more than a few of us in town who understood what was at stake. I told you things had changed for me. One thing that changed is my working, unofficially, with the gang here. On certain projects. Maine attracts...unique types of people. That shouldn't surprise either of you. You've spent time here. Well, some of us in town wanted to help. However, we could."

"With sides being drawn in this—whatever is coming—war? Readjustment?" Kath looked at Jotunn as she spoke. "There are certain creatures from the Otherworld. The Veil. Whatever you want to call it. They don't want to be caught up in what's coming. Some of them are too small, meek, to make a difference. Some are confused and don't know what is right. Some are trapped in the drift of events. Persecuted for being different. Or pressed into service against their will."

"They're trapped," Mal jumped in. "No safe place to simply be. As you've seen, there are some serious bad guys at play. Nowhere seems to be beyond the reach of either side. We've heard about your...abilities? And we know too well what the Dullahan and his like are capable of. Maine is a vast space and so much of it is empty forest. Wild. Secluded. Untouched by men. So—"

"We made a choice," Kath said. "Our intentions were good. Are good. All we want to do is give these folks a place to be themselves. To live free. No expectations. We've been creating a haven for them. Way north of here. Where no one will bother them. But getting there safely is complicated. You tried to hide from the ones who are chasing you. That didn't work out. And you have friends and power and resources. Now imagine being all alone and simply wanting to disappear."

"We help them do that," Mal continued. "Take them in, keep them fed and warm, pass them along our network. Give them hope."

"What?" Trout asked, sitting forward and absently soothing Jotunn with a gently bouncing knee. "You're saying you made a sort of Underground Railway? For Peripherals?"

"Yeah, I guess I am saying that," Kath replied. "There's actually a connection to the real Underground Railroad in Brunswick. "We've been home to good hearts for a long time."

"We were calling it the Underworld Railroad," Mal said. "Although Underworld isn't quite right."

"I voted for the Paranormal Parkway but lost," Kath shot back with a disappointed look to Mal.

"We should just stick with Underworld Railroad," Mal said soothingly. "Not that many people will ever even know about it."

"Right," Trout interrupted. "How did you end up snatching Jotunn, then? He doesn't seem like he wanted to be here." Jotunn shook his head vigorously in response to this. "Seems this Railroad of yours isn't doing much good if it's holding folks against their will."

"Dan, we didn't hurt Jotunn," Mal said. "We never would. But a house troll without a house who shows up unexpectedly overnight raises eyebrows. At least eyebrows that sense he's here. We needed to find out how he ended up under the swinging bridge."

"Blame me," Kath said. "I'm the one who sensed him. I'm the one who picked him up. But all we could get him to say was 'Trout' this and 'Trout' that. Not hard to connect the dots here."

"Truth," Jotunn muttered, barely lifting his face from Trout's neck. "No hurt. Just scare. Not want to lose friend." The troll looked at Sean. "My friends."

"Trout, he was never in any danger," Kath continued. "All we want to do is make sure everyone, especially Jotunn here, is safe. If the wrong people found him, human or not, bad things could happen."

"And what's the next stop on this Underworld Railroad?" Sean asked, as Kathleen grimaced, knowing she had lost the naming contest.

"Funny you should ask," Mal answered, shooting an apologetic look at Kath. "From here we send them to Monhegan, actually. Get them looked over, make sure they're healthy and up to the next stop, which is further up the coast."

"Quite a coincidence," Sean said. "You knew this when we saw you this morning?"

Mal shook her head. "I knew there was a troll in town. No clue he was with you until I got back to my car."

"They nice to me," Jotunn said, finally raising his head. "Just scared. Missed Trout."

Kath rose to lean on the other side of her desk. "We're on the same side. We all want what's best for the folks who need looking after. Now how about you tell us how you ended up bringing a lost troll with you to Maine to check on your hurt friends?"

Trout glanced at Sean. "Mind if I do this?" Sean nodded and motioned for him to take the floor. And with that, Trout told them how they had ended up at America's Stonehenge. How they had happened upon Jotunn and how he had joined them on the trek north. "Our thought was to get him to Monhegan and find him some new friends. Maybe a new reason to...be a troll. But the little guy may have other ideas."

Jotunn stared adoringly at Trout throughout the story and beamed at him when he had finished. "Trout my new *kildevand*. I protect Trout now."

Trout grinned back at the troll and mussed the hair on his scaly head before wincing and surreptitiously wiping his hand on his jeans.

"I appreciate the thought," Trout said. "I think Sean and I are trying to look after *you*."

"Funny," Jotunn replied, adjusting himself to sit more comfortably in Trout's lap.

"Right," Sean said, trying to get the conversation back on track.

"Let's say we're all on the same side. And I still have a lot of questions. Luckily, I know and trust you guys. So far. What happens next?"

"I'd say we fill Bert in on everything and, hopefully, if the boss man agrees, you all can go on your way with any help we can give."

A new voice spoke next, and all eyes turned to the door. Unnoticed by any of them, it had swung silently open, and a large figure stood in the entrance, nearly blocking out the light from the hallway.

"The *boss man,*" said a deeply resonant baritone, "already knows. And no, you can't leave." There was steel in the tone.

Sean and Trout shot panicked looks at each other and Jotunn burrowed his face back into Trout's shoulder. If the troll could have disappeared into Trout, he would have.

A tall, muscular man stepped fully into the office. His deep brown hair was perfectly coiffed, and his chiseled features showed resolve. He fixed both men with a stern look, lingering longer on Sean as if he could see straight into him. He looked more like a retired football player than the Artistic Director he was. Bert Clarke had arrived. Abruptly, he broke into a gleaming white smile.

"You're going nowhere until we grab a drink at Bionic and we catch up properly." He smiled at Mal. "I hear the staff there is amazing. Relax guys. And you, too, sir," he directed at Jotunn. "This may be the safest and friendliest stop you've had in a while. Make the most of it."

And just like that, the tension in the room flew out the doorway with a fluttering of anxious wings and even Jotunn returned the smile Clarke had aimed his way. It seemed Sean, Trout, and Jotunn would spend at least some more time in Brunswick. And it came as a great relief to all of them, although a shadow still lay over Sean. A shadow that Trout thought only he could sense.

Brandy and the others sat, completely satiated, in the center of the room. They could barely move; they were so stuffed. What Jay had downplayed as some odds and ends, had proven to be a feast. Jay himself remained full speed. He was now tending to Kelphit and Sandy, who had remained with their respective patients. Every few minutes, he cocked his head, listening for something, and as she watched him, Brandy realized that it had been more than fifteen minutes since Fintan and Sulevia had gone outside.

Brandy stopped to listen, also, and it seemed nothing had changed. The wind and rain seemed as heavy as ever and she was beginning to worry about their hosts. Bayard and Noodle were deep in a conversation about various pizza styles and were apparently oblivious to everything but the state of their stomachs.

Brandy rose and crossed to Jay, who was setting a plate of meats and cheeses for Sandy. And he was setting it quite well, Brandy noted.

"Were you a chef in your previous life?" she asked him.

"Nah," Jay answered, putting the finishing touches on the plate presentation before looking up at her. "Did a lot of cater waitering early on. Out of necessity, not choice. I was an actor. Dancer, singer, actor, to be precise. Served a lot of mediocre food to very rich people who didn't know any better."

"An actor, huh?" Brandy asked, leaning against the wall by Jay. "In New York?"

"Among other places," Jay said, setting the plate by Sandy, who nodded her thanks. "I was good, too. But—stuff happened. And I ended up here."

"What kind of stuff?" Brandy continued. "Tell me to shut up if I'm being too nosy. I have a habit of doing that."

"Not too nosy," Jay replied. "Just probably not the time or place to get into it. I'm guessing you're in the biz?"

"That obvious?"

"Takes one to know one," Jay said with a wry grin. "Or an ex one, anyway."

"Well, I'd love to hear more about your story. When the time is right," Brandy replied. "Trying to figure this place out. Maybe that will help."

"Highly doubtful," Jay answered. "I've been here a long time, and I still haven't figured it out."

Brandy became distracted by Cinder, who had paced to the front door, and was sniffing along the floor there. Only then did she realize that the wind had stopped. In fact, the rain had ceased, too, and a stillness had fallen over the building. Cinder let out a whine and pawed at the door.

"And it seems our hosts have done the trick," Jay noted. "I need to set something out for them. They'll probably need it after that."

As he rose and grabbed his bag of seemingly endless food, the door opened and Sulevia, followed by Fintan, entered. They were soaked through and looked exhausted, but the glimpse of the village green behind them that Brandy got showed a bright sun making it seem as if there had been no storm at all. No sign of clouds. No wind.

"I'll be damned," she said to herself, as the others congregated in the center of the room. Even Kelphit and Sandy, both holding their plates, joined the others to hear what had happened.

Fintan eased himself into one of the overstuffed chairs and sighed. Sulevia did the same on the sofa, allowing herself to kick off her shoes and settle into a corner with her feet tucked under her.

"Impressive," Brandy said as she approached them. "Guess there's more to you than meets the eyes. You two okay?"

Sulevia leaned her head back on the cushions, staring aimlessly at the ceiling. Fintan ran his hands over his face before lifting his head and smiling.

"That was not a natural storm," he said, finally. "There is more at play than we had foreseen. This island has always been inviolate. We tend the sick and injured, regardless of their allegiance. It's always been so. For someone to ignore that tradition—it's never been done. Lucky for us"—his eyes scanned the room—"all of us, we are well prepared for most eventualities. Most. But we will have to investigate who this was. And why. The next time will likely be more diffi-cult to counter."

"You tend to...anyone?" Brandy asked, head cocked. "Even those who would do you harm. Or the island. Or both."

Sulevia spoke without moving her head. "Yes. We were always set apart from any disagreements, or conflict. Healing knows no borders. Our allegiance was always to seeing the afflicted made whole. And that was all. This, though—this signals a shift in the Veil. It can only be so, because that storm came from no man. Or woman." She shifted her eyes to take in Brandy, and they were kind, but concerned.

Brandy thought she caught Fintan glance at Jay. It happened so quickly that she almost thought she had imagined it, but when she glanced at Jay, she saw him with his eyes downcast. There was something more at play here. Something she could not know, having just arrived.

"Both sides, huh," she muttered, but received no reaction from any of the others.

"Yo, Brandy," Noodle called, and she noticed that he had detached himself from the group and wandered to one of the windows, pushing the shutter open slightly from within.

She wandered over and made note that Kelphit and Sandy had remained by their wards even through the height of the storm and the return of the two island healers. Sandy was entirely focused on her work, but Kelphit was completely aware of everything that was being said.

Brandy reached Noodle, also making note that Cinder was still by the front door and had been joined by Bayard.

"What's up, Noodle?" she asked. "Need something?"

"Nah, I'm good," Noodle replied, never taking his eyes from what had caught his attention outside. "Just thought you would find this interesting." He nodded toward the village green outside.

Brandy followed his eyes and saw nothing out of the ordinary. The storm clouds had flown, leaving a brilliant blue winter sky behind. The trees, bare of leaves except for the plentiful evergreens, stood stolid and tall, surrounding the village with their always watchful presence. The pathways were dry and pristine, as well-groomed as they had been when the travelers had arrived.

Brandy took it all in and was turning to Noodle to ask what he had noticed when it hit her. There was no sign of the violent storm that had raged only moments before. No branches down, no run-off from the lashing rain, not even a puddle on the steps leading to the buildings.

"Well, damn," she said, sharing the surprise with Noodle. And as he nodded in response, she shook her head. "I don't understand any of this. Wind that leaves no damage. Water that isn't wet. What have we gotten ourselves into here?"

Noodle had no answer and stood silent. At the front door, Cinder threw her nose into the air, searching for a scent that only she could detect. With a glance over her shoulder at Bayard, she padded out the door and vanished into the trees across the green.

Clarke stayed in the doorway, refusing to take any of the other seats, even though they were offered.

"I'm good here," he said. "This is Kath's office. She's the boss in here. Do we have a place for them to stay the night, Kath? I'm thinking maybe not downtown given our troll buddy here."

Jotunn glanced up at Clarke, his initial skepticism thawing. He almost allowed himself to smile.

"On it, Bert," Kath answered. "And I agree that out of town may be best. Maybe the cottage?"

"Great idea," Clarke answered. "You'll love it. Out in the woods. Next to the water. Quiet. Very quiet. And the landlords, Kieran and Patricia Fanning live two doors down and have helped us many times when we have special guests passing through. They know what's what."

"Now it is about twenty minutes out of town, if that's okay," Kathleen said.

"But," Mal interjected, "it's north of town, so will give you a head start to Monhegan in the morning."

"Good point," Clarke agreed. "Whaddaya say? Accept our hospitality?"

Sean, still reluctant, looked to Trout, whose face was lit up in anticipation. Jotunn, too, seemed intrigued, and both of them looked exhausted.

"If it were just me," Sean said, "I'd push on, but it's not just me. And you all have been so nice. We'll just get on the road super early tomorrow morning, right?"

Trout and Jotunn both nodded in response, and the relief on their faces was so comical Sean chuckled.

"It's settled, then," Clarke declared. "Kath, give the Fannings a call and let them know. I'll get lunch sent in from Big Top and when we're done, why don't you head to the cottage, get some rest, and we can meet up at Bionic at say"—he glanced a question at Mal— "five o'clock?"

Mal seemed agreeable to that and, with a plan in place, everyone rose and got to work.

"Lunch in my office in fifteen, yeah?" Clarke called over his shoulder as he disappeared down the hallway without waiting for an answer. "I have to call Marcello. He's been texting me every five minutes wanting an update."

Mal paused on her way out the door and turned to Sean and Trout.

"I'm sorry if it seemed like I wasn't operating in good faith," she said. "I really didn't know anything about Jotunn when we had breakfast. At least, not in relation to you. I was genuinely happy to see you. And I'm genuinely happy to be able to help you."

"No need for apologies," Trout replied. "You're one of the good ones, Mal. We know that. It's good to see you."

"Thanks, Dan," she answered, but her eyes lingered on Sean, who remained silent but gave her a reassuring, if less than enthusiastic, smile.

Kath rounded the corner with a bag from the deli around the corner.

"Bert opted for take-out," she said. "He thinks you should go get some rest. I won't tell you what he said you look like. Now go! Get outta here."

Sean and Trout, with Jotunn still firmly clasping his neck, excused themselves and went to their car in the lot across the street, leaving the others to their tasks.

Trout turned to Sean as they got back to the Crosstrek. "You sure you're okay with this?" he asked. "I feel like you got railroaded into it."

Sean looked out over the parking lot. Ironically, the Brunswick rail station was on the opposite side. "Railroaded. Funny. But no, as much as I want to push on and get to Breena, I know this is best. It's hard to believe we were in that Stonehenge place and met this guy" —he nodded to Jotunn—"only last night. I'm exhausted. We need the rest. And now that Bert and Kath and Mal are in on things, maybe they can actually be some help. I don't know. Hard to think straight, honestly."

"Oh, hold up!" Trout suddenly exclaimed. "The hot food bar! Jimmy Masterson would hate if we missed it."

"Actually," Sean answered, "he'd hate to hear you call him Jimmy. But do what you gotta do. Jotunn and I can wait here. Probably not a bad idea to have something to eat at the cottage before meeting them later. That deli order won't last me that long."

"Well, Jimbo seemed inappropriate for him, so—Jimmy," Trout said, handing the troll to Sean and headed into the supermarket. Jotunn shot him a mournful look as he wandered away, before turning dubious eyes to Sean.

"I know, buddy," Sean responded. "Maybe we got off to a bad start. Let's get into the car and out of sight and maybe you can tell me some more about your old home in Massachusetts?"

The troll's eyes filled up with tears again, and Sean immediately regretted his choice of subject.

"You know what, skip that," Sean said, backtracking as quickly as his mind would allow. "How about we talk about that swinging bridge you were under? That used to be one of my favorite places here."

At this, the troll turned to Sean and flashed a wary smile. "Bridge nice," Jotunn said. "Old. Old to human, anyway. Not to me. But still nice."

Ten minutes later, when Trout returned from the Hannaford with a paper bag stacked with recyclable hot food containers, he opened the door and was surprised to find Jotunn turned sideways in the back seat to face Sean, opposite him, and speaking at breakneck speed.

"Bridge good for hiding," he was saying. "People no think to look under. Hear lots of talk when no one know you there." He paused to drag an already moist forearm across his perpetually oozing nose, then turned at the sound of the opening door. "Trout! Back so soon! Got food! Sean is friend now. Not as bad as I thought. Just grumpy. Lots of grump. Better now. Can we go to water house now? Jotunn want to see water."

"Well, this is a happy change," Trout said, sending a questioning look to Sean, who smiled and shrugged in response. "Yeah, he grows on you. Slowly. Like a fungus. Shall we get going?"

Sean climbed into the front seat and started the car. Carefully backing out of the space. Jotunn took his familiar seat in Trout's lap and was chattering away about the beauty of the swinging bridge and how surprising it had been to "actually like Sean."

Shaking his head, Sean pulled out onto Maine Street and turned left headed back out toward Cook's Corner. They would pass the turnoff for Wild Oats, but this time were headed further, out into the woods between Brunswick and the city of Bath. He had tried to put some sort of direction into the GPS, but Kath had warned him that the cottage had no actual address, and he wasn't likely to get much help. She'd been right. Nothing came up when he tried to get them to the general area, so he drove and looked for the landmarks they'd been given.

It was a straight shot out Bath Road. They passed nearly every strip mall iteration Sean could imagine, but on further inspection, he noticed a number of storefronts empty, staring back at him like the lifeless eyes of a shark. The store where he'd bought his beloved Red Sox hat a few years earlier was gone. As was the Big Lots store where he'd bought his first pair of reading glasses. Begrudgingly. There was the Applebee's where he had joined Bert and other theatre staff all those years ago. One of the only places open late after a show. Finally, they made a right-hand turn at the Schutty's Seafood truck and found themselves on a much smaller county road. Two lanes that wound and curved for a few miles before Sean realized he had just passed what must be the dirt road that led to the cottage.

Sean backed up, twitchy that a car could come up behind him while doing so, but he managed it, and they then started down a dirt track that put the car's all-wheel drive through its paces. Finally, the track ended, and they all turned to find a small red cottage tucked into the last plot of land before a spit of trees that separated them from the houses at the end of the next dirt track along the peninsula of land.

Jotunn was out the door before Sean could even switch off the ignition, and Trout laughed out loud to see the little troll scamper around the side of the house and toward the sparkling water of the New Meadows River in the backyard. Trout unfolded his lanky frame and hustled after Jotunn, worried that he could cause some mischief, or, worse, run into some of the neighbors. But as he rounded the corner of the cottage, he found the troll standing at the top of a small incline that led down to the water. Or, more accurately, toward the mudflat that lay exposed now at low tide. The air had the tang of the sea, and salt, and the vegetal scent of seaweed and grasses exposed by the receding water. A small lobster boat chugged up the river, already heading home after a full day's work that had begun before most people had even left their beds.

Halfway across the river on a small island, two bald eagles tussled over a fish one had caught, their cries echoing across the otherwise still serene landscape. Trout's breath caught in his throat, and he joined the troll on the hill. A moment later, Sean joined them and took a long, deep breath.

"Well, damn," Trout said quietly. "This is the nearest thing to Montana I think I've ever seen. Throw some mountains in there and I could actually be happy here."

"We just don't have air like this in New York," Sean replied. "I think my shoulders just went down three inches. And I didn't even know they'd been tight."

"Ginge, your shoulders have been around your ears since the day you closed your show and Ken disappeared. You deserve a breather."

"Ken..." Sean said. "Can't believe he's gone."

"I know, pal," Trout said, reaching a big hand out to lay on Sean's shoulder, before thinking better of it.

The moment was interrupted by an exceedingly strange hooting sound that erupted from Jotunn. He pointed at a rock outcropping to their left that was shaded by a massive elm tree whose branches dropped lazily over.

"Can I? Can I? Can I?" the troll asked Trout with pleading eyes.

"Go for it, little guy," Trout said.

"Just try to stay out of the mudflat—" Sean pointed at the deep brown mud field that sat between them and the rocks, but it was too late. Jotunn was off like a shot and capered through the mud, at times sinking in over his knees before extricating himself and plodding to the rocks where he plopped down and lazily played with the lowest branches.

"Okay, I admit it," Sean said. "You were right. We need this. I'll buy Bert a drink tonight for knowing what I needed more than I knew myself."

"Ahem," Trout replied. "Pretty sure I've been telling you that for at least the last fourteen hours."

"That's true," Sean agreed. "Sadly, you won't be there, so—"

"'Scuse me?" Trout protested. "Where am I gonna be?"

Sean pointed to Jotunn, who had flopped back on the rocks and was watching the clouds slip by overhead between the branches over his head. He looked like he was wearing a pair of deep brown overalls. Deep brown mud overalls.

"You're going to be figuring out how to clean a troll," Sean laughed. "Come on, let's leave him to it and check out this cottage. What kind of fried food smorgasbord did you get?"

"Oh, you are going to love it. Egg rolls. Fried cheese. Onion rings."

"Anything, oh I don't know, like a vegetable?"

"Onions are vegetables," Trout pointed out.

"Funny," Sean replied.

"Do I really have to clean the troll?" Trout asked. Nervous.

"Absolutely," Sean answered, disappearing into the cottage.

CHAPTER 7

The storm had indeed been banished and shown no signs of returning. Tensions eased and everyone had gone back to the priority—tending the ill. With little else to do, Brandy, Noodle, and Bayard had finally fallen asleep, scattered around the various chairs and sofas. Jay had offered to show them to a cabin that was available for them to use, but they had all declined, unwilling to leave Nick and McCloud. Jay had nodded in understanding and set about his tasks, shuttling in and out, bringing the healers whatever they needed.

Brandy was the first to rouse and immediately rose to check on the patients. McCloud was still unchanged. He seemed asleep, completely unaware of his surroundings. Fintan remained by the bed, monitoring the Scotsman. He acknowledged Brandy but had nothing new to tell her.

Next, Brandy ambled over to Nick's bed, and here there had been some change. Nick's complexion had improved, and his breathing was easier. He seemed to be resting more comfortably, too. His injured arm lay on top of the sheet and the angry crimson that had throbbed on it had settled into a less concerning tinge. It looked no different than one would have expected from such a wound.

Sandy motioned for Brandy to step aside and the two women moved closer to the front door where they could speak more freely.

"He's doing better," Sandy said. "It didn't look like that would be the case for a while, but Sulevia and Kelphit are something else. I thought I knew a few things about healing and natural remedies, but I've never even imagined the things they can do."

"That's the first good news I've had since this all started," Brandy replied. "What was the deal? Why was Nick so much worse than anyone else? He wasn't the only one to get nicked in the fight at the Fulton. But no one else reacted this way."

"I'm probably not the best one to answer that," Sandy admitted, "but from what I understand, the pike that got him was...different. It was likely the claw of a Barghest."

Brandy began to speak, and Sandy stilled her with a gesture.

"I'd never heard of them either. A creature from the north of England. Big, bad, black dogs with red eyes and a decidedly unpleasant temperament. Even Sulevia had never seen anything like this. Their blows cause wounds that never heal, which is what Nick is dealing with. Sulevia and Kelphit had to dig deep to find a solution. I'm out of my depth, but they seem to think he's turned a corner."

"Got it," Brandy said. "Thanks. Now if we could just get McCloud back, we could maybe get Ken back from...wherever he went in time."

"One step at a time," Sandy answered, glancing over her shoulder at Fintan by the Timestrider's bedside. "Oh, and glad you're here. I hate that I missed so much with everyone. Sounds like between the Outer Banks and Lancaster, you've all had a full plate."

Brandy laughed and melted into a hug with Sandy. "That's an understatement. But look at you now. All that learning you did is paying off."

"I don't think I had much to do with any of it, but I do what I can," Sandy said. She glanced back to where the others were still asleep. Even Cinder lay on her side next to Bayard, her paws galloping after some quarry in a dreamworld all her own. "Look, I think the imminent danger is past. You should go out, take a walk, sit on a log, contemplate the beauty of this place. Monhegan really is otherworldly. Sorry, that may not be what you want to hear. It's beautiful. That's all I mean."

"I think I'll take you up on that," Brandy said, glancing out the still partially open window. "Looks like the sun is on the way down. Should grab a moment while I can." She paused to give Sandy a squeeze. "Thank you. I really mean that. I thought we were going to lose Nick."

"I know you did," Sandy said. "So did I."

"Okay, I'm out. I'll have my cell with me if you need me, although I'm not sure it works here."

"Spotty at best," Sand replied. "But you can't go too far. It's an island."

"Good point," Brandy said, heading to her bag and fishing around in the bottom.

She opened the front door and saw that she had been right. The sun was nearly below the tree line and shadows were stretching across the ground. She turned in a circle, trying to decide where to go, before setting off in the opposite direction of the town below them by the harbor.

"It's an island," she muttered to herself. "How far can I go?"

Within moments, she had entered the shelter of the forest, and the air immediately felt cooler. Crisper. The ground beneath her feet was frozen again and she felt herself thrill to the sudden cold. Each breath stung on its way in. She felt good. Alive.

She followed what she thought was a trail. Barely discernible along the forest floor. But she could make out enough to keep pushing ahead. She climbed over a fallen tree. Pushed through a bush that obscured the supposed path. A squirrel, disturbed by her passing, chittered at her from a nearby tree trunk.

"Sorry, buddy," she said quietly. "Just passing through. Go about your business."

And then, abruptly, the trees gave way to a small clearing. Stones and logs scattered about. It seemed as if someone had created the space just for her to stop. And so, she did. She found a large rock, scrambled up its face and pointed herself toward the Gulf of Maine and the Atlantic Ocean, knowing that the next land she would see, if she could see it, would be the ancestral home of the people working to save her friends. The cliff in front of her was easily more than a hundred feet high. The waters stretched out in front of her to infinity. She fished in her pocket and drew out the earbuds she had taken from her pack and slipped them into her ears. The moment of solitude was needed, although she would never have been able to put that into words. She pulled up a music app on her phone and allowed herself to submerge in the one refuge that had always been there for her. Music.

Paul Weller sang about flying fish, and she marveled at how the universe seemed to always send her just the right song at just the right time. She closed her eyes and allowed herself to drift away. Off the cliff, over the sea, far away. To a place with no Dullahan. No violence. No sorrow. No tears. Nothing but her and the marriage of music, word, and listener. For the first time in many weeks, she almost felt like herself. Her old self. And she somehow understood that self was gone. Replaced by this new Brandy. Stronger. More determined. More fiercely devoted to her family. And her family of friends.

Friends.

That thought led her back to Ken O'Carroll. And the decision he had made when their only hope of traveling back through time to the present had malfunctioned. She had seen the look in his eyes. The resolve. But she didn't understand what he'd decided until it was too late. He'd sent her and Sean back to 2024 and stranded himself in the past. And now, he was gone. At least to her. They had tried to find some information on what happened to him in the past but found little. A cryptic message left at the Fulton Theatre that had waited for years to be opened. Some signs that he had found financial and career success. But she missed him. And she felt that she had somehow failed. To stop him from doing what he did. She was the rock at the center of their group. She should have come up with a solution. She still had to.

Ken was adrift in time. Stuck where he didn't belong, in order to save the rest of them. She sat alone. Missing her friend. It seemed impossible that he was simply...gone. Even after the problems they had faced with Ken, and there had been many in the last few weeks, he had proven that his old self was still somewhere in there. And he proved it by sacrificing his own life. Or the life he had known.

Paul Weller gave way to Colin Hay in her ears. He was singing about waiting for his true life to begin and she opened her eyes, taking in the vastness before her. The horizon where the ocean met sky almost seamlessly in the dying daylight.

Cocooned in her own thoughts, she was startled at movement beside her on her stone perch and jerked suddenly away from whatever it was. She felt a gentle touch on her arm and turned to find Fintan seated next to her, a knowing smile on his lips.

She hit pause on her phone's screen and removed an earbud, returning his smile with relief.

"I'm very sorry," he said. "I had no intention of disturbing you. Or frightening you. You have found one of my favorite solitude spots. Monhegan is very helpful in providing them."

"Just glad it's you, Finn," Brandy answered, allowing herself to relax again. "Didn't mean to swipe your place. Funny, I thought it seemed kinda lived in." She glanced again out to sea. "You have a good one here. Just woolgathering. Not your fault I was a million miles away."

"I haven't abandoned my duties. I believe I've done all I can for the Timestrider," he said, following her gaze. "For now. A Naga's spell is formidable. Very few could resist at all. He is very strong. I do believe we can call him back. In time. How he will be affected—that is anyone's guess."

A gull rose from the cliffs below on an air current, hovering before them. Then another. They paused to examine the two figures seated in the clearing before riding the wind up and away, eventually diving toward the waves below. As they disappeared, Brandy felt as if she was soaring herself. Out into the vastness. Untethered.

She and Fintan sat in silence for a few minutes, lost in their thoughts only to be pulled back to their little clearing by a sudden chirping beside them. Brandy turned and saw a squirrel. She was fairly certain it was the same one she'd seen earlier. It was so close to Fintan that he could have reached out and touched it.

"Friend of yours?" Brandy asked, chuckling.

"As a matter of fact," Fintan said, holding out his palm and allowing the squirrel to climb on and scurry up his arm to perch on his shoulder. "I've been on this island a very long time. Eventually, they see me as one of them. As much a part pf the island as this stone. Or that tree."

"Sounds nice," Brandy replied, watching the squirrel stretch and lay its head aside Fintan's. "I don't think I've ever stayed in one place long enough to know what that would feel like."

"There are few places like Monhegan. This is rare."

"Will McCloud be able to Stride again when he wakes up?" Brandy asked, suddenly. "If he wakes up, of course."

"I honestly can't say," Fintan said, and noticed the disappointment on her face. "I know you want him to be able to find your friend. But I can't tell you something I don't know. And I can't lie to you."

"I appreciate that," Brandy answered. "I do. I just...miss him."

They sat again in silence for a few minutes. The dying sunlight seemed one of the most beautiful sights Brandy had ever experienced. She was afraid if she spoke, the magic would be gone. And it did feel like magic. Seated here on the edge of a mystical island, with an ancient Fae next to her.

She noticed a robin, flitting from branch to branch, whistling and chirping. It's call incongruously upbeat in the growing darkness.

"I would have thought," Brandy said finally, breaking the spell, "that robins would be gone by this time of year."

"Many have migrated by now," Fintan said, smiling at the newcomer. "But not all. That is one of our residents. He stays year-round. Most people don't realize that happens. But it's not uncommon."

"Well, welcome, resident robin," Brandy said. "Welcome to the sunset. Pull up a branch."

The bird gave her a glance, fluffed its feathers against the cooling evening air, and settled down.

This time it was Fintan who broke the silence. It was his turn to gaze at the dying day, and he seemed to be debating whether to speak before beginning. Tentatively.

"I am always happy to see them. The robins. This one, in particular, because he stays with us and has become part of Monhegan. But for ages now, almost longer than I can remember, I've called them Lee-Thorps."

Brandy shot him a questioning look, but sensed he wanted to talk, so she sat back without saying a word.

"I had a friend. A dear friend. Robin Lee-Thorp. A distant relation to the Viscount Fairfax. We were inseparable. He was astonishing for a human, although I've always believed he had some blood from the Fae in his family."

He rubbed his hands across his face. He clearly was struggling to find the right words. An unusual thing to see in one of the Peripherals.

"As a joke, I began to call every robin I saw on the wing a 'Lee-Thorp.' It was lighthearted. A simple nod to a friend who meant so much. To me. He was witty, wise. A thinker. An explorer. An adventurer. A chronicler. He was...a jewel among humankind. Sadly, his human blood was too much for his Otherworldly gifts to overcome. He fell ill. And despite fighting to remain here. Fighting gallantly. He slipped away one day. His absence affected me more than the loss of anyone before then. From that day forward, I shared the story of the Lee-Thorp name whenever I saw a robin. They are and ever will be Lee-Thorps to me. And while he is gone and knows the secret that no living thing knows, he is remembered. People who know me now also call them Lee-Thorps. So, while he is no longer by my side, he is still near me. And his name endures. And even though I know the truth, my heart, my ancient weary heart, still soars every time I see one. Every time my soul whispers within me, *A Lee-Thorp!* And for that moment, he lives. His name lives. His memory lives. And he is here again."

Brandy now reached out to Fintan and laid her hand gently on his shoulder.

"Thank you for that," she whispered. "And from now on, they will always be Lee-Thorps to me, too. And I'll share that story. And his name will go on. And on."

They both turned again to the deepening darkness over the sea, the day almost entirely fled. They put their arms around each other. Two virtual strangers, who now had a bond as unlikely as it was unexpected. In the dying light, they watched shards of light glisten along the tops of the waves far below. A web of faerie lights. Otherworldly. Beautiful. And thought of lost friends.

Finally, night claimed the earth and they rose, silently, brushing off their clothes and turning toward the village. The squirrel remained on Fintan's shoulder and rode along as they left. As Brandy took her first steps from the clearing and into the deep shadows of the forest, she looked to the trees and realized that as they had sat silently, the Lee-Thorp had flown away.

Surprisingly, after Sean and Trout grabbed showers and a quick rest, they had found Jotunn lounging by the back door of the cottage, and their fears of a troll in need of a power wash had proven unfounded.

Jotunn was spotless. In fact, he somehow seemed cleaner than before he'd gone frolicking in the mud flat.

"Never figured trolls to be the self-cleaning type," Trout said, indicating the little creature. "But there you have it. His nose has even stopped drippin'."

"Do you think we can leave him here on his own while we meet Bert?" Sean asked, watching the troll facing the setting sun. "Last time we left him somewhere, he ended up getting abducted."

"I wouldn't say abducted," Trout said. "And to be fair, it might have turned out better for us 'cuz of it. Now we have some new pals on our side. Maybe we should just ask him? Probably a good idea to start trustin' the people around us. Even if they're trolls."

"Yeah, you're right," Sean agreed. "Not always easy."

"Nothing about life right now is easy, Trout replied. "But trusting is one simple thing we can do to help change that. 'We struggle with the complexities and avoid the simplicities.' Let's just ask him."

"Did you just come up with that?" Sean asked, turning slowly to Trout.

"Me? Pshaw," Trout said with a chuckle. "I'm touched you think I could. Nah, that was Norman Vincent Peale."

"Just when I think I have a handle on you, Dan Trout, you go and quote Norman Vincent Peale. But you have a point. Let's ask Jotunn if he minds staying."

"'Change your thoughts and you change your world,'" Trout answered.

At Sean's unspoken question, Trout smiled and said, "Also good old Norm Peale. Heckuva guy."

"Right. Let's go ask him."

"'Society is always taken by surprise at any new example of common sense.' Ralphie Emerson," Trout responded.

"Now you're just showing off," Sean muttered, heading out toward the back porch and Jotunn.

After explaining the situation to the troll, Sean and Trout were surprised when his response was to ask if he could stay behind at the cottage before they even had a chance to ask.

"Quiet here," Jotunn explained. "Too many people where you go. Rather be here. Met a nice heron. Want to talk more with him. No mean to hurt feelings. That all right?"

"You got it, buddy," Trout answered, as Sean grinned and shook his head. "You relax. We won't be too late. And remember Kieran and Pat down the road if there's an emergency. But try really hard not to have an emergency, yeah?"

Jotunn smiled in response and rose to wrap his arms around Trout's waist. "Trout friend. Thank you."

Much to Sean's surprise, the troll then repeated the gesture with him. Sean shot a surprised look to Trout who smiled and shrugged. Surrendering to the moment and finding that he was beginning to actually like Jotunn, Sean awkwardly returned the embrace.

Five minutes later, Sean started up the Crosstrek and they bumped their way along the dirt road back to the main road. In twenty minutes, Sean was turning off Maine Street in Brunswick and finding a parking spot not far from the front door of Bionic.

Night had truly fallen by now and the streetlights left pools of light along the brick sidewalks. Traffic was light. January in Maine was frigid, and this night was no different. Pedestrians were few and far between along the central business district. Mainers are smart and know how to get through the long dark months of winter.

As they entered, Trout holding the door open for Sean, they found the bar to be largely empty. Wood-planked floors throughout were well-worn and comfortable. Immediately to their left they saw two dartboards that had seen plenty of action. To the right was a collection of large barrels with stools around them. Beyond that, an open floor, presumably for dancing or events, but which sat empty and bathed in a blue glow from two light trees that seemed to be wishing for busier nights.

Mal waved from behind the long wooden bar that stretched

along the left side of the room. A row of gleaming taps and shelves of brightly shining bottles stretched down the wall behind her.

"I think I can squeeze you in!" she called to them as they approached her. "Kidding. Obviously. Bert and Kath are—"

"Back here!" Bert interrupted, emerging from the back of the bar. "We're here. Never sit with your back to a door!"

"Thanks, Mal," Sean said to her as he and Trout proceeded back to the stools that had been staked out for them.

"Great beer here," Bert said by way of welcome. "Sean, I think I remember you liking IPAs. I recommend the Puddle Jumper from Flight Deck down the road. Trout, what's your poison?"

"Don't worry, gents," Kath said. "We have some munchies on the way. The usual stuff but they do it really well here. Hey, Mal! Any chance you can join us?"

Mal exaggeratedly peered up and down the empty bar. "Yeah, I can probably swing that. Let's get you all set up and I'll be around."

Sean went to the bar and got his beer and a Flight of the Concorde Pilsner for Trout. Returning to the table he saw a lone man wander in and sit at the far end of the bar and take out his phone. He was on the young side, Sean guessed late twenties. The one feature that stuck out was that, despite the sub-freezing temperature outside, he was wearing a pair of Crocs.

Mal delivered a beer to him before coming around and pulling a stool up to the barrel table to join them.

"You okay to be over here?" Trout asked, motioning toward the newcomer by the dart boards.

"Oh, him?" Mal asked. "Not a problem. Crocs comes in most nights. Nice guy. Pretty low-key. Crazy to wear Crocs in January, but that's Maine for ya."

"Let's get down to it, guys, so we can just relax and have some fun," Bert said, sipping on a bourbon. "We have some things to share with you, and I'm hoping you'll share some with us. Yeah?"

Sean shot a nervous look at Trout, who mouthed *Ralph Waldo Emerson* to him and settled back on his seat.

"Yeah," Sean said after a deep breath. "Yeah, I think we should do that."

With that, Sean allowed himself to share more than he had in quite a while. The appearance of the Peripherals, the discovery of his hidden wells of power tied to his singing, the struggle against the Dullahan and all of its minions that had taken them from New York to North Carolina. He walked everyone through the adventures and misadventures in Lancaster, explaining their foray into time travel and its unfortunate result for Ken. He even, with a shy glance at Mal, explained his relationship, or whatever it was, with Breena.

He turned it over to Trout who filled in some of the gaps, including his love for Eleanor Dare. A conjuror who was trapped on the Outer Banks of North Carolina, largely because she had chosen to throw her lot in with Trout and Sean.

Throughout, Bert, Kath and Mal exchanged occasional glances, especially when the subject of the Fulton Theatre, time travel, or the Peripherals was mentioned.

As they slowed and finally ended, Sean and Trout sat back and took deep breaths.

"Whoa," Sean said. "Sorry. That was a lot. I guess it just felt good to be able to get it all out."

"In front of people we know," Trout continued, "and trust."

"And trust," Sean echoed.

Kath stood up from the table, announcing, "Don't know about you all, but I need another drink after that. Especially"—she glanced at Bert and Mal—"because I know it's our turn. Anyone?"

Everyone at the table raised their hand and said, "Please," so Kath and Mal rose and tended bar.

"While they're getting us set up," Bert said, "I think I'll share some of my story. Stuff they know and don't need to hear again."

"Go for it," Trout answered, staring into his glass as if there could be some remnant of his beer hiding in the bottom. There wasn't.

"As I mentioned," Bert began, "we have a...close relationship with the Fulton. Truth is, Pettirosso and I have been partners for...a very long time. In every sense of the word. You both know I used to be an actor. Marcello and I met then."

"I wondered," Sean said. "Something in the way you mentioned it earlier."

"Leave it to you to pick up on that," Bert replied. "Anywho, when I made the switch to taking over here, we had a heart-to-heart. A few. We saw a chance to do some good. As you found out, the Fulton is a magnet. It draws all types. From all over. This world and...others. Some mean well. Some need help. We decided to help."

"Marcello never said a word," Sean noted.

"You all had your hands full, from what I heard," Bert pointed out. "Time and place. Need to know. All of those cliches. But now you know."

Trout was leaning against the wall, fixing Bert with a meaningful stare. "I like it," he said. "I can see it. Good balance there with you two."

"It works for us," Bert said, smiling. "But to more pressing matters. As a magnet for so many, the Fulton was in a position to help those who needed it. And Brunswick has a history of its own. It was on the actual Underground Railroad. And there you have it."

"I didn't know that," Sean said. "I knew about Joshua Chamberlain. All of that. No idea about the railroad."

"Didn't Jimmy Masterson play Chamberlain here once?" Trout interjected.

"He did," Bert replied. "He was brilliant. But you're right, Sean. Most people don't know everything there is to know about Brunswick. Maybe that's for the best."

"Mal and Kath are sensitives," Sean pointed out. "We know that. What about you? How do you fit in? Other than the Marcello connection, I mean."

"I'm not a Fae, not directly," Bert said, raising his hands. "But I do have certain talents. Not completely unlike yourself. My voice, my heritage. Marcello believes I'm descended from a human/Fae commingling. but we've never chased it down. I've always...known things. Felt things. If things had been different, we could have switched places, Sean. But I have to be honest. I'm glad they weren't."

Kath and Mal had returned now and quietly taken their spots.

"Glad we missed that part," Kath said, elbowing Mal. "Heard it enough for a lifetime."

The women shared a laugh at Bert's expense, but it was clear the three were close.

"If I can continue," Bert said, raising his eyebrows at the women, who bowed in return, "Maine is a pretty special place. It's very connected to the earth. And it has a history that, like Brunswick, flies under the radar a lot. It was a chance to make a difference."

"So...who exactly is it that you help?" Trout asked.

"Anyone who needs it," Mal answered, nodding to Bert. "Not everyone is cut out to be a hero. Or a fighter. Some of the Others, just like humans, simply want to live their lives."

"But as you've seen," Kath said, "often some of these lesser Fae—"

"Maybe 'lesser' isn't the best label," Bert cut in.

"Good point," Kath agreed. "I just mean some of the Others who are smaller. In stature. Or strength. Or temperament. Gentle may be a better way to describe them. If everyone was a hero, well, it wouldn't mean much, would it? Everyone has a part to play. Need the mountains with the valleys."

"Never thought about it quite that way," Trout said, hoisting his new beer.

"We didn't really have the luxury of thinking about much of anything," Sean replied. "It's been one calamity after another since we started this. I went to Lancaster to get away from it. But I guess there's no escape for me."

"Sadly, Sean," Bert said, "you are just too much in the thick of it. That time travel *was* Marcello's attempt to get you out of harm's way. But we know how that turned out."

"Speaking of which," Sean sat up straighter on his stool. "We really do need to hit the road early in the morning. That Monhegan boat leaves early. And I want to check on Nick and McCloud and then get on with things."

"Bit of good news on that front," Kath said. "I arranged for a boat to take you over in the morning. So, no need to worry about the ferry schedule."

"Nice one, Kath!" Trout replied. "One less thing to worry about."

"There is a small catch," Mal interjected. "We have a couple of new friends to send along with you. If that's okay."

"Like Railroad, refugee type friends?" Trout asked, leaning in.

"Yeah," Bert said. "But the good news is you get me, too. No offense, but we gave our word to get them there safely and one of us needs to go along. My turn."

"Even better," Sean said, nodding. "We can pick your brain on the way. Who will be joining us?"

"You'll see in the morning," Kath answered. "They'll get in later tonight. Fewer people that know, the better. They're staying out by you, so you won't be slowed down getting out."

"I was going to have them stay with me in town, but with everything going on, we thought it better to put them out there. They attract attention. You attract attention. Just being cautious."

"Cautious is good," Trout said. "Cautious is my middle name. What say you, folks? One more and then call it a night?"

Crocs at the end of the bar had gotten up and was throwing some darts lazily, but his heart didn't seem in it, and he quickly sat back down at the bar. His feet didn't quite reach the ground, and his legs were swinging like a small child at the grown-up table on Thanksgiving. Of course, that just made his Crocs all the more noticeable.

No one else did wander in as they lingered over their last drinks. No one seemed in a hurry to leave. The whole evening just seemed so...normal. Pleasant, even. Sean and Trout relaxed in a way they hadn't for what seemed an age. The conversation drifted to the latest Broadway news. Then the latest Broadway gossip. Then the latest Fulton gossip. And ended with Trout making a passionate argument for Bert hiring him for the upcoming summer season. And Sean. But the case really centered around Trout.

By ten o'clock, even Trout had to admit that he was done. The afternoon rest at the cottage had long worn off. Sean had forgone the last drink, knowing he had to drive, and he was drooping closer to the tabletop with each passing minute.

Finally, Bert rose and stretched, calling it a night. Kath stared wistfully at the tap handles but knew when to say when. Mal excused herself and went to give Crocs his tab and exchange pleasantries. He paid up and wandered slowly out. They could see him pause when he reached the street before turning right and moving off toward Maine Street.

After their goodnights, the group split up. Kath wandered off in the direction of the offices. Bert climbed into his SUV and cruised off. Mal gave the guys a hug and turned to her side work. Technically the bar didn't close until midnight, but she would be out early tonight. No patrons. Frigid temperature. Everything pointed toward an early night.

Sean and Trout ambled out to the Crosstrek, both climbing in with weary sighs. If they had been in a show, they likely would have another hour before their work was done, but this night, they were exhausted and looking forward to the serenity of the cottage in the woods.

Twenty minutes later they turned onto the dirt track that led to the house. As they passed Pat and Kieran's house, Trout pointed out Bert's truck in the driveway.

"Guess those new folks really are going to be staying close by," he said.

"One thing I'll say," Sean answered. "Folks around here can keep a secret."

They parked, and as they crossed to the front door, they both stopped to take in the full moon that made it feel like afternoon. The river beyond the cabin glistened in the moonlight, boats moored not far from the shore bobbed on the incoming tide like the audience at a

Saw Doctors concert. At least, that's what Sean thought when he looked out.

Before they reached the door, a pair of glowing eyes appeared at the corner of the building. Before either of them could react, Jotunn came racing out of the darkness toward them, leaping into Trout's arms. As much as a small troll can leap into a very tall man's grasp.

"Back! Back!" the troll cried. "Gone so long. Worried. Nice here, though. Not as nice as Trout here, but nice. And Sean! Sean friend now, too. Moon big. So bright. You smell like ale. Smells good. Bring any for Jotunn?"

They were all laughing as they entered the cottage. Sean thought he hadn't been so relaxed since before his Broadway show had closed and the Peripherals entered his life.

As the door closed behind them, Jotunn threw his nose in the air, and Sean noticed it was running again.

"Others are coming," the troll announced. "Wind brings them to me."

"All good, little guy," Trout reassured him. "We'll have some new friends to meet in the morning. But tonight? We sleep."

The door closed behind them with a snick. None of them bothered to lock it. Not out here. In the woods. By the river. Under the moon.

Mal had been wrong. The side work took longer than she expected. And at the last minute, two other regulars had wandered in for a late nightcap. Not a big deal. They were friends and good tippers. And honestly, it broke up the monotony of closing the bar entirely by herself.

She wiped her hands with her bar towel as she closed the door behind the latecomers, calling, "Night, Ames. Night, Bunny!"

She scanned the bar, making sure all was in order. It was. She rarely made mistakes. And never when she was in charge. She gathered her coat and bag from the back room and crossed the empty and darkened dance floor toward the front door. Crocs had left a dart on the bar, and she absentmindedly tossed it toward the board as she headed out. She didn't look back, so never saw that she had thrown a bullseye.

She reached the door and reached for the light switch, pausing when something seemed different. The air suddenly felt still. She looked out the window. The streetlight on the corner with Maine Street had blown and was stuttering a strobe in the night. Odd.

As she was watching, the next light closer to the bar started to flicker. It fluttered for a moment before falling dark. Something was wrong. Very wrong. The night was clear and cold. There was no weather affecting anything. And even then, Maine knew bad weather. This was something else.

She opened the door just a few inches and put her ear to the gap. Nothing. She was getting skittish. Silly. Maybe a transformer. Nothing more, nothing less.

She stepped out onto the sidewalk, and she turned to lock the door behind her, she heard it. Could that be a horse? She paused. It was definitely a horse. She spent enough time on a farm these days to know what she was hearing. But it made no sense. Who would be riding a horse in downtown Brunswick at almost midnight on a Tuesday night?

No one. That's who. Because the next thing she heard convinced her to duck back inside and shut off the outside lights. As she did, another streetlight stuttered and went out.

She fished her phone out of her bag and texted Kath immediately.

Lock the doors. We have company. Not the company we expected. Will be there ASAP. Follow the plan.

Mal rushed into the back room and grabbed a rucksack that had been stashed at the bottom of her locker for quite a while. She had never needed it before. Had hoped she never would.

When she reached the front door again, the noise had grown

louder. Underneath the slow and deliberate clop of a horse moving along the main street, was the unmistakable sound of something metallic being dragged down the street. She knew the sound of tire chains. A common sound in Maine during the winter months. This was not that. This she thought she recognized, while also thinking it must be wrong. Metal links being strung along. A very different kind of chain. The clattering sent its echoes into the otherwise silent town. Christmas was over, so this was no Jacob Marley paying a visit to a local Scrooge.

A horse appearing at almost exactly midnight, with a rider trailing a chain behind. It could only mean one thing. Their Railroad had been found out. A Dullahan. Must be. Maybe *the* Dullahan. Had come to Brunswick.

CHAPTER 8

Just before midnight, Sean woke with a start. Bad dream. Dreams. Plural. In the first, he'd been in some sort of hospital. But a hospital from long ago. Basic. Spartan. And eerily silent. He'd been there to visit a family member. A dream family member, no one he actually knew in life. The patient had been fine when he arrived, but things went downhill fast. Within minutes, his dream family member had been slipping away, turning a ghostly grey color. Flesh sagging. Fear radiating from their eyes. But silent. Everything silent. He'd run into the hallway calling for help, only to find that the same scene was playing out in every room. Every doorway stood open with a panicked visitor calling for help as patients in every room slipped away.

He'd shaken himself out of that dream. Sweating. Anxious. Took a breath when he realized it wasn't real and tried to go back to sleep. With no success. He'd gotten up to grab a glass of water and let his heart rate return to normal. He crossed to the bathroom, noticing Trout asleep on the sofa in the living room. Jotunn sat beside him, face pressed to the cool glass of the window, the moonlight giving him an almost angelic sheen. A smile spread across his ridiculous troll features.

He got to the bathroom and pushed the door open, but it crashed into something on the other side. Startled, Sean pushed more cautiously on the door to ease it open past whatever was in the way aside. To his even greater surprise, he felt resistance again and then it was shoved, forcefully, back at him, slamming shut. Something was inside. But what? Or who?

He turned to make sure he had seen Trout and Jotunn. He had. They were both exactly where he'd seen them. The only two others in the cottage. And both continued as if he weren't there. The door creaked open just a bit, and he felt himself being drawn into the bathroom. He was powerless to stop it, and as he tried to call to Trout, no sound came from his mouth and panic set in once again. His feet dragged across the floor of their own volition.

He sat up in his bed. Another dream. Two dreams back-to-back. His subconscious was doing somersaults tonight. He'd had enough dream manipulation back in Lancaster when he'd had to combat the Shadow People and the Hide-Behinds. Scanning his room, he sensed nothing. Deep breath. Calming breath. This really was just a case of bad dreams.

He threw the heavy covers off of him. The comforter was almost too hot, even in the drafty cabin. He slipped to the floor and quietly entered the living room. Trout and Jotunn were exactly as he'd seen them in his dream. Odd. Jotunn faced the river out back, the moon shining on his upturned face. Sitting quietly, there was a simple beauty to him that Sean had never noticed before. He walked to Jotunn and placed a hand on the little troll's shoulder. Jotunn showed no sign of surprise, in fact he leaned his head onto Sean and together they basked in the moon's glow while Trout snored quietly beside them.

The moment was broken by a clatter from down the road, in the direction of Kieran and Pat's house. A moment later, they heard an engine start and speed away down the dirt road. Sean guessed it was Bert, heading out to welcome the latest refugees.

Sean pressed his hand against the window, enjoying the taste of the frigid outdoor air on his palm. Refreshing after the massive comforter. He gave Jotunn a gentle squeeze and together, they both turned to give the sleeping Montanan a look, and then smiled at each other. Sean, feeling an unexpected fondness for the troll, gave a small wave and wandered into the bathroom for some water and then made his way back to bed.

The dreams had left their mark, though, and sleep was elusive. He lay in the dark, listening to every small scratch and patter from outside, along the walls and on the rooftop. The nighttime denizens of the forest going about their business. He closed his eyes. Still no sleep. Was that quiet scritch a raccoon? A squirrel? Was that distant cry a fox? A lynx? A Shadow Person? His mind whirred.

Finally, the forest sounds gave way to the thumping of his heart. It became the only thing he could hear. His heart. Inevitably, it led him to thoughts of Breena. Beautiful, elusive, impossible Breena. He knew she had feelings for him. Had. It felt so long since they were together. The first days of knowing each other and the intoxicating danger that mingled with mutual discovery. Her miraculous appearance on the battlefield of Bodie Island in North Carolina. He could still feel the kiss they'd shared. Its honesty. Purity. Those things can't be faked. The heart knows. But now family—and Fae—politics had interrupted. Feelings or not, she may be forever out of his reach. If that was true, this entire enterprise was a waste of time. His and his friends'. He knew he had treated them badly. Especially Trout, who had been nothing but a steadfast friend. Trout deserved better from him. All of the Grumbles did. He didn't feel in complete control of himself. And every part of the situation screamed for him to control himself. Too many people depended on him. Too much hinged on his growing power and how he chose to use it. But he had to know. If Breena was being held against her will, he would free her. If she had turned her back on their love, he would know the instant he saw her.

A romantic or a fool? The difference could be razor thin. His heart beat. And beat. His mind turned. And Orpheus never did welcome him to the land of sleep.

When Brandy and Fintan returned to the community hall, they were greeted with a buzz of activity. While McCloud still lay in his bed at the far side of the main room, Nick was sitting up in his. Bayard, Noodle, Sandy and Kelphit were clustered by him. His color was returning; the unhealthy clay-like grey had been replaced with a flush of pink. His injured arm sat across his lap, and Brandy saw his fingers wriggle a bit as she broke into a run and skidded to a stop by him.

"Hey, hey, hey!" she crowed. "Look who decided to join us! Dammit, Nick, don't you ever do that to us again or I'll cut you myself!"

Nick chuckled and extended his uninjured arm to Brandy. "Good to see you, too," he said. "I'm feeling much better, thanks for asking."

"I assumed you were by the simple fact that you're, you know, conscious. And not the color of New York snow after a week in a C-Town parking lot."

"Strangely specific," Nick replied, "yet effective."

"He responded quicker than any of us expected," Kelphit said. "Remarkable."

"What's remarkable," Sulevia interjected, "is your healing knowledge, Kelphit. I thought I knew almost all there is to know, and you have proven me very wrong."

"The most important thing is that he's back!" Sandy said.

"I don't feel all the way back," Nick insisted. "But it's nice to feel anything, honestly."

Drawing the others away from the bed, Bayard took Brandy's arm and crossed to the sofa. "There's more news. We got an email from Trout. He and Sean have been trying to reach us, but none of us have service on the island. They're headed to see us, actually. Apparently, not all is going to plan for them, but they want to see how the patients are doing. Nick's timing is good, in that regard. They'll be here in the morning."

"Good news all around," Brandy said. She noticed Fintan had crossed quietly to McCloud and stood by his bed. She gestured in his direction, and the others took note.

"No change there," Sulevia noted, quietly. "I fear the Timestrider will need to find a reserve within himself if he's to return. The Dreamworld can be very enticing. It takes enormous self-control and awareness to fight back. If he were human, he would be beyond anyone's aid."

"I feel pretty useless, honestly," Noodle murmured. "Can I do anything for anyone? Anything?"

"None of us know when we will be called or how we will respond," Sulevia said, turning to Noodle. "You are not here accidentally. I believe that. You must, too."

Noodle nodded, but his face belied his lingering doubt. Still nodding, he passed Nick's bed, patting him gently on a foot before leaving through the front door.

Bayard started to follow Noodle out, but Jay stopped him.

"Why don't you let me keep him company," he said. "I know my way around here. And we still don't know what sent that storm. I'll look out for him. You get some more rest."

Bayard paused. He had only just met this man, but he trusted Fintan and Sulevia. And Kelphit. He paused, but finally nodded, coming to some sort of decision.

"Of course," he said. "Mind if I send Cinder out with you? She needs to stretch her legs. Not good being cooped up."

"You bet," Jay agreed. "I love dogs. Especially when they're wolves."

With that, Jay and Cinder left the building, and the room settled into a nighttime quiet. Nick had fallen asleep, and the others murmured quietly. Fintan remained apart, vigilant by McCloud.

Jay was surprised to find that Noodle had only made it as far as the front porch of the community hall. He'd taken a seat and was stargazing. The night had arrived crystal clear and blazing with stars.

"Incredible, isn't it?" Jay asked, taking a seat next to Noodle. "I'm from Chicago, as I'm sure you guessed. Nothing like this there. I have hard time believing there's anything quite like *this* anywhere."

Cinder paused briefly but had no intention to sit on a staircase and followed her instinct, dashing off into the forest with a woof as farewell. The two men watched her until she disappeared, becoming a shadow that flashed in and out of the starlight as she explored and smelled and...lived.

"Oregon gives it a run for its money," Noodle answered, face still upturned. "That's where I'm from. But being on an island makes it... different. Lonelier. Quieter. Maybe more peaceful?"

"I get that," Jay said. "I mean, I must. I came here and stayed."

They both allowed the silence to sit between them. It wasn't awkward. The island seemed to cast a spell over both.

"A bit worried about that storm," Noodle said finally. "That happen here often?"

"Storms?" Jay asked. "Yes. A lot. But like that? No. No one and nothing would ever dare to do anything like that. At least, that's what we thought. Something is up. Something bad."

"That seems to be an ongoing theme for us," Noodle said. "You wouldn't believe what we saw in Lancaster. I'm not sure that I believe it. And I was there."

"Oh, I could tell you some things that might match it," Jay replied. "But you know what? If something bad is coming, and I think something bad *is* coming, whaddaya say we just...enjoy this. For now. For a little while."

"I say, that's a great idea," Noodle said. "Best idea I've heard in a long time."

So, they sat and turned their faces to the heavens where a billion points of light shone down on them. Light that had taken ages to reach them here, on this night. On this island filled with magic and mystery.

It had been only hours since Monhegan had felt the fury of some sort of unnatural attack. Something mighty had set its sights on this place. Or these people. Most likely both. But here, tucked under this blanket of stars and surrounded by the dense embrace of the woodland, they felt secure. Sheltered. Protected. And they relaxed into another companionable silence.

Cinder flashed between the tree trunks, and her joy was infectious. For this moment, all three allowed themselves to be here. Now. Whatever was barreling toward them would have to wait.

Mal slipped quietly out the front door of the bar. Her heart was pounding, and her breath misted in front of her face. She had plenty of experience helping small, frightened Otherworld creatures along their way to sanctuary further north in Maine. She considered herself a den mother of sorts. A nurturer. And though she had always known danger was a possible outcome of their activities, she had allowed herself to almost believe it wouldn't happen. She had never let her guard down entirely, but neither had she honestly believed it would come to this.

She chose to walk to the Maine State offices. No sense starting her car and drawing attention to herself. The hooves had moved along and were fading into the distance, but all else was still. She'd get there just as fast on foot.

Kath was there alone, though, and Mal was terrified what she would find if she didn't get there as quickly as possible. Kath was formidable, but like Mal had become used to being a gentle guide. With Bert off tending to their newcomers, Mal was Kath's only ally.

She hoisted the bag onto her shoulder and stayed close to the walls of the buildings, moving along Dunlap Street toward Maine. It was mostly unnecessary. The streetlights were out, and deep shadows had fallen across the town. She got to Maine Street and turned left, but felt too exposed, so slipped down Lincoln, left on Union, before working her way to Middle Street and approaching the theatre headquarters from behind.

Brunswick was dark and still. Too still. It was if someone had cast a spell over the citizens. Every window was black. No cars passed. Not a delivery truck. Not a stray student, back early from break, making their way home.

Her work boots sounded like hammer blows with each step, and she was sure that she had given herself away when she spotted the offices ahead. They were impossible to miss. Kath had turned every available light on and flooded the area with brilliant white.

Good. She wasn't too late.

Using a set of keys that had been given to her for emergencies, she slipped into the back of the building, through the scene shop, noting that the doorway had been treated with herbs and marked with symbols of guarding.

Moving through the silent building, she called out quietly for Kath, only stopping when she heard the front door open. A moment later, she heard Kath's booming voice ringing through the night.

"Yeah, yeah," Kath called. "I know who you are, and you don't impress me one bit. I'd get out of this town, if I were you, before the big guns get here and do it for you."

Mal knew Kath well. Maybe as well as anyone else in her life, and while her words were firm and sure, Mal could sense the tight fear in them. She hurried through the hallways. Hard to believe it was only hours earlier that they'd sat here with Trout and Sean. She glanced into Kath's office as she passed and noted it wasn't even quarter past twelve. She hoped they would see the sunrise.

She reached the entrance, reached into her bag and drew out two pouches she stuffed into her coat pockets and then slowly drew out two short black daggers and a chalice.

The daggers were both black-bladed with silver hilts that ended in green crystal balls. One bore a silver gilt moth, with traces of green tourmaline throughout. The other was similar, but in blue and with a female figure on the hilt and an Egyptian scarab where the moth lay on the other.

As Mal reached for the door, she heard a rasping voice answer Kath. It scratched like gravel and reminded her of winds setting up the clacking of dead marsh grasses in the wetlands behind her house. It stopped her midway to the latch, and she couldn't stop a shudder from snaking down her spine. The voice oozed evil. It was a voice rarely used and never ignored.

"You were dead the moment you stepped beyond that door," it hissed. "You are nothing. Meaningless. We are here for others."

Mal glanced out the front door, but couldn't see whatever was speaking to Kath, but she could see Kath. And what she saw stole her breath.

Kath stood alone on the sidewalk in front of the building. In one hand, she held a six-foot harpoon. It looked lethal, but Mal recognized it as a replica prop from the production of *Captains Courageous* a few seasons back. The blazing light that enveloped the offices reached only so far. The supermarket just a few feet away across the street was a black void. All that existed seemed to be Kath, the office, and the scene playing out. A gentle flurry of snow had begun, and the effect was of a nightmare snow globe. The world beyond shrouded. Nonexistent. Just the drama unfolding on the sidewalk.

Mal wasted no more time. Kath looked so small and alone, her neck craned to look up at whatever she faced. She wouldn't face it alone.

"What's up, Kath!" Mal called as she exploded out of the door. "Little late for business on a Tuesday night. Hey, I've got something for you!"

Kath turned to Mal and the look of relief on her face was nearly heartbreaking, but nothing compared to the determination behind it. Mal tossed her, gently, the dagger with the scarab on the hilt.

"Mal, damn glad to see ya," Kath replied. "Maybe don't throw any more sharp objects at me, but I can put this one to good use."

Mal strode to Kath's side with much more confidence than she was feeling. She gave Kath a shoulder squeeze before turning to her left to see what they were dealing with and what she saw snatched the breath from her body.

Less than ten yards in front of them was a figure beyond any nightmare she had ever suffered. A headless figure sat astride a massive black stallion. The figure was ashy grey, with skin that sloughed off it whenever it moved. Mal stared, agape. The figure carried its head in its left arm, and the face matched the deathly pallor of the body. The skin was stretched tight across the face, thin as parchment and making a rattling sound with every movement it made. And it was manic. Large eyes blazed a terrible crimson and its mouth, which stretched from one side of the head to the other, bore deadly flashing teeth. A hideous smile. In its right hand, it held a whip that snaked on the ground behind the rider and his voluminous black cloak. The whip appeared to be made of a spine. If it weren't so startlingly long, it could have been human. Everything Mal had ever heard of the Dullahan had done nothing to prepare her for the terror that faced them now.

Mal's hesitation lasted only a fraction of a second. She quickly reached into one of the pouches in her pocket and drew out a handful of powder. Cupping her hand before her face, she blew the powder into the night air between them and the Dullahan. It blossomed outward and mingled with the lazy snowflakes, settling on the sidewalk. Simultaneously, Kath took the prop harpoon and scratched a semicircle in the gathering snow on the sidewalk.

"You're not welcome here, big ugly," Kath stated plainly. "Go now. We can just pretend this never happened."

The laugh that erupted from the Dullahan sounded like wind whipping through a barren graveyard. "More amusement," it purred. "Your gestures mean nothing to me. You accomplish nothing."

Kath laughed in response. A reaction so surprising that Mal shot her a look of surprise.

"Yeah, I didn't really think a fiberglass harpoon would stop you in your tracks," she said lightly. "But it did buy us some time. And that's all I really wanted."

The roar of an engine shattered the night, and a familiar SUV came roaring across the Hannaford parking lot, jumping the curb and briefly going airborne before crashing down the small verge, across the far parking lot and coming to a skidding stop a few feet from the two women.

The driver's side door opened, and the familiar figure of Bertram Clarke emerged. His eyes were flashing with an anger Mal had never seen in him. He reached back into the truck and drew out a baseball bat with a sizeable metal spike driven through its end. He waved it in front of him as if he was a batter approaching an at bat.

"Hi, ladies," he said. "Hope you don't mind my crashing your party." He glanced at his truck, where it lay steaming in the frigid night. "Literally. But I hate to miss a good scrap."

"The more the merrier," Kath answered. Clearly relieved.

"Lookin' good, Bert," Mal chimed in.

The Dullahan spat at them. "More blood for me," it said, lashing out quickly with its whip, shattering three of the lights along the building's wall before the others could react. Darkness settled even closer to them. A spotlight on the center stage of their conflict.

"My companions prefer to work in darkness," it said, laughing again in its horror cackle.

From the newly settled darkness behind the horse came the sound of claws, clacking on the cement sidewalk. Large claws. Slowly, emerging from the blackness, two sets of eyes. While the Dullahan's eyes glowed a poisonous crimson, these blazed a hellish ruby. Deliberately, with no sense of urgency, two massive canines stalked into the light. Bigger than any dog Mal had ever seen, their heads came easily up to her shoulders. Their teeth were bared and dripped a yellow viscous fluid. They were as black as the night they had just left.

Kath and Mal both instinctively stepped back, but Bert let loose with an incongruous laugh. Loud and light and unworried.

"You think I would just show up with only trusty Frank Thomas here?" He waved the bat in front of him again. "I mean, pretty sure the three of us could take the three of you, but why risk it? I see your two puppies and raise you. Four wolves."

The other doors of the SUV swung open slowly. Four figures stepped out. Tall, athletic, coiled with unleashed power. Almost as one, they all raised their faces to the others and Mal and Kath both gasped. Their eyes gleamed a bright hazel, one in particular blazed so brightly that Mal felt the need to look away. While the forms were human, the heads atop were distinctively lupine. They moved with an economy of motion, yet before any of the others assembled could react, they had gathered around Bert and the women. One moment they were at the truck, the next on the sidewalk, coiled and ready for violence.

"Thought you might like to meet my pals, the Wullivers," Bert said, unable to hide the smile that crept onto his face. "Be a good beastie. Take your pets and get away from my friends and my theatre. While you can."

Without a glance at the Dullahan, the canines backed up silently until they had been engulfed again by the black of the night. The Dullahan held its head aloft and the gruesome mouth spat on the sidewalk. Slowly, it, too, withdrew into the darkness.

Before it disappeared, they heard it rasp again. "Mistake after mistake. You delay your end. Nothing more."

Silence.

Exhalations.

"You and your friends got here just in time," Mal said, bending at the waist and taking ragged, stuttering breaths.

"*Our* new friends," Bert replied. "And yes. Of course. I have a bottle of good Scotch inside. Shall we?"

As they all turned and entered the building, Kath turned to Mal. "What was that powder stuff? Never seen that one from you before."

"Pretty sure it was baking soda," Mal said quietly, with a look of shock on her face. "Not at all what I had planned. I grabbed the wrong bag on the way out."

While Kath processed that information, they both stopped in their tracks as the newcomers morphed from their wolf shapes into simple humans, with no sign of anything unusual about them.

Mal shook her head and was the last to walk through the front door.

The group, now seven strong, settled into Bert's spacious office. Kath and Mal sat close to each other, huddled in a corner. Bert sat at his large mahogany desk. He smiled broadly. The Wulliver family perched around the room. Much to Mal's and Kath's surprise, they all now appeared entirely normal. No sign of the wolf forms that had so changed the course of the encounter outside.

"Um, Bert?" Kath spoke first. "Little info here would be a spiffy thing." Her eyes were large, and she was on the edge of her seat, eyes flicking from one side of the room to the other.

"Take a deep breath," Bert said, his smile never faltering. He reached into a drawer and sat up with a bottle of Maker's Mark bourbon in his hand and proceeded to fill glasses from a set of cut crystal on his desk. "Meet the Wulliver family. These are the newcomers I told you were arriving tonight. And lucky for us they did. Although I would have preferred introducing you under easier circumstances."

The lone woman in the family sat forward in the chair she had claimed. Silver hair framed an ageless face. Her eyes remained the brilliant hazel that set her apart from the men in her family. Her movements were controlled, agile, but her face was open. Kind. Amused, even.

"Hello, Kath. Mal," the woman said in a clear, calm voice. "Bert has told us a lot about you."

"You've got an advantage on us there," Mal said quietly, not relaxing into her seat one inch.

"My name is Carolyn. Carolyn Wulliver," the woman continued. "We had arranged through Bert, here, and Marcello Pettirosso in Lancaster to arrive here tonight. We're here to help."

"No offense to the two of you," Bert said. "Things seem to be getting more heated here. Everywhere, really. It's only a matter of time before our arrangement here is discovered. Was discovered." He grimaced slightly. "And I think we need to make sure that whoever comes to us in need is assured of safe passage on their path. So..." He gestured widely to the newcomers.

"We certainly never meant to frighten you," said another man, seated next to Carolyn. "I'm Finlay, Carolyn's husband. And here we have Craig, Carolyn's brother, and over there we have Donal, my cousin."

Craig nodded politely while Donal grunted in response. Craig was very similar to Carolyn, although his hair remained a midnight black, with flashes of white peeking through the thick mane in places. Donal was strikingly different. His hair was a deep chestnut. He was shorter, thicker and more muscular than the others. His air was more belligerent. Truculent. Although it didn't seem to be aimed at any one person in the room, he still set the two local women on edge. They both sank deeper into their seats and closer to each other.

Carolyn reached over to place a hand on Mal's arm. Gently. "We're friends of Sean Curley's. All of the Grumbles really. But Sean and I became close during his time in Lancaster. If he were here— and we expected him to be with us when we met you—he'd vouch for us."

"I don't get it," Kath shot a barely controlled glance at Bert. "Why are you here? And how is a family of werewolves, no matter how well intentioned, supposed to put our refugees at ease?"

Craig winced, and Donal growled while rising and pacing his

corner of the office. Finlay huffed at him and gestured to the windowsill he'd been occupying, and Donal resumed his seat.

"Common and easy mistake," Finlay said, eliciting another guttural comment from Donal. "We're not werewolves. We're shapeshifters. We are always in full control of ourselves. No full moon needed. No silver bullet to stop us. Just simple folks that happen to have a different ability."

"They're Fae," Bert broke in. "Make no mistake of that. But they are misunderstood and have fled persecution many times. They're not so different from a lot of the folks we help. Stagecoaches in the old west had guardians. Shotgun Riders. Well, meet our version of Shotgun Riders."

"Our family has been around a long time," Carolyn said. "We've moved from one place to another. Started in Scotland. The Highlands. Kept getting pushed north until we finally gave up and came here to America, where people were trying to find peace. Been in Pennsylvania ever since."

"If you finally found your place, why are you coming here?" Kath asked. "Not trying to be a pain in the ass, just trying to fit it all together."

"I like that one," Donal said, gesturing to Kath with a jerk of his chin.

"Perfectly understandable," Finlay answered. "A bunch of things really. First, we're all getting older. We're tired. There's war coming. We feel it in Lancaster. There's a new generation of Wullivers there. They've earned the right to lead this fight. They're ready. Readier than we are."

"And we," Carolyn said, "think we can be of more help here. All we've ever wanted was to be left to ourselves. It seems that's what you help people find."

"And honestly," Craig spoke for the first time, "Maine sounded more appealing at this point in our lives. We want to be closer to the earth. We're not naïve enough to think it's going to be easier here. Just different."

"And it is definitely time for a change," Donal growled.

"Whatever your reasons, your timing is pretty perfect," Mal said. "Thanks for saving our skins."

Bert sipped his bourbon and made note that he was the only one partaking. "Come on, gang. Or should I say 'pack'? Let's drink to a new partnership. We're going to help a lot of people. Oh, and I think you're underestimating me and good ol' Frank Thomas." He patted his baseball bat, perched on his desktop. "We've broken a lot of bones in our days. We had that Dullahan right where we wanted him."

"Shut it, Bert," Kath said, chuckling. "We were toast, and you know it. But...ummm...that Dullahan is still around here somewhere. Should we be letting Sean and Trout know what's up?"

"We should and we shall," Bert replied, downing his bourbon, and nodding to Finlay, Kath, and Donal who had all followed suit. "We'll actually do one better than that. Wullivers, you and I are heading out to the cottage. We're taking them to Monhegan. Our first escort mission, yeah?"

Bert slapped his thighs and rose from the desk. The Wullivers nodded in agreement and began to get ready to leave.

Mal held up a hand as if she was a pupil in a schoolroom. "What exactly are we supposed to do here?"

"Hold the fort," Bert answered, putting in his large black puffy winter coat on. "You'll be fine. Hard part is over."

"I sure hope you're right," Kath muttered. "That Dullahan has to be somewhere."

Mal and Kath followed the others out to the street, where Bert's SUV still stood, blocking the street. Bert climbed in and made sure all of the Wullivers were in before turning around.

"We're stopping at my place for provisions and a debrief," Bert called out the window. "We'll aim to get to the cottage by five. You need anything, give a shout. You've got this!" And he rumbled up the street toward his house, which was only a few blocks away.

Mal and Kath stood numbly on the sidewalk in front of the office.

Most of the lights had been shattered by the Dullahan's whip. The glass lay scattered around the sidewalk and across the small garden outside the doorway. Kath kicked at some of the bigger pieces listlessly.

"We can deal with this in the morning, yeah?" she asked, taking in the mess that surrounded them.

The adrenaline was finally easing, and both women were ready to find a comfortable place to set themselves down.

"Come on," Kath said, starting for the door. "I'm resetting the alarm. And that bottle of Maker's looked pretty full to me. Let's drink to the end of simpler times."

CHAPTER 9

Brandy had tossed throughout the night. Sleep eluded her. Something felt wrong. She should be used to that, by now. She wasn't. She had staked out one of the chairs in the community room but couldn't get comfortable. Nick had fallen into deep sleep. Sandy rested in a seat by his side.

Kelphit posted himself by one of the windows and Brandy had no idea if he was awake or asleep. Noodle, however, had taken another of the seats and a gentle snuffling snore rose from his side of the room.

Bayard and Cinder had disappeared hours ago, presumably prowling the island and exploring every tiny crevice they discovered. They both were happier roaming.

McCloud lay in his bed. Unmoving. If not for the rise and fall of his considerable chest, there was no sign that he was still in there.

The locals had left before midnight, returning to their homes. Or so Brandy
assumed.

Finally, she could no longer sit still and quietly rose, pulling on her boots and rustling quietly through her bag. She hefted her war club, given to her by Kelphit before they had confronted the Dullahan and his evil cohort on the beach at Montauk Point. It had served her well. Surprisingly so, helping to dispatch a Wendigo that had threatened Sean in the midst of the chaotic melee. She took a close look at the club, appreciating its craftsmanship. Its balance. She had no training. No expertise with the weapon, but it had suited her somehow and it eased her mind to hold it again. She knew somewhere in Nick's bag was his matching club, also given by Kelphit and she felt a longing for her friend to be healed. To join her again with his club in hand and his phone in the other hand as he looked up some seemingly useless but ultimately important bit of trivia.

But Nick lay motionless across the room. Thankfully there was some optimism, at least. More than they had felt before they arrived in Monhegan. She would take that and be grateful.

Kelphit remained by the window, not reacting to her movement. The moon shone through the window and from where she stood, he looked every bit the ancient and powerful wise man that he was. Slipping the shaft of the club into her belt, she grabbed her coat, hoisted the rucksack over her shoulder, and let herself out through the front door.

Emerging onto the front steps, she took a deep breath and for the first time really felt the purity of the place. Pristine air. Something she was completely unaccustomed to enjoying. She stopped to stare at the sky. Millions of glittering stars winked back at her, as if they shared some joke that no one else could understand. Not for the first time, she wondered why she lived in Manhattan, with its noise and clutter and crowds and tension. She knew why—because she was an actor and that's where the work had always been. But, oh, the things she gave up for that. And the price she asked her family to pay, as well. Her husband, Mick, had never complained. And lord knew he could have.

She picked a direction and wandered off. Her legs needed to move. She needed to be away from these buildings. She needed to be away from even these people. They were her friends. Some of the dearest she had. And Sean and Trout were on their way. That was good news. But it added complications, too. Sean seemed to draw trouble in his wake like a string of tin cans behind a "Just Married" car. And he seemed...different. Breena was lovely, but love could be a bitch. She wanted to exhale. Nick looked to be getting better. McCloud was...holding. But then there was Ken. He was gone. Likely forever. And she would never shake the belief that she could have changed that outcome. The enormity of the last few weeks was crashing over her, and she felt close to drowning in it. She moved.

She glanced at her phone screen and saw that she still had three hours until sunrise. Plenty of time to shake these feelings. Plenty of time before Sean and Trout arrived. She had to find her center again.

Surprising even herself, she moved toward the populated village by the harbor. No one but the odd fishing boat would be stirring at this hour. She wanted a better look at where they were. Who the new neighbors were.

In less than ten minutes, she had arrived back at the fork in the path that led to the dock. She turned left instead and found herself moving away from both Fintan's village and the artists' galleries and houses that dotted the landing area.

She continued on, passing the Inn and a food truck parked incongruously next to the clinic, which looked more to be a first aid hut than any source of real medical attention. On she went. She pushed herself uphill, increasing her pace. Punishing herself, although she wouldn't have been able to voice exactly why. The Monhegan Brewing Company appeared on her right, a beer garden created with a wall of old lobster traps. She made a note to visit if and when the opportunity presented itself. But on she trudged, her breath beginning to come sharper and a stitch in her side threatened to force her to stop. A sign for Lobster Cove was all she needed to redouble her efforts and plow forward.

Some of the cottages she passed glowed with a warm yellow light. Islanders rose early and were stirring when many New Yorkers were still finding their way home. The gravel path shifted to mulch and eventually dirt. More than once, she thought she had taken a wrong turn. The boughs over her head cutting off all views of the sky and stars above and she felt...cut off from everything. Adrift on land. Floating along on this strange little island in the middle of the sea.

Suddenly, the trees gave way to an open sky and the stars that had greeted her when she had first started welcomed her back like old friends and assured her that she was on the right course. She paused at the edge of the forest, halfway between the canopy and expanse of sky that seemed somehow impossibly endless. She felt suddenly small. Inconsequential. She took comfort in that. She wasn't *that* important. There was a relief in knowing that.

She shuffled her feet in the sand of the path, enjoying the feel of it. Of knowing that she was near the edge of the island. Another shore to explore, much as she felt she was on the edge of the earth, staring at the immensity of the heavens above her. Felt it pulling her up. Out.

She continued toward what she now heard was the pounding of the surf somewhere in the darkness ahead. It pulled her, like standing by the window in a tall building and feeling the urge to step out and down. Down. Down.

She skirted tidal pools, once misjudging and feeling a shoe slip below the surface of a pool that had been so still and dark that she still couldn't see it after she had pulled her foot and dripping shoe free.

A large shape loomed out of the night in front of her. She moved toward it, curious. As she neared, she realized it was a shipwreck. A rusting hulk, disappearing with each tide that pulled at it. With each storm that lashed it with winds that blew sideways and found nothing on the empty beach to slow their violence.

She made her way to it and found a seat on one of the protruding spars. She noticed a cross in the distance, placed on the summit of a small hill. A life preserver placed over it. A memorial to those claimed by these waters.

She pulled her war club from her belt and began to toss it in the air. Practicing for what she couldn't say but feeling alive and brave. And protective of her friends and family. And everyone who needed protection. From evil. From the world around them. From themselves.

She began to carve the air in front of her with the club. Putting more of herself behind each stroke. Trying things she had never thought to try before. She felt powerful. Needed to sense the solidity of the club. What it bestowed upon her and how it connected her to Kelphit, and Nick, and everything that had crashed into her life over the last few months. It belonged only to this new Brandy. It mattered.

Suddenly, the club slipped from her grasp and clattered away along the shelf of rock where she stood. She scrabbled after it, just missing, before seeing it tumble over the side of the ledge. She heard it striking the cliff as it fell. And then to her surprise, she heard a splash.

She rushed ahead cautiously, craning her head over the side of what proved to be a far more substantial drop than she expected. In a pool at least ten feet below her, she saw the gleam of the silver spike on her club winking from below the water. It was beyond her reach, and she had barely finished cursing her stupidity when another wave arrived, eclipsing the pool. When it receded, the club was nowhere to be seen.

She laid her head on the cold and salt-crusted stone. Gone. The one thing she had to show for the new her. Swept away. Lost. She sent a silent prayer out for it to come back to her. To whom she did not know. But still she sent her plea to the skies above. To the celestial watchers twinkling eons away. But the stars remained silent. Watching. Blinking.

It took her a moment to realize that there were sounds emerging from the surf. Sounds that were not the ebb and flow of the waves. Sounds that drew closer. Every internal alarm began to ring. She was no longer alone. But she was defenseless. And the only thing she could think of worse than being perched alone on this spit of rock above the ocean, was not being alone. And her prayers turned to curses.

Trout's alarm woke him just before five and he slowly stirred, only to find Sean already awake and sipping a cup of coffee at the kitchen counter. He didn't see Jotunn, and spun in a panic, afraid the troll had wandered off just when they needed to be getting ready for Bert to arrive.

Without turning to him, Sean said, "He's out back. He wanted to say goodbye to the heron."

Trout sat up on the sofa and looked over the back out the window and there was Jotunn. He stood by the bank of the river, gesticulating wildly and talking animatedly. From time to time, he gave a slight hop and was clearly excited.

Ten yards into the water, a massive great blue heron stood, perfectly still, scanning the water for passing fish. The bird glanced at the troll occasionally and cocked its head before letting loose with a guttural croak that was entirely at odds with the elegant, fluid bird.

Trout grinned and felt a wave of regret as he checked the time again. He rose and crossed to the window, his socks allowing him to slide the last few feet a la *Risky Business*. He tapped gently on the window, and in the faint glow of the approaching morning, Jotunn turned and saw Trout. The troll's cry of joy could be heard clearly. He jumped again and pointed from the heron to Trout and back again, before shambling up the embankment and into the back door of the cottage. Once again, he looked as if he had been professionally groomed. His nose pristine and free of discharge.

"Trout up! Trout up!" he cried, the door slamming behind him. "See bird friend? Big. Funny."

"I saw that, bud," Trout answered with a laugh. "You seemed very excited. Looks like you're gonna miss him, yeah?"

"No miss," Jotunn said, pausing to think. "Him free. We see again if want. Want him stay here. Him happy. That make me happy."

Sean turned slowly on his stool at the counter. "I think I underestimated you. There's a good heart in there."

"Oh, yeah, good heart," the troll replied. "Still young. For a troll."

Trout laughed and Sean shook his head. Jotunn grabbed Trout's massive hand and led him toward the kitchen, patting the stool next to Sean.

"You want me to sit there?" Trout asked.

"Yeah," the troll answered.

"Okay," Trout agreed, taking seat. "But you know we only have a few minutes until Bert and our guests get here, right?"

"Me know," Jotunn said, climbing with some effort onto the counter opposite the two men. "Need tell you something. Secret. Feel bad. Waited long. But Sean—nicer than I think. Time to tell."

Sean and Trout exchanged a glance before Trout took the lead. "What is it, little guy? You know you can tell us anything. We've got your back."

"Sorry. Sorry," Jotunn said, his eyes brimming with tears.

"Hey, Jotunn, whatever it is, it's okay," Sean assured him. "We can handle it."

The troll began to cry now, hard and with a stuttering breath. "That it. That the secret," he managed between sobs. "Me not Jotunn. Well, yes. But not *my* name. Name of my people. We are all Jotunn. Like you. Human. We Jotunn. But you...you are Trout. You Sean. I am Dünker. Name is Dünker. No tell you at first. We keep name secret from all but family. Best friends. You now best friends. So—me Dünker."

The little troll turned a face full of fear toward Sean and Trout, who looked again at each other.

"Oh, wow," Trout said finally. "You don't have ta feel bad. Dünker. Look, we just feel honored that you decided to trust us with that. I get it. Everyone has things they keep close to their heart.

That's nothing to feel bad about. It's just smart. Happy to now know."

Sean pushed himself back from the counter and put an arm around the troll's shoulders. "Thanks for trusting us. We'll keep your name a secret. Just between us. To the world you are Jotunn. To us— you're Dünker."

Dünker broke into a wide smile. "Knew you would understand. I thanks you for not being angry. Just for us three."

The lights of an arriving car swept across the front door of the cottage. Glancing at the clock above the stovetop, Sean saw it was one minute past five. Bert was punctual. He had to give him that.

Dünker swung himself down from the counter and stuck his nose in the air. "Big man is here. Has others with him. Strong others. Not human."

The troll scurried across the room and hid behind the couch. His eyes and mottled ears the only parts of him showing. Sean and Trout shared a chuckle and went to open the door.

"Just more refugees," Sean called over his shoulder. He reached for the doorknob and paused when he saw the window filled with the shadows of four figures. He had been expecting one or two. And he had assumed they would be small in stature. Needing protection. But what he saw was anything but that. The four shadows had slipped nimbly onto the front stoop. They seemed bundled with energy. Bert's sturdy figure followed slowly behind the others.

A loud rap sounded from the door. Behind him, he heard Dünker's sharp intake of breath, and a rustle as he fell to the floor completely. Sean even noted that Trout had stopped moving toward the door.

"Uh, Sean," Trout said quietly. "Something seems off here. How well do we know Bert? I mean really?"

"It's Bert," Sean answered, with a hitch in his voice. "But yeah, this isn't what I thought."

The door rattled with another hearty slam and a voice called out.

"C'mon, man. Quit you're diddling in there and get the door open. It's freezin' out here."

Sean cocked his head. There was chorus of laughter from the doorstep. Something was familiar, but that voice belonged to another place. Not here. Sean inched the door open, peering through the crack and it burst inward, sending him staggering back toward the counter.

A pile of bodies followed, tumbling over one another and pushing each other out of the way to reach Sean and Trout. It was Trout who recognized them first, Sean still denying his own senses.

With a Big Sky-sized hoot, Trout grabbed two of the nearest newcomers in a massive bear hug and dissolved into laughter.

"What the hell are you lot doing here?" he cried.

Finally, Sean allowed the truth to hit him. Quietly, he said, "Carolyn? Finlay? What's going on?"

"What about Craig and me?!" Donal cried. "I know it took us a while to warm up to each other, but I'm here, too, you ingrate!"

Sean laughed. The Wullivers laughed. Trout was still lifting Finlay off the ground. Bert finally made it through the door and, taking in the scene, found himself laughing, as well.

The little troll peered over the sofa, torn between wanting to join the laughter and an urge to run for the back door and escape into the river.

"It's all right, Dü— Jotunn," Trout said, motioning for him to join them by the door. "These are our friends. The Wulliver family from Lancaster, Pennsylvania. But what they're doing here I haven't a clue. Friends, Jotunn! Friends. All is well."

Slowly, the troll inched out into the clear. The look of confusion on his face causing Trout to beckon him again.

Dünker sidled up to Trout, keeping the big man between himself and the newcomers.

"Smell all wrong," he whispered to Trout. "Look human. Smell animal. Smell wolf. Smell danger."

Trout crouched by the troll. "It's okay," he assured Dünker.

"Friends. Helpers. Remember, we're friends, you and me, yeah? They're friends, too."

"Smell old," the troll continued. "Old world. Otherworld."

Carolyn took note of the hushed conversation and approached slowly, hands outstretched and upturned. "I haven't had the pleasure of meeting you yet, friend," she said. "I'm Carolyn. Wulliver. Originally from the Highlands of Scotland. You're not the first Jotunn we've met. And a pleasure it is to meet you."

The troll's mouth fell open and the look of shock on his face caused a ripple of laughter that spread to all in the room.

"Friends," Dünker said quietly. "More friends. Never had so many. Ever."

"Well, you do now," Carolyn said, as Finlay came to her side.

"How?" Sean asked, still staring at the Wullivers. "Why are you here? You don't need saving. And I know you don't run away. Ever."

"Good points, Ginge," Trout agreed. "I thought we were waiting on some meek helpless little folk or the like. What gives?"

"Can we save the heartwarming reunion for the ride up to New Harbor?" Bert interrupted. "We have a boat to catch."

"Shotgun!" Carolyn called as they crowded out the door into the frigid morning.

Sean was the last to leave and paused before closing the door behind him, taking in the little cottage where so much had happened in so little time. Dreams. An awakening in terms of Dünker. A reunion both in Brunswick and now here with friends from a different place in his life. He took a breath, turned out the lights, and headed out to the car.

As they pulled away up the dirt road, Sean's Crosstrek following Bert's big SUV. Pat and Kieran watched them on their way from their front window. They held hands briefly before getting to work. The next visitors would be here soon.

Brandy backed slowly away from the edge of the cliff. She bumped into the remains of the shipwreck. Without taking her eyes from the water, she reached behind her and felt a scratch as her hand scrabbled along the rusted hull. She hoped she was up to date on her tetanus shot. And then she hoped that she would be around to find out after whatever was rising out of the water was done with her.

She tumbled over the wreck, placing it between her and the water, She looked frantically from side to side for something—anything—that could be used to defend herself. She finally settled on a fist-sized stone, hefting it and knowing immediately that it would be next to useless.

The approaching sound grew louder, finally drowning out even the crashes of the waves.

Slowly, agonizingly, something rose. First a hand appeared over the edge of the rocks. Then another. And finally, a man climbed over and stood. He was taller than seemed possible. Finally reaching his full height, he towered at least ten feet in the air. His black hair fell past his shoulders, and was drawn back and plaited, leaving his face, with its chiseled jawline and piercing brown eyes, free to take stock of where he had arrived. His skin was dark, deeply tanned, and he wore the clothes of a man of the earth—natural colors, tanned leather, rough-spun cotton.

Recognition hit Brandy.

"I know you," she said. "You saved us from the kelpies."

He paused to consider her.

"More than just kelpies. But yes. And I have heard you, Brandy Johns," he said, and though his voice was not raised, it echoed across the rocks as if the words had been a full-throated cry. He turned and, though she had fallen flat to the ground, looked directly to where Brandy was hidden. "Why do you cower? You called. I came. What is it you have lost?"

Brandy slowly rose from behind the ship. She'd faced creatures of all kinds over the last few months, but never alone. She was scared. And she knew that he could sense that.

"Sorry to bother you," she replied. "Didn't really think anyone would answer. Let's just say this never happened and go on our way, yeah?"

"If what you seek is what you claim," the man said, "it would be reckless to leave it to be found by others. Come. Tell me. I will do what I can. These are my waters. I must."

"It's just an old club," she protested. "Not worth the fuss, really."

"I heard you," he replied. "A club created by the wise Kelphit is not a thing to discard lightly. It is a rare and generous gift."

"You know Kelphit?" Brandy asked, raising herself slightly to get a better look at the man. He was intimidating, but a closer look at him revealed eyes that looked kindly at her. He had taken a seat on the ledge and dangled his feet over the side, like a child on a swing.

"We know of each other," he answered. "I hope to meet him. He has spent time on this island, but my waters are wide, and we have never shared a fire."

"He's a good man," Brandy said. Inching further from her hiding place.

"And wise," he answered. "There is nothing to fear here. At least, not from me. My name is Gluskabe. I will put your mind at ease. I will return with your club."

With that, he slipped silently over the edge and disappeared. Brandy moved cautiously to the cliff, unsure if she was more frightened of the fall or the giant Gluskabe. As she peered over and into the waves below, her breath caught. Gluskabe was disappearing below the surface without a ripple.

She sat back on her haunches. It would have been nice for someone to warn her that there was a giant cruising the waters of the island. She had assumed Kelphit would give her the heads-up regarding something like this. Although, upon reflection, he had been busy since they arrived.

The faintest of glows began to crack the horizon, although night still claimed the sky. The wind had died almost entirely, barely a twitch now. It was still cold, but the adrenaline rush of a giant had managed to warm her up.

Within five minutes, the water below her began to boil and froth. Gluskabe emerged, not troubled by the water, the darkness, the cold. He seemed as placid as someone walking back from a trip to the refrigerator. Brandy's senses were at war with each other. On one hand, a giant had climbed from the sea. Large enough to crush her, she was sure, war club or no war club. And she had no war club at the moment. On the other hand, he had instantly put her at ease. If she could compare him to one person she knew, it would be Kelphit. And Kelphit was one of the finest men she had ever known.

And so, she sat back, while the giant approached. Neither fight nor flight winning the internal battle.

Gluskabe strode through the waves to her and leaned on the cliff as easily as some leaning on a bar to order a beer. He was smiling at her. Pleased.

"I think I have found what you seek," he announced. Slowly, and with some pride, he lifted his hand and placed it on the rocks by her side. When he removed his hand, he revealed a length of darkly worn wood. Something between a staff and a club. Longer than Brandy's club, it bore intricate carvings. One end showed a scene of blooming flowers and fruit, while the other ended in a vicious looking knot of wood, worn and stained. It carried the air of great age.

Brandy saw Gluskabe's expectant expression and felt inexplicably guilty to tell him the truth. "I'm sorry," she said. "It's much more impressive than mine. I'm sorry. But thank you. Really. I'll just head back now. You've done enough."

Gluskabe looked—very briefly—disappointed, before nodding slowly and holding his hands out. "No," he declared. "I will find what you need. Patience."

With that, Brandy watched as he disappeared below the waves again, with one hand throwing a farewell. Again, Brandy sat back and waited. She was inclined to simply leave, but the giant had been incredibly accommodating and eager to help. Not only did it seem rude, but she questioned the strategy of angering someone over twice her size. And clearly from the Otherworld. So, she made herself as comfortable as she could.

Again, within five minutes, the water thrashed and bubbled as Gluskabe rose once more, his smile even broader this time. The sequence repeated itself and he placed something next to her, covering it with his massive hands.

Brandy raised her eyebrows in question, and the giant let loose a laugh to suit his size. He removed his hands and exposed a mace. A length of bronze, smooth with age. It was studded with angry-looking spiked protrusions, and its bulbous head was fashioned into the head of a ram with magnificent, curved horns.

Brandy looked at Gluskabe again only to find another grin of pride. Not only did she feel awful telling him it was once again not what she was looking for. But she'd read enough to know that lying to powerful creatures of this sort never turned out well.

"I'm so sorry, Gluskabe," she said, trying out his name for the first time. "This is even grander than the last club you showed me. This is not mine, either. But someone must be missing it. It's beautiful. And looks...intimidating."

The giant stepped back and considered her. His kind eyes now looked more contemplative, and she wondered if she had somehow offended in a way she hadn't anticipated. Without a word, Gluskabe patted the rocks next to her and pursed his lips, before nodding again to himself and turning to the open water again.

The rush she'd felt at the giant's arrival was fading and Brandy began to feel the cold seeping into her, so she stood and paced along the cliff edge. Morning crept closer and the horizon glowed a purple and crimson swathe across the sky. Brandy muttered to herself and cursed her luck, or lack thereof. But she did it silently, in no mood to attract more attention to herself.

Moments later, she saw Gluskabe rise again. This time, his hand appeared first, clutching a length of iron, gleaming and deadly looking. Intricate scrollwork snaked along the blade, reaching a hilt that was bell shaped and curved in what seemed to Brandy's untrained eye to be Celtic.

Before the giant even reached the shore, Brandy strode to the cliff edge with her hands upraised. "Gluskabe!" she called. "That's not even a club! That's a sword, and a beautiful one. But it's not mine. I can't take that."

Gluskabe didn't slow a bit on his path toward her, and he focused squarely on her in a way that made her squirm uncomfortably.

He presented the sword to her, hilt first. "This isn't yours?" he asked, pinning her in her place with his gaze.

"No, I'm sorry," she said quietly. "Mine is a much humbler club. This is a beautiful sword. I can't let you look any further. I've taken up enough of your time."

Gluskabe placed the sword gently on the broken rocks at Brandy's feet. He nodded again to himself, before lifting his other hand and presenting to her the war club she had been given by Kelphit. It was simply made. Bound together with leather straps, a silver spike jutting out from the head.

Brandy felt her breath catch and she nearly cried out. That's it!" she said. "You're a miracle worker. I can't believe it!"

"I told you these are my waters," Gluskabe answered. "I know what lies here. And who deserves what." He paused before handing her the club. "It is a fine club. I see why it means so much to you. But you, Brandy Johns, have proven yourself true. Many would have taken the other, grander, items I brought to you. But you chose honesty. Something I find sadly rarer with the passing years. And so —I give you all of these. The items I've brought here have been carefully chosen. Kelphit will know them. And Fintan and Sulevia. Bring them with you and my thanks and respect go with you, also. Know that Gluskabe is here. And will be here when I am needed."

The giant turned swiftly, more swiftly than she had seen him move thus far. In the space of a breath, he was gone with not another word and leaving no trace on the water's surface that he had passed.

Brandy stood in stunned silence. She stared at the assembled artifacts he had just gifted her. All of them seemed to glow in the first kiss of dawn.

She gathered them, surprised at the weight. She turned her back to the water and began the hike back to the village. She needed answers soon, knowing that the boat with Sean and Trout would arrive soon. A friendly water giant...Just when she thought she had gotten a handle on things, she found out how very wrong she was.

———

Bert took the lead in his SUV with three of the Wullivers joining him. He knew the roads and had driven to New Harbor often. Sean, Trout, and Carolyn followed in the Crosstrek. Dünker curled up by Trout. The further along the route they ventured, the smaller the roads became, and Sean was actively doubting Bert's sense of direction. It was a short drive, less than an hour, when the two cars pulled into the parking lot of Shaw's Fish and Lobster Wharf. The sun had yet to fully rise, so their headlights swept the parking lot and the docks beyond when they arrived. A number of fishing boats were already on their way out of the harbor.

Carolyn had used the ride to fill Trout and Sean in on the events of the night before. The appearance of the Dullahan. The Barghests. The revelation that the Railroad was likely a secret no more. They arrived in New Harbor with a greater sense of worry. And urgency.

One boat was docked and running, its lights giving a ghostly appearance. It was a handsome boat, well maintained. Nothing extravagant, but exuding an air of stability, literal and figurative. Sean zeroed in on it immediately and couldn't help but think of a scene from one of the *Jaws* films. He had no idea which one, but was certain it wasn't the first, and best.

Any thought of horror movies was dispelled when a far-too-awake voice broke the pre-dawn silence. "Bert? Bert Clarke? Get your butt down here and let's hit it!"

Bert, still emerging from his truck shouted back, "Yeah, yeah, Andy! Just chill yourself. I'm a theatre person, it's a miracle I'm here this early, at all!"

Bert led the procession toward the boat. With the Wulliver family, there were nine of them, and Sean looked dubiously at the size of the boat.

"You thinkin' what I'm thinkin'?" Trout said, leaning closer to Sean, while Dünker looped a clammy hand into his back pocket to stay close.

"Yeah," Sean answered. "There's a lot of us for that one. Guess we'll see what Captain Andy there has to say."

As they drew near to the dock, Bert called out. "Permission to come aboard, Captain?"

"Permission...hmm..." came the answer from a sandy-haired man standing by the rail. "Now that I'm getting a good look at you all, I'm not so sure. The rest of you know this big guy well. He looks like trouble."

"Jerk!" Bert called back, and the two of them dissolved into laughter, while the rest of the arrivals looked uncertainly at each other.

"Get on up here," the ship's captain signaled for them all to join him. As they tromped aboard, Bert wrapped the fellow in a bear hug and turned to the others.

"Folks, this is Andy Plummer," he announced. "Sailor extraordinaire, guide of unmatched skill, and owner of a questionable sense of humor. Andy, these are—well, the folks I told you about."

"Ignore him," Andy said. "I'm hilarious. Welcome aboard. You can stow any gear in the cabin. Make yourselves comfortable. There's coffee on and I've got some donuts from Frank's on the counter."

"Are we good to leave our cars where they are?" Bert asked.

Andy took a look out at the parking lot, and replied, "Sure are. Shaw's is closed for the offseason right now. I'll let them know. Speaking of cars"—he stopped and turned to Trout—"you must be Dan Trout. I've been keeping an eye on your Bronco. It's right there in the corner under the light. She's a beaut. If you ever want to let her go—"

"Not a chance!" Trout answered. "That's my baby."

"I figured," Andy said with a chuckle. "Had to try, though. I have your keys below, just a sec."

"No need," Trout called, practically vaulting back to the dock. "I have another set. Come on, Jotunn. I've got a treat for you. Ever had a massage?"

The little troll looked confused, but seeing Trout disappear from the boat was all the encouragement he needed, and he followed as quickly as his little spindly legs could carry him.

A moment later, they heard the engine of the Bronco growl to life.

"Looks like you are a couple folks extra from what I was planning," Andy said, surveying the party.

"I don't have to go," Bert offered. "I'd love to get out there. It's been a while, but I can wait."

"No need," Andy replied. "Emma! Alex!"

Two young people appeared from the stern, neither could have been more than twenty-five years old, questions on their faces.

"You can take the morning off," Andy told them. "Don't worry. You'll get paid. Just be here when I get back for the next group. Rest of the day as usual. Sound good?"

They both agreed and leaped ashore easily.

"See you in a few hours," Emma called as she and Alex trotted up the dock and disappeared around the corner of Shaw's.

"Great kids," Andy commented, watching them go. "Hope I can hold onto them for at least another season. Good crew is hard to find."

"You okay coming back from Monhegan on your own?" Bert asked, as the others made their way into the cabin.

"Sure am," Andy answered. "Thanks for caring. Welcome aboard the *Acheron*, the finest boat you'll take today." He crossed to the wheel and sent a blast of the horn into the early morning quiet, calling Trout back to the dock. "We leave in five!"

Bert stood next to him and raised his eyebrows while cocking his head to the side.

"What?" Andy asked. "You can help me shove off in a sec. I've always wanted to tell you to shove off, by the way. But what's the look for?"

"You're not even going to mention the little creepy grey guy following Trout around?"

"No need," Andy said, checking the equipment in preparation for leaving. "I've learned after all these years hanging out with you it's best to just accept things. Also, you won't believe what I tell you about the trip I took out there. With your friends."

CHAPTER 10

Brandy was practically jogging as she started toward the healers' village. She'd gotten turned around more than once in the forest. It was much darker beneath the branches that shrouded the trails. She realized how tired she must have been when they arrived the day before, because almost nothing looked familiar. At one point, she twisted her ankle on a stray root, and her progress slowed. She could feel her foot swelling as her boot grew tighter and tighter. She glanced at her bag where the newfound artifacts were stowed. Awkwardly, as none of them fit cleanly. None of them seemed large enough to serve as a crutch, and that seemed inappropriate somehow, so she left them in place and scanned the forest floor, finally finding a fallen branch that would do the trick.

Slipping it under her shoulder, she continued on her way, hobbling awkwardly. The bag over one shoulder and the makeshift crutch under the other arm, made her progress slower than ever and she cursed her stupidity for falling.

She stopped often, sitting to try to minimize the swelling, but it was a losing battle. She checked her phone and saw that she was in danger of getting back to the village after the boat with Sean and

Trout arrived. Damn. Nothing was going according to plan, and she was about to add to everyone's problems instead of being the help that she had intended. Stupid.

Everything felt like it was going wrong when she finally caught a glimpse of the village through the trees. The lights were still on, but daylight had begun to sneak through the boughs overhead. She allowed herself to gather her thoughts. And sigh with relief. She'd made it. And she had so many questions for Fintan and Sulevia. Who was Gluskabe? And what exactly were these things he had given her? She couldn't shake the feeling that all of it was important. Very.

Somehow, she had gotten turned around and was coming to the cluster of buildings from the side opposite where she had left. As she limped out of the tree line, she saw a group leaving the community center. She recognized Bayard and Noodle, with Cinder prancing eagerly next to them. Fintan was with them and Kelphit followed him closely, their heads close together in discussion. Even Sandy was there, walking slightly behind Kelphit. This meant that Sulevia was the only one left inside tending to the patients. And maybe Jay would be there, but she had no idea what to make of him. She'd taken too long. She would have to wait for them to return, and the inevitable fuss that would accompany the reunion would delay her answers even longer. Stupid.

Maybe she could talk to Nick about it if he was still awake. She didn't know Sulevia and was a bit intimidated by both her and Fintan. Although she would never admit that to anyone other than Nick. And Trout. And maybe Noodle. And Bayard. Funny, something in her balked at the idea of sharing it with Sean. He seemed so out of sorts when they had been finishing in Lancaster. Something had felt...off. She felt ashamed of the thoughts. They had been through so much. Sean had saved them many times. Saved her. But there was no denying her intuition.

She stood just past the edge of the forest and watched them disappear in the direction of the harbor. Shaking her head, she trudged slowly forward, struggling up the wooden stairs that led to the main building. Damn, that ankle was not doing well.

She stumbled in through the door. Sulevia was at the far end of the room with McCloud. But Nick was sitting up in bed, and when he saw the state of Brandy, he cried out and tried to stand. Jay, who was sitting in the center of the room, jumped up and motioned to Nick to stay where he was.

"No, no, no," he shouted. "You stay there, buddy. You're nowhere close to getting out of that bed. And you"—he turned to Brandy—"stop where you are. I've got you."

He rushed to her side and slipped his arm under her shoulder, while placing her improvised crutch by the doorway.

"Let's get you to that sofa, yeah?"

"Thanks. 'Preciate it," Brandy answered. Wincing as she mistakenly stepped on the injured side.

Sulevia saw what was happening and, wiping her hands on her dress, hurried over to where Brandy was settling. Sulevia carefully removed Brandy's boot, and Brandy hissed in pain as the blood rushed in where it had been held back.

"Well, I feel like an idiot," she spat out between deep breaths.

"Not at all," Sulevia answered. "Those trails are tricky at the best of times. And the predawn darkness is definitely not the best of times to go exploring. But no worries. I'm up to this challenge. I'm sure it doesn't feel minor at the moment, but this is not the biggest challenge we've had here. You'll be fine. With some time."

Sulevia sat back on her haunches and when she reached to move Brandy's bag out of the way, Brandy clutched it to her lap before placing it next to her. Away from Sulevia, who gave her a curious look.

Sulevia's look went unnoticed by Brandy, who was distracted by Nick calling to her across the room.

"Just couldn't stand me getting all the attention, could you?" he said, grinning. "Should have known not to leave the city girl on her own out here."

"Yeah, bite me," she replied, wincing and cursing as Sulevia worked on her ankle. "Wouldn't even be here, if it weren't for you."

Nick widened his eyes and gave her a chance to reconsider her comment.

"Okay, yeah," she said quietly. "That was over the top. It just hurts. Let me get squared away and I'll hobble over. Got something I want to tell you."

Nick gave her a thumbs-up, while Sulevia focused on Brandy's ankle.

"Don't mind me," Jay said. "Think I'll go help with luggage when the crew gets here. Hey, no one get hurt while I'm gone, 'kay?"

<hr>

Brandy had just managed to get to Nick's bedside when the doors burst open and the crowd from the harbor noisily entered the room. Trout immediately made his way toward Nick and Brandy, while Sean wandered in the opposite direction, talking intently to Fintan and Kelphit.

Trout paused, surprised to find Sean walking away, shrugged, and moved to Nick's bed.

Brandy leaned into Nick and quietly whispered, "I'll have to tell you later. Don't say anything to anyone, yeah?"

Nick didn't respond but was clearly thrown off by the request. Any confusion was set aside when Trout, followed by Noodle, reached the bed and hugs and hellos were exchanged.

"Well, wouldja look who's sitting up and looking mostly alive!" Trout shouted with far too much volume for the situation, but even a scornful shush from Sulevia could do nothing to calm him.

Nick laughed. "They tell me I might even make it. Whatever clipped me back in Lancaster had some sort of poison curse thing on it. Gotta thank Brandy and the rest for getting me here so fast. Anything happen to you? I thought you guys were looking to find a portal to the Otherworld. What's up?"

"Well," Trout said. "You're not going to believe it, but—"

It was then that Nick and Brandy both noticed a pair of clammy hands with long claws clutching Trout's knees. Then a tentative hooked nose, practically a beak, came sniffing from around him and a pair of cloudy, worried eyes turned to the tall Montanan.

"Friends?" Dünker asked quietly.

"What the hell—" Nick shouted, pushing himself back in his bed as close to the headboard as he could squeeze.

Brandy, too, jumped and found herself moving in the same direction as Nick, meaning away from the troll.

"Friends, Jotunn, friends," Trout said quickly. Then turned to Nick and Brandy. "It's okay, gang. He's harmless. Just a buddy we ran into on the way that needed a hand. All good."

"Buddy," Dünker said quietly, holding still to Trout's legs.

Noodle moved to the bedside. "It's cool. Jotunn here is fine. Promise. And he loves this guy here," he said and gestured to Trout.

Nick relaxed on the bed, but Brandy remained wary and slowly moved her bag under the bed with her uninjured foot. The motion set her off balance and she almost fell, catching herself on the bedpost. Everyone immediately noticed her bandage.

"What happened to you?" Noodle asked in alarm.

"Yeah, what gives," Trout added. "We heard about your trouble on the trip over, but no one said anything about you being hurt." He turned to cast a look back at Bayard, who was deep in conversation still.

Sandy rushed to the bedside dragging a chair behind her. "Heard what happened," she said, with a gesture to Brandy. "You should be sitting."

"Thanks, Sandy. Long story," Brandy said, looking at the floor. "Involves an early morning walk, a dumb city gal, and a pissy tree root."

Before anyone could comment, Nick, looking over everyone's shoulders caught a glimpse of the Wullivers hanging back by the doorway.

"What?" he cried. "What are you all doing here? Carolyn, Finlay! Get over here!"

The Wullivers sheepishly glanced around the room. Sean had been, by far, the closest of the Grumbles with their family, but he had quickly become drawn into a deep talk by the far window. They tentatively approached Nick's bed.

"Well, hot damn," Brandy said. "You all are a sight for sore eyes. A pleasant surprise, for once. What gives? Never thought I'd see you away from Lancaster."

Carolyn and Finlay looked at each other as Donal and Craig remained behind.

"No sense hiding it," Carolyn said. "We don't need to tell you that the world is—let's just say—changing. So, we're here to help. Lancaster needed new blood. We needed...more space. Trees and grass. Air."

"Pettirosso was in touch with Bert, over there, and we agreed to head up to keep an eye on the Underworld Railway, or whatever they decide to call it. Lots of vulnerable creatures will be coming this way. Just trying to live their lives. Lots of bad folks will try to stop them. We're here to stop the bad folks."

Jay, who had quietly approached and found a place to lean on at the windowsill, nodded and spoke. "Nice to hear. I think this island is pretty well covered, but the road here? As we learned yesterday, anything can happen. Hey, I'm Jay. I live here."

"Nice to meet you, Jay," Trout answered. "You look familiar."

"Glad to hear it," Jay answered. "We did that monkey musical together. I had a mask on most of the time."

"Right!" Trout shouted again, earning another look from Sulevia. "You were the dancing monkey. Jay! Funny guy. What the hell are ya doing here?"

"Long story," Jay answered, glancing over his shoulder out the window.

"He's been promising to tell us," Brandy said. "Nothing yet, though."

"We have time," Jay replied, still looking out the window. "Hopefully."

Sean was animated. More animated than Bayard or Kelphit had seen him before. His energy seemed out of context with their surroundings and nothing they were saying was deescalating things.

"Look," Sean persisted. "I see Nick. He looks better. That's good. McCloud back there? Seems the same. Not sure what I can do about that. Gotta let that one go. You all are better positioned for that. What I need from you is information. I need to find a way to the Otherworld. Not a portal. At least not one that is known. I've heard there are subterranean paths. Caves. I thought we'd found something at that mini-Stonehenge place, but no go. Any suggestions? I don't have time to waste."

Bayard placed a hand on Sean's arm, trying to slow him down. Sean's voice was raised. He was clearly not focused on what was around him, but on where he wanted to get. Both Bayard and Kelphit exchanged looks.

Bert looked concerned. He hadn't been around Sean for some time, and this was not the person he remembered. He and Fintan exchanged a look. A look that Sean couldn't help but notice.

"Okay, yeah," he plowed on. "I get it. I don't seem all that concerned about my friends, but I thought that's why we *sent* them here. That's your job. We came here to check on them, yes, but also to drop off the troll. And then find out from you where I can find what we need. What I need. Breena is being held somewhere."

"And Kallan," Kelphit said, quietly.

"Yes, yes," Sean raged. "Kallan, too. Why does everyone want to assume the worst of me. Yeah. Kallan, too. Stop judging me and help me. How do I get to them?"

Fintan, who didn't know Sean, reacted differently. He walked to the nearest window, his arms behind his back. He faced the trees outside, and spoke slowly, cautiously.

"There are a few such places," he said. "How they stand now? I couldn't say. We are focused on this island. Preserving it and the lives who make their way here. It has never been our goal to travel back there."

"Can you help me or not?" Sean asked, his voice brittle as the dead pine needles on the forest floor outside.

"Yes," Fintan answered after a delay. "With information. But we cannot travel with you. Nor in good conscience advise any others to go with you."

"Fine," Sean spat back. "None of you could do anything to help me anyway. Just tell me where to go and get out of the way."

Bayard was leaning against the wall now, a few feet away. He was startled to sense a difference in the attitudes of Fintan and Bert toward Sean. Yes, they didn't know him well, but there was a reluctance to offer much to him. To even approach him physically. After a moment, he realized that they were afraid of Sean. Even Fintan, who had seen so much and lived so long. And suddenly, Bayard understood how very perilous Sean made the entire situation. His power was like none they had seen, and he hadn't even plumbed its depths yet. If he veered in the wrong direction, if he fell victim to the urges that had led Ken O'Carroll astray, everything could fall apart. Everything. Cinder was sticking close to Bayard, never taking her eyes off of Sean.

Bert was watching Bayard and Kelphit closely, clearly looking for some direction from those who knew Sean best.

"Sean," Bert said, "do you think it might be best if you paused things here for a day or two? Fintan and Sulevia are masters of the healing arts. And you already know Kelphit. You are obviously exhausted. Wouldn't catching your breath, studying the options, letting your friends recover, give you a clearer view of the path forward?"

Sean's shoulders sagged. He looked at the faces around him and seemed to give Bert's words real consideration. The air was charged. Breaths were held.

Across the room, Trout's voice was raised as he reminded Jay of something they had shared onstage and the group around them laughed. Relief in the sound.

It broke the moment and Sean turned to those around him.

"Yeah, Bert," he said icily, "it probably would be best. But if you didn't realize, we *don't have time.* You weren't in Lancaster. You didn't lose a friend. Lost somewhere in time. Watch him sacrifice himself. There is no time to waste. Breena won't be sacrificed. Not while I breathe. If someone would just *tell me what I need to know*, I can get on with fixing things. Trust me, no Dullahan, or Red Cap, or Hide-Behind, hell, not even that guy Balor, will stop me. I don't care what your relationship with Pettirosso is, Bert, or how many people you make feel better here. None of that matters. Just let me do what I have to do if all of you are too cowardly to jump in."

Sean's voice had risen throughout, and he ended shouting into the sudden stillness of the room. Trout's group had fallen silent as Sean's voice rose.

Silent looks made their way around the room. Words went unspoken, but decisions were made.

Fintan nodded slowly. Decision made.

"Jay," he called across the room. "Our new friends will need something to eat. If you could help us?"

Jay nodded and made his way to the door, giving a hooded look toward Sean as he took his leave.

"I suggest we all gather," Fintan continued. "There will be information for all to hear and, in my experience, everyone will have something to contribute."

Carolyn began to cross the room to calm Sean, but he slammed his hand against the wall and stomped toward the seating area. At that, Finlay touched her arm and shook his head. Carolyn turned back to Sean and there was sadness in the look she sent to him. Sean paused mid-step. He ran his hands down his face.

And then he turned and stormed out the front door, letting it slam behind him. The blast of cold air that swept into the building as he left was nothing compared to the chill of his exit.

No one but Nick noticed Brandy nudge her bag even further under the bed. At least, that's what Brandy thought.

———

Everyone but Sean gathered together in the center of the room. Nick tried to get up but was shushed and told to stay where he was by Sulevia and Sandy. He gave in grudgingly and was asleep almost as soon as his head hit the pillow.

"We obviously have some problems, folks," Bayard said. "Sean is cracking under the pressure. I don't think we can trust him to make clear decisions right now."

"No, we can't," Kelphit agreed. "However, what makes this more complicated, is that he's correct. We don't have time to waste. So how to balance the need for recovery with the need for a rapid solution?"

"If we can even find a solution," Trout said. "No offense to you Peripheral types here, but Sean is by far the most powerful of us all. If we can't count on him, what are the options?"

"Strongest or not," Brandy broke in, "he's not right. If we can't trust him, he's worthless to us. He needs a reset. This isn't the Sean we know. I don't know *who* that guy is."

She looked around the group and saw nods of agreement coming from her fellow Grumbles.

"It seems to me," Noodle said, quietly, "and tell me to be quiet if I'm out of line, I'm the new guy here. But isn't fixing people exactly what you do here? Will a day or two make that much difference?"

"You have as much right to speak here as any of us," Fintan replied, fixing Noodle with a kind look. "And you are right. What we must do, is find a way to convince Sean that what is in his best interest is to rethink and strategize. And to do so without antagonizing him. While he is the strongest of us, I think it's been proven that no one should, or even *could,* be doing things alone."

"I'm not about to let that happen," Trout said. "I've come this far with him. I'll stick it out."

"And so will I," Bayard said, his eyes on the floor. "We're already two down from your Grumble fellowship. I won't see more lost."

"Yeah, I'm in too," Brandy said, slapping her knees and standing to pace. "No matter how much of an ass he becomes. I learned my lesson with Ken. I'm in 'til the end."

"Maybe I can talk to him," Sandy suggested. "I'm the one of our group that has some experience with healing and how these things happen. Maybe he'll listen."

"I actually had a different idea," Sulevia said as the front door opened and Jay appeared balancing platters of food and drink. She glanced at Fintan and Kelphit and both men nodded. "Jay came here once in distress. He found healing. If anyone can understand what Sean is feeling, I believe it's him."

Crossing to the assembled group, Jay nodded his understanding.

"I wondered if you would work yourself around to that," he said. "Yeah. I get it. I can give it a shot."

Bert crossed to Jay and put an arm around his shoulder. "Thanks, Jay," he said. "I know it's no small favor to ask." He turned to the rest. "I'm sure Marcello told you all in Lancaster that Sean was our best hope, but not the only. And certainly not the first. Jay, here, was once in a very similar position as Sean. He discovered great power and attracted the wrong kind of attention."

"Yeah, yeah," Jay replied. "Thought I was a big deal. But it all got to be too much. Too much. I wanted out. I just wanted quiet. And I found it. So, I stayed. Here. Where they found a way to patch me together again when I thought my pieces were way too Humpty Dumpty for that. And the world kept spinning. Things went on. Bad guys did bad stuff. Good guys did good. Most people did nothing. And eventually everyone just...forgot about me. Except these crazies here. Let me go talk to him. No guarantees, obviously."

Jay settled the platters on the table and stood up. Looked pointedly at Fintan and turned to leave.

"Thank you," Sulevia called after him and he waved without turning around. And was gone.

"Son of a—" Trout said, shaking his head. "Monkey mask Jay was the original chosen one? And I know *both* of them. Hot damn."

The Wullivers had remained silent throughout. Watching. Finlay now stepped forward.

"We're here to guide and guard those who need asylum and when they travel on," he said. "We won't go with Sean. But our duties have started, and we'll keep you safe on this island while you figure things out. If you need us, we'll be nearby."

With that, the family filed out the front door, shifting to their wolf forms as they did.

Not for the first time that day, Noodle's eyes grew wide. Trout gave a full-throated howl. Sandy shook her head in wonder.

While everyone watched the Wullivers go, Brandy caught Kelphit's attention and motioned for him to quietly meet her by Nick's bed. None of the others paid much attention as the two excused themselves. There was food to be had and a lot that needed discussion.

———

Brandy stopped at the head of Nick's bed and leaned against the wall by the window. Slowly, she reached her good foot under his bed and dragged her bag out just enough for Kelphit to see. The hilt of the sword peeked out of the open top and the other two artifacts bulged inside.

Kelphit turned a questioning look to Brandy.

"I wasn't sure who I should tell," she began. "Or even what to say. I think what I have in there is probably pretty important, but things seem a little dicey right now. Tempers running high."

"Wise," Kelphit said. "You have piqued my curiosity." He paused to take in the room and check once again on the still sleeping Nick. "Meet me behind the building. Bring what you have found there."

"Thanks, Kelphit," she answered, the relief clear in her voice. "I knew you would be the right one to ask."

"That remains to be seen," Kelphit said, gently. "But I hope to be a clear head and good counsel."

Brandy gathered her bag and held it close to her chest as she made her way quietly to the front door. She kept her eyes down and slipped quickly out.

When Kelphit followed her a moment later, Trout made note but his hunger and current discussion with Bayard and Noodle kept him where he was.

Brandy was waiting by a picnic table set toward the edge of the central village clearing. She watched as the compact and agile Kelphit approached. She'd rarely seen him so animated. He saw her and increased his pace.

The day was clear and cold. A light breeze set the branches around them to sing a gentle whispered song. Birds sang somewhere out of sight, and Brandy closed her eyes, enjoying the moment of serenity.

She heard the light tread of Kelphit coming closer, and though the ancient healer was a gentle and wise presence, she knew that what she was about to tell him would change things. How they would change, she had no idea. But she knew that whatever was in her pack was important.

She shook her head, pausing one last time to listen to the sounds of the island around her. She wasn't good with things like this, but she thought she recognized the song of a robin amongst the cries of the gulls. She corrected herself. A Lee-Thorp. She smiled to herself and placed the bag on the table next to her as Kelphit arrived. He sat on the side opposite the bag, giving her space, although he was still unaware of what they would discuss.

"You have me intrigued," he said. "If I saw what I believe I did, you have a tale to tell."

Brandy slowly unzipped the backpack and placed the three items —the sword, the club, and the mace—on the table between herself and Kelphit. She heard him take a sharp breath. He reached tentatively toward the artifacts but thought better of it and instead moved away from them.

"I know these things," he said quietly, "although I've never seen them. We should do this somewhere more secluded. Follow me and we shall talk as we go."

Brandy packed her bag again and followed Kelphit deeper into the forest. While walking, she told him of her time by the shipwreck. She talked of practicing with her club, a gift from Kelphit himself, she pointed out. She told him of losing it into the sea. And she told him of the appearance of Gluskabe, and all that followed.

Finally, they came to a fallen tree that provided them with a seat far from any of the others. The trees reached over them protectively. A canopy of needles and branches above while the ground around them was littered with moss-covered stones and intricately woven roots thrusting up through the loam. Silence embraced them as Brandy finished her story.

Kelphit sat silent. He glanced to the boughs above. Then to the green and brown mottled earth at their feet.

"You have done well," Kelphit responded finally. "I know of Gluskabe. He is noble and powerful but tolerates fools and liars not at all. Had you lied, he would have known, and things would have gone much differently. You passed a test you did not know you were given. Good. As to these"—he gestured to Brandy's still closed bag— "you have been given wealth and strength beyond your knowing. May I?"

Brandy placed the pack at his feet and motioned for him to help himself.

He reached in and withdrew the mace.

"This," he said, his voice catching. "Astounding. This is Tishtrya's mace. Tishtrya is a Persian God with dominion over rain and fertility. There has been no word that Tishtrya has fallen, so I can only think that this was given freely, for Gluskabe to bestow as he saw fit. Whoever wields this controls the wind and the rain. This alone would be a gift beyond imagining."

Brandy found herself unable to respond to what Kelphit was telling her, a state with which she was very unfamiliar. She held the mace in her hand, its ram head now seeming far more ominous than a few moments ago. Brandy was hesitant to hold it and set it aside quickly.

She slid her hand into the bag and slowly drew out the club. It looked to be a simple branch, slender with a sturdy knot at one end and with subtle carvings of plants and flowers on the opposite end. The wood was nearly black with age, but the wood felt substantial. Solid.

"This looks familiar," Brandy said, relieved that the second item seemed so normal, for lack of a better term. "My parents visited Ireland when I was a kid. They brought me back a shillelagh. Traditional fighting stick. Mine was painted black, and didn't have any of this carving, but is that close?"

"Close, but far short of the mark," Kelphit answered, taking the club in his hands and cradling it gently. "This is nothing less than the Lorg Mór, the club of the Dagda, Lord of the Tuatha. One end deals death while the other"—he held the narrow end with the carving toward Brandy—"can heal. Some even say it can resurrect. That Gluskabe possessed this and has given it to you is a riddle. The Dagda has not been seen in many years. Was this given freely? Taken? Found? It will be of great interest to Fintan and Sulevia, especially. It could change their entire hospital here, if the legends are true. It will be the subject of much discussion."

"But," Brandy protested, "it just looks like a stick. Why would Gluskabe give me these things? He doesn't know me. I don't get it."

"It would seem to me, and I hope I have the opportunity to discuss this with him, that Gluskabe has decided—at the very least, he has chosen—to help Monhegan. Even if his help goes no further than that, it could change...everything."

"That's not even the one I thought was impressive," Brandy said, her breath catching as she reached into the bag one last time and drew out the sword. "I figured a sword was deadlier than a club and a stick, but now I don't know."

Kelphit received the blade from Brandy and turned it gently in his hands. He leaned in closer, examining the hilt and the guards.

"This will need more study," Kelphit said finally. "This is beyond my knowledge. It is clearly Tuatha in origin, the scrollwork is plain to see. But, unlike the other two, this is a piece of less renown. That is not to say of lesser power. This blade is made to destroy. The others have at least some aspects of creation to them, which is why I am sure of what they are. Fintan will know this. And Sulevia."

"Why does this last one scare me more than the other two?" Brandy replied. "And why the hell would this Gluskabe guy give them to *me*? I'm small potatoes."

"And yet these *were* given to you, not to Sean. Not to Trout. Not even to Bayard. There is something to that, but I don't know what. Yet." Kelphit rose and indicated for Brandy to replace the weapons in the bag. "Keep this to yourself. For now. Our hosts may have insight that I do not. I think it wise to gather as much information as we can before sharing this with Sean. He is under enough pressure. Agreed?"

"Oh, hell yeah," Brandy said, quickly. "That guy is about to split apart from whatever is eating him. Last thing he needs is some ancient killing machines to push him over the edge. I mean, I don't even want to touch them."

"And yet, I think you must," Kelphit replied. "Gluskabe had his reasons. It is not my place, or the place of any other, to take them from you."

"Ah, great," Brandy grumbled, hoisting the bag again. "Like I didn't have enough on my plate. Whatever. I'll take 'em. For now. But figure this out, yeah? These things seem like game changers."

"Possibly," Kelphit said. "But there is great magic in the world. If we have these, what do our foes have?"

"Man, K, you can really burst a bubble, you know that?" Brandy said with a grimace.

Their walk back to the healers' village passed quietly, but Brandy found her pack much heavier than it had been on the way out.

Sean was sitting on a bench by the Monhegan Lighthouse when Jay found him. He was facing out over the town below, with the harbor behind it and the sea stretching beyond. The air was crisp, and the grass crunched underfoot with the brittle frost of winter.

"Hey, man," Jay called, walking up behind Sean and stopping a few feet away, sharing the view. "Love it up here. Can't get near it in season, but this time of year you feel like you have the whole world to yourself."

Sean didn't turn at Jay's arrival but sat still facing the opposite direction. "I'm surprised they sent you," he said. "Figured it would be Brandy. Or Trout. Hell, my money would have been on Noodle before you."

"I'm full of surprises," Jay replied, crossing to the bench and perching on the arm. "Guess someone thought I had something to offer, under the circumstances."

"I doubt that," Sean said. "Doubt it very much. Just because you did some shows back in the day, doesn't mean we have anything in common. In fact, I don't even really care how you ended up here. This is just a quick stop on my way to somewhere else. So—no offense, but you can just head back and tell them you gave it a shot, but no dice."

Jay pointed to a nearby outcrop of rocks that ended in a steep drop to the village below.

"Some of my favorite islanders live there," he said.

"In the rocks?" Sean asked. "Is this the part where I ask what you mean, and you tell me a heartwarming story? Because I'd really rather just not."

"I don't know if it's heartwarming," Jay answered. "Just a nugget of information. Do with it what you will."

"I doubt if I can shut you up, so have at it."

"Well, you know that the island attracts people who need healing," Jay said. "Human, Fae, all sorts."

Sean nodded absentmindedly. Never taking his eyes off the horizon.

"But it's also other creatures of the world who make their way here," Jay continued. "We've seen seals, eagles, osprey. Even had a whale who came to the back side of the island once looking for some help."

"Make a great special on the Discovery Channel," Sean said. "You should pitch it to them."

"Maybe twenty years ago," Jay replied. "Not so much anymore. Anyway, one of my favorite little families lives in those rocks. Couple of puffins."

Sean turned halfway on the bench. "I do like puffins," he admitted. "But you're not hooking me that easily."

They both sat, contemplating the bustling harbor. One of the Hardy Boats was just arriving.

"Why are they here?" Sean finally asked. "This time of year, they should be back out to sea, not here."

"Yeah, they should," Jay agreed. "They're mates. Came here a while back. She had an injured wing. He was fine. The healers did what they could, but they couldn't fix her up. Not well enough to leave. So, she had to stay. And he did. To be with her."

"Seems like unusual behavior," Sean said, despite himself.

"Yeah, well, it is," Jay said. "But even puffins have a place in the Otherworld. Kind of. Legend has it that they are the reincarnation of monks. Or people who live a life of true service. Not all puffins, but some. Goes way back to the Celts. They even call them Little Friars."

"I always thought the way they walk makes them look like they have a lot on their minds. Hunched over. Leaning forward. Like little professors."

"Or little monks," Jay replied.

"I guess so," Sean agreed. "Like little monks."

"Well, the point is, not everyone who comes here knows they need it," Jay said. "Or plans to stay. But life happens. Like with Tuck and Marian."

Sean finally turned all the way to Jay, the question plain on his face.

"Just names I gave them," Jay confessed. "Friar Tuck, you know."

"Maid Marian wasn't with Friar Tuck," Sean said.

"That we know of," Jay answered. "Who knows what happened after the story ended. Besides, I thought it was funny. Unlikely couple in an unlikely place. Like my Little Friars."

"Okay, dammit," Sean said, turning back to face the harbor. "You win. Why did you stay? Your mate have a broken wing, too?"

"I wish it were that noble," Jay said. "I stayed because I was too weak to face going back."

"I don't understand," Sean said quietly.

"No way you could," Jay answered, now looking out over the harbor himself. "I was visited by some of the Fae. The ones you call Peripherals. They sent one of their contact teams to me. Guess they thought I had some potential. Maybe could be of use to them."

"Wait," Sean said. "Contact teams? What do you mean?"

"Pretty much what it sounds like. They have teams of Fae that set out to identify and recruit humans they think have talents. It used to happen a lot more, apparently. They've started ramping it up again lately. Mine was a couple years ago. They like to get you when your emotions run high. They came to me on opening night of a new show. I was—ripe for the taking. Flying high."

Sean thought back to his first encounter with Breena and the rest of the Peripherals. It had been closing night of the Grumbles' show. Emotions were definitely running high at that point.

"They choose a primary contact," Jay continued. "Someone they think will really connect with the—subject? Target? Well, they chose well with me. Too well. I fell for my contact. Hard. Before I knew what was happening, I couldn't keep my emotions out of any decision I made. She was my complete opposite, but you know what they say about that."

Sean felt a lump in his throat. His pulse raced. Jay could be describing how he met Breena. His mind was reeling. Had anything she'd told him been real?

"What was her name?" Sean asked, afraid to know the answer.

"Odette," Jay said, his eyes still on the horizon. "She's everything I'm not. Somber, disciplined, stern. I was hooked."

Sean's eyes closed, half from relief, and half in dismay. Odette had been one of the Peripherals he'd met. A fierce, focused, Teutonic warrior. He couldn't imagine her inspiring love in anyone, let alone the loose, jokesy Jay, but life and love were strange.

"Did you meet her?" Jay asked, sensing Sean's reaction. "You did. Did she contact you, too?"

Sean shook his head slowly. "No. I mean, I did meet her, but she wasn't my...contact."

Jay sagged onto the bench; relief mingled with pain. "But you fell for someone," he said. "I can see it. I'd tell you to let it go, but I know it's pointless. You gotta figure that out on your own. Who was it?"

Sean hesitated before finally whispering, "Breena. Her name is Breena."

Jay sat with that for a moment.

"I don't know her," he said. "Not one of my team. Not sure how you could have resisted Odette, but hearts do what they want. Unless they're manipulated by the Fae, I guess. I've considered that, too."

"What about the rest of the team you had?" Sean asked. "Kallan? Bayard? Alara? Were they in it?"

"Nah," Jay said. "Don't know any of them. You better believe I would have had a reaction when I saw him if Bayard had been in on it."

"That makes sense. They told me they were the lowest of the low," Sean recalled. "They were sent because no one else could be spared. That they were all expendable. Did they say the same to you?"

"No," Jay said. "Sounds like one of their cover stories. Mind games. They're good at it." A pause. "But after what happened with me—maybe it could be true. Maybe they just gave up on all of us. Humans. I was supposed to be a sure thing. My failure...probably didn't go over too well. I'm guessing it made Odette look bad, too. She'll never forgive me for that. Stubborn German temperament."

"But why did you end up here?" Sean asked. "What went wrong? You loved Odette. Did she love you? Why come here?"

"Oh, man, that's the million-dollar question, isn't it?" Jay said. "Did she love me? I have no idea. I could never read her. Not really. Probably part of the attraction. I never did make good choices in that department. But the first time we met a baddie? I wigged out. A minotaur. What the hell do I know about them? Nothing. Forgot everything they taught me. Lost control of my talents. Only thing I could think about was protecting Odette, which was, of course, the last thing she needed. *Her* of all people. Definitely not one to be taken care of. The whole thing went to shit. They decided they couldn't trust me. I failed the test. And when they told me they were sending me back to my regular, boring life? When it was clear Odette would go and I would probably never see her again? I fell apart. They dropped me on Monhegan. Been here ever since."

I'm so sorry," Sean said. "I didn't know any of that. They told me there had been others before me, but I never thought it through."

"How was she?" Jay asked anxiously. "Is Odette good? Was she with anyone?"

"She's fine," Sean assured him. "We went through some tough moments, but she came out okay. Don't think she was with anyone, but it didn't really come up."

"Gotcha," Jay said with some relief. "Well, you did better than me. Obviously. I'll stay here, I guess. Doesn't seem like I belong anywhere else now. Damaged goods. At least I can offer to help the healers. My powers are pretty good when I don't get all turned around by emotion. I hope they trust me."

"They sent you out here to talk to me," Sean pointed out. "They must."

"True," Jay said. "Hey, look, Tuck is back. Delivering a snack to Marian."

Sean turned toward the rocks and saw a flash of black and white flutter into a crevice.

"Wow, they're faster than I expected."

"Oh, yeah," Jay agreed. "Tough little suckers, too. They look cute and goofy, but they're survivors. Live most of the year out to sea. Normally. Rugged doesn't cover it. Another legend says they can predict the weather. I think they just know when a storm is coming. They'd have to, living at sea. But I guess making it legendary and magical is more fun."

"I guess there are much worse things than coming back as a puffin," Sean mused.

"I guess so," Jay agreed. "Live a life of service and get rewarded with that? I wouldn't mind."

A quiet moment passed as they waited for Tuck to reappear. He did and flashed off toward the water, back on the hunt.

"You know," Jay said, watching the little bird flit into the distance. "They sent me out here to make you feel better about staying a day or so. I have no idea if I did that, but I did want you to know my story. Not sure anyone else really can understand. But yeah. You should probably hang here for a bit. Clear the head. Rely on your friends. They obviously love you. Let them."

"I fell for mine, too," Sean admitted. "Breena. It's why I've been such an ass to everyone."

"I know," Jay said. "Spotted it a mile off. And look. Just because mine was a disaster, doesn't mean yours has to be. But you should weigh all the information first. I really hope she cares for you. That's the world I want to live in. Which is how I ended up here. But I have a feeling about you."

More silence.

"Thanks," Sean finally said. "I have a lot to think about. But at least now I feel like I can make a better decision. Let them know I'll stay a day. We'll take it from there."

"Good decision," Jay replied, slapping Sean's leg as he jumped to his feet. "See? You're already making smarter decisions than I ever did. Sit here a while. Say hi to Tuck when he gets back. I'll tell them to give you some space."

Sean nodded his thanks and watched Jay disappear back down the path toward the village, before turning his attention back to the harbor and the swirl of emotions Jay's story had left in him. He wasn't at all sure what was real anymore.

He popped in his earbuds and let the earthy tones of Gordon Lightfoot ease his worries. "Early Morning Rain" took him away. The longer he listened, the lower his shoulders fell until they were almost —*almost*—relaxed.

CHAPTER 11

J ay arrived at the healers' village just after Brandy and Kelphit
had returned and called everyone to gather at the tables on the
green. Everyone but Nick and McCloud were present. Even
Sandy had emerged from the community center and stood perched
on the front steps, half in and half out, unwilling to completely leave
the patients on their own.

Kelphit had taken center stage and stood by the wooden table,
Brandy's bag laid out in front of him. Fintan and Sulevia sat at the
opposite end of the table, their focus squarely on the bag. Bert stood
nearby, tossing a pinecone in the air and seeming perfectly relaxed.
Trout was holding back on the edge of the group. He alternated
between looking in the direction Sean had left and soothing Dünker,
who had attached himself to Trout's lower leg. Noodle sat at the
neighboring table, his sketch book splayed in front of him and his
hand flying across the page.

It was Bayard who caught Jay's attention most. He was well
beyond the circle of the others. He rocked slightly from foot to foot,
as if he could barely control the urge to run. As if the energy coursing
through him was desperate for some release. Cinder was beside him,

leaning on his thigh, her ears pinned flat on her head. She looked poised to either dash into the woods and run herself tired, or leap onto the table to confront…something.

Jay paused at the edge of the trees. He couldn't quite hear what was being said, but tension sat heavy across the group. Concerned, he picked up his pace. All eyes turned to him as he neared the tables and cleared his throat slightly, making sure they knew he was there.

"Yo, this looks like a pretty heavy meeting," he called. "If you're still worried about Sean, you can chill. I talked him down off the ledge. He just needs a few minutes to gather himself, but he's cool. Look like he'll stay for a little, and everyone smarter than me can help him come up with a plan. Poor guy is a big ball of regret, love, guilt, confusion. Hope. It's a lot."

Sulevia rose and motioned for Jay to join her. "We all thank you, Jay," she said. "I'm sure that wasn't easy. In your absence, Kelphit and Brandy have come to us with…some new information."

"Hit me with it," Jay replied, taking a seat between Sulevia and Fintan.

"You may want to rephrase that when you see what it is," Brandy said, from Kelphit's side.

"I think it best to tell them how this came to pass," Kelphit interrupted.

Brandy nodded and gave them the full story of her encounter with Gluskabe. The Peripherals of the group all sat taller at the mention of that name. Bert seemed to startle at the first mention of it, and his pinecone hit the ground. Trout was unreadable, but Dünker emerged from his lock grip on the Montanan and nervously smiled. Noodle's hand paused briefly before attacking the sketch book again.

At the conclusion of Brandy's story, Kelphit reached into the bag and withdrew the mace with the ram's head atop it. He placed it delicately on the table. Both Fintan and Sulevia took sharp breaths. Bayard stepped slightly away, Cinder moving as one with him.

Fintan crossed to Kelphit and cautiously lifted the mace.

"You're correct, of course," he said, nodding to Kelphit. "Tishtrya's Mace. Not seen in many years. So many that some of us believed it was lost forever. Perhaps that would have been best. But here it is. It conveys the strength of nine men. Likely more. And controls the weather. At least in that it can create cyclones and rain. Why Gluskabe would bring it here, now...I don't know."

"It will take wisdom to consider how or if we should use this. It is not a thing to take blithely," Sulevia said.

"Gotta be honest," Brandy replied. "I'd feel a lot better if you Peripheral types took these things off my hands. I have no clue what to do with them."

"And yet," Fintan said, "they were given to you specifically. We must find out why."

Kelphit nodded. "I've told her as much. And there is more."

He carefully lifted the club out of the bag and placed it next to the mace. This time the reaction was even more pronounced. Sulevia and Fintan audibly gasped and rushed to the table. Bayard's eyes widened and he slid even further from the group.

"The Lorg Mór!" Fintan cried. "How can it be? Why is it here?"

Sulevia looked as if she wanted to speak, but no words came. Her hand shook as she reached for the club, before thinking better of it.

"It is the Lorg Mór," Kelphit whispered. "Astonishing."

"Friends," Fintan continued, "this is one of the greatest treasures of the Tuatha De Danann. The war club of our chief, the Dagda. It is of inestimable value."

"And power," Sulevia said quietly.

"Yes, and power," Fintan continued. "It both gives and takes life. One end deals death. The other, with its etching, can heal. Some believe even reverse death. It can't be an accident that it would appear here, on our island of healing."

Jay, still seated, had never heard Fintan speak in such reverence. And he felt the stirring of fear.

"These two I was sure of," Kelphit continued. "But this last, I confess, is beyond my knowledge."

He lifted the sword from the bag and placed it alongside the other two weapons. It gleamed in the bright winter sun. It looked ice cold. And deadly.

Bayard cried out and turned to walk toward the woods behind him, Cinder at his side. He stopped halfway there, and paused, unsure whether to stay or go. Trout made to follow, but Kelphit shook his head. It was Sulevia who tenderly lifted the blade, slowly raising it above her head so it caught the sunlight even more spectacularly. It flashed and everyone instinctively shielded their eyes. A thrum of energy rumbled through the clearing. Sandy at the door to the infirmary rushed back inside, presumably to check on the patients.

Sulevia gently lowered the sword back to the table and rushed off to one of the surrounding cottages, muttering to herself so quietly that no one could make out what she was saying.

"Dayum," Trout said, craning his neck to get a better look, then reconsidering and staying put. Dünker retreated again behind Trout's leg.

"Did anyone hear that?" Brandy said, scanning the village for something that could have set them all on edge.

"I didn't *hear* anything," Noodle responded, his hand never leaving the page in front of him. "But I sure *felt* something."

Sulevia emerged from her cottage clutching a book under her arm. She rushed to the table and placed the heavy tome next to the blade and began ruffling through the pages. Finally, she found what she was looking for and stopped. She leaned in, her fingers tracing something on the page. Suddenly, she stood straight and fixed Fintan with a look.

For his part, Fintan had remained rooted where he was and seemed to hold his breath. When Sulevia turned to him, he let out a small cry.

"This is, without a doubt, the Singing Sword of Conaire Mór," Sulevia announced. "It belonged to a high king in Ireland long ago. Little is known of it, but it was said to lead the bearer into battle singing a song of destruction. None could withstand it. With the death of that king, the sword was lost."

"Some believed," Fintan said from his seat, "as I did, that it had been hidden. Its power too great to risk in the world. In lands where bards and poets held such influence, this sword in the wrong hands could have changed the path of nations. A violence magnifier."

Bayard surged to the table, his eyes wide with alarm. "This cannot stay here," he said, emphasizing his points by striking the table repeatedly. "The second age of bards is here. We're watching it happen. The sword must be hidden. Again. Until we, and more importantly our friends, have a better understanding of what they can do." He turned to Trout and Brandy. "I love and respect you. I hope you know that. But not everyone is as worthy. We've already seen that even steadfast hearts can be turned by power. Ken proved himself vulnerable. And, as much as I care for him, Sean, the greatest hope and greatest danger of all, is in the midst of...something. None of us know how that will go."

A pregnant pause followed. Jay rose and crossed to the community center doorway, shaking his head. Brandy half rose from her seat, ready to make an argument, but abruptly sat back down. Noodle's hand never left the page in front of him.

The lengthy silence ended only when Sean appeared from the trees. His steps were light, and his entire demeanor had shifted from the dour anger that had sent him off not too long ago.

"You guys were right," he announced. "And Jay was the perfect one to talk me around. A short break will do me good." He noticed tension in the group. "Hey, what gives? Did I miss something?"

His eyes took in the table and settled on the shining blade in the middle of it.

"Damn, that looks scary. Fill me in?"

While the other Wullivers prowled the nearby forest, alert for any threat, Carolyn stood just within the shade of the forest, watching the group as they first saw the weapons and then erupted in concern at the reveal of the sword. Their words carried to her sensitive canine ears, and the silver-grey fur along her neck stood up as she heard the alarm and fear in the raised voices.

She was quite sure that Cinder, and likely Bayard, too, sensed her presence, but for their own reasons they allowed her to observe silently.

It was not the first time she had seen power threaten to derail good intentions.

She headed silently back into the forest to reflect on what she had seen and how she could help. And to gather her family in case they would be needed to hold the group together. Something she had never considered before.

Sean sat in disbelief after Kelphit and Fintan, supported by Sulevia, filled him in on everything he had missed. His incredulity came not from the fantastical events and powerful weapons that had come to Brandy (although if he was honest with himself, he did wonder why Gluskabe had chosen her and not him), but from the wariness he sensed radiating toward him from everyone assembled. His closest friends, and some of the beings he most admired, had lost their faith in him as a decent and reliable person. It hurt. A lot.

When they had finished, he leaned forward on the table. The afternoon sun shone down, and he felt himself flush, despite the winter chill. He rubbed his face, exhaustion mingling with shame. Because as hurt as he was, he knew that they were right to doubt him. He had doubted himself until his talk with Jay.

His deep auburn hair, growing darker with each passing year, ruffled in the breeze. He brushed it out of his eyes and looked around the assembled group. Dünker remained buried in Trout's leg, but the others watched him with varying degrees of concern. It hurt even more as he realized they were still on edge, waiting to see if he would try to claim the sword and wreak violence. Only Jay seemed at ease. He had spoken his piece and had seen Sean's response.

Sean covered his face with his hands, running them from crown to chin. Then back. As if he could erase his behavior of the last few days. And how it had affected his friends' opinion of him.

"Look, I get it," he said, lifting his face to look each person squarely in the eyes in turn. "I haven't been myself. I let things get out of hand. I tried to escape my responsibilities by running to Lancaster. It didn't work and all I accomplished was to put even more people in danger. I wasn't even there when I was needed most. Then the appearance of Breena. And Kallan. It pushed me over the edge. But Jay"—he nodded toward him—"really did get through to me. I'm going to pull myself together. And I know I need you all to do that. And that you've all sacrificed to keep me going. So, look...I don't want the sword. I don't want that kind of power. I never wanted *any* power. It just happened. So...please...relax about that. Someone else should carry that burden. Responsibility. However you want to look at it. You all can decide that. I just want to sit with you all and come up with a plan. I need to find a way into the Otherworld. A back door. And there is no other group of people I trust more to help with that. I'm sorry I was an ass. Old Sean is back. But before any of that, I want a nap. Anyone got a spare bunk for me?"

Brandy and Trout were the first to reach him and each threw their arms around him. Even Dünker peeked out from behind Trout with a tentative smile. Bayard was not far behind, a reflective grin on his face. Bert clapped his hands and let out a whoop. The healers visibly relaxed and placed the weapons back in Brandy's bag. Out of sight.

Noodle remained where he sat. He, too, smiled, but his pencil never stopped weaving its way across the sketch pad on the table.

"Of course," Fintan eventually said. "My manners are lacking.

Again. Please, allow me to show you to a cabin. Let me know if you need anything at all."

As Fintan led Sean away, Kelphit took Brandy's bag and moved off toward the community center with Sulevia in tow.

Dünker crept out in full view and peered up at Trout.

"Trout-friend," the little Troll whispered hoarsely. "I can go see trees? Maybe see ocean?"

"Of course, pal," Trout answered. "You don't need to ask me. You're free to do what you want. Go on! Take a looksee around. Stretch those little bowed legs. See something pretty."

"Free?" Dünker said, quietly. "Free. Go see trees. Birds. Thank you, Trout-friend!"

The troll scurried off, waving one arm in the air and wiping his nose with the other. Bayard shared a quick glance with Cinder, and with the slightest of nods from both, Cinder slipped quietly into the forest where Dünker had gone.

Fintan returned to the village green without Sean, who was presumably already into a much-needed nap.

Noodle rose from his drawing and looked at those remaining. "If no one minds, I'm going to take a stroll down through the town. I saw a few art galleries that looked interesting. I'd love to talk painting with someone."

"I think that's a fine idea," Fintan said. "It seems everyone could use a short break. Shall we meet again in the hall in, say, two hours? We do still have much to discuss."

"Great idea," Bert agreed. "Mind if I tag along, Noodle? I don't know much about art, but I do know the Webers who run the Brewing Company. Closed this time of year, but I'm betting they'd be happy to share some goodies they have in there."

Noodle paused for only a second before agreeing that it sounded like a fine idea, and the two meandered off toward town, falling into a deep discussion on the latest Broadway season and its hits and misses.

Watching them leave, Fintan laid a hand on Trout's shoulder.

"I'm glad to have the two of you here," he said, including Brandy. "I want to talk to you about Jotunn. It's highly unusual for a troll to attach so completely to humans. They are a secretive and elusive breed. How well do you know him?"

"Well, shoot," Trout replied. "Not well, but he seems innocent enough. I thought he might want to stay here on the island with you lot, but I got a hunch he'll push on with us now."

"Damnedest thing I've seen," Brandy added. "Just took a shine to this big oaf and tagged along. Can't explain it."

"I see," said Fintan. "I don't want to be out of place, but I thought you should know. Jotunn is a family name. Common. Trolls guard their true selves very closely. I don't want to imply anything sinister. But trolls are secretive. Very. It's no surprise that he would use that name, but he may be hiding more than just that."

"Ohhh," Trout replied. "He and I had a heart to heart a while ago. Sean and I know all about him."

Fintan raised his hands and seemed surprised. "Say no more. If he has shared that with you, he has taken you into his truths. I'm surprised, but it speaks clearly that he is connected to you. And before you offer, I do not want you to share that name with me. That is between you and him. And rightfully so."

"Right," Brandy said. "I have no idea what you're talking about. Just met the little fella." She gave Trout a sharp dig in the ribs.

Fintan laughed, nodding. He suggested they both take the opportunity to either explore or rest. Without hesitation, they both retreated to cottages on the outskirts of the village and fell fast asleep within minutes.

Noodle and Bert tromped through the forest trail, across the open fields, past the lighthouse, and finally into the town itself. Noodle made note of The Barnacle on their right as they passed the dock area and briefly considered stopping in. The building looked old, rustic, and sturdy. All things that appealed to him at this point. When he saw a group of new arrivals head into the shop, he thought better of it and kept crunching along the dirt path toward a row of small shops that quickly proved to be art galleries. His eyes growing larger the nearer he got.

Bert had been chattering away throughout, but Noodle had been lost in his own swirl of thoughts. He clicked back into the moment as they neared a particularly cozy-looking gallery.

"So, yeah, that's when I knew," Bert said, "that Maine was the place for me. Haven't looked back since. Never saw me becoming a freedom fighter for wayward Fae, but no complaints there, either. What are the arts if not a place where the vulnerable find a haven? Guess we just took it a step further. Well, a bunch of steps. I can*not* wait to get my hands on some of that beer."

"Bert," Noodle replied, never taking his eyes from the gallery ahead, "want to pop into this shop first? Looks intriguing to me."

Bert took a moment to size up the framed paintings in the window, before deciding.

"Do you mind if I run ahead?" he asked. "The beer is calling me. Can you hear it?"

Noodle laughed. "Totally cool. I'll just be a few minutes. Need an art fix."

As Bert continued through the town and eventually up the hill toward the brewery, Noodle paused to stand in front of the front display window, soaking in some original works there.

One large painting showed a boat, impossibly small against the angry sea, struggling toward the harbor. A tiny spot of perseverance in a landscape hellbent on stopping it. The piece next to it stopped him in his tracks. It was a quilt, but like none he had ever seen. It was so full of detail it could have been a painting. It showed the sun rising over the water and stony shore of a Maine vista. The sky was an explosion of color—purple, green, pink, grey, blue. He looked at the small brass plate at its base and saw that it was titled "Song of

Light," which seemed like the most serendipitous thing he could have imagined.

He opened the door and entered the gallery. It had clearly been a home at some point, but now was filled from floor to ceiling with paintings. Many original, but some prints, as well. In addition to a handful of quilts, there were sculptures and some ceramics. The subjects covered every bit of life on Monhegan. Wildlife, flowers, forests. Sailing, swimming, fishing. From realism to abstract and every other style he could imagine. Noodle was captivated, nearly overwhelmed by the assault of color and style. And the sheer creativity on display, no two pieces even remotely similar.

He was so transported that he nearly jumped out of his skin when he heard a rich alto voice come from the rear of the store.

"Welcome," it said. "If you see anything you like, just let me know. Don't mean to ignore you. Just caught up in this interview on the TV. Take your time. Slow day. January, you know."

Noodle let his pulse return to a normal rate before heading back toward the voice. Turning a corner, he came upon a tall, elegant woman seated behind a counter stacked with all the tools needed to frame and hang art. A small TV was flickering in the corner, the volume low enough that Noodle hadn't noticed it over the softly playing ambient music.

"Don't mean to bother you," he said quietly. "I'll just take a peek around."

The woman rose and flashed an open, brilliant smile. She had tightly curled hair that was in the midst of turning an elegant, mature grey. Her brown eyes shone brightly with easy laughter. And something a bit deeper than that.

"No, no, not at all," she said. "My gallery, my job to make you welcome. It's just this is a live interview, and I haven't figured out how to pause it. Welcome to Foxglove Gallery. I'm Taren Hargens. This is my place." She paused for the briefest moment, before continuing. "Help yourself. If you haven't heard about this, it's the latest Stewart Garland piece. Rachel Shaddow is talking to him."

"Did you say Stewart Garland?" Noodle asked.

Taren smiled. "Sure did. Pull up a stool if you're interested. Got about another ten minutes to go. Sorry, I just think he's great. And he says so much I agree with. He's kicking off a concert tour this week."

Noodle found a stool on the patron side of the counter and set himself down. Sure enough, when he focused on the screen, and Taren lowered the music in the gallery, he found the familiar face of his pal, Stewart, seated opposite the legendary television journalist.

"You've basically come from nowhere," Shaddow stated. "How do you explain that? And how do you handle so much success so quickly?"

Stewart ran his fingers through his impressive mane of still-black hair and leaned forward in his seat.

"I'm not exactly sure how to answer that," he said, with a shy smile. "I just think the whole premise is off base. There's nothing about me or my career that came out of nowhere. Or happened fast. I've been performing at the highest levels of theatre for...over twenty years. And even though most people don't recognize my name, they may know my face. I've been on television many times. And Broadway. I've heard it said that making it to Broadway is like making a National Football League team. It's that competitive. So...I've been doing this a long time. Four hundred and sixteen shows a year. That's the Broadway schedule. It's grueling. Athletic. Most actors don't take vacations because they love what they do. But also, because our profession is so tenuous. We save all that vacation time and cash out when the show closes. For when times get hard. And they get tough for all of us at some point. Even though showbiz is obsessed with youth and looks right now, and I guess always will be, those things don't last. But young performers rarely understand that. Until they have no choice. It's just most people don't know how hard we work. And how long it takes most of us to find any footing. I didn't come out of nowhere. I came from a life of hard work and persistence that prepared me for the opportunity if—and that's a big if—I ever got the chance to step forward and *really* show what I can do. I'm good. Very good. But I'm not so egotistical as to think there aren't hundreds of others who can do exactly what I'm doing. A lot of them maybe even better than me."

Shaddow chuckled quietly and placed her notes on a table beside her chair. "I think I should ditch my notes and just have a talk with you," she said. "Your humility, which you just put on full display, is one of the things that people admire the most. It's pretty rare today. How do you explain that? And why do you think people have responded so wholeheartedly to your message of peace and love. Generosity. Kindness. Things that, frankly, have been uncool for a long time."

"Isn't that so sad, though?" Stewart answered. "Why is it uncool to care about other people? Isn't that one of the best legacies we can leave behind? And make a difference here while we're doing it? Maybe I'm here to make uncool cool again. Or maybe, I'm just being me at the right time."

"Why is this the right time for that message?" Shaddow followed up.

"I think it's always the right time for kindness," Stewart replied. "For me, personally, I've been watching as good old common decency slid into irrelevance over the last—let's just say—many years. I have good friends—my best friends—going through a lot right now. I wanted to be there to help them, but they convinced me that my going on this tour and hopefully reaching people, is needed. I feel like I'd be letting them down if I gave it any less. And I don't like to let my friends down."

"So that's you personally," Shaddow continued. "What about the world at large?"

"Just look around," Stewart replied. "Which I know is what you get paid to do. Reality television. Our politics. Big corporations. It seems like everything has been rewarding behavior that pushes others down to propel yourself up. Honestly, I think—I have to *believe*—that people want a change. We don't all have to be Mother Teresa, but maybe we should stop rewarding the Genghis Khans.

And I don't think I'm the only one who feels that way. So, if I can change—or embolden—some hearts to listen to their angels and not their demons, and do it by singing some songs and making some jokes and telling some stories? Well, I'm here for it. And judging by the reaction, so are others. It's not rocket science. It's just common decency. And common decency shouldn't require an act of courage."

"Stewart Garland," Shaddow said, rising and extending her hand. "Thank you. I wish I had more time to talk to you. I hope you'll come back. Best of luck on the tour. Doesn't sound like you need it, but still...Folks, Stewart will be coming your way soon, starting with the Hollywood Bowl on January 20, followed by a six-month world tour."

Taren leaned forward and turned off the television.

"Thanks for indulging me," she said, turning a smile to Noodle. "I just love him."

Noodle was silent for a moment. He knew Stewart from New York and was very aware that the friends he had referenced were the Grumbles. He wasn't as close with Stewart, but he knew him and had been surprised at how affecting his words had been.

"I get it," he replied. "He's got an important message. Hope I get the chance to see him on the tour."

"Oh, that would be a dream," Taren said. "I used to live in New York. Probably saw him in a show, at some point. But, well, I'm here now. I heard the call of the island, and the rest is history."

"Wow, that's quite a change. New York to Monhegan," Noodle replied. He glanced around the gallery. "But I get it. Monhegan is beautiful. I've only been here since yesterday, so I haven't met many people, but if they're anything like the island itself...it seems like a special place. What did you do in New York?"

"What didn't I do," Taren said, with a laugh. "Did some singing. A lot of singing actually. Some acting. Taught. Eventually, I became a life coach. It just...made sense to me. And I'm good at it. I always supported artists of all kinds. When the city started to be too noisy for me—you know what I mean, right?—I stumbled on Monhegan thanks to some friends up here. Fell in love with the place. Opened the gallery to be a cheerleader for artists I thought should get more attention. Still a life coach. Sing in a local choir, but just for fun now. Oh jeez, listen to me. Rambling on. I do that sometimes."

"Not at all," Noodle said. "I think that's all interesting. And yeah. I get it."

"I think I've been chasing peace all my life. Personal peace. Can't control the rest of the world. Yeah. Chasing. Probably why the life coach thing started. And this island…made me feel quiet. Still. And the artists. The art. Put me at peace. I know art is different things to different people, but for me it's always been a refuge. So, I stayed. Oh, I'm rambling again. Sorry! What about you?" Taren asked. "What brings you to the island? Especially this time of year."

"Some friends were in a jam, and I wanted to help," Noodle said. "Glad I did. I like it here."

"A jam, huh?" Taren said. "They up at the healers' village? No better place to be if you need help."

"Oh," Noodle stammered, surprised. "I guess I didn't realize people knew about that place."

"A lot of us do," she said. "Not everyone, but most. People here tend to be pretty in tune with the world around us. Plus, the whole life coach thing. They've asked me for help. Well, once. But I thought that was pretty cool."

"Wow, very cool."

"And you?" Taren continued. "Where are you from? What do you do? Enough about me."

"I'm from New York," he answered. "A lot of that going around. And…well, I draw. Probably why I was drawn to the gallery. No pun intended."

"Ha!" Taren exploded with a guttural laugh. "Good one. You draw? Like what? Cartoons? Engineering plans? Lots of things to draw."

"Yeah," Noodle said, drawing it out. "I do a lot of work for the Broadway and theatre community."

"You're kidding?" Taren said, her voice even louder than it had been. "Do you know Stewart Garland?"

"Actually, yeah, I do. He's a sort of friend."

"I cannot believe this. Wait. Are *you* famous? Should I know you?"

Noodle laughed and looked at the floor. "*Should* you know me? Nah. But you might know some of my stuff. Most of my work gets shown under the name Noodle."

"Holy shit!" Taren shouted, reaching new decibel levels with each statement. "Noodle! I *love* your stuff! Come here. Wait until you see some of these artists I have here. You will love them. Can I get you to sign something? How long are you staying? Can we have a reception for you here? Come here! Look at this!"

And she was off to a corner of the gallery, digging through stacks of prints and pulling some that she swore would be of interest to Noodle.

For his part, Noodle was a bit embarrassed by the effusive attention, but quickly found himself grinning from ear to ear, unable to resist Taren's infectious enthusiasm. And not long after that, he really was swept away by the art she was showing him.

Their discussion veered from painting styles to local artists, to the challenges and rewards of living in New York. And moving away from New York. It didn't take long for them to sit down on their stools again and jabber away as if they'd known each other for years.

That's how Bert found them when he wandered back to the gallery, his arms filled with various cans from the brewery. Taren welcomed him, declaring any friend of Noodle's was welcome there. More chattering ensued. A couple of the beers intended for the healers' village disappeared in the process.

When Noodle and Bert wandered back to the village almost an hour later, Noodle saw the island around him in a completely different light. And he loved to play with light in his drawings.

<hr>

The village was buzzing with activity when Bert and Noodle got back. Trout and Sean were emerging from the cottages where they had rested, and Sandy stood on the steps of the community hall gesturing for them all to hurry and join her inside.

Sean shook his head, trying to clear the cobwebs. Trout jogged across the green to join him and together they made their way to Sandy. Noodle was not far behind, but Bert was struggling under his armload of beer, so the others returned to his side to help. Together they all followed Sandy into the hall.

The healers and Bayard were gathered in the center. A large table had been brought in and on it was a large map spread out and held down by small crystals at each corner. The three weapons gifted by Gluskabe occupied the rest of the table. All of the Peripherals were huddled, heads close together and in the middle of an animated discussion. When they saw the others returning, they broke apart and stood by the map, waiting.

"What's up, folks?" Sean said, approaching. "Didn't think we were going to have any heavy talks while all of us normal folks were away."

Kelphit shot a displeased look at Sulevia before responding. "Neither did I," he replied. "And I'm relieved you have returned. There is some disagreement on how we should proceed. Your opinions would be welcome."

"Our apologies," Fintan said. "We had no intention to cause discomfort. But Sulevia and I both believe"—he ventured a glance at the other Fae—"that, while the mace and blade will require much debate on how best to be used, the club, with its healing qualities would serve best remaining here."

Bayard, still looking out the window over Nick's bed, spoke without turning to the others. "I don't have an argument with that, necessarily. I think Fintan is shading his words a bit. What they proposed was to use the club to attempt to heal McCloud. Even without considering that all of you were still away, I think, and I believe Kelphit does, too, that more study is needed before we experiment on anyone. Particularly the only Timestrider alive."

"And more importantly," Kelphit added, "I think this perfectly displays why deliberation must be sober. These items have been here only a few short hours and already they are causing friction between normally reasonable minds. The lure of power, even when intended for good, is strong. Possibly too strong even for the Fae to resist."

"Nonsense," Sulevia interrupted, almost immediately holding her hands up in apology. "That was harsher than intended. Our point was simply that Gluskabe clearly intended for these to be here. Now. With us. There is nowhere else positioned more precariously than us in the coming struggle. And no one more qualified to use the club than the elders of a community that is devoted to healing. Imagine the good that could be done if McCloud were to wake and join us."

"And imagine," Bayard said quietly, finally turning to face the others, "if something were to go wrong and McCloud were lost. Yes, he is a Timestrider, but he is also a living being and deserves the respect and caution any of us would receive in the same situation."

The Grumbles stood in silent shock. Sean was focused on what it would mean should McCloud come back. Maybe they could find Ken and bring him back to now. To his true timeline. The very thought sent a surge of adrenaline through him. A chance to right what he saw as one of his greatest failures.

"There is no danger to McCloud," Fintan said, trying to calm the moment. "Either he wakes or stays as he is. Not trying, though...He is sure to remain lost."

"What I'm hearin'," Trout said, "is y'all want to throw a Hail Mary here. I'm not too happy that you were ready to do it without us, but...maybe it's not the worst idea? The mace and the sword are still up for discussion, though, right? 'Cuz, I have a feeling they're gonna see some scuffles in the very near future."

"We have no desire for those weapons here," Sulevia assured

them. "Our only wish is to heal those in need and protect our island home."

Sandy timidly stepped to the table and fixed her eyes on Kelphit. "If the risk to McCloud is small, would it be so bad to try?"

Kelphit sighed. "My fear is that we don't yet know the risk," he said, glancing at Bayard. "But there is no better gathering of healers than those here now."

"I'm still against this," Bayard said loudly, his hands in the air. "I've seen power corrupt before. And I've seen the unanticipated results of even the best of intentions. I'm not a healer, but I fear I will be one of the ones who will have to clean up the mess should things go wrong."

"I hear you, friend," Fintan responded. "At the first sign of danger, we will stop. But we must try. If not now, when?"

Bayard nodded, but without conviction.

The Fae looked at each other, and without saying a word, reached agreement. Silently, Kelphit walked to where his bags were leaning against the wall and put on his wide leather belt and its various attached pouches.

Bayard shook his head and crossed to the far side of the room. Loudly. With Cinder padding along behind.

"Maybe I should put these on ice for now, then?" Bert said, holding up some of the beer he'd brought.

"Yeah, that's probably a good idea," Sean answered.

"Although I could use one of those right about now," Brandy said, looking wistfully at the cans as Jay hurried out to find some ice.

"You and me both," Trout agreed, checking to make sure his own war club was handy.

Sean chewed his lip and stepped to Nick's bedside, watching as the healers headed toward McCloud's bed, Fintan bearing the club. The Lorg Mór, the Great Club of the Tuatha, was about to join the struggle.

CHAPTER 12

The breeze outside was picking up again, rattling the wooden walls, but the sun still shone in the dying light of late afternoon. Kelphit hurried about McCloud, placing stones in a very specific pattern around the bed. Sulevia held a large book in both hands, thumbing through the pages in search of something. Fintan stood by the head of the bed, the Lorg Mór clasped firmly before him. The narrower end, the portion with the intricate etching and floral patterns rested on the mattress next to the Scotsman's face.

As one, all three of them began to chant quietly, each in a separate language, none of which were recognizable to any of the Grumbles. Faintly, at first, and then brighter and brighter, the club began to pulse with verdant light. The chants became more urgent, gaining speed.

Outside, the sun was dipping below the tops pf the trees, and darkness crept in through the windows on skeletal shadows thrown by empty branches. The wind continued to pick up, but all eyes were fixed on the Timestrider. The green pulsing glow snaked down the length of the bed, encircling the patient.

The healers were struggling now. Perspiration showed on their faces, and Sulevia began to flush, her face turning a deeper shade of pink, then red.

Sean, noticing the toll their exertions were taking, gestured to Trout and Brandy to join him, and they approached the healers, making a semicircle behind Fintan and the club. Sean began to sing quietly, his eyes closed and his face set and determined. After seeing what he was attempting, Brandy and Trout added their voices to his, and quickly a bright white light took shape around them and sent tendrils toward Fintan. More specifically, toward the Lorg Mór.

Nick, still bedbound, was determined to add his voice. His mellow tenor seamlessly joining with the sound the others were making. Noodle, too, began to wordlessly sing, and gestured with his head for Bert to help him. Together, they took hold of Nick's bed and slid him closer to the others.

Bayard shook his head and remained on the opposite side of the room. His arms flicked back and forth and with each motion a pair of deadly looking daggers slid from his sleeve into his hands. This continued as he paced from wall to wall.

Jay was the only one who seemed distracted. He glanced repeatedly out the window as the darkness settled in and then continued. Getting somehow darker than a simple dusk should be.

Sandy stood dumbfounded, watching the healers, her mouth agape. At the moving of Nick's bed, she shook her head and rushed to Nick's side, also adding her rich soprano to the glorious sound in the room.

The white and green lights entwined. Pulsed. Took hold of McCloud, gradually covering him completely and finally raising him ever so slightly above the mattress. The light grew brighter. And brighter. The singers, one by one, had to shut their eyes against the brilliance they were helping to create.

A small but insistent tapping began to come from the window. Something was rattling the pane in its frame. With the growing wind, it seemed likely to be the empty branches around the building scraping along the exterior.

Fintan's arms began to shake. The club pulled him forward until it was resting on McCloud's chest. Fintan was helpless and could do nothing to steer the club. In fact, the club began to draw more and more light from the singers. All of them began to struggle to reclaim control of their sound, but the club took hold and tightly. Only Sean seemed to be able to retain some control of himself, and even he began to strain.

Kelphit dropped to one knee by the bed, leaning over and propping himself up with one arm. Sulevia let the tome she was holding drop to her side, her breath coming in ragged bursts.

The tapping at the window continued, growing in volume and frequency. This didn't seem like the random scratching of wind-blown boughs. Jay moved silently to the front door to investigate.

On the bed, McCloud was settling back onto the mattress. The green and white light slithering along and around him, finally sinking into him completely. He arched his back and gasped for air, the first signs of life he'd displayed since he was first felled by the Naga's curse in Lancaster weeks earlier.

Suddenly, the front door flew open, the blinding lights of the mystical club ceremony bursting into the village green beyond. Jay appeared in the doorway and in his hand, he held a small bird. It was Tuck, the island's puffin. The little friar.

Bayard crossed quickly to Jay and the puffin, leaning down and laying a hand on the sturdy little creature. As he did, McCloud sat bolt upright in the bed, a wild look in his eyes as he struggled to focus his eyes. He looked around the room, finally settling his eyes on Sean and finding some relief there.

Bayard lifted his head from the bird, and rushed to the bedside, where all eyes were fixed now on the Timestrider, who still gave a gentle, but quickly receding, green glow to all around him.

"Our time is up," Bayard called, pushing his way into the circle around McCloud. "A storm is coming. And this is no natural storm. We need to act. Now."

McCloud pushed himself backward in his bed, trying to crawl as far from the others as he could, half turning as if he could climb through the wall behind him and disappear.

"And who the hell are ye?" he cried. He looked at Sean. "You seem familiar, but the rest of the lot of you I've never seen. Where am I? And how did I get here?"

"No memory. His mind is blank," Fintan said quietly. "Wiped clean."

"I don't think you appreciate what I'm saying," Bayard said, grabbing Fintan by the shoulder. "Something has sent this storm. It's nearly here. We must decide our course. Now!"

<hr>

Fintan was silent for just the barest moment, his eyes flickering between Bayard and McCloud. His indecision didn't last, as he quickly turned to Sulevia and Kelphit.

"We must get Sean and the others off Monhegan before the storm arrives," he said quietly. "We don't have time to wait for Andy to bring his boat out. Find Taren. She can take them. But first, we must gather the information they need on where to access the Otherworld."

From the doorway, Jay called out. "I'll go to Taren. Do what you need to here." He turned to leave, still holding Tuck. When he crossed the threshold to the green, he held the puffin closely before releasing him to return to his craggy home and mate, and then Jay disappeared into the darkness and the mounting wind.

Sean stepped to Fintan, waving his arms in front of himself. "There is no way I will leave you when things get dangerous. I'll stay and defend the island and then find my way to Breena. I just went through that whole awakening with Jay. I can't just cut and run. That would be against everything I said I learned."

Fintan turned to Sean, but it was Sulevia who spoke. "Sean, as admirable as that is, you have no choice. If you are on the island when the storm reaches us, you could be stranded here for too long. While having you to fight by our side would certainly be a help, we are perfectly capable of defending ourselves. If we call the mists of Hy-Brasil, we need to know we can remain hidden as long as necessary. If you are here, we cannot do that. You and your companions must decide who will stay and who will go."

"We can't split up again," Sean answered. "We finally made our way back to each other."

Nick spoke next, still in his bed. "I can't go, Sean. I'm sorry. I can barely cross the room, let alone go hunting for portals to the world of the Fae. I would only slow you down. I hate it, but there's really no alternative. And maybe I can help here. I hate to be separated. Again. But you need to go."

"I'm sticking with you, Ginge," Trout said, standing by Sean. "I've come this far."

"Me go with Trout," Dünker said, from behind the Montanan.

"And I have a feeling you'll need me," Brandy said, joining them.

Sandy stood in the center of the room, looking from Nick to the still-cowering McCloud. "I have to stay, I think," she said, her eyes pleading with the others. "I'm so sorry. But I'm a healer. My work here isn't done."

Noodle hadn't moved. He stared at the floor by his feet. "I'll stay," he announced quietly. "Something about this place has gotten into me. I think it has things to teach me. And if what happened in Lancaster is any indication, Nick and I make a pretty good team in defending a place. You don't need me, Sean. But I think that I need this place."

Nick nodded to Noodle and raised a thumb in approval.

Bert raised a hand. "I need to catch a ride back to the mainland," he said. "If trouble is coming, I need to be with my people. My theatre. My town. I wish I could be more of a help, but maybe being on the front line down there is the best way for me to serve."

Bayard had remained by the front door, facing out. Lightning flashed, throwing a shadow of the Peripheral and Cinder racing across the hall.

"This storm is close," Bayard called to the others without turning. "And will be far worse than we think. There are evil voices on these winds. Whatever happens needs to happen soon." He turned to face the room. "I will go. The island is in good hands, but if you do reach the Otherworld, you will need one of our kind. And it's time we got our house in order. I won't leave that solely to my human friends. As capable as I know they are."

Sulevia handed the mace to Trout and the sword to Brandy. "I think these should go with you. We've seen what the Lorg Mór can do, We can save many souls here with it. And maybe it will help defend the island, as well."

"Aw crap," Brandy said. "I really don't think I should be trusted with this thing."

"Don't sell yourself short," Trout said, slapping her shoulder. "This is awesome! I've got an enchanted axe and now a magical ancient mace. We'll be unstoppable!"

Brandy simply shook her head.

Fintan clasped Sean's forearm. "This is all happening faster than we expected. Remember what you learned here. And find Breena. And may finding her bring with it truth. And a way forward."

Sulevia clasped Sean's other forearm. "I had hoped to give you more guidance, but I offer you this. Go to Owls Head. The lighthouse. The Keeper will have the information you seek. If things go as I believe they will, remember that the devil makes many promises but keeps few. It may be the littlest people who provide the answer."

A peak of thunder shook the building and Bayard at the front door shouted, "We must go! Now!"

The Grumbles quickly gathered their belongings, bags and backpacks stuffed in haste. When they reached the door, Kelphit was there to hug them each tightly.

"I will remain," the wise man said. "This healer still needs healing. And this island may have a use for me. But watch for me. I think we will see each other again."

Jay appeared at the far end of the clearing waving his arms. An angry rain had begun to fall, and he was quickly soaked through, his dark hair matted to his head.

"Taren will be waiting in town! You need to move!"

The departing Grumbles reluctantly filed out, picking up their pace as the rain lashed into their faces. Each stopped to cast looks back to the friends they were leaving.

When Sean reached Jay, he stopped and took him by the shoulders.

"You don't have to stay here, Jay," he said. "Come with us. You can do anything you want. Together we'd be unstoppable."

"Thanks, Sean," Jay answered. "I appreciate that. Really. And you're right, I could go. I finally feel that I don't *have* to stay here. But I'm choosing to. I owe them that much. And I owe it to myself. I don't have to stay here because I'm afraid. I'll stay because I can make a difference."

"Your call," Sean said. "But thanks for everything. You were the voice I needed. When I needed it. I hope I see you again."

"Well," Jay responded, "I learned just as much from you. Now, go. Do what has to be done."

Sean nodded once. Decisively. And disappeared down the path after his friends and toward the harbor as the wind gathered its strength, and another flash of lightning showed Jay racing back to the village hall, the wind throwing him inside the building where he slammed the door shut behind him.

Taren's boat was much smaller than the *Acheron* that Andy Plummer owned. In fact, Brandy, who knew next to nothing about boats, seemed downright afraid to board.

Taren stood on the deck, by the wheel and called to Brandy, who was hesitating on the dock.

"She's not much to look at," Taren called, raising her voice above the rising wind, "but she's the most reliable boat on Monhegan! If we want to make it, though, we have to go now."

Taren pointed to the sky to the south where a tower of black storm clouds was whipping its way toward them. Deep within the cloudbank flashes of lightning flickered and the distant thunder could be felt through the deck of Taren's boat, *Funny Girl*.

Carolyn appeared, running down the hill toward the dock, followed by the other Wullivers.

"You can't get rid of me that easy!" she shouted, as they jumped nimbly onto the deck of the boat.

"Oh, man," Trout said. "Who was supposed to tell Carolyn to meet us. And the Wullivers?!"

"Cinder made sure she knew," Bayard replied. "I would never have left without them."

"Yeah, you see how easy they got on board?" Trout said, turning back to Brandy.

"Yeah, yeah, made it look real easy," Brandy complained. "But they're frickin' wolf shifters, so it *would be easy for them,* you massive turd."

Sean stood at the rail and held a hand out for Brandy.

"Now or never, Brandy," he shouted. "We won't get another chance!"

"Come on, Bran," Trout added. "Even Dünker managed it. Once you're on board you'll feel a hundred percent better!"

Shaking her head, Brandy took a deep breath, grabbed Sean's hand, and leaped, landing hard on the deck. As soon as her feet touched down, Taren gave a nod to Bert, who threw the last line clear and pushed off.

The enclosed water of the harbor was tossing them about as they made their way toward open water, but nothing could have prepared them for the violence of the sea when they emerged from the protection of Monhegan.

Taren pushed the little boat as hard as she could, calling for everyone to find something to hold on to. The *Funny Girl* was tossed about like a toy in a bathtub. But they had managed to escape before the island fell under the black clouds.

Taren guided them toward New Harbor, but the going was slow, as the waves pounded. Brandy turned a decidedly unhealthy shade of green, and Trout wasn't faring much better. Bert seemed to be an old hand with the boat and scuttled back and forth helping Taren as needed.

Sean seemed completely unfazed, and stood in the stern eyeing the incoming storm as if he could defeat it by sheer will power.

On the opposite end of the boat, Bayard and Cinder stood toward the bow, both looking toward the mainland as it crept slowly, so slowly, closer. The skies in that direction shimmered a pure blue, no sign of the angry storm they were fleeing. For all the world, it seemed the storm was being sent specifically to lay siege to Monhegan.

The waters calmed a bit as they put more distance between themselves and the violence behind them, but it was nothing like the calm-as-glass waters they'd enjoyed on the first trip out.

It was a tense nearly two-hour journey, and when the boat finally docked, Brandy made a beeline for the restrooms dockside, her shade of green somehow even worse than it had been.

"This is her chance," Trout said after Brandy's rapid exit. "She should audition for Elphaba."

"Play nice, Dan," Carolyn said. "Not everyone is made for a rough, open-water dash."

Bert had fallen behind everyone and now picked up his pace, cellphone held to his ear.

"Sad to say, I need to get back to my theatre," he said. "Some questionable storm clouds down that way, too. And Kath tells me there's been a massive arrival of various Fae hoping to escape what's on the way. If you Wullivers are up for it, it sounds like we could use your help getting these poor folks out of harm's way."

Carolyn broke away from the others, and with a quick glance to Finlay, turned back to Bert, nodding.

"It's what we came here to do," she said. "Let's start doing it."

"We're off then!" Bert declared. "I'd stay and help you all out, but it sounds like we all have our work to do. Let's get this over with and raise a glass when it's over. Hope it goes without saying, you run into trouble, we're there."

"Thanks, Bert," Trout replied. "I will take you up on that toast. Good luck with those refugees."

Dünker peered out from behind his usual spot behind Trout's leg.

"Help them," the troll said quietly.

Carolyn crossed to Dünker and knelt next to him.

"We will," she said, placing a hand on his grey and quivering arm. "You landed with the good guys. You look after your people, too, yeah? We all need to work together."

"No worry," he answered. "Will take care of them. Especially Trout. No one hurt them."

"Excellent," Carolyn said, rising to join her family and Bert climbing into his SUV.

"You're headed up the coast," Bert called. "Things get darker and less crowded that way. Be careful. Not that I think you have anything to worry about."

The Grumbles and Bayard, with Dünker still clinging to Trout, waved the others off, and the parking lot felt emptier and quieter after the massive truck pulled out. They breathed in the silence, steeling themselves, each in their own way, for yet another trek into the unknown.

"Well," Sean said, finally, "Owls Head is just over an hour away. It'll be full on night when we get there, so I hope this Keeper is up for an after-hours visit. Don't think we can wait until morning."

"No arguing that," Trout responded. "My question, though, is are we taking the Bronco or the Crosstrek?"

"We could take both," Sean suggested. "In case we need to go different directions, at some point?"

"I think the last thing we will want in the days ahead is to get separated," Bayard replied. "My guess is this will take all of us together to get through."

Brandy shuffled back from the direction of the bathrooms; her shade slightly less chartreuse than when she had left.

"I think Bayard is right," she said, her voice scratchier than normal. "Plus, the Bronco has more space for Cinder. And those seat massagers. And seat heaters. And refrigerated compartment. And—"

"Yeah, yeah, I get it," Sean answered. "You made your point. Bronco it is. I'll let Bert know my car is here."

"Actually," Taren said, arriving from securing her boat, "I could use it. I think I'll need to spend a couple days mainland based on that storm. Okay if I borrow it to get to a friend's house?"

"That's actually great," Sean said. "I'd feel a lot better that way. Take good care of my baby."

He threw the keys to her.

Together, they all turned to look back in the direction of Monhegan. Darkness had swallowed the waters between them and the island. But in the distance, flashes of orange and yellow strobed the night brightly. The storm looked otherworldly and violent. Unlike any they had seen.

As the two vehicles pulled out of the parking lot, everyone's heart was heavy. Fearing for what was happening to their friends ten miles at sea.

Back on Monhegan, the winds raged outside of the community hall. Lightning flashed across the black sky, and the tapestry of stars above was wiped away by the blanket of roiling, bubbling clouds that had so suddenly enveloped the entire island.

Kelphit was standing over a table, his stones scattered across the surface, his face a mask of concentration. He took some powder from the bag on his belt and scattered it over the stones.

"They are away," he said to no one and everyone all at once. "Taren has escaped the storm, and they will make New Harbor. The gale is too massive to turn now. Unfortunately, that means we are about to experience its full effects."

Noodle was furiously humming and drawing in his pad. He had used this to great advantage during the siege of the Fulton Theatre, but here he gained little traction. His voice all but drowned out by the howling wind. Growing frustrated, he slammed his pencil down onto the page and paced away from his chair.

"I'm sorry," Nick called to Noodle. "I don't think I have the strength yet to do what we did in Pennsylvania. I've tried to write about the storm, but nothing is coming. I'm still not right."

Fintan and Sulevia increased their volume and pace and seemed to be finding some success in protecting the building. As they continued, their glow expanded and reached the cottages around the green. Silence fell, and everyone was able to catch a breath.

Noodle saw that McCloud was still cowering in his bed. His mind was clearly still wiped clean. The Timestrider would be of no help. With renewed determination, Noodle returned to his sketch pad and began to angrily draw. He outlined the little healers' village and made it peaceful. Tranquil.

As he did, the shimmering light from the two Tuatha healers snaked across the floor and up the legs of Noodle's chair before sliding onto and *into* the drawing, which then began to glow itself.

"Hey, guys," Noodle called, "I think this may work. Something's happening!"

The drawing brightened and as Nick craned his neck to look out the window, he saw the village shift to reflect what was on the page. Order was being restored, but beyond the light that had descended on the village, the storm still screamed at them and threw itself against the dome.

Jay appeared again at the front door, which easily opened now to his touch.

"Well, we're good," he announced, "but the town is completely exposed. Those nasty water horses are throwing themselves at every boat in the harbor and the waves are reaching up the hill. Pretty sure the Barnacle will go soon. Can't be long before other buildings follow. We have to do something to help them."

Before anyone could answer, a voice crawled into the building. It wasn't loud, but every person present heard it clearly. The voice was refined, smooth. And filled with venom.

"Giving succor to my sworn enemies?" the voice snarled. "You are no longer neutral, and as such will feel my wrath. Your services will not be needed much longer in any event. You have chosen your path. And chosen poorly."

Sulevia and Fintan faltered in their chant, and their light followed suit.

Kelphit rushed to their side.

"Is that...?" he asked.

"Yes," Sulevia answered.

"Balor, King of the Fomorians, is behind this attack," Fintan said. "We *may* be able to protect our place here, for now. But the humans below—we cannot."

"I don't know who this Balor joker is," said Jay, "but we have to do something for them. This isn't their fight."

A great shaking took hold of the building, as if massive hands had begun to shake the entire village. And Nick, still watching out the window, saw exactly that happen, as hands the size of his bed pounded the ball of light around the buildings.

"Hey, I've dealt with this guy before," he shouted. "We're in big, big trouble."

The Bronco pulled out of the parking lot in New Harbor and turned left toward the highway, waving goodbye to Taren as she turned right in the Crosstrek to head to her friend's house.

"Okay," Trout said. "according to the GPS, it's just over an hour to Owls Head. Anyone have any idea what to expect up that way? We're headed further north than I've been."

"Technically, it's all part of Down East," Brandy said. "I've never really understood it, but I've been corrected so many times, it's stuck in my head."

"But we're headed north," Trout persisted.

"Yeah, it has something to do with sailor lingo," Brandy explained. "Anything on the coast is Down East. North is inland. It's a Maine thing. Don't blame me."

"Whatever," Trout answered. "Wherever we're going, I've never been."

The Bronco rumbled up Waldoboro Road, eventually turning onto Route 1. It wasn't even nine o'clock, but it felt like midnight as they cruised along in the pitch dark of the Maine countryside. Eventually, Brandy dozed off with her face pressed to the cool window to her right. Bayard turned his eyes to the sky and watched as the countless stars of a Maine night sky stared silently down at them. Cinder, too, had fallen asleep in the rear compartment. Her nose quivered, chasing dream smells.

"Sulevia said something cryptic to me as we were leaving, Sean said, his face glowing from the dashboard instruments. "Everything happened so fast, I didn't really think about it. She said the devil breaks his promises. And then something about Little People? Any clue what she means?"

"Well, I'm the one driving," Trout replied, "so, a little busy here. If only you had a device that could connect you with every bit of information that ever existed."

He nodded to the cellphone in Sean's hand.

"Smartass," Sean said. "I don't even know what to search for."

"Start with the devil in Maine and go from there," Trout

answered. "You have...forty-seven minutes to knock yourself out. Then we get to Owls Head."

Sean's face now glowed from the dashboard and his phone screen. He muttered a few "hmms" and "huhs," until Trout finally interrupted him.

"Mind sharing?" he said. "You're driving me crazy."

"And you're driving me to Owls Head," Sean quipped.

"Ha, ha," Trout deadpanned.

"Right, sorry," Sean said, lifting his head from the screen. "There's a kind of scary amount of material on the devil and Maine. Starting with the Puritans, who thought this was devil's country. Probably just because there weren't many folks up here then."

"Well, many of *their* folks," Trout pointed out.

"Good point," Sean agreed. "They just labeled it that because of their ignorance. Apparently, all of Down East was called that. So maybe that's what Sulevia meant?"

"Seems pretty flimsy to me," Trout said. "But who knows? There was a lot going on. My guess is we'll find out as things unfold."

"Probably," Sean said. "I mean there's a Devil's Back, Devil's Bog, Devil's Elbow...the list is pretty long."

"What about Little People?" Trout asked.

"No clue," Sean replied. "I thought of the Little People we saw briefly in Montauk. Maybe something with the indigenous folks up this way?"

"That's better than I would have done," Trout admitted. "All I know is we need to get to this lighthouse."

"You're right," Sean said. "One step at a time. Music?"

"Absolutely," Trout answered.

Sean turned on the stereo and scrolled through the stations on Trout's satellite radio service, He finally settled on a station of Emmet Swimming music, shooting a questioning glance toward Trout.

"Ah, man," Trout said, grinning and shaking his head. "Blast from the past. Nice."

Sean leaned back in the very comfortable lumbar-supporting upgraded seat and let his phone screen go dark, as Emmet Swimming sang about a broken oar, which seemed appropriate as they traveled toward the unknown. The next song came on. It was called "South Bristol, Maine" and the two friends shared a surprised look.

"I had no idea. Really," said Sean.

"There are no coincidences," Trout answered. "Not anymore."

Finally, they turned off Route 1 and onto the charmingly named Buttermilk Lane. They cruised onto North Shore Drive and then turned left at Main Street and arrived in the town of Owls Head itself.

"Almost there," Trout announced.

Brandy stirred in the back seat and Bayard pulled his focus back into the truck.

A left on Lighthouse Road took them past a small park on the right, nestled along the waterfront. A moment later, they passed the entrance to the Owls Head Lobster Company, the sign done up under a pile of colorfully painted lobster trap buoys.

"This place looks pretty nice," Brandy said, her forehead still pressed against the window. "And that reminds me. I'm starved."

"Same!" Bayard called from the opposite side.

Even Cinder added a wistful whine from the very back. Dünker remained silent, as he had been for the entire drive.

"Yeah, we'll stop for something after we get to the lighthouse," Trout said. "Definitely should have done that before now."

"Mid-week in January in the booming metropolis of Owls Head, Maine?" Sean chimed in. "Maybe this lighthouse keeper has something we can buy."

Silence settled into the Bronco as Trout turned into the gravel parking lot that signaled the lighthouse ahead. If the drive up had seemed dark, the lot was as if someone had poured the blackest ink across the scene. Thick trees reached over the area, and it took a moment for Trout to spot a sign at the edge of his vision.

"Looks like we hoof it from here," he said, pointing. "Shall we?"

They climbed out of the truck, the three Grumbles' creaky knees sounding like popcorn as they stood. The boat journey and then the Bronco had taken a toll. Bayard, though, brimmed with energy and helped Cinder clamber over the back seat and out into the night. She immediately threw her nose in the air and cast her senses out into the forest. She huffed quietly and cocked her head slightly, glancing up at Bayard.

Dünker stayed where he was in the back compartment and shook his head. Even when Trout extended a hand to help him down, the little troll refused.

"No go out there," he said. "Strange smells. Not safe. Trout should stay here with me."

"No can do, bud," Trout answered. "But you stay. You'll be safe here. We'll be back in just a little bit. Promise."

"Should listen to Dünker," the troll murmured.

But they didn't. Together, the five started toward the path that led into the woods and to the lighthouse. The only sound was the crunching of the Grumbles' feet on the ground. As always, Bayard and Cinder were completely silent. Within a moment, the dense trees swallowed them, and three cellphone flashlights lit up to send their feeble beams onto the trail in front of them. Like a shot, Cinder padded off into the trees. Bayard shot her a glance, shrugged, and continued after the others.

A breeze off the unseen water to their right set the branches over their heads into a whispering chatter. It was impossible for them not to feel as if they were being watched. Even Bayard had the sense of... something watching from behind the trees. Shadows lengthened and danced around them. More than once, Trout spun quickly around to try to catch whatever or whoever was stalking them. Brandy shouted when she thought she felt something brush her shoulder.

Sean was reminded of the earliest of his encounters with the Peripherals, when he felt as if every move he made was observed by... someone. Suddenly, he had the feeling that there was something in the limbs above them, but when he turned his eyes upward all he could make out was a suddenly bright moon breaking through the clouds. Peeking through a gap in the boughs overhead.

As suddenly as it had embraced them, the forest disappeared, and they found themselves in the open. Up an incline, they saw a warm orange glow spilling from the window of a squat building just off the path. Other than that light, there was no sign of anyone nearby. No smoke rose from the chimney of the building. All was completely silent.

Beyond the building, the faintest shadow rose into the air. The Owls Head Light.

"Must be the Keeper's house," Trout said, lowering his voice to match the noiseless night around them.

"It's the logical place to start, anyway," Sean agreed.

Brandy had turned to stare into the darkness in the woods behind them. Bayard followed her gaze but said nothing. He gently took her shoulder and pointed her forward.

Sean walked quickly toward the door of the house and saw that it was also marked as the information center and gift shop. The Keeper must live toward the back, which made the lone light in front more logical.

Sean knocked on the door. Quietly, at first. Then louder when there was no response. He checked his watch. It wasn't even half past nine. Even in rural Maine, surely there must be someone awake. He stepped back to look at the other windows, but all remained black.

"Sean," Trout said. "Uh. Look."

Turning back to the one lit window to the right of the door, he nearly leaped backward when he saw it now occupied by a small girl. She sat and stared at the group. Her eyes were keen, but cold. Unreadable.

"Hi, there," Sean said. "Are your parents home?"

She stayed where she was. No sign at all that she had heard him.

"We're trying to find the Keeper," Trout said. "The healers on Monhegan sent us."

"It's a bit of an emergency," Brandy said, stepping up next to them.

Still nothing from the girl.

Bayard now stepped next to the others.

Now the girl turned her head ever so slightly to look directly at the Peripheral. The faintest hint of a smile found its way onto her face.

"Can you tell us where the Keeper can be found?" Bayard asked.

Slowly, the girl raised her hand and pointed toward the lighthouse up the hill to their right.

"Thank you," Bayard said.

"To the lighthouse we go, then," Sean said, starting up the hill.

A dog began to bark in the distance, and they all stopped where they were, mindful that Cinder had been gone for some time. A scrabbling sound erupted from the trees to their left, and a flash of auburn streaked into the open. It was Cinder, running full speed until she skidded to a stop by Bayard. The hair along her back stood straight up and her brilliant amber eyes flicked between her people and the trees.

"Great," Trout said. "Something's out there that spooked Cinder. I didn't think that was possible."

"I'm not sure that she's spooked, as you call it," Bayard said, rubbing the wolf's ears. "I think she came back to warn us."

"That doesn't make me feel better," Brandy said.

"Doesn't matter," Sean said, continuing up the incline. "We still need to get to the lighthouse."

The others followed, but Trout and Brandy were focused behind them, while Bayard gave his attention to Cinder.

When Sean reached the stairs that led up to the light, he stopped suddenly, causing the others to come to an abrupt halt.

"Come on, Ginge," Brandy muttered. "We're spooked enough without you pulling stunts like that."

Sean shook his head and held his finger to his lips, telling them to be quiet. He lifted his hand and pointed to the steps. As they all watched, a set of damp footprints proceeded to climb toward the lighthouse. Footsteps. But no feet. Just phantom prints ploddingly making their way up.

"I believe the Keeper knows we're here," Bayard said, taking the lead and following the footprints toward the tower.

"You have got to be kidding," Trout replied. "Why can't anything just be normal?"

Reluctantly, the others followed Bayard up. Cinder loped behind them, keeping an eye on the trail beyond the information center. From the shelter of the trees, a low growling could be heard.

"No one said it would be easy," Sean said, as he followed close behind Bayard.

CHAPTER 13

Nick still sat in his bed, watching helplessly as the giant hands of Balor continued to pummel the protective light around the village. They seemed to swell and grow as the minutes passed. Eventually, Balor pressed his enormous face to the dome, an eye the size of a Volkswagen blinking slowly as a deep and threatening laugh echoed throughout the healers' village.

Unlike when Nick had seen him in Lancaster, Balor now was monstrous. No pretense of nobility surrounded him. No airs of civility. No manicured appearance for anyone watching. Instead, he was enormous, standing over thirty feet in height. He shimmered with an orange flame, flickering up and down his body. Gone was the crown with one baleful eye set in it. He had one lone eye now, crimson fading to a dead, lifeless black at the center. He was here not to parlay, but to destroy, and he cared not one bit if those on the island saw his true self. He expected none of them to live to see the morning.

Noodle was furiously drawing on his pad, which still glowed with the healers' chanting, but a great rending sound thundered through the village. One of the windows blew out, and with it the winds, finally finding their way through weaknesses in the protective light, came whistling into the hall. They ripped the pad from Noodle's hands, and as his pages flew around the room and out the window, all of his work began to fade.

Noodle dashed to McCloud's bedside and shook his shoulders. Sandy, who had been trying to sing with Nick unsuccessfully, followed him.

"You have to help us!" Noodle screamed into the Scotsman's face. "You're the only one who can!"

But the Timestrider stared back at him with wide, panicked eyes and seemed unable to find his voice, let alone to find a way to unlock his powers.

Jay stood in the center of the room watching all of this unfold. The wind buffeted him, threatening to lift him off the floor, but he braced himself. For a moment, he stopped seeing the room around him and retreated into himself.

When he snapped back to himself, he nodded once, decisively, and crossed to Fintan and Sulevia.

Jay looked them squarely in the eyes. The healers responded instantly, shaking their heads and grabbing his arms. But Jay was not moved and nodded again.

"This is it," he said to them. "This is why I stayed. I was never like Sean. I was always me. Jay. And I'm the one who can do this. The only one."

Sulevia began to object, but Jay drew her in close, silencing her.

"You know it's the only way," Jay continued. "I *want* to do this. For you. For all you've done for me. For all the good you have yet to do. For the poor people in town, who think this is nothing more than a bad storm. I want to serve. It's what I've always wanted. But now, I know how."

Fintan grimly shook Jay's hand.

"I would stop you if I could," he said. "I would stop you if I had any other answer."

"I know you would," Jay said, returning the clasp. "It seems like such a small thing to say, but...thank you."

"It's not small," Fintan replied. "And I will answer you with the only words that I know to be larger: You are loved. We love you. I love you."

Sulevia withdrew from Jay's embrace and held his face in her hands.

"Return to us, if you can," she said, her eyes full.

"You know it, Suly," he answered, a lopsided grin creeping onto his face. "Catch you later. I've got a king's butt to kick."

Kelphit watched soberly, while the others heard what was happening but didn't fully understand.

"Hey gang," Jay called, as he reached the front door. "Take care of each other, yeah? Hopefully, this won't take too long."

He opened the door, and the wind immediately ripped it from his hands. He turned one last time and shrugged to all the others, before turning and walking into the maelstrom, his hands raised to protect his face.

He reached the trail to take him into the woods and toward the town below. As he approached the spot where the protective dome ended and the storm thrashed unfettered, he stopped. He turned back to the village. The place that had taken him in and restored him to himself. Given him the family he had never really known. He closed his eyes briefly, turned, and pushed his way out into the violence.

He turned his head toward where he had seen the form of Balor battering the healers.

"Yo! You two-bit cyclops!" he shouted skyward. "Stop picking on sick people and doctors. Come get a real Chicago ass-whipping!"

He turned and continued along the path, starting to sing as he did. With each step his voice rose in volume, and as it did, his own golden glow enveloped him, seeping into him. By the time he emerged from the forest he looked like a golden statue, shining, impervious, timeless. He paused by the lighthouse and looked down the hillside to the harbor below. The kelpies had intensified their attack and many of the boats, those that hadn't foundered, were listing and slipping under the waves.

Amongst the kelpies, Jay now saw the figures of women gliding through the tumultuous waters, wreaking havoc. They grabbed loose pieces of boats, haunting the edges of the harbor looking for humans to drag away. Luckily, the storm was so violent that the townspeople were all sheltering inside, but not for much longer as their livelihoods and investments were reduced to scrap.

Jay, continued to sing and, as he did, he began to weave balletic movements with his arms, and his golden skin grew harder, brighter. This was something that Sean had never been able to do. His gifts not lying in the world of terpsichore. As Jay did this, he lifted off the ground and guided himself through the shrieking winds, down the incline and to the edge of the harbor.

By now, the kelpies and their female accomplices had taken note. Many shrank from his brilliance as he approached, but a brave—or foolish—few turned to this new threat and threw themselves at him. His feet never touched the ground, and he never slowed. He carved through any who approached him, reducing them instantly to nothing, banishing them to whatever realm had spawned them.

He felt the power now, coursing through him. He laughed, and there was a touch of madness to it, had any been there to hear. He sent himself high into the air with a leap, soaring, reveling in the freedom. And he knew—without the slightest ego or doubt—that he was invincible. That none could withstand him. The only thing able to bring him down would be his own choice. His own decisions.

His feet touched the waters of the harbor only long enough to send him careening toward the small island of Manana on the opposite side of the harbor. He knew it to be uninhabited now and thought briefly of the famous hermit who had once lived there. The idle thought was a flicker and then gone.

He found the old Coast Guard fog station atop a hill, and placed his hands on the foghorn, sending its mournful call over both islands, a booming war cry that echoed and drowned out even the gale winds, driven by his golden power.

"Balor!" Jay cried, standing on the summit of Manana Island. "Your turn! I already finished off your foot soldiers. All up to you now, big boy!"

Balor, still slamming himself into the weakening globe of light over the healers' village, turned at last to Jay, defiant across the harbor. And he saw his followers scattered and fleeing. Already the harbor was settling down under the golden glow Jay had spread as he'd passed.

With a growl and a final slap at the healers, Balor, King of the Fomorians, turned and took the bait. With less than a dozen steps, he had crossed to Jay and, raising both fists high in the air, brought them down where the seemingly small figure stood waiting.

Jay smiled. His motions became more focused. His voice louder. Higher. Beautiful. And terrible. As he rose once more off the ground, he turned to face the giant and raced through the air directly at him. And into him.

The air above Manana Island exploded in light and fury and wind. And the rage continued for some time, while the villagers quaked in their homes and the kelpies, the few still alive, fled to the depths of the ocean.

Back in the healers' village, everyone but McCloud had gathered at the front door as soon as the hammering of Balor's fists stopped. Above the trees, they watched as the golden light of Jay grew, and pulsed, and grew more. The angry calls of Balor echoed over and through the trees. First filled with madness, then anger, and finally the unmistakable pitch of fear.

The golden light flared. The entire world seemed to explode, and the watchers could see nothing but the blinding lights for long minutes.

Finally, the world returned to itself. The winds calmed. In the harbor, the waves disappeared. The air cleared and the bluest winter sky appeared.

As their eyes were restored, Sulevia clasped Fintan's hand. And Fintan grasped Kelphit's. Nick, Noodle, and Sandy held each other.

"And so goes a good man who found his purpose in the end," Sulevia whispered.

"What about Balor?" asked Nick.

"Not dead," Kelphit answered. "But beaten. And sure to never darken this island again."

"Jay?" asked Noodle.

"Somewhere else now," Fintan said. "A place of his own choosing. But always a part of us. And Monhegan."

They turned back to the hall and began the task of restoring it to order. Hearts heavy. And full.

A few days later a third puffin appeared in the cliffs of Monhegan. And the healers found themselves often wandering the paths on the edge of the island, watching for the newcomer. Filled with tears. And joy. And hope.

———

Bayard stood by the door to the small lighthouse. It was closed tight, but a light shone inside the tower.

The tower was small by lighthouse standards, standing only thirty feet tall. However, it was situated on an eighty-foot cliff, setting it over one hundred feet above sea level. The tower was simple. A white brick cylinder with a black cupola on top, a small walkway ringing it. Its white light flashed out into Rockland Harbor and Penobscot Bay, and this night the foghorn sounded every twenty seconds.

As the group crowded into the entrance, Sean was surprised to see a ladder with seven open rungs leading up to the light room. The sound of busy hands filtered down to them. The Keeper was clearly at work above them.

Bayard apologized to Cinder, explaining that she would have to wait below as he grabbed the ladder and hoisted himself up. Trout took pity on the wolf and made sure the door was left open enough for her to come and go as she pleased, but she showed no inclination to distance herself from Bayard.

Sean followed up the ladder and Brandy and Trout reluctantly followed suit.

"I bet this place is beautiful in the daytime," Brandy said, looking down at Trout. "Whaddaya say we come back to Maine when the world gets back to normal?"

"Don't you mean 'if' it gets back to normal?" Trout answered. "And, yeah, that would be great, but I'm headed to the Outer Banks when this is done. I've already been away from Eleanor for longer than I wanted."

"Well, I'll send you a postcard," Brandy said, emerging into the upper light room.

Bayard and Sean were standing behind an older gentleman. He was working hard at polishing the plentiful brass fixtures. He was dressed as an old-time sea captain. A dark blue suit with gleaming brass buttons and spit-shined black work shoes. His thick white hair was swept back over his weathered face, all lines and crags that told of a life spent in harsh conditions. A thick beard, impeccably trimmed, fringed his face. His deep-set eyes flashed green when he eventually put down the rag he was using and turned slowly to them. Sean's breath caught when he realized the one most remarkable feature of the man: as the light turned ceaselessly, it shone through him with each pass, and Sean looked twice to confirm that he was, indeed, seeing through the man and out into the night beyond the 360-degree windows that ringed the tower.

"I believe you are the Keeper?" Bayard said. "We were told we could find you here."

"Told?" the man replied. "I find that hard to believe. Isabelle has not spoken to a soul in many, many years. But she did let me know to expect you."

His voice was deep, rich, and rolling like the waves that could be heard crashing on the bluffs just beyond them. But it was a kind voice, with a barely contained mirth that seemed eager to burst forth like the laughter of the gulls who wheeled on the unseen breezes over the trees.

"That's true," Sean admitted. "But she did point us in your direction. And maybe more to the point, Sulevia and Fintan sent us here from Monhegan. We need your help."

The Keeper's eyes widened briefly, and he turned back to the large Fresnel light, lifting his cloth and resuming his work.

"Did they now?" he replied. "I don't believe they've ever done that before. I'm not sure if that speaks more to their faith in you or the seriousness of your situation."

"Maybe both," Trout said, moving forward and examining the light, touching the glass around the lamp.

The Keeper rewarded him with a swat from his cleaning cloth.

"I'm beginning to doubt that," the Keeper replied, but there was laughter below his words. "Tell me. If I can help, I will. But I must warn you, I have been closed in this tower for a very long time. Why don't we step out onto the walkway. The night is clearing, and I think you will be more comfortable."

They shuffled outside, single file through the doorway. Somehow the Keeper was just...there.

"Thanks," Trout said, the last to arrive. "Was feeling a little cramped in there."

"I saw," the Keeper replied. He turned to Bayard. "You I know. Not personally, but I know you are Fae. My apologies to your wolf. I can do many things, but I cannot give her thumbs to climb a ladder."

Bayard dipped his head in acknowledgement, considering the old man anew.

"You three," the Keeper continued, turning to the Grumbles, "are less clear to me. There is strength in all of you. But you, carry a heavier weight, young man. And show the signs of a strength I have never seen." He took Sean by the arm and led him to the rail, facing out over the waters below.

And Sean told him. Everything. From the chase along Long

Island, to the chaotic fighting in the Outer Banks, to the siege in Lancaster. He told of the appearance of Balor. The Dullahan. The countless minions they had at their call. He told of the uncertainty surrounding Breena and Kallan. Their fates at the mercy of their captors. He told of Monhegan, and the storm that had forced them to flee back to the mainland with the advice of the healers in their ears.

When he finally finished, the Keeper said nothing, but turned his eyes to the glimmering night above them. He stood frozen so long that Brandy elbowed Trout, worried that he had fallen asleep. Or forgotten that they were there. But before Trout could react, the Keeper's eyes focused again on the tower and the group assembled around him.

"I believe you," he said quietly. "More's the pity for all of us. Not much happens along this coast that I don't know, but I have been too removed lately. That will change. But I do have some harsh truths for you."

"Truth I can handle, not so sure about the harsh part," Trout muttered.

Bayard silenced him with a glance and motioned again for the Keeper to continue.

"To begin," he said, "the storm on Monhegan has run its course. The healers and your friends are safe. All but one. But that is a story for another to tell you. Balor was the guiding force, and he has been sent on his way."

"Wait," Sean said, holding his hands up. "What do you mean 'all but one'? Someone didn't survive? Who?"

Brandy moved off to the side, pulling her cellphone from her pocket and quickly tapping at her screen.

"Nick was pretty weak," Trout said, concerned. "And McCloud was even worse off. Probably one of them. Can't imagine any of the healers getting hurt. But there will be holy hell to pay if it was Sandy. Or Noodle! No, not Noodle! He doesn't deserve anything like that—"

Bayard again held out his hand to stop the Montanan, as Brandy returned.

"I've got service," she said, "but the island—I can't reach anyone. You remember how bad it is there. And if they just had a storm?"

Sean kept his eyes fixed on the Keeper, and in a moment of clarity, he understood what had happened. And why. He closed his eyes. There would be time for reflection and grief. But that time wasn't now. He wanted the others focused. And he needed to come to terms with it himself, and so he stayed silent. But the Keeper had seen his realization and nodded in return.

"I also know of your encounter with Gluskabe," the Keeper said, turning to Brandy. "And I know what he gifted you. He hasn't involved himself in the ways of men for as long as I can remember. I will not interfere with the doings of him. But I will say this: that blade holds more power than anything I've ever seen. The hands of a Bard, and yes, I will call you that, should hold it only under the greatest duress. And even then, you"—he turned to Sean—"should avoid it at all costs."

Sean nodded and stepped to the rail, gripping it and feeling the cold unmoving iron helped to ground him and he closed his eyes tightly, trying to think only of what lay ahead. Of what must be done.

"Sulevia mentioned the devil and Little People," Sean said. "Can you help us understand what she meant? I need to find a path to the Otherworld. To Breena. And Kallan. We need to know the truth in order to move ahead."

"I can't see the future," the Keeper answered. "But I do know this coast. And I understand the lesser pathways you seek. I find it interesting that you say *you* need to find the path. *You.* Who stand here surrounded by friends who have given much to stay by your side. Beware the urge to do this thing alone. No good will come of it."

Sean continued to hold the rail. His eyes fixed somewhere in the dark night ahead and showed no sign he had heard.

"Better listen to him, Ginge," Brandy said. "Don't be a jerk. Again."

"We've come this far," Trout agreed, also stepping to the rail by Sean. "We're in it to the end."

"The end," the Keeper replied. "Hm. At any rate, I can help to guide you, using Sulevia's words, but I can only offer my opinion. You will face many decisions once you leave here."

"Of course," Sean said, finally stirring. "We just need to be pointed in the right direction."

Bayard approached the rail. "Tell us of the devil," he said simply.

"Ah," the Keeper answered, turning to the Peripheral. "The devil has many names and many forms. But I will tell you this, and I believe it was what Sulevia meant: The Devil's Oven is a cave. On Mount Desert Island. It is a treacherous place. At the whim of the tides. It has long been a dangerous, and therefore unused, entry to the other world. There are many places that have adopted the name of the devil—caves, trails, glades. But this cave is what you seek. What Sulevia cannot know, especially given recent events on Monhegan, is that the Devil's Oven has recently attracted the attention of a Wendigo. A Skinwalker. And rumor is that it is not alone."

"We are way too acquainted with Wendigos," Brandy interrupted.

"Aw, man alive," Trout chimed in, "last thing I want is to tangle with one of those things again. Especially now that we're down Nick and Stewart."

"Great," Sean said. "If this Devil's Oven is guarded, what do we do?"

"And this is where Sulevia's wisdom provides for you," the Keeper answered. "While there are many beings who could be called 'Little People,' I believe she was providing you with an even lesser-known pathway to the Fae realm. In Way Downeast, where the sun first meets the land each morning, there is another cave. It is called Gulliver's Hole. But this cave comes with another set of...complications. There are Others who have made that area their home. They live in secret. And they are vulnerable. And protected."

"Protected?" Sean asked. "Protected from what? And by what?"

"Protected from harm. By anyone. And anything. All of us. By the Watchers," the Keeper replied.

"Well, if it's not a Wendigo, I vote for the Gulliver place," Brandy said.

Trout hung his head and let out a chuckle. "Little People. Gulliver's Hole. Sulevia gave us everything we needed. It was right there."

"Let's hope no Lilliputians tie us down," Sean said. "Although, that would at least be something new."

"Keeper?" Bayard asked. "Do you think this is our best path?"

"I do," he replied. "But remember, I cannot see what is to come. My physical life ended long ago, but my work is never done."

"Yeah, what's up with that?" Brandy broke in. "What's *your* story? How did you end up here?"

"I'm the Keeper," he answered. "That's all you need know. Be careful. Be wise. Be kind. Listen to the water. And now—I'm very tired."

As they watched, he slowly slipped away, rippling and fading until where he stood was empty. The light of the tower continued to spin, illuminating them all at intervals, but the quiet that fell was complete. The waves a hundred feet below fell silent.

They all looked around at each other. With a shrug, Trout started for the doorway.

"Man, life is so freakin' weird, right now," he said, entering the tower and heading for the ladder down. "That almost felt normal to me!"

"I'd really like to know his story," Brandy added, following. "Don't know about you guys, but I liked him. We've met some pretty cool dead people lately."

"And more than a few I'd rather not run into again," said Bayard.

Sean stood at the rail for a moment as the others exited. He looked down at the rocks below and exhaled as the sound of the waves returned. The stars above glimmered along the waters of Penobscot Bay below, glittering and shimmering. He felt the unmistakable urge to lean out, over, to fall, fall. To let the water claim him.

To disappear. Like leaning against the window in a tall building and feeling the pull of the earth below. But the feeling passed, and he shook his head.

"I'm coming, Breena," he whispered. "I hope I'm right. About you. About everything. But either way I'm coming."

As he turned and followed the others, he could swear he heard the faintest trace of her voice reaching him and saying, "I know."

When he caught up with the others, they had reached the top of the stairs outside the lighthouse and paused to wait for him. Cinder had rejoined them and stayed close to Bayard. He joined them and made sure to close the door firmly behind him.

"Thanks, Mr. Keeper!" Trout called to the light thirty feet above. "Appreciate you!"

The others sent silent thanks as they turned to the path back toward the information building and the path beyond it to the parking lot.

As the neared the building, they all noted that it was cloaked in darkness. No light in the windows. No little girl appeared to bid them farewell.

An eruption of barking rose from the forest in front of them. Exactly where they had to walk.

"Who says rabid dog and who says wolf?" Brandy asked.

"Could be Cujo," Trout said. "Stephen King is from Maine."

"Not helping," Sean said, punching Trout's shoulder.

At just that moment, the barking turned to a strangled yelp and cut off suddenly.

"See?" Trout said, heading down the path. "Everything's weird."

They hurried down the path to the parking lot. The tension in the air had fled, like air being let out of a balloon. They walked easier, their arms swinging jauntily. Within five minutes, they were back at the Bronco where they agreed to find a place for the night and to make plans to head to Gulliver's Hole. As they opened the doors, a wide-eyed Dünker popped his head over the back seat.

"Happy!" he cried. "Happy. Safe. We go."

And they did.

Bert and the Wullivers pulled into Brunswick later than they'd planned. A stop in Bath to pick up something to eat had revealed just how tired they were, and they allowed themselves the indulgence of lingering over a meal at The Cabin, a log-cabin-themed Italian pizza spot. A couple of glasses of wine for the Wullivers went down easy, and the short drive back to Brunswick featured some very relaxed wolf-shifters.

Pulling onto Maine Street from the interstate, it was just after nine o'clock and the town was nearly entirely empty. Thursdays in January mostly were. But everyone in the big SUV sat up straight as they grew closer to the Maine State Music Theatre at the far end of downtown.

Something was off. There was ordinary quiet, and there was the quiet that came with tension. The feeling that the atmosphere was stretched too tight. Ready to snap. Or burst.

The Wullivers rolled down the windows and scented the night air. Bert touched the large screen on his dash, checking to see if he had any messages from Kath or Mal that he'd missed while relaxing. He did.

It was short on detail but long on misgiving.

Come quick. Newcomers. Trouble. No time.

Bert increased his speed and turned hastily toward the offices. The building was lit up like a candle. That was a sure sign that something was off. Bert pulled into the small lot by the loading dock and jumped from the truck, rushing through the nearest door. He jogged through the scene shop, into the hallway that led to offices, but skidded to a halt immediately.

He knew this building. Every creak, breeze, and echo were seared into him over long years of work, and sweat, and devotion. He knew instantly that the building was empty. Slowly, he moved cautiously to his office door. It was open, but as he expected, it was silent.

He heard a tap coming from the window at the main entrance and poked his head out of the door to glance up front. Carolyn was there, her nails clacking on the picture window, and as he neared, she jerked her head away from the building. Behind her, he saw her family, and all had shifted into their wolf shapes. She did the same as he approached.

He let himself out, back onto the familiar sidewalk in front.

"This way," she said, and without waiting for a response turned on her heels and began a loping pace down Maine Street again and the Bowdoin campus where the theatre stood.

"Should I get the truck?" Bert called in a stage whisper.

"This is quicker," Carolyn said, increasing her speed.

"And there's no parking up there," Finlay added. "That huge white truck of yours isn't exactly unobtrusive."

"Lots of scents flying around," Donal said, falling into line with the others. "Probably smart to keep a low profile until we know what's cookin'."

Within five minutes, they were standing on the swath of green grass outside the theatre itself. The glass tower that housed the stage door was cloaked in dark masking, a recent addition that added privacy for actors and technicians as they arrived at work, but on this night prevented them from seeing if any lights were on inside.

The campus around them was quiet. Most students were still away for the winter break. The academic buildings all locked up tight. Beautiful in the orange glow of the streetlights, red bricks and archways almost gave the sense of stepping back in time. Almost.

"I don't hear a thing," Bert said. "And I sure as hell don't smell anything. I'm texting Kath."

Finlay grabbed his hand to stop him. Bert, not used to being challenged, bristled for a moment until he saw all of the Wullivers focused on the stage door.

"Inside," Carolyn said. "We go first."

The wolf Wullivers crept silently toward the building. As they drew near the door, Donal slipped silently to the left and around the building toward the campus lawns. Craig, with barely a nod to the others, did the same on the right.

Carolyn tried the door and slowly opened it. Cautiously. Finlay, his hand raised again to stop Bert, entered the building and paused. Bert followed him in, and Carolyn entered last.

As the door closed behind her, darkness blanketed them and the stairwell in which they found themselves. The stairs down led to the basement where the technical offices and shops lay. The stairs down were a gaping maw of blackness. No sound rose. No light escaped.

The stairs leading up reached the stage level at the first platform. The faintest glow seemed to reach Bert's eyes, and he thought he could hear a hushed murmur coming from that direction.

Carolyn and Finlay, though, showed no hesitation, and began to pad up the stairs toward stage left and the stage proper beyond. Trusting their senses more than his own, Bert followed.

As they entered the stage, any doubt Bert had was gone. The ghostlight—a simple bare bulb placed atop a pole that lit the stage at night when it was otherwise empty—was sending its gentle glow to the corners of the space. That was perfectly normal. Ghostlights were an old and revered custom in the theatre. But its light was dancing and flitting with shadows, as if an ensemble of dancers was performing choreography in a macabre and startling rehearsal.

A moment later, Bert heard quiet voices. Hushed but intense, they sounded urgent. And afraid.

Bert tried to push his way forward to the stage, and for the third time, Finlay held him back. Finally, Bert's temper got the better of him and he turned angrily to the shifter. Carolyn inserted herself between the two.

"We should go first," she whispered. "Safer. Stay close."

Taking a ragged breath, Bert nodded and threw an apologetic look to Finlay, who grinned and shook it off.

The two shifters moved ahead, and after a few more short steps, the trio emerged into the stage left area and stopped in their tracks. Even the Wullivers were taken aback by what they saw.

Kath stood within the glimmer of the light center stage. She was deep in discussion with—Bert wasn't sure what his eyes were showing him. Beside Kath stood a small figure. Less than three feet in height. It was covered in spiky, thick hair. Had exaggerated features. Ears and a nose too big for the rest of its face. It was wearing simple, rustic, leather boots and a tunic of the same.

Kath's hands were raised in a soothing gesture while the small creature seemed agitated and gestured behind it.

As his eyes adjusted to the dim light, Bert caught sight of Mal, sitting cross-legged at the farthest reach of the pool of light. In her lap was another, though vastly different, diminutive figure. This one was clearly female, wearing a deep orange dress, with intricate bead-work cinching it tight at the waist. She had elaborately plaited hair, swept back and falling down her back. Her ears were long, ending in points, and her face shone with kindness and intelligence. And fear.

But it took a moment for Bert to make sense of the most striking aspect. On her back were a large set of wings. In shape, they resembled those of a butterfly. Grand yet fragile. Their pattern, though, was entirely unique. Orange, mirroring the dress she wore, they seemed to shift and shudder. Bert felt dizzy as he watched it, as if he were staring into the depths of a flame. Orange giving way to ochre, to copper, to gold, and back again.

Bert was forced to shake his head to break from the beauty of those wings, and as he raised his eyes, he realized that the entire theatre was abuzz with voices. There were a few dozen small beings scattered across the stage of varying sizes and appearances. But it was when his eyes found the seats in the audience that the situation became clear. Many seats held figures. They leaned close to each other and murmured. Many gestured to the stage, where Kath and Mal were clearly trying to calm the crowd.

A line of creatures waited at the stairs that led from the auditorium onto the stage, hoping for a turn with one of the two women.

Finlay and Carolyn looked first to each other and then to Bert, surprise written clearly on their faces. Bert returned their surprise before taking a step onto the stage. Into the ghostly luminescence. Dozens, possibly hundreds, of faces turned to him. Mal surged to her feet, taking care to cradle the woman on her lap in her arms.

Kath, though, was the first to speak. "Hey, Boss," she said. "Glad you got the message. So—uh—I think it's safe to say things have taken a turn. They're telling us this is just the first wave. Looks like that mass exodus is happening."

And at that, the voices of the hundreds of creatures rose filling the theatre with the sound of a rushing brook. With the sound of breezes in the forest trees. In languages not familiar.

But when Carolyn and Finlay, the two shifters, stepped into the light, the chorus became agitated, and fear swept the crowd. They were different. Yet somehow Fae. The assembled group sensed the shifters were dangerous. Bert raised his hands to settle the moment, and nervous mutters replaced the noise.

All eyes turned to him. But he had no idea what he should say.

CHAPTER 14

As Trout steered the Bronco out of the Owls Head Lighthouse parking lot, the gravel clacked under the tires. There were no more sounds from the forest behind them, and Sean kept glancing into the back hatch area where Dünker had quieted and curled up next to Cinder. The two were forming an unexpected friendship. Something about the set of Dünker's face as he rested caught Sean's attention. He looked...different somehow.

The events of the last hour quickly eclipsed whatever thought about the troll he'd been gnawing, and he pulled out his phone. The Keeper had said something about a place where the sun first hit the land. His fingers flew across the screen, chasing down a bit of information. As he was doing this, he felt a pang at the absence of Nick. Normally, they would have let Nick search like this. But Nick lay in a bed, far out to sea and hopefully well.

The Keeper hadn't told them explicitly, but Sean knew who had been lost on Monhegan. It could only have been Jay. He could *feel* it. They had connected during their talk. Their stories so similar, yet so different. Different sides of the same coin. Sean felt Jay's absence keenly. And couldn't help but wonder how his own story would end. And if there were others walking similar paths out there now.

He did worry about the others left on Monhegan. Nothing he could do about that now.

Ah, here. Gulliver's Hole was up the coast, outside a town called Lubec. In a park with a lighthouse. Of course. Another lighthouse.

He hadn't given himself time to reflect on hearing Breena's voice at Owls Head. Just wishful thinking? Or proof that their connection was still alive? And real. He pushed those thoughts away. No time for it now. Use it as incentive, but don't put too much into it. Yet.

"This Gulliver's Hole is outside a town a few hours away," Sean announced to the others. "I don't know about you, but I don't think I have it in me to drive three more hours tonight. Thoughts?"

They drove past the Owls Head Lobster Company, now closed for the night, and Sean saw the others look longingly at it as it fell into the rearview mirror. His fingers flew across his phone screen again.

"Right," he said, when he'd gotten no answers. "Rock Harbor Pub and Brewery. Less than fifteen minutes away. Who says no?"

More silence, but Sean noticed Trout working the navigation system, and as soon as the directions appeared on the screen, he hit the gas, and the truck took off like an arrow.

Shortly, they found themselves in the surprisingly bustling downtown area of Rockland, Maine. It was clearly more of a hard-scrabble working area than some of the more tourist destinations they had experienced up to now. Sean found himself liking it instinctively.

They easily found parking directly next to the pub and clambered out of the Bronco. Bayard led the way. His newly discovered penchant for popular human food on display. He'd been disappointed when Sean told him that the pub didn't serve pizza. After all, it had been over two days since he'd had any. But the promise of something new had placated him and now his enthusiasm led the Grumbles to share an amused look.

Trout stopped to make sure that Dünker was well situated in the hatch area and the troll fixed him with a look of pure adoration before snuggling under a large blanket kept for emergencies. If a troll in your truck didn't qualify as an emergency, well, what did? If all went well, the troll wouldn't wipe his nose on the blanket. The promise of a surprise snack seemed to mollify Dünker into accepting Trout leaving again.

Cinder chose to stay in the truck, although she had been given the option of exploring the area. Much like Bayard and the other Peripherals, she was more at home in open spaces. This city did not qualify. At least she knew the truck. Had adopted it as her den away from home. And the scent of Bayard was a comfort.

As the group entered the pub, the long bar ahead and to the left was ringed with locals. Regulars. Fishermen and dock workers who sought refuge here after long hard days. They gave barely a glance as the four newcomers found spots at the bar far from the door and away from the cold wind that whistled in every time the door opened.

The bartender, a burly, sandy-haired fellow with a prodigious beard that matched his attitude sauntered over to them and waited expectantly. As they scanned the beer list behind the bar, he let loose a sigh clearly aimed at pushing them along in the decision-making.

The Grumbles were no newcomers to this situation and Trout was the first one to jump into the void.

"First time here," he rumbled. "Whaddaya recommend?"

The bartender, taken aback at being asked for an opinion, turned fully to face them. Recalculating.

"What do you like?" he ventured, cautiously.

"Beer," said Brandy, earning a chuckle from some of the locals a few seats away. "Really," she said, "I like anything but a gose. That Ginger over there"—she gestured to Sean—"tried to kill me with one once. Worst thing I ever tasted."

"It wasn't that bad," Sean replied, earning more chuckles from down the bar.

"I hate those, too," the bartender answered. "I'll bring you a few of our greatest hits and you can fight over them." He started toward the taps before stopping and turning back. "I'm Pete, if you need anything. Any of these jerks at the bar tell you anything about me, it's a lie."

Bayard sat back in his stool and considered the others.

"That was...remarkable. And strange," he said. "Just when I think I understand your kind..."

"Yeah, humans are pretty darn weird," Trout agreed. "But we make the best of it. Usually."

Peter returned with four pint glasses and placed them on the bar.

"IPA, double IPA, stout, and a session IPA. That last one is for the ginger with no soul who gave you a gose."

At this the entire bar gave a laugh and Sean, suitably chastened, put his forehead on the bar and raised his hands in surrender.

"Kitchen closes in fifteen," Pete the bartender said. "If you're eating, better keep that in mind." And he was gone again.

"Can we order before we talk?" Trout asked. "I'm starving."

Bayard nodded his head vigorously and Brandy agreed.

After consideration, they ordered and settled into their beers. Each took a moment to savor. To breathe. To mull over their evening.

Brandy worked her cellphone, sipping the double IPA she'd claimed. "If we're stopping somewhere tonight," she said, "and I assume we are from what you said earlier, may I suggest Rockport, just a bit further? If no one objects, I'll book a couple rooms and we can take our food back there. Rockport Harbor Hotel. Bit pricier than our usual, but I'm guessing we all need it."

"I'm in," Trout replied. "In fact, my treat. We've earned it." He sipped his IPA and made a guttural noise of delight.

Bayard was sipping the stout. He nodded but was so involved with his beer that he couldn't speak.

Sean agreed that it made sense, and the idea of a comfortable bed and down pillow had him dreaming already.

It didn't take long for the food to arrive, and the beer was giving them all a sleepy, happy, tired feeling.

"You okay to drive, Trout?" Brandy asked as they gathered their things and headed to the door.

"Hell yeah," Trout said. "That beer hit the spot but I'm a big boy. In fact," he stopped and crossed to the back of the bar, returning a moment later with a six-pack of the Storm Surge IPA. "A nightcap for the room. Let's hit it."

Settled back into the Bronco, with the smell of buffalo mac 'n' cheese and fish tacos filling the cabin, they headed back into the dwindling traffic.

They decided mutually to hold off on talking until they had settled into the hotel and eaten. Poor decisions were often made on an empty stomach.

In fifteen minutes, they had reached the hotel. Ten minutes later, they were checked in. Another fifteen minutes saw them done with their meals and Bayard singing the praises of fried pickles and buffalo chicken dip. Dünker had been quite happy with his chicken alfredo, before quietly leaving the room to wander the now-deserted waterfront outside the hotel.

Each of them grabbed a beer before adjourning to the balcony that overlooked the harbor below. The moonglow on the harbor was bright enough that they didn't turn on a light, enjoying the peace of the moment. The gentle wind sent breaths glittering across the water below them. It was almost impossible to fathom what they had seen in the past few days. And what lay ahead.

"Lubec, Maine," Sean said. "Just over three hours from here. We can get a late start and still be there by lunchtime tomorrow. Gulliver's Hole is in the state park outside of town. It's tricky, like the one the Keeper mentioned in Acadia. We'll have to time it with the tides. But, maybe just as important, we have to figure out what he meant about the folks given asylum there."

"I have no idea what to expect," Brandy said. "But I really hope we aren't about to make life harder for some vulnerable people."

Trout took a swig of his beer. "I don't know what the alternatives are. Even the Keeper made it sound like this was the only way. Wish we had Kelphit to bounce things off."

"Sadly, I'm the only Fae here," Bayard said. "Wisdom isn't always my strongest suit. But I agree. It seems we're backed into a corner. And, honestly, with the boldness of that attack on Monhegan, I don't think we have time to muck around."

"I agree," Sean said. "So, we're agreed? Tomorrow, we go to Lubec and find our way to the Otherworld?"

"You make it sound so straightforward," Brandy said, "but yeah, I guess so."

Trout slammed his beer down on an end table suddenly.

"Well, I'm an idiot," he said.

"Agreed," Brandy replied. "What specifically have you done this time?"

"I left the bag with the mace and sword in the truck. I better go grab that."

"Gee, you think so?" Brandy said, shaking her head. When he looked at her, she pointed to the door. "Go!"

Trout got up and headed into the room. Sean rose to follow him.

"I'll walk you down," he explained. "You all should get some sleep. My mind is going a hundred miles an hour, though. Maybe a walk and some sea air will help me unwind."

Bayard watched Sean closely as he exited the balcony. He looked ready to say something but thought better of it and returned to his beer.

At the Bronco, Trout quickly unlocked the driver's door and reached under the seat. His eyes widened in surprise, as he pulled out a wrapped Christmas gift. With a quick look to Sean, he put the box back where he'd found it and, for one panicked moment, frantically cast his hand about under the seat. He let out a hearty breath and withdrew his hand, the bag containing the weapons in his hand.

"Sorry," he said, turning his face up to see Sean standing just behind him. "That's...a gift for my sister. Ronnie. Veronica. I'll get it to her when this is all said and done."

"No need to explain," Sean responded, turning to lean with his back against the truck's fender. "Gotta say, Dan, I can't seem to get my mind right. Too many thoughts. Too little time. Sorry, no need to bother you with it. I just need to stretch my legs."

"Never a bother, Sean," Trout said, straightening up. "Ever."

"You're a good man, Dan," Sean replied. "But I know that's not entirely true. Lost myself for a bit there. Thanks for sticking with me."

"Was never a doubt," Trout said. "Been through too much to give up now. I know you, Sean. Even when you seemed you didn't know yourself. Take your walk. Clear your head. Tomorrow will be a big day."

Surprisingly, Trout drew Sean into a bear hug that lasted longer than felt entirely comfortable. Truthfully, he wasn't very comfortable with physical affection of any kind.

Eventually, Sean broke the hug. Looked at Trout, half-smiled, patted him on the arm and started off.

He walked past the boat club on his right. Past that, he caught a glimpse of a pedestrian bridge that led him over a small canal and down to a park on the shore of the harbor. It was quiet. Night fell fast and early in most of Maine, especially in January, so the streets and paths were deserted.

Rockport Marine Park, he read on the sign as he entered. He found a set of benches by the water, and though the cold was starting to find its way into the seams of his coat, he sat, wrapping his arms around himself to buy a few more seconds of warmth.

Why had he been so awkward when Trout had hugged him? He'd never been like that before. Before when? Before the last few months? No, it had started before that. Before the demands of everyday life and the stresses of being an artist in a society that placed little value on them had taken hold of him.

There had been a few moments of released emotion with Breena. But not as many as he would have once allowed. A kiss on the beach in Montauk. A more passionate embrace after the battle of Bodie Island in North Carolina. Too few.

He'd had few relationships that lasted. Few that had depth. His peripatetic lifestyle prevented it. At least, that's what he'd always told himself. He thought of Jennifer Blevins. That was a relationship that should have grown. She was an actor, too. She understood. In theory. Beautiful. Talented. But he'd sabotaged that chance at happiness. Why?

He thought of others more recent. Kat in Lancaster. He'd noticed the spark. But by then the swirl of events had pulled him away. And Mal, in Brunswick. Beautiful, kind. Sensitive. But...he always created the barriers. Convinced himself it would be too complicated. But wasn't life complicated?

So, what was it, then? Fear of loss? Disappointment? Maybe.

And why was he willing to go to such lengths for Breena? The attraction was unmistakable. And they connected in ways he'd never known. But deep down, although he knew the feelings were real, he wasn't sure about her. And beyond that, about them.

The one woman with the greatest obstacles between them had become the one he *had* to fight for.

And yes, he knew there was more at stake. Much more. But he hadn't asked to be "the one," or at least the "latest one."

That line of thinking led him to consider Jay. He knew—in his bones—that Jay was gone. That he had saved Monhegan and in the process...found himself. The knowing was bittersweet. He knew Jay had done what he thought was best. And right. But he also resented that he would never have the time to truly know Jay. That other, earlier, version of what Sean was becoming. And someone he would have cared about deeply.

He had experienced so much loss. Too much. And now he thought of Ken. Another friend who had sacrificed himself for others. Stranding himself fifty years in the past so that Sean and Brandy could come home. But it hurt. Would always hurt. How could someone be there.

And then suddenly...not. There was still so much unsaid. So much to live. He'd found himself wondering what Ken would think about each new unbelievable thing they'd stumbled upon. The old Ken. Before he'd lost himself. The Ken he'd rediscovered before his last decision.

No more loss. He was determined. Trout. Brandy. Bayard. Cinder. Nick. Noodle. Stewart. Sandy. So many who had trusted him. Followed him. Needed him. There could be no more loss.

A statue on the other side of some hedges caught his eye, and he shook his head free of the cluttered thoughts and emotions. He needed focus. That was the only way to avoid more loss.

The cold blowing off of the water sent him wandering toward the statue. To his surprise, it was a sculpture of a seal. He read a plaque placed on the ground with the help of his phone's flashlight function. It was Andre the Seal. That information tickled some far corner of his brain. Had he read a children's book about this?

He read the sign. A seal pup adopted by the harbormaster here years ago. Instead of returning to the wild, Andre had chosen to stay with the man and their enduring friendship of over twenty years had inspired books, films, television programs. Ah, that's why it had sounded familiar.

Sean thought of his visit to Ireland a few years back when he had witnessed the dolphin Fungie and his unique relationship with the town of Dingle. Always appearing when boats cruised out of the harbor. A relationship that had existed for over three decades, if he remembered correctly.

Inevitably, his thoughts wandered to Bayard and Cinder. Their bond had been apparent almost from the moment they met, and he doubted they would ever be parted by choice.

He'd never had a relationship with an animal like that. He loved them. Had longed for a pet for years, but his profession and lifestyle had convinced him it would be complicated. And ultimately unfair to the animal. But others were able to do it. Was it just an excuse for him to avoid another kind of attachment?

Was that also why he continued to sabotage his personal relationships? Making things seem complicated in order to avoid commitment? Breena was the first thing he'd ever felt compelled to fight for. Even in his career, he'd always just...done what came. Dammit. It was time to fight. For something. For her. Even if she proved to be something other than he hoped, at least he would have fought.

He was uncomfortable with his own thoughts and nearly laughed out loud. Tomorrow he would try to enter the land of the Fae, and here he was thinking things that would be better saved for a counseling session or a Dear Abby column.

He rested a hand on the limestone statue, petting Andre's head, and whispering "good boy" to him. He'd heard seals called sea dogs before. Now it made sense.

Something, or someone, passed by the streetlight behind him, throwing a shadow over Sean and Andre. He turned, half expecting to find Trout or Brandy there. He'd been gone a while and, well, there had been a lot of unusual things happening to them lately.

But when he turned, there was no one there. He looked in both directions of the park. Nothing. Even the calls of the gulls, that had greeted him when he first arrived, had silenced.

In fact, now that he was noticing, every sound around him had stilled. The wind had died. The waters become flat.

And the streetlights themselves seemed to flicker and dim.

Suddenly, he felt very exposed. The expanse of the harbor stretching into blackness behind him. The park well-groomed, but open.

The feeling reminded him again of when he had first begun to awaken to the Peripherals shadowing him. But that had been because they had decided to step forward and explain their existence.

This was something else. Whatever had caused these feelings was decidedly *not* interested in being detected. In fact, had he not developed a sense for things like this, he doubted he would have noticed at all.

He wasn't afraid. He felt secure in his ability to take care of himself, but he was getting tired. And if something was stalking him, which is what it was beginning to feel like, then what was happening with his friends?

With a farewell pat to Andre, he began to make his way back to the hotel. He did notice the lights brighten as he left, and the feeling of being watched traveled with him. It wasn't until he was back in the room that he relaxed, and the feeling skittered to the edge of his senses and disappeared.

He found his friends asleep. All except for Bayard, who sat on the balcony, sipping another of the Rock Harbor cans of beer. Sean squeezed his shoulder as he took the seat next to him, and ruffled Cinder's ears in greeting.

No words were spoken, but all three were on alert. Cinder's ears forward and twitching.

If any of them noticed the faintly glowing eyes staring up at them from the sidewalk below, they didn't say. And when the eyes became hooded and faded to nothing, they rose, almost as one, and made their way into the room.

Bert had spent a life on and around the stage, but he had never experienced stage fright the way he did when the theatre became still and fell silent. All eyes on him. He knew whatever he said next, it had best set them at ease or disaster could fall on everyone here.

"Friends," he said, gesturing for seats to be taken. "My name is Bertram Clarke. I run this theatre, with quite a bit of help"—he nodded to Kath and Mal—"and together, we are the next stop for you on your way to your peaceful new life. I welcome you. *We* welcome you. I know times are chaotic right now. I know it can be a scary thing to feel the need to leave your homes and seek a better life. A safer life. For you and your families. My husband, Marcello Pettirosso, probably sent many of you here. Even if you don't know me, you know him. He can be trusted, and I hope you will trust me. Normally, we would arrange for you to travel to an island up the coast from here. Monhegan. But events are moving faster than expected, as I'm sure you've noticed. So, we will arrange to take you to another stop on our Underworld Railroad. A place filled with many who share your predicament. Who want what you want. A place of quiet, and beauty, and safety. You are now traveling beyond the reach of those who would harm you. You are with friends now. You are with family."

His heart was pounding, and he was sure that everyone could see the sheen of sweat that appeared above his upper lip. For someone who was normally unruffled by even the most contentious board meeting or stressful Opening Night, this was definitely new territory.

Kath worked her way to his side. "We've got all kinds of folks here," she said. "Pukwudgies we've seen before. They're from our neck of the woods. They're the little hairy ones. The beautiful dark folks with the butterfly wings? Those are Aziza. They've come all the way from Africa. Even some others from the Shinnecock Nation down south."

"I have no idea how we're going to get them all moved," Bert said. It would take dozens of trips with my SUV. Even adding your car, it will be weeks."

"Should we stash some of them out at Kieran and Pat's? It's quiet out there this time of year," Kath suggested.

"I'll give them a call in the morning," Bert said. "Good thinkin'. I guess we should just make them comfortable here for the night."

Mal had wandered over while they were talking, still holding one of the younger Aziza in her arms.

"We have a plan?" she asked.

"Bunk here tonight. Hopefully out to the cottage in the morning," Bert replied. "It will be crowded, but there should be plenty of outdoor space for them to—"

Before he could finish his sentence, they heard the stage door crash open off stage left and down the stairs. In fact, it sounded as if it had shattered the glass in the door. The sound of raining glass shards continuing after the initial concussion.

The shifter Donal rushed onto the stage, skidding to a halt as he saw the assembled crowd. His clothes were torn across his chest. A trickle pf blood ran down the side of his face and his breath was heaving.

"Hide-Behinds," he choked out. "Red Caps. Even Max Stubbe is out there with some of his family. It's bad. Real bad."

"Max Stubbe?" Bert asked, looking to Finlay.

"Another shifter," Finlay explained. "He and his family are decidedly not friendly. They fought against Pettirosso in Lancaster."

Carolyn was looking over Donal's shoulder, concern on her face.

"Where's Craig?" she asked.

Donal shook his head once, and Carolyn gasped.

"How?" she whispered.

"Last I saw him, he was facing off with Stubbe," Donal explained. "There was a group of Red Caps flanking him. He threw himself at them all so that I could make it back to warn you. I'm sorry. We didn't really have a choice."

Carolyn turned away and could do little to hide the tears that fell at the news.

"Right," Bert said. "Change of plans. Can we get this crowd out of here, or is it already too late?"

"We're down to three shifters," Donal answered, "but we can carve a path. Hold them. But not for long. If we're getting them out of here, it has to happen fast."

"Stubbe will pay," Finlay seethed. "But first things first. Let's get these people to safety. Bert, you and the ladies get going. We'll handle things here."

"First, no," Bert said. "I stay and fight for my theatre. So, there are four of us. But we don't have a way to transport them, and I don't think they'll be outrunning a pack of shifters."

Mal raised her hand as if she was in a class. "I may have an idea," she said, quietly.

"I'm all ears," Bert said quickly.

"The bar just bought a couple of party buses," she said. "We're planning on some brewery crawls in the spring. Just old school buses, but I have the keys. And they're just sitting there. Not being used until April." She turned to Kath. "Can you drive a bus?"

"I'm from Boston," Kath said. "I can drive frickin' anything."

Mal turned back to Bert and raised her eyebrows.

"Do it," Bert said. "Can they get out the loading dock?"

"Yes, I think so," Donal said, sagging to sit on the stage.

"Yes? Or you think so?" Bert demanded.

"Yes," Donal replied. "Yes. But not for much longer.

Carolyn stepped up next to Mal. "I'll go with them. You'll need everyone else here." She turned to Mal. "Hi, I'm Carolyn. Ready for this?"

"Hi, I'm Mal," she answered. "And absolutely not. But we can't wait for me to be ready, so—"

"Go," Bert said quickly. "Be careful. You're our only hope."

"Obi-Wan," Kath said quietly.

"You're going with them, Princess Leia," he shot at her.

"I think I have my fake harpoon here somewhere," Kath replied. "We're good."

"Just be careful, will ya?" Bert said.

"Don't worry, Boss," Kath said, grabbing his arm. "We've got this."

The three women took off at a jog.

Bert couldn't help thinking that maybe he should have taken one of the magical weapons from Monhegan, after all.

One of the Aziza had approached Bert and the shifters. She was strikingly beautiful, with wings of iridescent blue and green, but her eyes flashed brightly.

"I am Selam," she said. "And though we are small, we are not helpless. And though we are refugees, we are not powerless. We will help."

Bert nodded slowly and shot a look at Finlay.

"I'd say no," Bert replied, "but I don't think we have that luxury. Thank you."

He strode into the wing and reappeared a moment later with his baseball bat.

"And we have Frank Thomas on our side, too," he announced. "Let's shore up that stage door and keep an eye out for those buses. And if we have to, we'll crack some skulls. No one messes with our theatre."

Finlay and Donal followed him as he headed toward the exit stairs. After a moment, a contingent of the Little People, from all clans, moved along behind them.

CHAPTER 15

The morning came and with it a quiet watchfulness. No one mentioned the unease from the night before, but neither did they relax completely. Sean found himself looking out the windows often. Whatever had unsettled them last night seemed to have moved on. At least for now. Recent events, though, had taught them to never truly relax.

They took their time packing up for the drive. Lubec's tides were against them, and they likely wouldn't be able to attempt Gulliver's Hole that day, but getting there and checking the lay of the land was important.

The Bronco pulled out of Rockport at eleven in the morning. The drive to Lubec would take just over three hours if the traffic was in their favor, and traffic on these roads at this time of year was sparse, at best. The roads became smaller and fellow travelers rarer the further along the coast they drove. At one point, they cruised past blueberry farms, all empty land and snow cover at this time of year. And something called the Wild Blueberry Heritage Center. The building looked like an enormous blueberry, and Sean would have absolutely stopped if he hadn't been on his way to rescue the woman he loved and save the world. He did love some mimetic architecture. No sooner had that thought formed than he realized just how much of a nerd he truly was.

The weather took a turn as they continued. After their experience on Monhegan, all of them began to get twitchy as the clouds ahead shifted from puffy white, to grey, to deep angry rolling black. Each of them threw their senses out, trying to pick up on any unnatural energy coming their way, but none of them found a thing. Even Cinder lifted her head but quickly returned it to her outstretched paws and drifted back to sleep.

Finally, the black clouds let loose, and a cold mist fell, shifting not long after to a driving, drenching, miserable downpour. The windshield wipers made a rhythmic thump as they worked hard to keep up with the torrent.

Trout, though, seemed completely oblivious. In fact, he turned the satellite radio to a station for XTC, cranked up the volume and began to sing along as "The Ballad of Peter Pumpkinhead" played. Sean turned in his seat and caught Brandy's eye, grinning. Within moments, they began to sing along, fully aware of the song's message of the government resenting a good man who comes only to help others. By the time it was finished, all three had descended into their own thoughts.

Bayard, though, had never heard the song and had been carried away with the bouncy tune and seemingly frivolous lyrics.

"I enjoyed that one!" he cried. "More like that, please."

Shaking off his unease, Sean shot him a thumbs-up. "The Mayor of Simpleton" played next and Bayard continued his happy bouncing, while Sean considered that he had to give XTC a close listen again. When he had time. After.

The three hours passed quickly, and the Bronco rumbled into the outskirts of Lubec just after two o'clock in the afternoon. The rain had settled into a steady, morose curtain that dampened everything, literally and figuratively. Not a soul was seen as Route 189 turned into Main Street. Incongruously, they passed a t-shirt shop, a Dollar

General. They passed the turn for the West Quoddy Head Lighthouse, barely visible under the conditions. All made note of it, but no one said a word. They would head there soon enough.

Eventually, the houses grew closer together and they began to feel as if they had actually reached the town. Trout pointed out his window at a street corner.

"Well, that's damn cute," he said.

At first, Sean saw nothing but a tree stump on the edge of someone's yard. On second glance, though, straining to see past Trout and through the heavy rain, he realized the stump had been decorated. Someone had created a faerie house out of it. It was four levels, complete with a shingled roof. Small figures scampered about the exterior. Climbing a ladder. Waving from a window. Tending a garden. Sharing a drink at a picnic table. He was reminded of the time Sandy Dale had scattered little faerie houses around her neighborhood in New Jersey. In hindsight, they all should have seen that her path would lead somewhere else eventually. Sean made note of the street corner. Interesting.

They'd agreed over the last few months that there were no coincidences. He reminded himself of that.

Shortly, they reached the end of the road and turned left along the Lubec waterfront. The entire downtown consisted of only a few short blocks, and from what they could see there were some gift shops and restaurants along with a smattering of art galleries

In the opposite direction on the street, Bayard had spotted the small local brewery and made a sound that sounded remarkably like Cinder whimpering.

Brandy chuckled and patted him on the arm.

"Maybe later," she said. "If you're good. And they're open."

Bayard turned back around in his seat and pouted. An ancient, Otherworldly truculent child. For a moment.

Cohill's Inn rose to their left and they all spontaneously thanked Sean for booking them there. It was a simple three-story structure perched on the corner of town overlooking the water. A quick search told them that the Indian River lay to their left and Deep Cove just to the right. There was a memorial park of some sort across the narrow street. Even in the deluge, they could see the spot was stunning.

Trout made a quick U-turn and parked in front of the inn. There was no traffic, and no scarcity of parking. As they climbed out and grabbed their bags, Bayard gave a small yelp and pointed. The ground floor of the inn held a pub, and it was one of the few businesses with lights on.

"I think I love you," Bayard said, turning to Sean.

"I know," Sean replied, with a laugh. "Let's see if you still say that after tomorrow."

As Trout gathered his things, Dünker rolled out of the back hatch. He jumped from foot to foot, peering into the darkness over the harbor in front of the truck. He stuck his nose into the air, wiping the ooze of it away as he took prodigious sniffs. A broad smile, full of his yellow and broken teeth, lit up his face.

"Good smells, Trout," the troll enthused. "So good! I can go? Want to run! Smell! Find friends. Find smells."

"You don't need to ask me, little buddy," Trout answered, ruffling the straggly tuft that passed as hair on the creature. "Knock yourself out. But I'd be extra careful with meeting new friends. We don't know this place yet."

Dünker yipped with happiness and disappeared into the darkness to the left, where a parking lot gave way to some fishing docks and then trees.

The group spilled into the small office area and rang the bell on the counter. An older woman appeared eventually, shuffling slowly.

"Curley party?" she said, more than asked. "Must be. Only guests tonight. We normally close up this time of year, but you know the right people. Bertram Clarke put in a good word for you."

She gave each of them a long, uncomfortable looking over.

"Four of you and one dog," she muttered, looking at a computer screen on the counter. "I've got you in two rooms. Top floor. All water views. And we'll be keeping the pub open late tonight. The locals are a bit restless, so it will be good for everyone. Mr. Clarke has picked up your bill, just so you know. Very generous." She gave them another looking at, and each of them felt distinctly judged.

"Thanks," Sean said, stepping forward. "I'm Sean Curley. They're under my name. We'll be sure to thank Bert."

The woman's eyes widened when Sean used Bert's first name, but it was unclear to him if it was because she was impressed or disgusted. Maybe a touch of both.

Keys in hand, they all gathered their belongings and headed up the staircase to the left of the counter. On the third floor, they headed to their rooms, comparing keys.

"Brandy, you and I are in number nine," Sean said. "Hope that's okay. I put you two in number eight." He gestured to Trout and Bayard. "But really, it's just us and we can come and go as we want. I just didn't think it was good for any of us be alone. Not this close to the end. Hopefully the end."

"Fine with me!" Trout boomed. "C'mon, horse boy! Let's check this room out. We scoping the town out after?"

"Let's do that," Sean said. "Wanna say fifteen minutes?"

"Done," Trout answered, guiding Bayard to their door.

Sean wandered one door down the hallway and opened the door, catching his breath at what he saw. "I think you're gonna be happy, Brand."

The doorway led to a huge room with windows on two sides, a 180-degree view of the water with Canada just across the way. It seemed close enough to step over. The tiny Mulholland Point Lighthouse was on the far bank, barely visible in the slacking rain. As the sun tried to break through, a golden glow escaped and glimmered in the foggy aftermath of the storm.

Brandy entered and dropped her bag before she even reached the windows.

"Nicely done, Ginge." she said. "I don't often give you compliments, and there's a reason for that. But this time—well done."

They stood next to each other and watched as the sun struggled its way into the afternoon sky. Brandy grabbed Sean's arm and pointed at the water. In the swirling waters of the tide, a group of seals had gathered to body surf the whirlpool that had formed beside the stone jetty just outside. They watched in awe and delight as the group frolicked and flashed through the rising waters.

As if something had just occurred to him, Sean turned to Brandy. "Do you think any of them are—?"

"Our selkie friends?" Brandy asked, getting the gist of his question. She turned and considered the seals again. "I'm not getting anything. But Bayard will know better than me."

Sean nodded. Placing a hand on the glass and putting his head on it, trying to peer down the street to the right. Suddenly, he stood up straight. That sense of being watched was back. Unmistakable.

He felt Brandy stiffen at the same time. All of a sudden, the huge picture windows felt a little *too* big. Instinctually, and without saying a word to each other, they grabbed the two curtains and drew them across both windows.

"There's something about this place," Brandy said, quietly. "It's beautiful, I'll give it that, but..."

"Yeah, I know," Sean agreed. "Something's up. But isn't it always lately."

<hr>

Bert walked quickly out the stage door. He swung his baseball bat in lazy circles at his side. "Okay, Frank," he whispered to the bat. "We've been through a few things, but I think this is going to be a big one."

Finlay and Donal emerged from the door behind him, shifting into their wolf forms and taking up positions on either side of Bert. Both nosed the air and growled long and low at what they sensed.

They were surrounded by a scattering of old trees, some forty or fifty feet tall. They cast writhing shadows around the paved footpaths and manicured lawns that were normally used by students.

But all three men knew that tonight, something much more diabolical waited in the shadows.

Something flitted between two trees off to their right. All three of them saw and turned their eyes in that direction. Something clattered in the distance. Metal on metal. Not a sound for a January night in Brunswick, Maine.

Donal took a lithe step in the direction of the shadow they'd seen, but Bert stopped him with a shake of his head.

"We hold here," he said quietly. "We have to keep the loading dock behind us clear for the buses."

Donal gave a curt nod of his head and fell back into place. Finlay turned to take in the loading dock. He nodded to Bert and indicated the floodlights that illuminated the dock.

"I see what you're getting at," Bert said. "I'll kill those lights. Kath and Mal know where they need to be."

He slipped quietly into the building, and as he did, a long howl erupted from the copse of trees deeper into the campus to their right, past the shuttered concession stand. A pair of deep ruby-red eyes flickered into sight. Then another. And another.

"Stubbe," Donal growled. "He took Craig. We end him tonight."

"We will," Finlay said, his voice so filled with barely disguised fury that Donal cast a surprised look at him.

The lights behind them, over the docks, cut out with a click. They stood now in darkness, the lights along the path pools of light in an ocean of blackness. Bert returned and took up his place between them, noting the red eyes that now were creeping closer.

An angry orange flame burst into life behind the approaching Stubbe and the other shifters. It wove lazy circles in the air before cracking through the air, connecting with one of the tree branches above them and setting it instantly alight. The tree was quickly engulfed in flames. Orange, red, purple fingers of violence, climbing the old tree and creating a massive torch to light the way of their attackers.

The enormity of what they faced struck them, and three figures standing in the way of the advancing creatures felt small and insignificant. Ahead of them they saw a phalanx of Red Caps, marching in formation, their brutal pikes arrayed on their shoulders.

Around them, the trees teemed with the faint hints of Hide-Behinds, moving unseen and inexorably forward. Likely dozens of them, but the exact number unclear.

The wolf shifters, Stubbe and two others strode confidently in the fore, raking their long claws along each tree as they passed, leaving scores along the bark, delighting in violence for the sake of violence. The three defenders raged inwardly, almost able to hear the cries of the ancient trees as they were mutilated, and their neighbor fell victim to flames.

And behind it all, at last, the Dullahan itself emerged. High on his horse and with his demon Barghest hounds at his side, low to the ground. Stalking. The flaming whip continued to leave macabre trails of light in the air above it all.

"Here we go, gents," Bert said to the others. "Don't expose yourself unnecessarily. We just need to hold long enough for the buses to get here and loaded. Once that's done, we get back inside and come up with Plan B."

"Sure," Donal answered, baring his fangs. "Piece o' cake."

The Red Caps were upon them a moment later. Bert sent two to the ground with huge swings of Frank Thomas, before an uppercut sent a third sailing backward where it landed with a clatter and lay still.

On either side of him, the shifters were a blur of anger and violence. The Red Caps were no match for their reflexes and precision. Maybe, just maybe, they would be able to get out of this in one piece.

No sooner had Bert allowed himself that thought, than Stubbe and the enemy wolves were there, teeth gleaming in the reflection of the orange flames. They threw themselves at the defenders and, combined with the remaining Red Caps, began to drive Bert and the shifters backward toward the stage door. The loading docks were threatened, but even worse, the defenders were in danger of being overwhelmed.

As the low murmur of big engines could be heard across the campus green, Finlay fell to his knees, Max Stubbe standing over him with a dagger in one hand, fangs poised to drive downward, and a wicked grin creeping across his twisted face. To his right, Donal was slashed across his back by one of the other wolf shifters who had flanked him. He arched in pain but kept his feet. Barely.

Bert was swinging his bat with one hand and throwing haymakers with the other, keeping the Red Caps off balance, but he was distracted by the injuries suffered by his friends, and as he tried to turn to Finlay's aid, a pike found its way inside his defenses and sent his bat flying out of his grip.

Suddenly, the rustle of dozens of wings settled over the melee. The air was filled with the iridescent flutter of the Azizas' rainbow wings. Surprising the attackers from above, they dove and plucked the pikes from the hands of the Red Caps, raking their nails along their faces, quickly blinding them as blood streamed from their brows. Many of them began to turn in circles, flailing with their arms as they tried in vain to clear their vision.

And then the Pukwudgies joined the fray. Rushing into the battle with small knives and spears at the ready. Many, with a flick of their hands, threw gravel from the paths into the eyes of the Red Caps, blinding them further, and within moments the attackers were fleeing.

But the Dullahan and the Barghests were not so easily dissuaded and continued to advance, secure in the knowledge that the Hide-Behinds were creeping throughout the trees. And now, punctuated by the screams of the Little People caught unaware, the Hide-Behinds began to grab and drag them away. Even a few of the Aziza were plucked out of the sky, disappearing behind a tree, falling into shadow with strangled cries.

The Little People of the Shinnecock Nation now flowed out of the doorway. They clustered and chanted, sending a low ground mist across the green. Where it touched a Hide-Behind, the invader became tangled in it and swept away. The tide seemed to be turning. Again.

Bert found an opening and lunged to recover his bat. Turning, he was faced with an impossible choice. Both Finlay and Donal were still at the mercy of Red Caps. Finlay on the ground, trying to ward off his attacker, while Donal had been driven against the wall of the theatre, where he sagged to one side and looked sure to fall at any moment.

Bert hesitated. How could he make this decision? Whoever he abandoned would surely be lost.

"Dammit!" he shouted. "Donal! Hold strong! Be there in a sec!"

With that, he turned to Finlay, who was closer, and sent a vicious swing of the bat into the Red Cap who was poised to drive its pike into his chest. The attacker crumpled like an empty suit of armor. Finlay shook his head, took the hand Bert offered, and together they turned to Donal.

It was clear they were too late. Donal had sunk to one knee, his head bowed. Waiting for the inevitable.

And then, a figure rose behind the attacking Red Cap. Rose impossibly high and snarled a curse.

"Nae!" it cried. "You get your dirty, stinking self away from him!"

A set of claws, large, sharp, lethal, pierced the creature from behind and lifted it into the air. The Red Cap didn't even have time to cry out. It was dead before the figure tossed it limply to the ground, and stepped to Donal's side, lifting him easily.

Donal looked in disbelief. Salvation literally from nowhere. And then the figure stepped into one of the pools of the streetlights. The wolf head was battered. Bleeding. Torn. But recognizable.

"Craig!" Donal gasped. "I thought…"

"Me, too, cuz. Me, too," Craig said weakly. "But I knew you couldn't do this without me, ya big marshmallow."

Donal laughed and wrapped Craig in an embrace.

Suddenly, four beams of light raced their way across the paths and lawns and the roaring of engines exploded into the night. Two repurposed school buses jumped the curb and rattled across the grass toward the loading dock behind the defenders.

The strafing headlights dispelled the last of the Hide-Behinds, and any remaining Red Caps took to their heels when they saw their fellow fighters dispatched by Bert and Craig.

And that left the Dullahan and his canine lackeys. The Dullahan and his horse fairly pranced in their approach, the whip still weaving shapes in the air.

"The one I seek isn't here," the creature rasped from the back of its mount. "A waste of time. And none of *you*"—it held its head aloft and fixed them with its gaze—"have anything I need or want. You are nothing. Will be nothing. All of the Fae who have chosen the human side...prepare to die. I would do it myself, but you are not worth my notice. And humans? You are already dead. You just don't realize yet. Your desecration of this world is at an end."

One of the buses gunned its engine, and gears could be heard grinding as it jerked forward, aiming directly at the Dullahan.

The specter huffed dismissively, and waved the whip in a circular motion behind the horse. Almost instantly, a glowing circle lit the night with fire. With barely a glance, the horse stepped backward through the portal, followed by the black mongrels.

The bus bumped its way across the grass exactly where the Dullahan had been but found the space empty by the time it arrived.

A primal scream rose into the night as the bus's door accordioned open. Mal jumped down and out.

"And stay out!" she screamed at the void the Dullahan had left behind. "Stinking piece of shit!"

Kath emerged from the other bus and rushed to Mal.

"Easy, easy," Kath said. "Impressive. I had no idea you had that in you."

"Oh," Mal replied, turning angry eyes to Kath. "I'm full of surprises."

Carolyn came bounding out of the first bus, ready to fight. She almost seemed disappointed to have nothing to do.

As the defenders gathered their wounded and dead, they prepared to board the school buses.

"They could be back any time," Bert explained. "I don't trust any of them. Best get you on your way. Whatever happens, we will hold the line here. Tell the others in Lubec, we are now their southern guards."

As the college green became a bustle of activity, no one noticed the eyes watching from behind a tree further into the campus. And no one noticed when they flickered and disappeared. But Bert paused to look back over his shoulder and gave a brief nod before rejoining the others.

───────

Sean and Brandy left their room and found Bayard and Trout already waiting just outside the front door of the inn. The sun had made a late day breakthrough, and the dying light, the golden hour, bathed the beatific scene in an otherworldly sheen. The lighthouse across the channel had emerged from the fog and flashed its light into the gathering dusk.

The street through town to their right was nearly deserted. The only sign of life emanated from the brewery just over a block away. The four set their feet in that direction. Five minutes later, which included a stop to watch a bald eagle perched atop an abandoned building by the water, they made their way into the taproom.

It felt more like someone's living room than a brewery. Well-loved upholstered chairs and couches lay scattered about the room. The bar was at the far side of the space, and they headed there. Despite a smattering of locals, it was easy to find stools and they settled themselves to wait for the bartender.

The locals made note of their arrival, and if the glances lingered a little longer than they expected, it wasn't an unfriendly atmosphere.

Much the opposite. The attitude from the others seemed to be one of curiosity rather than belligerence.

Scanning the beer menu, they each made their selections, and when the beers arrived, they adjourned to a small couch and two chairs that were nestled in a far corner. Sipping their beers, they all made complimentary note of the quality, with Brandy, who had ordered an Imperial IPA by the name of Bailey's First Mistake, particularly taken by her beer. At 9 percent ABV, it would be one and done, but the others let her have her moment.

One of the locals rose. A gentleman who seemed to be north of seventy years old opened a case at his feet, emerging with a worn and well-loved fiddle. He began tuning his instrument and was soon joined by a young lady who had been sitting at a long table in the room adjoining.

With unspoken agreement, the two finished tuning and, at a nod from the older man, they launched into an Irish reel. Toes around the room set to tapping and it took no time at all for the newcomers to join in with the rest. Sean and Trout relaxed instantly. This was an atmosphere they understood, and they sank deeper into their sofa.

Bayard was watching the players closely, a broad grin spreading Cheshire cat-like across his face. For the first time in days, he seemed relaxed. Much more like the freewheeling Bayard of old. "Old" being just a few months past. Cinder, stretched out at his feet, gazed lovingly up at him, yawned, and drifted to sleep while her tail thumped on the floor, nearly matching the rhythm of the music.

Only Brandy seemed removed from the moment. Staring intently into her mug. Eventually, her eyes rose to look out the front window to where the tide was racing past just across the street.

While the music played, and the four travelers allowed themselves a brief chance to breathe, the streetlights came on with a juddering click.

Eventually, one of the locals couldn't contain his curiosity and sauntered up to the newcomers.

"Don't get too many strangers in here this time of year," he said, with a distinct old-school Maine accent. "Hope you don't think me rude if I ask how you ended up all the way up here in January?"

"Not at all," Trout said, rising to shake the man's hand. "Dan Trout. From Montana. We came here on the advice of a friend. We're outdoor enthusiasts. Hoping to take in the lighthouse. Do some hiking. And now, I would add drinking some excellent beer while listening to equally excellent music to that itinerary."

The man stepped back to take in the tall westerner. "You're a long way from home," he noted. "Pleased to meet ya. Brad Nadler, here. Mind if I park myself for a spell? You're closer to the fire and it's feelin' pretty cozy about now."

"Help yourself," Trout replied. "Glad of the company. We've been cooped up in a truck together for a few days. Change of pace is welcome."

"I can see you're the charmer of the group," Brad said to which Trout chuckled and Sean shook his head. "Every group of friends needs one."

The players shifted gear, launching into a slow and weepy rendition of "The Fields of Athenry" and the bar fell silent for the duration. At the conclusion, Brad rose, drained the last of his beer and cast a look around the circle. "Anyone need anything?"

Everyone shook their heads except Brandy, who checked her nearly empty mug and turned to Brad. "I'll take one of whatever you have. And it's on me. I have a tab."

Brad smiled widely at his good luck and shuffled off to the bar.

"We should head back to the inn fairly soon," Sean said. "Grab some food before the music starts tonight?"

The others nodded in agreement, but they, in fact, did not leave for quite some time. It turned out, after further discussion with Brad, that the music at Cohill's was simply an extension of the music here at the brewery. Everyone, including the musicians, would simply get up and wander down the street. After an hour, and another beer, the three Grumbles had consumed enough liquid courage to join the fiddle players for a rendition of "Carrickfergus." As they sang, a subtle golden glow covered the floor like a low fog. If any of the locals noticed, they didn't mention it.

When they finished, the room stayed silent. The wind outside whistled down the empty street until, almost as one, the room rose and rushed to the singers to shake their hands. And just like that, they were welcomed unreservedly into the heartbeat of the bar. The brewery. The town.

At seven thirty, with the brewery awash in the golden light from the numerous duets, trios, ballads, and up tempos the room had experienced, the bartender waved a towel and announced the festivities were moving down the street to Cohill's. A collective cheer rose up, and the crowd gathered their belongings and began the shuffle to the street.

Night had fallen, and so had the temperature, causing coats to be donned as everyone hit the night air. Sean walked slowly, bringing up the rear and marveling at his friends, who had all managed to ingratiate themselves so quickly with the locals. Brandy was deep in discussion with a woman wearing paint-spattered overalls and a paintbrush stuck into her wildly unkempt hair. Trout was still deep in discussion with Brad Nadler, comparing the strengths and shortcomings of Maine versus Montana. Bayard was riling Cinder up, who had found a German shepherd larger than she was to romp with. The owner of said shepherd followed, laughing heartily and trying to keep up.

Before they reached the inn, an impromptu version of "The Rattlin' Bog" kicked off and the golden light returned, stretching nearly the length of the tiny downtown area.

Sean stopped in the middle of the street. As usual, he felt removed from the festivities around him, and wished he could set aside those feelings and just enjoy the moment. He caught a glimpse of that when he lived in a song, letting the notes, the lyrics, flow through him. He sighed, a cloud of breath floating out and up to dissipate as it reached the streetlight overhead.

He turned to take in the quiet of the town behind him. All of the shuttered storefronts managing to feel cozy and welcoming even closed tight. Something caught his eye. Something small, close to the ground, rustling just outside of the glow of the streetlight, but following the golden musical light on its path to Cohill's.

His first thought was Dünker returning from his exploration of the area, but on reflection, the shape he'd seen was smaller than the troll. Quicker. More elusive. If he had seen anything at all. He strained his eyes to try to catch the movement again. He found more than he'd expected, as the space he was watching began to heave with movement. More than one something was there. Watching. Following.

Sean suddenly realized the group had outpaced him and the leaders were already headed into the inn and the warmth of the blazing fireplace in the pub. The orange-yellow light spilling from the doorway was distinctly different from the golden hue of their music, and combined, they turned the end of town into a sparkling crown to the Main Street. He felt isolated. The rustlings at the edge of the light were growing louder, closer, trying to flank him, attracted to the end of the street like moths to a candle.

Sean turned and hurried after the brewery crowd. As he did, something else caught his attention. Behind the ground level shuffling, something bigger lurked. Something very big, indeed. Sean was sure his heightened senses had allowed him to detect whatever it was. He saw it in his mind more than with his eyes, and again he was reminded of his first encounters with the Peripherals, when he had felt pursued, observed, exposed. This was worse. He knew much more now of how the Fae operated. Something this big that could escape his detection, and the detection of his friends, was new. And dangerous.

He couldn't get back to Cohill's fast enough. He'd let his guard down after their escape from Monhegan. He thought the only thing to fear was the path to the Otherworld, but clearly, he had misjudged. There were still plenty of threats here and now. Had he, once again, placed his friends in more danger than he'd expected?

He cursed himself not for the first time, and he expected not the last.

As he finally reached the inn, he rushed through the front door, letting it slam behind him and hoping it would prove sturdy enough to keep out the things that were lurking in the night. He turned right, into the pub, and was greeted with a scene of pure revelry. The music had resumed, and surprisingly Bayard was leading a rendition of the French chanson "La Vie en rose." Sean stopped in his tracks. He had never seen the Peripheral so...happy.

Sean quietly slipped onto one of the barstools and ordered an Allagash White. A classic Maine beer, but after one sip, decided it was best to switch to tea. The memory of the scratching outside and the looming trek through the Fae portal tomorrow sobered him quickly.

He sat and watched his friends. The sheer joy emanating from them. The smiles that turned their ways when the locals interacted. Something in the windows behind them shifted, and Sean was about to raise an alarm when he saw the familiar mottled face of Dünker peek over the sill. The troll caught sight of Sean and waved happily. Sean grinned. That damn troll's giddiness was contagious. When it wasn't trying to wipe its nose.

Dünker spread his arms wide, pointing to the side of him, and as Sean glanced in that direction, he stood up from his stool. Slowly at first, but with increasing speed, small pairs of eyes popped up beside the troll. Behind him. In every direction.

The music faltered, as more people noticed what had become impossible to ignore. Dozens of creatures were waiting outside the windows. Lined up on the sidewalk and stretching around the corner to the swath of grass there.

Bayard, Trout, and Brandy quickly made their ways to Sean at the bar. Concern was etched on all of their faces. With a further curse of himself, Sean realized they had left the magical weapons locked in the rooms.

Stupid. Stupid. Lazy and foolish.

Quietly, every face in the pub turned to face the Grumbles and Bayard. The laughter had fallen silent with the music. The air crackled with tension. Violence didn't seem imminent, but it felt near. The most surprising thing was that not a single townsperson seemed concerned. Or surprised by the faces at the windows.

Brad Nadler stood and shot an apologetic look at Trout.

"Well, this is unfortunate," he said quietly. "We really enjoyed your company. But this"—he indicated the audience at the window —"changes things. Should have known better than to let the music get out of hand. They always come to the music. You all need to take a seat. We'll have to talk this through."

There seemed to be no room for debate.

On Monhegan, there had been an uncomfortable détente since the storm. Gluskabe had been patrolling the waters around the island, though there had been no more sign of Balor or any of his minions.

Nick continued his recovery. Each day the use of his arm increased. He and Noodle decided to create together to bolster the defense of the island. They had done well in Lancaster with the saving of the Fulton Theatre. Nick's writing and Noodle's drawings melded together and became manifest in the world outside the hall.

With their continued work, the island began to feel more secure. Nearly impenetrable. Kelphit, Fintan, and Sulevia, with Nick's continued improvement, focused more on McCloud's situation. The massive Scot continued in a fog of amnesia. He could recall nothing of his past and had completely lost any sense of his time-traveling past. Sandy fussed about the healers' village, keeping everyone comfortable and studying every move the ancient healers made.

In this context, the loss of Jay was felt sharply by everyone. His ability to cut through pretense had disarmed more situations than they had realized while he was still there. There was silence now where his flippancy had once been. At times, the silence spoke so loudly to his loss that it became almost unbearable.

After much discussion and debate, the healers made the difficult decision to recall the mists of Hy-Brasil to hide their village. Not the entire island, as the humans in the town had done nothing to deserve being disappeared. But the healers' village, now that it had been declared a target by none other than Balor, King of the Fomorians, would need to reconsider how it existed in the world. This meant that only the injured and infirm who had powerful connections would be able to access the healers. It was not what they wanted. But it was necessary.

Nick decided to send an email to Sean and the others before the island was shrouded. The healers assured him and the other humans that they would be returned home when affairs on the mainland were more settled. "When" felt a bit like "if" to them, even though they valued all that Monhegan was.

The youngest puffin appeared often at the windows, seeming to prefer the village to the craggy cliffs where the other two puffins spent the majority of their time. The newcomer strutted along the windowsills, more like a little general than a little friar. His presence helped. And he knew it.

They named him Chicago.

Kath and Mal decided they needed to stop for the night. They were a caravan of two. Two repurposed school buses packed to bursting with hundreds of Little People. Fae. Refugees who had placed their trust in the Underworld Railway and had instead been attacked, placed in mortal danger, and seen too many of their loved ones perish defending the very place that was supposed to defend them. They needed to decompress.

And Kath and Mal were tired. More than that. They were exhausted. It would be dangerous for them to push through the night. And, despite Kath's claims to the contrary, she *couldn't* drive a school bus. Not well, at least. And she definitely shouldn't drive one in the middle of the night, on blackened country roads, with a gaggle of restless passengers, and too little sleep.

Mal was fine. Kath would do better in daylight.

Mal had checked her maps app before they had left Brunswick and put a mental circle around Toddy Pond. They had opted for the "scenic" route on Route 1. It only added ten minutes to their journey, but they had no idea what they were going to find in Lubec or along the way.

The attack on the theatre had materialized seemingly out of nowhere. They couldn't assume that they would have a clear path all the way to the town.

The buses rattled along the state highway. Not the most comfortable of vehicles for long drives, the passengers were just relieved to be on their way.

At Toddy Pond, Mal found a public boat ramp just off the roadway. It was empty and there was just enough space to park up and let the Little People catch some rest. They had been through so much just to make it to Brunswick in the first place. Exhaustion caught up with them and most fell into a deep sleep where they were. Others wandered out into the silence of the night, sitting quietly in the cold air, watching the waters lap gently on the shore. A few even took flight, brightly colored and delicate wings soaring over the pond, dancing in the starlight and chasing moonbeams across the water's surface.

Kath climbed down from her bus and stretched with a resounding crack of…something. Neck? Back? Whatever it was, it had sounded both painful and relieving. She grimaced at Mal, emerging from her bus.

"I could have made it to Lubec, you know that, right?" Kath said just a tad too loudly.

"I know that," Mal said, calmly.

"You're humoring me," Kath complained. "I hate when you do that."

"I'm not," Mal insisted. "I genuinely think it's best for everyone to stop for a while. Much better to arrive in daylight. Bert can let whoever needs to know that we're on our way."

"You're still humoring me," Kath whined.

"Little bit," Mal said with a grin.

Kath shook her head and returned the smile.

"Hopefully," Mal said, "we'll get there tomorrow and find our friends safe and successfully back from whatever they needed to do. Let's manifest that."

"Manifest shmanifest," Kath grumbled. "But yeah. That would be good."

They both turned and watched the dance of the Azizas in the night sky. Intricate. Beautiful. Startling. A reminder of why they took the chances they did.

They reached out and held each other's hands. And watched the most remarkable ballet above Toddy Pond.

CHAPTER 16

Sean sat at the bar, fiddling with his glass of iced tea. He pushed the glass around in the small puddle of condensation on the bar top. The others sat to his right. Trout was finishing off Sean's Allagash White.

"No sense in it going to waste," he said, pulling the pint over to hm.

Brandy was rocking back and forth on her stool, which had one leg shorter than the others. She said nothing, but her face betrayed her concern. And curiosity.

Bayard was the only one who seemed unfazed. He continued to play with Cinder, who had simply accepted the faces outside as perfectly normal.

The townspeople had adjourned to the small reception area, and though they had closed the door behind them, their voices could be heard, muffled. At times they rose in what could only be anger.

The faces at the window had disappeared. Even Dünker was nowhere to be seen.

"Shoulda known it was too good to be true," Trout said, swirling the last of his beer around his glass. "Beautiful town, nice people. Is it too much to ask to have one pleasant night before we head to the Fae Kingdom?"

"Apparently it is," Brandy replied.

The door swung open, and everyone sat up in their seats.

Brad led the locals back into the bar. Some were definitely unhappy. That much was clear.

As the others took seats around the pub, Brad sat at the bar next to Sean.

"Right," he started. "We clearly have some things to explain to you. It was either that or kill you, but we opted for the simpler solution."

When the Grumbles reacted with alarm, Brad laughed and did a small drumroll on the bar.

"Just kidding!" he said. "Trying to lighten the mood. Maybe the wrong tone to set. Not my forte. Relax. We were never going to kill you."

"Great," Trout answered. "I feel so much better. Say, can I get another Allagash? It seems like I might need it."

"Help yourself," Brad said, indicating the tap handle on the other side of the bar.

Trout reached over and refilled his glass, before settling back onto his stool.

"We called Bert down in Brunswick," Brad went on. "He clearly knows us here, so we had to check up on you. He explained what's going on, although I suspect he left a lot out."

"I'm not even sure *I* understand everything that's happening," Sean said.

"You should know, Bert just had a touch of trouble down in Brunswick," Brad said. "I know you know about the Underworld Railroad. Well, we have been the end stop for it. But the other side is finally zeroing in on us. They showed up down his way and apparently things got rough."

"Is everyone all right?" Trout asked, putting his beer down. "We have some good friends there with him."

"They got through it," Brad said. "But they were pretty lucky. One of the shifters got dinged up pretty bad. That could be touch and go."

"Which one?" Sean asked quickly.

"I think he said Greg? Craig?" Brad replied. "Hopefully that will turn out okay. But you should know the Dullahan was there. Along with a lot of other nasties. It's important because we are the last stop on the Railroad. This is where all the refugees are sent."

"Makes sense," Brandy said. "Isolated. Beautiful. Space for them to roam."

Brad nodded. "At first, the town didn't realize it was happening. But we're pretty tight knit here and eventually we noticed too many little things to ignore. Little houses. Gifts left on doorsteps. Chores done by...no one. We put out gifts in return. One thing led to another. Once we contacted them—or more accurately, they made themselves known—we grew together in a pretty special way. We look out for them. Keep their secrets. We're part of the Railroad now. We take protecting them seriously."

A woman at a nearby table rose and said, "They are our wards. If anything happens to them because of you, you will have an entire town very angry with you."

Bayard finally turned in his stool to face her. "We hear you. We're here to help, not hurt. Hopefully, we'll be out of your way in the morning. We want nothing more than for these poor souls to find peace."

The woman nodded and sat, but she was clearly far from entirely satisfied.

"Jessi, we talked about this," Brad said, hands raised. "Bert made it clear we should help these folks. They're the good guys."

"We have good intentions, at least," Brandy said.

"Our worries are that you being here will draw too much attention," Brad continued. "If this place is discovered, we'll have to relocate them all. That's not a small project. We weren't even aware of the portal in Gulliver's Hole. It must have been unused for a very long time."

"We'll be gone in the morning," Sean reiterated.

"You should also know that there is another group on its way here," Brad said. "A very large group. Maybe doubling the number of refugees we have. Your friends Kath and Mal are driving them up. They should be here sometime tomorrow. However, the Dullahan is on the loose. I have a bad feeling things are about to get messy."

Brandy suddenly looked up at Sean. "That gnome house we saw on the way in!" she said. "We thought it was just a quirky decoration. Maybe...?"

"Interesting," Brad said. "Most people can't see that. Seeing as we're all on the same page now, maybe we should let our guests in. They're dying to meet you. And play some music. No reason not to."

Bayard was grinning as one of the locals crossed to the door and opened it. What had been a low hum underneath their discussion erupted in high-pitched squeals and cries. Into the room poured a host of creatures of all shapes and sizes, although most were less than three feet tall.

Some were covered in thick fur, looking for all the world like sentient hedgehogs. Some looked like the Little People they had seen in Montauk months ago. The most striking were of a deep ebony shade, with beautifully colored wings, like a swarm of butterflies, who soared and flitted about the room.

Last of all, Dünker came bounding into the pub. His face, the color of old cheese, was radiating joy. He stood taller than most of the newcomers and was reveling in their company, running from one group to another, singing and slapping backs. In the midst of it all, he turned to look back at where Trout was sitting at the bar. He smiled then and waved. A full body wave that shook him from side to side.

In mere moments, the music started again. This time, it was the townsfolk joined by the dozens of tiny Fae. The pub became a festival of light, and music, and guileless joy. All these creatures, from different homes, cultures, traditions, united. United in the simplest of things that they all shared. A community that had every excuse to be angry, or sullen, or defensive, had chosen to find the good in their situation.

Sean stood and made his way to Brad, who had joined a table of musicians playing some Counting Crows and eliciting a sing-along. Briefly, he joined in, and grinned as the room began to fill with golden light again.

He asked Brad if he could have a word, and the two stepped behind the bar where the crowd was thinner.

"I was just wondering," Sean said, "what happens if trouble does show up here? There must be some sort of defense in place, right? I can't believe the Railroad would just drop these people here and—that's that."

"No, you're right," Brad said, angling himself away from the rest of the room. "There are arrangements. We should have known this day would come, but we've probably been a bit naïve. There are others to step in if needed. But I hope we never need them."

"I thought I saw something out there," Sean said. "On the way from the brewery. Something...big."

"If so, they may be gathering already," Brad replied. "It's very rare for anyone to see them. If that's what it was."

"We'll be out of your way early," Sean said. "I really hope we haven't made things worse for you."

"Not your fault," Brad said. "If Gulliver's Hole is what you say, this day was always coming. Better it be you than someone with worse intentions. Sunrise tomorrow is just after seven. Not saying you should get out that early, but it really is an experience to be there when the sun rises and hits the coast for the first time."

"Yeah, I've read about it," Sean said. "I think I'd like to see it."

"You should relax while you can," Brad said, pointing into the pub. "Nights like this don't happen often here. And may never again. Sing. Make friends. Have that beer you turned down earlier."

"Thanks, I will," Sean said, facing the festivities.

Trout had the little troll on his lap and was telling tall tales about his mother punching a bear in Montana. His audience was rapt and howled with laughter.

Bayard was in the midst of the Little People, singing and placing them on Cinder's back to take wild rides around the room.

Even Brandy had shaken off her malaise and joined a table with a mandolin and an Irish flute.

Sean felt the pull of the frivolity. But his feet carried him to the window facing the street. The brilliant light spilled out, making it difficult to see very far. But he couldn't shake his unease at the memory of the large shape he had seen. What had they stumbled into? And how many lives would be upended, or worse, by their decisions tomorrow.

Finally, Brandy came and dragged him back to the music. Eventually, he allowed himself to relax. And he sang. And was happy.

Sean woke early. The sun was still down, and a brisk wind was whistling down the street outside the window. He heard Brandy in the other bed before he turned to see that she was very much happily, and noisily, asleep. She'd pulled her covers up around her, and only a small piece of her face was poking out. The noisiest piece.

He couldn't help but smile at her. The night had stretched long. Many beers were shared, and songs were sung, and Sean had learned more than he'd ever expected to know about Little People of the Fae. Pukwudgies, Aziza, The People of the Shinnecock, Menehune, Brownies, Jogahoh, even Leprechauns. All assembled under one roof. The memory was a swirl of color and joy and... sadness.

Every one of them, including himself and his friends, had wound up here because their way of life was threatened. And while, for at least that one night, they had found refuge in each other. In their shared fears and hopes. In their desire for a quiet, gentle life. The melancholy beneath it all was proof that everyone knew the end of the story had not yet been written.

Sean swung himself out of bed and checked the time. Sunrise was over thirty minutes off, and he would have time to drive out to the West Quoddy Head Lighthouse to see the first rays of the day. The first rays to hit the contiguous U.S.

And maybe it wasn't a bad idea to see where it was they would all find themselves later in the day. The park that housed the lighthouse was also the home of Gulliver's Hole. And if the Keeper had been right, their best hope of gaining access to the Otherworld.

He slipped quietly out of the room and down the staircase to the front door. The Bronco was parked out front and Trout had left the keys with the front desk in case anyone had needed them. Considerate, but also probably influenced by the beer haze of the end of the night.

He was shocked at how every evidence of the night before was gone. No empty glasses though the door in the bar. No tables moved about the floor. Not even plates full of scraps left in the bus tubs in back of the wait station.

As he climbed in and fired up the big truck, he didn't see the curtains of the room next to his twitch. The room in which Bayard and Trout were staying. He also didn't notice the curtains of the lobby office open slightly before closing quickly. It wouldn't have mattered. He needed to see West Quoddy. And somehow, he knew he had to see it alone.

The drive was a quick quarter of an hour. Along the way, he passed the Grand Manan Channel on the left and many stunning vistas of small coves and marshes. If he hadn't been on a schedule, he would have stopped any number of times. But he was, and he pushed on.

The glow of morning revealed a ground fog as he pulled off the road into the parking area, the red and white tower of the light becoming more visible in the rising dawn. He parked and climbed out of the cab, his feet hitting the gravel parking lot with a crunch that sounded like a cannon blast in the total silence. He almost apologized for the disturbance before reminding himself that he was the only one here.

An eagle on an early morning hunt sailed slowly over, and Sean stopped to admire it. The January chill of Maine took no time in seeping into his bones, and he was reminded that he was still existing on the clothes he'd packed for Lancaster months ago. Probably should have picked up a heavier coat along the way. You know, in all his spare time.

He started down the hill toward the lighthouse, its light flashing over him every fifteen seconds. The foghorn called out every thirty seconds, a plaintive sound disappearing over the nearly invisible waters beyond. His feet crunched on the frost-covered grass as he made his way toward the water. Again, he felt guilty for disturbing the pristine silence of the scene.

He found he had just enough signal to look up some facts about the spot. "Quoddy" means "fertile and beautiful" in the native Passamaquoddy language. He was sure that in better conditions that would prove true. This morning, though, it seemed like a grey-swept impressionist painting, full of softened corners and mingling hues.

He reached the lawn by the Keeper's House and the tower, standing to peer out over the sea far below. The sound of the waves the only evidence to his senses of what lay at the foot of the rocks.

He knew that the park stretched off to the right. Hundreds of acres of trails through forest and bogland. Along cliffs and through trees to a rocky beach. It was at the bottom of one of those cliffs that Gulliver's Hole would be found. Tide would be low by early afternoon, and that is when they would need to make their attempt at entering.

What would they find? Would they find a path to the Fae lands? Would Breena be there? Would she be happy to see him? Or had she thrown her lot in with the opposition? He had so many questions. So many doubts. About everything including himself.

This was why he knew he'd had to come alone. Too many thoughts. Too many fears. Too many hopes.

It was while he was lost in those musings that he suddenly was ripped back to reality. To where he was standing. He sensed it before he heard it. And then it was there. The almost whisper-soft brush of footsteps over the grass. So much quieter than his clumsy boots had been.

He didn't turn. Whoever it was, was already beside him. Had eluded his heightened perception almost entirely. Without turning, he said, "Friend or foe?"

There was a lengthy pause. Finally, a deep, thrumming voice answered. "Neither. But I am friend to your friends, so that seems a good place to start."

Sean turned and nearly gasped when he discovered who had joined him. He had seen many things in the past few months and weeks. But nothing quite like the massive form that stood now next to him.

It was the shape of a man, but well over ten feet tall. Covered entirely in hair, long flowing brown hair, it was dressed in a simple cloak with dark woven pants. Its feet were bare, and like its face, entirely covered in hair. The face that turned to consider Sean was keenly intelligent, and the deep-set eyes seemed to be obsidian black, but shining with intelligence. And purpose.

"It was you I saw last night, wasn't it?" Sean asked. "On the street when the crowd was headed to Cohill's."

"No," the creature answered. "It would have been one of my tribe. You would be the first to ever sense one of us without our consent. Interesting."

Sean nodded. "But you, or your tribesman, was outside the pub during the music."

"We were all there," the voice rumbled back. "We enjoy a session as much as the next, but we have a job to do."

Sean was silent for a moment, letting this news simmer. Pieces were clicking into place.

"You work for the Railroad," Sean said, finally. "You protect the refugees."

"We do," he answered.

"And I would think my being here is upsetting a lot of your work," Sean continued.

"It is," came the answer. "But this is a day we always knew would come. We are not unprepared. That does not make the situation easier."

"I never wanted to hurt anyone. Or expose vulnerable people to danger," Sean said. "But this is the only path that was shown us. It seems this is the only place where we can do what we must do."

"Not the only," was the answer. "But the most logical. For now."

"I'm sorry," Sean said, turning now fully to the man.

"I know," he replied. "But that will not change things. We are sworn to protect those who seek peace."

"I don't want to stop that," Sean said, realizing that his voice sounded much more pleading than he'd intended.

"And so you won't. We'll make sure of that."

"Can I ask who you are? Can I help?" Sean asked, his voice sounding even more plaintive. Who was this person?

"You can," came the answer.

A lengthy silence followed. Sean almost wondered if the question had been forgotten. He turned a questioning look at the newcomer.

"It's not a simple answer," he said. "I am a Guardian. I always have been, but I, and my kind, have been called to service as the worlds continue to collide. The drift of time seems to be unstoppable now. If I were to break your neck now, which make no mistake, I could, I may be able to halt things. But even then...maybe not. And besides. That is not our way. We are the Guardians."

Sean nodded slowly, feeling the truth of the words. "And who exactly are *you*? And who makes up your tribe? And thank you for not killing me."

"You may not thank me for that before it is all done," the man said. "I am a Woodwose, in your language, although there are many names for us. Green Man, Sasquatch, Yeti, Bigfoot, Almas, Orang Pendek. Your kind has given us many names over time. We have always existed to protect. Mother Earth was our first charge. And she remains that. Not an easy task with your kind doing all they can to destroy what makes her...perfect."

Sean acknowledged that with a rueful shake of his head.

"But now there are threats to...others. And we answer the call. You may call me Greenwood. That is the simplest way for you to pronounce my name."

"Thank you for sharing that with me," Sean answered. "I always wanted to believe your kind exist. The world just seems better with you in it. To me, anyway."

"We are a secretive people," Greenwood said. "We never wanted attention. We never wanted to know you. No offense. We only wanted to preserve the green spaces, the natural spaces, of the world. But it was not enough. We were not enough. This place was chosen because we hoped it would be removed enough. And then the nearly miraculous relationship with the town developed and gave us hope. But if the fight arrives here, as we now think it will, the refugees will be moved yet again."

"You keep saying 'we,' and mentioned another tribesman was there last night," Sean said. "How many of you are there?"

"Enough," Greenwood replied.

As if on cue, a shower of pebbles and small stones began to fall around Sean. None of them actually struck him, but more than one came close. At the same time, a percussive knocking echoed around the small clearing where they were standing. Finally, a chorus of guttural cries went up from everywhere around them. Full-throated and animalistic, they flew around the space, echoing and eventually sailing out over the water.

Sean turned slowly and was somehow unsurprised to see the entire tree line filled with figures as massive as Greenwood. Some larger. They were of varying shades—some a dusty white, some grey, some deep pitch black. The stones slowed and stopped, but many of them continued to thump their massive hands on the tree trunks where they stood.

"Ah, I see," Sean muttered.

"We will not harm you, Sean Curley," Greenwood said. "But neither can we give you aid. We exist solely to protect those who deserve and need protection. You are not that. And here we will intervene only for the refugees. That said, you do not need to worry for them. They will be well cared for. You and your friends should focus only on yourselves."

"Good to know," Sean said. "Thanks for the warning. Or advice? I'm not really sure what that was. Hey, do the townspeople know about you? Just curious who is in on things."

At that moment, the sun lifted its head above the horizon and the Gulf of Maine was lit like a flame, a tongue of orange sunlight reaching across the water to where he stood. The lighthouse warmed, as if reaching out to the new day, and far out on the water a single lobster boat chugged slowly back to the harbor while seals on the distant rocks turned their wise faces to the sunrise.

"Just wondering if I can say anything to them. The townspeople?" Sean asked again, after giving the rising sun the moment it deserved.

Silence.

He turned to find Greenwood gone. Sean spun to take in the edge of the forest, but it, too, was empty. If it weren't for the scattered stones and rocks around his feet, he would have doubted the entire experience.

Shaking his head yet again, he started up the hill toward the Bronco. The warmth of the morning was reaching him now and the low fog began to burn off. He made the short drive back to town, thinking about tall tales and legends, and how truth was often found somewhere along the way to them.

He turned on the stereo and played Lyle Lovett. Because that cowboy-poet almost always made him feel better while making him feel wiser. He needed both right now.

Sean was surprised to find himself following two school buses down Main Street when he got back to Lubec. The town seemed small to have *two* school buses. When he saw them pull up in front of Cohill's, it dawned on him. Kath and Mal had arrived. This was confirmed when Mal stepped off the first bus, shielding her eyes from the bright morning sun. She seemed unsure of where to go, but spotted the Bronco and waved, her shoulders relaxing noticeably.

Sean pulled up behind the buses, killed the engine, and jumped down to the sidewalk.

"You're in the right place, Mal!" he called. "Welcome to Lubec. We had word you were coming."

"Glad we made it!" she called back. "And wait until you meet our passengers!"

"Wait until you meet the townsfolk!" Sean returned.

Kath emerged from the other bus, her red tangle of curls a testament to the night they'd spent outside at the pond. She quickly popped on a pair of sunglasses.

"Cripes," she said. "Is the sun brighter up here?"

Trout, Brandy, and Bayard tumbled out of the inn, rushing to greet the newcomers. Trout being sure to introduce the others, somehow dumbfounded that they had managed not to meet already.

Brad appeared walking down the street from the direction of the brewery. He seemed to be the de facto leader of the town, and Sean doubted much happened without his knowledge.

Sean saw that the tide was going out and the seals were back, riding the whirlpool by the jetty. This time, though, he was sure he spotted at least one selkie, the shapeshifting seal-people they had encountered in Montauk. He breathed a sigh of relief. They could use all the friends they could find at this point. He made eye contact with Bayard and nodded toward the water. Bayard followed his gaze and nodded. Confirmation.

Brad arrived and spoke quietly to Mal and Kath. The buses were abuzz with chatter from the passengers. Sean caught a glimpse of some of them, faces pressed to the windows, curious to see what their new home would be. Not entirely unlike the students who used to ride the buses, curious and eager. Sean felt a pang at the knowledge that this may not be their final stop.

Brad broke away and entered the inn. Within five minutes, the street began to fill with the locals, all coming toward the new arrivals. Most came bearing small gifts: baked goods, keepsakes, hats, even a growler or three of the local beer. Obviously, Lubec had firmly embraced their role as the final stop on the Railroad. If not for the air clearing of the night before, Sean was sure he and his friends would have been excluded from this scene. He was glad to witness it. It added to his resolve to see things set right.

Hugs and welcomes out of the way, Sean motioned for the others to follow him inside, leaving Mal, Kath, and the townsfolk to sort the new arrivals. They climbed the stairs to room number nine, where Sean and Brandy stayed.

Trout whistled long and low when he came in the doorway and saw their windows looking out over the water.

"Well, damn," he said, "even I would have bunked with Brandy if I'd known this was the situation."

"Gee, thanks," Brandy replied.

Sean perched on the windowsill, the little lighthouse across the canal in Canada over his shoulder. Bayard fixing a curious stare on him.

"Oh, and thanks for bringing the Bronco back in one piece," Trout joked. "Find anything out?"

With a quick glance at Bayard, Sean said, "Actually, I did. Quite a bit."

And with that, he shared with them all he'd discovered. The lay of the lighthouse, the park, the quiet of the landscape. And, most importantly, the existence of the Guardians and what it meant for their success. Ot more succinctly, what it didn't mean.

"What you're saying is, we're on our own," Brandy said, when he had finished.

"Yeah, pretty much," Sean agreed.

"But we are absolved of worrying about the refugees," Bayard pointed out. "That was weighing on me. Greatly. Not a small thing."

"He's right," Trout said. "I mean, and Fae types around that are *not* out to get us—a good thing, right?"

"Can't argue with that," Sean admitted. "Tide is in by one o'clock. I think we need to be ready to head into the cave then. The longer we wait, the more chance we meet more bad guys. That Dullahan is out there. We know he doesn't take a break."

"I agree," Bayard said. "But I do have some questions. Do we know where the cave actually is? Or are we going to have to search? That's the first thing."

"We know exactly where it is," Sean answered. "It's well marked on maps. We just don't have any information on its current state. How accessible it is. Someone will have to get down there first to scope it out."

"Not easy, from what I was told last night," Trout said. "Steep cliffs, tricky tides. I'm probably too big to do it, but I'm happy to try."

"I'm the logical choice," Bayard cut in. "No offense, but I'm definitely the most physical of us. Yes, I know you're a senior citizen Olympian, Trout. But still."

"Too bad one of us can't fly," Brandy said. "That would make the whole thing a helluva lot easier."

The conversation halted when they heard a gentle tapping on the window. The second-floor window. Turning as one, they all stopped short. There was a face at the window. A beautiful dark Aziza, though not one they recognized from the night before. Her iridescent wings were lazily fluttering behind her. Cinder's tail was wagging in rhythm, and Dünker could barely stand still at the sight.

"Um. I fly. I couldn't help but hear what you were saying," she said quietly. "I'm Selam. I helped your friend Bert. I think I can help you."

"Couldn't help but hear?" Brandy guffawed. "You're eavesdropping at our window fifteen feet off the ground!"

The little Aziza grinned in response and Sean held a hand out to still Brandy.

Against his better judgment, and with images of Greenwood foremost in his mind, Sean opened the window. As the precocious Aziza made her case, she wore them all down. Not long after, they had the shape of a plan. Well, the shape of a shape. But it was something.

They retreated to gather what they needed. They would leave for West Quoddy and Gulliver's Hole in thirty minutes. It was time.

***

The Bronco pulled away from Cohill's full to bursting. And it was a collection of creatures Sean would never have foreseen. Trout drove with Sean riding shotgun. In the back, Brandy sat behind Sean and continually waved her hands about her hand, fending off the excited flutterings of the Aziza, the little Aziza. In the bed all the way in back, Dünker excitedly placed his hands and face on the rear window, and when Trout asked him to move to clear the view, the troll did so but left a greasy smear on the window that was too murky to penetrate. Cinder sat with her head over the rear seat headrest, her tongue lolling, a smile on her face, luxuriating in absentminded ear scritches from Bayard.

Sean couldn't shake his misgivings. All of the creatures in this truck meant so much to him. Even the newest addition. He was particularly worried about her, because her enthusiasm caused him to fear that she didn't understand the gravity of their task. That, and he wondered if Greenwood and the Watchers would interpret this as a threat to her safety. Was he creating more problems by including her? He hoped not, but knew he was in uncharted territory. For the first time in a while, he had felt weak beside Greenwood. In the presence of all the Watchers.

He hadn't enjoyed the feeling, but maybe, just maybe, it was a good reminder to not take anything for granted. Nothing.

As they pulled into the gravel lot Sean had left not long before, he found his eyes scanning the edge of the lawns, searching for any sign of the Watchers. He knew it was futile. Even with his experience of detecting the Peripherals, the Watchers were cut from a different cloth. They would only be seen when they chose to be seen.

But he was also alert for anything else amiss. The Dullahan, with his armies of Red Caps and Hide-Behinds could easily be in the area. And Balor had been sent on his way, but not defeated. The word from Monhegan had been very clear on that point. He also knew they were in the natural environment of the Wendigo, the indigenous Skin-walker. Just one of them had nearly been enough to finish them when they crossed paths in Montauk.

Although the parking lot remained empty, having companions with him somehow made the park and lighthouse less empty. Less foreboding. The lighthouse was closed for the season, but the park remained open. They were lucky to find it quiet. So far.

Sean had brought a map of the park up on his phone. Referring to it, he stopped the group at the edge of the parking area.

"My bad," he said, holding the screen up for others to see. "There's actually a parking area at the head of the trail we need. Better drive over there. If we need a fast escape, the quicker the better."

"Yessir!" Brandy said, snapping a salute at Sean. "Just kidding, Ginge. Lighten up. You're absolutely right. I'm all for a clean getaway."

They made their way to the Bronco, but as they were piling in, all of their Fae companions paused. Cinder's nose was in the air, quivering. Dünker's eyes became hooded and fearful. Selam fluttered nervously by the truck, her wings no longer languid and relaxed, but twitchy. Agitated.

It was Bayard who commanded the most attention, though. He

stood, entirely still, his wrists flicking his long blades in and out of his sleeves. He closed his eyes, listening, sensing, rather than seeing.

"We're not alone," he said quietly. "I don't know where to focus. There is...so much."

"We never thought we'd sneak through this unseen!" Trout called, gunning the engine. "Sooner we get to it the better, I say!"

Bayard nodded once and followed the others into the truck, never taking his eyes from the trees.

They traveled backward on South Lubec Road, turning left on an unpaved park road. The only other visible park road, for that matter. It ended in a looped parking area. The drive took less than five minutes, and once again Trout pulled up, this time facing out over the Gulf of Maine.

Brandy gave a whistle. Trout's mouth fell open. Even Bayard seemed impressed by the vista. They all slowly disembarked, eyes on the water ahead of them.

"Well, I don't know how this can be a forgotten portal, or a forgotten anything for that matter," Trout said, striding forward onto a grass swath between the lot and the trail that led off to the right, into the forest. "This is one of the most beautiful sights I've ever seen. And I'm from Montana."

The others silently agreed. The waters were a brilliant blue, almost turquoise, with shades of brilliant azure and deeper royal blue. If they hadn't known better, they might have thought they were in the Caribbean.

The trees were tall, weathered, knotted survivors. Many had been bent throughout the years by the sea winds and looked to be leaning over, reaching long arm-like branches inland. One particular tree, though, stood tall and straight. Solitary. Some sort of pine.

"I hope we don't rain down destruction on this place today," Sean said quietly. "This is a place I could spend the rest of my days just...looking."

Over the trees, the light from the tower continued to swing past them, barely visible in the daylight, but refusing to let its presence go unnoticed.

"'There is something about a lighted beacon which suggests hope and trust and appeals to the better instincts of all mankind,'" Trout spoke into the wind.

"Emerson?" Sean asked.

"No, Edward Rowe Snow," Trout answered.

"Who? You are a mystery, in a riddle, wrapped in a conundrum," Brandy said. "How do you know this crap?"

"That's what I do. I drink and I know things. Actually, this time I just read it on the website," he answered, holding up his phone.

"You are such a jerk," Brandy said, while Sean and Bayard laughed.

"Don't think we can put this off any longer," Sean admitted. "We go to the right. The Coastal Trail. Anyone has second thoughts, no shame. Stay with the truck. And if you see something, say something. Don't hold back. You ready?"

The response was underwhelming, but no one climbed back into the truck. The little troll clung to Trout's back like a toddler. Cinder's nose alternated between the wind and the path in front of them. Selam floated above them as if this had been her home for years. It took only a few steps for the forest to swallow them.

The trail, once clear of the public parking area, turned to dirt, and though the morning sun was still climbing in the sky, they quickly fell under the shadow of the trees that lined the path. The company marched onward; the trail surprisingly easy for them. Enough so, that Trout let Dünker down to scamper at their feet. The path was still moist from the early fog, but despite the occasional muddy spot, they found the going quick.

Sean was still holding his phone in front of him, watching the park map that he had located.

"Pretty soon, we should come clear of the trees on the left and reach some of the cliffs and rocky paths heading to the water," he said. "I thought it would be a much longer walk, but things seem to be moving pretty fast. In fact"—he paused briefly—"yeah, the beach with all the boulders should be just up here."

They maneuvered around a few more corners, and just as he'd said, the trees to their left fell away and the water, cerulean and navy, stretched away to the horizon.

"Good lord," Brandy said, "why isn't this place on every tourist brochure? I have never seen anything so pristine. It's stunning."

Bayard was silent but nodded his agreement. It was obvious, though, that he was preoccupied with locating whoever or whatever was in the park with them. Cinder, too, was preoccupied, yipping at Selam who kept trying to get him to play with her.

"Yup, rocky beach right there," Sean said, face still in his screen. "Now we start uphill, and we should be...almost...there."

"Might want to get your face outta that phone, Sean," Trout said. "First, it's really beautiful, and second, the last time I saw Nick do that on a cliff he almost went over the side. Just saying."

Their collective memories flashed back to Montauk, on their first adventure together, and the strangled cry as Nick almost went over a hundred-foot cliff because he'd blinded himself with his phone screen.

"Point taken," Sean said, putting his phone away. "Couple more turns and...keep your eyes for a 'foaming sea pocket.' The Keeper said there was a cave opening at the back of it. That's Gulliver's Hole."

"You have no idea how hard it is to not make jokes," Brandy quipped. "Foaming Sea Pocket...Gulliver's Hole...You're serving them up on a platter."

"Focus, Brandy," Sean said, but couldn't hold in a laugh.

In no time at all, they found themselves high above the water, staring down the tumbled boulders to the crashing waves so far below. As the waves receded, they could hear the stones being slammed against each other and a rattling, booming accompaniment was added to the scene.

"Tide looks pretty much out," Trout said, nodding to the exposed rocky shore. "Good timing."

The cliffs had become more pronounced and the trail, with no handrails in most places, suddenly felt a good deal more dangerous. Instinctively, Sean and Brandy hugged the trees on the right side of the trail. Bayard and Trout, on the other hand, seemed drawn to the edge, walking closer and staring at the drop.

As they reached the highest point, Sean stopped and pointed.

"There," he said, his voice full of tension and excitement. "That froth of surf right there. That has to be it."

They all gathered at the spot above where he'd indicated. The way down, if it could be called that, was steep. Steeper than any other spot until now. It looked almost impassable from this vantage, but they knew that adventurous hikers made it down to the bottom, so they would have to find a way.

"Selam," Sean said, quietly, "this is your moment. Do you still feel like you can fly down to check for the cave? Don't worry if it's too much, we'll find a way."

"Silly," Selam replied with a laugh that scattered like petals on the wind. "This is easy. And it's beautiful here. I *want* to go!"

Before anyone else could respond, she rose up into the air, catching a draft and sailed out over the cliff edge. Sean knew she was in her element, but still felt his throat catch at the sight. It may have been a mistake to include her, but it had seemed the best way. At the time.

Selam turned and gave them a shy wave as she reached her highest point before turning and diving in a fluttering descent. She sailed around three trunks and boulders the size of Trout's Bronco on the way. Quickly, she disappeared from view, and everyone held their breath, waiting for her to reappear.

And there she was! Finding an air current and riding it effortlessly to the cliff top where they stood waiting. Her smile was contagious, brilliant white in her midnight skin.

"It's there!" she cried. "It's small, and there are large stones everywhere to avoid, but the cave entrance is clear. The climb down is possible. It may be difficult for you, but not impossible. Let's go!"

Not for the first time, Sean was afraid that she didn't fully understand the gravity of the situation, but there was no denying that this would have taken much longer without her.

"Right," Sean said. "I think that Bayard should go first. You're clearly the most agile of us all."

The Peripheral nodded, absently staring into the woods at their backs.

"Trout, what's happening with Dünker" Sean asked, quietly.

"I was thinking he might want to wait in the truck," Trout answered, looking to the troll. "Tough going from here."

"No! No!" came the answer, as he clung to Trout's leg. "Stay with Trout. Stay with Sean. No hide in car. I know rocks. Know climbing. Useful. Not leave Trout. Friend."

Trout stopped to consider. "Okay," he said finally. "You ride piggyback with me. If it gets rough, you can help show us a path. But you stay. With. Me."

The troll cackled high and loud, wiped his nose on Trout's jeans and held on tighter.

Sean turned an expectant eye to Bayard. Carrying Cinder down would be considerably more difficult than hoisting Dünker on his back.

Bayard nodded once and kneeled by the wolf, petting her head tenderly. "I'm afraid you need to stay here," he said quietly. "We can't risk you getting injured on the way down. And I'll be so worried about you, that I may not focus where I need to. And truthfully, if we do find our way to the Otherworld, I'm not sure if you could join us. And I can't abandon you in a cave alone. I'm so sorry, my friend. Stay by the truck. Watch for trouble. I'll be back in no time."

Cinder whined, and looked as if she was about to protest, when Brandy gave a cry and slipped a few feet down the rock face. She grabbed out and caught herself on a tree trunk as she slid past. If she had missed that trunk, it could have been a long fall for her. The group jumped to help her, but without her reflexes she would have been gone.

"Shit," she said. "That could have been really bad."

Trout reached a long arm down and leveraged her back to the cliff top.

"And we were worried about Sean and his phone," Trout said, setting her down. "Glad you're okay. Don't do that to me!"

"To you?" Brandy barked back, before gasping and hopping sideways as she tried to put her feet down. "You have got to be kidding me. Same one I hurt on Monhegan." She tried her weight on the foot again. "Dammit. Sean, I think I sprained something."

Sean pursed his lips and thought.

"Right," he said, finally. "Adapt or die, right? Change of plans."

CHAPTER 17

Brandy was distinctly unhappy as she hobbled along the top of the cliff face, a broken branch she had found pressed into duty as a crutch. Her ankle continued to swell, and she kept reaching to loosen the laces. Soon the boot would be too constricting, no matter what she did. She peeled her sock back and grimaced to see her ankle turning purple. She snapped back to her feet, gingerly, and limped over to where the others were readying to start the descent.

"I saw that," Sean said, as she approached. "That ankle looks bad. You should just go back to the truck and wait. You'll be a sitting duck if anything comes at you here. It's not like you can help us once we head down."

"I didn't come all this way to sit in the car while you guys do all the work," she complained. "I can at least warn you if I see anything. At least give me that. Let me be the rear guard. Or whatever you want to call it."

"Fine," Sean said. "It's against my better judgment, but I guess I'll just add it to the growing list."

"You'll have Cinder," Bayard said, ruffling the wolf's tail. "You two take care of each other. Remember what I said: we're not alone here. So be alert. It may be a blessing in disguise that you stay up here."

"I don't see it that way," Brandy replied. "And my ankle definitely disagrees. I should have kept the damn magic club. I could heal myself. All I have is that mace and whatever it does."

"Hey, Brand," Trout said, approaching, "at least, you have something powerful to guard our flank. I'd give you the Singing Sword, but I have a feeling we're going to need it where we're going. Just stay safe, yeah? We're about to shake some trees pretty hard. Don't want anything falling on you."

You just mind yourself, Trout," Brandy answered. "We'll be fine up here. Just go. Get some answers, and let's move on."

"That's the plan!" Trout said, grinning as he started down the rocky cliff, Dünker clinging to him.

Sean gave Brandy an apologetic look. "I know this isn't what we planned. But we're all in it together, however it plays out."

He, too, followed Trout over the edge and headed toward the rocky shore below.

Bayard gave a last look at Cinder and started down, before turning back and giving the wolf a quick hug. "Stay safe," he whispered.

There was a very rough path between the largest boulders that only became obvious when they grew closer. For just a moment, Sean thought maybe they had overestimated how tricky it would be, but he rounded a corner and stopped short when he found the others standing still, contemplating a larger drop than they had yet faced.

Selam flew overhead and called out to them, "No, not there. It leads nowhere. To your right and past the trunk with moss on the upper side. You'll see the path pick up there!"

Sean waved his thanks, and she flew off, scouting ahead. As bad an idea as including her still seemed, he realized they would have been dealing with worse than a sprained ankle without her. Glancing to the others, he saw Bayard returning his look and he knew the truth of it, too.

Scrambling as directed, Bayard found the tree trunk and continued on toward the beach. The rest of the way continued in much the same way. Every time the climbers found themselves stuck, the little Aziza appeared to guide them. It took them forty minutes, but they did eventually reach the shore, Selam landed to dance at their feet.

"Told you! Told you!" she cried. "We make a good team. Little doesn't mean helpless!"

"Far from it," Bayard said, shaking her small hand. "You're the hero of the day. We are all in your debt."

"The cave is over here," she answered. "Follow me. It's deep. The doorway you look for must be hidden far inside. I will find it!"

She flew quickly off, despite Bayard's attempt to get her to slow down and wait for them.

She disappeared twenty yards along the beach. One second, she was there, the next she turned toward the cliff face and... vanished.

The others hurried after her. The troll was excitedly pointing at every new thing he saw. It was all Trout could do to keep him on his back. Sean put his head down and hurried after the Aziza, anxious to get to the real work.

And so, it was only Bayard who heard a rustling in the trees above them. And further up, where he had left Brandy and his beloved Cinder, he heard a rushing sound like the wind ripping through the forest. And in that rushing, he heard the tramp of many feet. Heavy feet, shod with heavy boots. Even all this way down the cliff, he could feel the ground shake beneath him.

Be safe, Cinder, he thought, sending the wish out into the morning.

Twenty minutes after the others had disappeared over the edge, Brandy grew restless pacing back and forth on her damaged ankle.

She began to strike her makeshift crutch on one of the boulders by the side of the trail.

Cinder cast a disapproving look her way, and stayed where she was, seated at the edge of the descent, her nose twitching in the air and her ears pivoting with each new sound from the forest.

Cinder and Brandy both froze suddenly when an answer to Brandy's thumps found its way back to them. Somewhere in the trees, something was pounding on a tree, the hollow knocking ricocheting to and around them.

Brandy stopped immediately and turned to the wolf.

"Obviously, you heard that, too," she said quietly.

Cinder showed that she did with a cock of her head, rising to her feet and turning to face the woods behind them.

"Well, Bayard did say we aren't alone here. Guess it was just a matter of time."

No sooner were the words out of her mouth than the sound of marching feet reached them from a completely different direction. A lot of feet. Coming from the opposite direction of the parking area, further into the wilds of the park.

"But that I really don't like," Brandy whispered. "Any ideas?"

Cinder took a few steps in the direction of the steps, nose held high. She began to growl, low and angry.

"They're getting closer," Brandy said. "We're completely exposed here. Into the trees? But we need to warn the others."

Cinder moved to stand at the precipice and lifted her head to howl. A high, piercing keen that cut through the wind where they stood. But would it reach them so far below, with the waves crashing next to them?

Slowly Brandy and Cinder backed into the cover of the trees. The ground off the path was loamy and thick. It became wetter as the path grew farther away. It was harder to move and even more difficult to keep silent. They found a small, sheltered space between the trees of a clustered copse, and settled in. Aware of every breath they took.

On the beach, the others reached the mouth of the cave. It looked more like a hole in the cliff than like a cave leading anywhere and Sean felt an adrenaline rush of panic. What if they were wrong? What if this was the wrong place? What would they do?

Any thoughts along that path were dispelled when he saw Selam reappear at the opening.

"Friends," she called, "it's exactly as you said. And it's beautiful. Follow!"

She hovered for a moment, her wings catching the sunlight as it bounced off the rushing waves behind them. Her face was lit by the purest smile Sean could ever recall, and he wondered if all Aziza were so joyous, or if she was just an exceptional individual. He suspected some of both.

They followed her slowly into the opening, picking their way cautiously among the slick, wet stones of the beach. This was far more treacherous than the descent had been. Random waves crept into the opening and eddied around their feet. A reminder of what happened when the tide came in. And of how cold Maine was in January.

Bayard allowed the others to precede him into the cave. Dünker was kicking Trout's side, willing him to go faster, and Trout played along with a game of giddyup.

Bayard paused before he entered the darkness. There was something—something beyond the pounding footsteps they heard from above. This was closer. Quieter. More sinister. Stealthy enough to escape almost any detection. But he was a Peripheral. He sensed whatever it was. Just barely.

He sent a call out to the animals nearby, asking for information. He wanted to know more, but his friends were already disappearing around a corner. And he knew they would need him. Soon.

Cinder's hackles were raised, but she knew better than to make a sound. Brandy watched the path, not daring to blink. The sound of boots was almost upon them, and she silently drew the mystical mace out of her pack. So much had happened in the few days, that she hadn't had a moment to look at, or practice with, the weapon. Something she regretted now.

Around a bend to their right, shapes began to emerge. She recognized them from the descriptions of the Fulton Battle that she had heard. Red Caps. Dammit. At least two dozen. Large, goblin-like creatures, all carrying crude but deadly iron pikes. They were clad in sturdy, basic leather with thick, clumsy boots designed to protect and inflict harm. They all wore hats in various shades of red. Brandy knew that the deeper the shade, the more kills that creature had to their credit, as their habit was to soak their caps in the blood of their fallen enemies. As they drew in front, just where the others had gone over the cliff, they suddenly stopped and faced the water.

Brandy realized that they were setting up to wait for Sean and the others to return. To ambush them when they had finished what they needed to do in the Fae kingdom. Diabolical. After all they would have come through, they would finally arrive at the trail again after the difficult climb, only to be greeted by this.

Brandy rested her forehead on the shaft of the mace. What had she gotten into? What good would she be with only one good leg and a red wolf to pit against...all of them.

Cinder sensed her unease and nosed her good leg. There was no quit in the little wolf. Brandy couldn't afford to give up either.

She knew what she was about to do was possibly the dumbest thing she had ever tried. But she had to do something before her friends walked, or rather climbed, straight into a trap. *If* they even managed to get back.

She took a deep breath. *Stupid. Stupid.* But she didn't really have a choice.

"Yo!" she shouted. "Yeah, you! Freaky Red Caps! Not a chance I let you hurt my friends, so I give you ten seconds to clear out or it's gonna get messy!"

A ripple ran through the ranks as the Red Caps turned to the sound. They seemed startled at first to find someone lurking behind them, but quickly began to chuckle, a low, barking, ugly laugh, as they realized it was only one person. A woman, hobbling on one leg. And a dog. The laugh was unnatural. It didn't belong in this place of such indescribable beauty. Brandy hated that it was here. That they were here.

They were truly ugly. Long, lank hair fell to below their shoulders. Their skin was sallow. Their eyes were small and cruel. Large teeth jutted from their mouths.

Two of the Red Caps separated themselves from the ranks and approached Brandy and Cinder. The others turned away, dismissing the intruders already. They were large, clumsy looking things, but moved with a speed that surprised Brandy. She put her weight on her good foot and readied herself with the mace as they drew closer. Cinder coiled herself to spring.

What had she gotten herself into? She couldn't take on even these two, let alone the entire squadron. She swung the mace in front of her, warning the Red Caps off, but they didn't even pause in their approach. And there it was again. That ugly cackling. Now they were really pissing her off.

She raised her face to the sky and screamed. Long. High. Loud. And this time the two Red Caps did hesitate. For just the barest fraction of a second. But then they resumed.

Brandy knew she was in trouble.

"Cinder," she said quietly, from the corner of her mouth. "Go. Hide by the truck. Bayard and the others have to know what happened."

But the wolf stood her ground. A low whuff told Brandy that Cinder had no intention of leaving.

"Stubborn wolf."

Out of the corner of her eye, she saw something happening to the mace. It had begun to glow. Faintly. She barely noticed, and the approaching Red Caps definitely hadn't.

Maybe, just maybe?

She'd never tried anything like this before, but she quietly began to hum. Her mouth pressed to the mace.

As she did, the weapon began to glow a deep grey, the color of storm clouds when they appeared on the horizon in the deep heat of summer. She was encouraged and pressed on. Cinder seemed to understand and shot a canine smile at Brandy, while taking up a position to her left, guarding her wounded side.

The glow of the mace grew, and with it, Brandy's tone. Gradually, the tone shifted to a song. A wordless melody that simply...came to her. And with the increase, the Red Caps began to take note.

With a final full-voiced shout-song, Brandy raised the mace high in the air, and out of the corner of her eye, she thought she saw flickers of white light along it. She aimed the mace at the Red Caps, thinking to give them another pause.

She gave them more than that.

The end of the mace erupted in fire and wind and the two Red Caps managed to look surprised before they were incinerated.

"Well, hot damn," Brandy said. "Thank you, Gluskabe."

Cinder rewarded her with a surprised glance, but before they could enjoy the small victory, the rest of the Red Caps turned at the sound. Seeing their two companions reduced to dust, they shifted en masse and began a more deliberate advance on Brandy and Cinder.

"Seemed like a good idea, at the time," Brandy said to Cinder. "If nothing else, I hope this is about to be loud enough for them to be warned down in the cave."

With another wordless melody, she pressed her head to the mace again. The magic in her voice was clearly working with the mace because she had no idea exactly what she was doing.

Cinder suddenly whirled and looked into the forest to their backs, growling.

"Aw, man," Brandy said. "What now?"

She risked a backward glance and caught the flash of a shadow disappear behind one of the trees. And then another.

"Hide-Behinds?" Brandy shouted to the sky. "Okay, Cinder. I don't see myself getting out of this, but you can. Please listen. Run. Wait near the truck. Tell them I tried."

Again, Cinder went nowhere. In fact, she moved closer to Brandy.

Brandy turned toward the approaching Red Caps, knowing that when she looked away the Hide-Behinds would creep closer.

She unleashed another blast from the mace and ten Red Caps fell to dust. But they were immediately replaced by another ten. Behind them, she saw more of them filing down the path. There were far more than just two dozen.

Another blast of the mace flashed. This time the lightning was accompanied by a blast of wind and lashing rain. The Red Caps that weren't immediately eliminated were pushed, flailing, across the ground relentlessly, until many disappeared over the edge and tumbled to the rocks below.

"I think I'm getting the hang of this!" Brandy cried, readying the mace again.

A particularly large Red Cap, with a hat so deeply dyed red it looked black, kept its feet and reached an arm's length of her. Instead of thrusting with the point of its pike, it swept her feet from under her and she fell. Hard. On her injured ankle.

As that happened, she sensed the Hide-Behinds nearby. Cinder spun, trying to keep her safe on two fronts and falling behind. She jumped and grabbed the Red Cap by the throat, sending it reeling away, grasping at the wound.

"Well, this sucks," Brandy gasped, her ankle blazing with pain again.

From the corner of her eye, she saw a green shimmer form between the trees nearby.

"What now?" she whispered. "Bit of overkill, don't you think?"

A figure took shape in the glimmer, and she realized she was looking at a portal. A portal that looked somehow familiar. But in the melee that raged around her, she didn't have the bandwidth to figure out why.

The figure strode forward. It was a man. One she didn't recognize. He was tall, with dark hair swept back, and eyes that quickly took in the situation. He was dressed in a suit that looked outdated. Something from the 1960s. He had a thin tie, impeccably polished black shoes, and the strangest hat she had seen. Wait. No. She *had seen* it before. It couldn't be...

The man lifted a bottle, and behind it placed some sort of can and a stream of liquid shot out into the forest. As it did, the Hide-Behinds, who had nearly reached Brandy and Cinder, began to scream in agony and immediately fell away to nothing where they had been drenched.

Brandy felt something shift in the air behind her, and before she could turn, heard a familiar voice say, "Told ya I'd see you in the funny papers."

She whirled to see Ken O'Carroll, their friend who was lost somewhere in time—had been lost—raise another bottle and send a spray of liquid at the remaining Hide-Behinds, sending them in the opposite direction.

"What the..." Brandy said.

"I fixed the chronovisor," Ken said, with an enormously satisfied smile on his face. "Well, with some help from my pal, Kelvin. Say hi, Kelvin!"

The other man raised a hand and shouted a greeting.

"Ran into him in the sixties," Ken said. Then whispered, "He's CIA."

"But, how—"

"We can talk about that later," Ken interrupted. "Why don't you use that magic club thing to finish off the Red Caps first? Nice trick, by the way. I don't have long. We're still figuring some time travel things out."

Brandy, still in shock, but grinning from ear to ear, turned and dispatched three dozen Red Caps with a flick of her wrist and a beautiful alto note.

CHAPTER 18

As they crept further into the cave, the footing became surer, but the boulders grew larger and the space they had to navigate became more cramped. The light from the beach outside faded with each step, and Sean and Trout both used the flashlights on their phones to light the way, but with little results. Above them, Selam floated, offering encouragement and promising them that the portal would be visible soon, but the longer they walked, the less Sean was sure they had made the right choice. Maybe the Devil's Oven cave had been worth the risk, after all.

After what seemed an eternity, they turned a final corner and came to a solid rock wall. As they had traveled farther in, the ceiling grew lower and lower so that by the time they reached the end, Trout was bent over at his waist and still couldn't quite manage to approach the wall. Dünker had long since climbed down from his back and now scurried around his feet, urging him in and grabbing his hand to pull him forward.

"Well," Trout said, "I'm glad we got here finally, but I don't think I'll be a whole lotta help. Can't squeeze myself in there."

"Let me see if I can find the doorway," Sean replied. "Hopefully, it's bigger than this space and you can get through. If not...head back to Brandy?"

"That doesn't sit so well with me. I came here to stick by you," Trout answered. "But you know I'll do what's best. Can't make myself smaller than I am."

Bayard had been tracing his hands along the rock face, trying to sense a crack or opening. Anything that would lead them toward the portal. As a result, he was completely distracted and barely noticed when Selam, who had been hovering overhead, tried to get their attention.

"Friends," she said, quietly at first, then repeating herself more loudly. "I think someone is with us..."

After a moment, her words penetrated Bayard's focus, and as they did, he became aware of a foul stench. Something was rotten. Dead. Decaying. Something that had not been noticeable until they stopped moving and whatever it was caught up to them.

Bayard spun at the wall, looking back the way they came. As he did, Sean, who was still preoccupied with finding the doorway, said without turning, "Do you guys smell something...off?"

What little light was still filtering in from the entrance suddenly grew dimmer, and a silhouette moved into view. A massive shape. Lank. long-limbed. Two red eyes blinked into view as it turned its full attention to them.

"Wendigo," Bayard hissed.

They hadn't run into one of the native terrors since their conflict on the beach of Montauk months ago. It had not been an easy encounter, and they'd barely escaped. They all knew that they were in Wendigo country now. It would be much more difficult to escape the gnashing teeth and insatiable need for flesh. The woodlands were their natural habitat, but there was no doubt that this Wendigo was there for them. Had hunted them down specifically to stop them entering the portal.

Trout reached immediately for his backpack and the Singing Sword that he'd stowed within. Finally, time to see what it could do.

But in the cramped space, he couldn't reach the clasp. He scrambled for it, but it was no use. The only way to reach it would be to go back out where the cave opened up. Back where the Wendigo waited.

Bayard and Sean were behind Trout, blocked from reaching the blade and reaching the Wendigo. They were trapped. Penned in. There was nothing to stop the creature from picking them off one by one.

Out of nowhere, Selam dove at the Wendigo, her luminous wings reflecting what little light there was in the cave. But she was not built for speed, and her size made her no match for her opponent. The Wendigo flailed at the little Aziza for a moment, but she couldn't evade it, and she was quickly held aloft in its talons, the antlers on its head scraping the rock ceiling as it cried in hunger and victory, poised to finish her.

"No!" Sean cried, trying to get past Trout to come to her aid, but the way was too tight. "Selam!"

And then there was another figure behind the Wendigo, even taller. And broader. It grabbed the Wendigo by its neck with one hand and gently plucked Selam from its grasp with the other, setting her free to fly up. It then took the Wendigo and smashed it repeatedly on the rockface on either side, and a few times on the ceiling for good measure. It then tore the antlers from its head and tossed them to the ground.

"Puny Wendigo. Come, little one," a deep ground-rumbling voice said. "You've done your part. Time to go."

Selam fluttered to the outstretched hand, and a massive fur covered head thrust itself forward into the light from the cellphone flashlights. Sean nodded.

"Greenwood," he said, "I'm glad you're here. Thank you."

Trout was staring in wide-eyed awe. This creature dwarfed even him. Bayard, too, looked mildly surprised. Apparently, the Wood-wose were adept at avoiding other Peripherals, too.

"You know my purpose," Greenwood rumbled. "I will take her to safety now. But I have watched you. I would help you if it were allowed. Know that there are more of these Wendigos on the way. Find your portal and go. If you make it back, you will find the refugees gone. Look for us in the North. We'll share a French 75 and breathe free air."

With that, the Sasquatch-like Guardian nestled the Aziza in the crook of his arm and turned toward the exit. He dragged the Wendigo's body behind him, and after a moment, they heard a guttural cry and then a splash. Greenwood had disposed of the creature. But now they knew there were more on the way.

"He was impressive," Bayard said in the following silence.

"Me like him," Dünker added, smiling.

"Wouldn't want to make him mad. What's the hell's a French 75?" Trout said.

"I have no idea. Let's go. We better find this portal," Sean announced. "Five more minutes. If we don't find it, we get out and try another cave."

As he said it, the stench of Wendigo began to drift to them again. This time stronger.

Brandy hadn't moved. She was frozen in place, a war of emotions playing across her face. Ken? Here? How?

"I know it's a bit of a shock," Ken said quickly, hands raised. "I spent a long time back in the sixties just lost. I'd given up. Figured that was it for me. And, you know, it wasn't so bad. I found some shows to perform in. Made some friends. Set money aside for my kids to get. Later. But I just assumed the chronovisor was busted and that meant I was, too. But then I started thinking...what if I could fix it? The visor? And my next thought was how ridiculous that was. I can't change a lightbulb, let along fix a time-travel helmet. But someone else might be able to. If I was stuck, what about those people we'd read about? The other scientists who disappeared?"

The other man had approached and now said, "That's where I come in. Kelvin Cevasco. Pleased to meet you." He held out a hand.

Brandy shook his hand reflexively, still too stunned to speak.

"I worked on the original project," Kelvin offered. "But my prototype was completely destroyed when I got stranded." He paused, staring at Brandy, who was still silent. "She okay?"

"Yeah, she's fine," Ken replied. "Just surprised. Anyway, Brand, turns out that if you start asking questions about a very specific project that nobody knew about back then—well, you find one of the only people who could possibly help. Kelvin."

Kelvin gave a little wave but turned to Ken again when he got no response. "You sure she's okay?"

"Hell yeah," Ken said. "She's a tank. Can take anything. So Kelvin and I took my broken visor, experimented on it, and found the components we needed to make it work. At first, we could only make small jumps. An hour or two to start. Then a week. And eventually bigger and bigger."

"Problem is," Kelvin cut in, "the equipment we had wasn't specifically intended for time travel. There was a lot of hit and miss. But we *think* we have it at a place that's manageable. But we don't know enough yet to understand how what we do affects other things. The whole time-space continuum. Think Doctor Who or Captain Kirk. So, we're trying to make our travel around really important events."

"Like saving your ass today," Ken said. "We've seen what would have happened if we hadn't been here. Not pretty. But look, we need to jump out of here. Clear the way for what happens next. I'd jump to help Sean, but we don't think we can jump to the Fae kingdom. Honestly, we haven't tried, but this is pure science. No magic involved. And that sounds like a very bad idea. So far."

"We're not ruling it out," Kelvin added. "Just not ready for it yet."

"Hang out by the top of the cliff there," Ken said. "You should be good now. The Red Caps are gone. The Hide-Behinds are long gone.

Isn't it weird that alcohol drives them off? That's, like the lamest bad guy to send after us. Grumbles like their drinks."

He and Kelvin shared a laugh, and it was as if Ken only then remembered the bottle in his hand.

"Elmer T. Lee," he declared, holding up the bottle of bourbon. "Criminal to waste it that way, but when you can time travel...well, let's just say I can still find it cheap. Have a slug, looks like you need it."

Robotically, Brandy took the bottle and downed a mouthful.

"Try not to tell the others, yeah?" Ken said, moving a few feet away. "We may need to keep the element of surprise. And like I said, still not sure what the repercussions are. Saving you was worth the risk. Hey! Did you guys get my letter back at the Fulton? About the money and stuff?"

"Yeah, yeah," Brandy said, still visibly stunned. "Pettirosso opened it in front of us. They named a theatre after you."

"I know! Isn't that cool? Look, we gotta go. Taking some risks still being here. Be careful out there. Peace out, Brandy! See you soon. In the funny papers."

Ken winked at her and turned. He and Kelvin flipped some controls on their oddly colander-like helmets, waited for their green shimmering lights to appear, and stepped through. And were gone.

Brandy hadn't moved a muscle. And didn't for quite some time.

Sean was frantically running his hands over the back wall of the cave. The stench of the incoming Wendigos was nearly overwhelming. Bayard felt the time running out and rushed to Sean's side. Sean was singing, sending his light into the stones, looking for cracks, weaknesses, anything. Bayard flicked his wrists and used his blades to explore the tiniest of openings, but nothing was appearing. Nothing glowed. There was no sign of a portal anywhere.

Behind them, Trout had walked a little further toward the

entrance, allowing himself to stand. As of yet, nothing had appeared in the halo of light by the cave opening, but the smell was unmistakable, and the murmurings of the waves had been joined by something...else. Dünker had perched himself on a rock near Trout's head and tapped nervously, watching Trout.

"Guys," Trout called back. "Could use some good news about now. Don't think we have much longer."

"We're trying, Trout!" Sean called back. "Nothing is happening."

"Well, I'm getting ready for some Wendigos over here then."

Trout drew the Singing Sword from his pack, able to reach it now that he'd backtracked toward the entrance. He could get the blade out, but that was about it. Even here, he had no room to swing the sword, and it dangled useless at his side.

"Did you just do something?" Sean called. "What did you just do?"

"Nothing," Trout answered. "Took out the sword, but I still can't swing it, so that's not gonna be a lot of help."

The light at the entrance shifted, was obscured. This time, though, it was not one figure that appeared, but a host of them. It was impossible to tell how many from their shuffling shadows, but it would be a challenge no matter how many there proved to be. One Wendigo had almost taken them down.

"The sword!" Sean cried. "There's a light in the rock. It must be the sword."

Bayard rushed to Trout's side. "Give me the sword," he said. "It's showing us the way. I'll be back before they Wendigos get here. If the portal opens, we'll never see them."

Trout paused, just for a moment, and handed over the sword. As Bayard disappeared with it, Trout reached into his pack again and withdrew the axe Kelphit had made for him all the way back at their first encounter in Montauk. The axe he had thought enchanted, but now was less sure. Axe in hand, he turned to face the approaching enemies.

Sean grabbed the sword from Bayard as soon as he got to the rock face. He held it in both hands, focused every bit of energy he had on it, and began to sing. His clear tenor echoed in the cave, bouncing from rock to rock, magnifying as it did.

Instantly, golden threads of light appeared throughout the stone. Sean redoubled his efforts, and the threads widened. Began to spin, gaining speed as they did. Sean knew what he was seeing. Had seen it in other places. A portal to the Otherworld was opening. The light soon engulfed the entire wall, and a maelstrom of energy crashed and spun in front of them.

"Trout," Bayard called, "get up here. It's happening!"

The entire back of the cave now began to bow inward, pulsing, until it collapsed into a tunnel stretching into what should have been the side of the mountain, but now led somewhere else.

"Dan!" Sean shouted. "Dan!"

He and Bayard turned and saw Trout stopped behind them, his arms resting on the ceiling of the cave a few yards away.

"Hate to say it, friends," he said, a somber look on his face. "I can't fit. That tunnel is even smaller than the wall. And I can't get to the wall."

The sound of the approaching Wendigos was now unmistakable and threatened to drown out their calls to each other.

"I guess I'm the rear guard," Trout said, coming to a decision. "Get Breena, Sean. Get the answers we need. I'll handle these Wendigos. Just close that portal tight behind you." He turned to the little troll. "Dünker, it's time for you to go. Go with Sean. You'll be safe there. You've been a good friend. Go. Be happy. You deserve it."

Dünker shook his head slowly.

"Dünker no go. Stay with Trout. Said I would take care of you. I stay. Trout not be alone. Not for this."

"There's no time!" Trout shouted. "Please, go!" Then quietly, "Please."

But Dünker simply turned to face the cave entrance and didn't speak again.

"Dan!" Sean called again. "Take the sword! You can use it against them!"

"I can't swing it in here, Sean," Trout said, slowly turning toward the oncoming swarm. "Go. Once a Grumble always a Grumble. Love you guys!"

Sean hesitated. How could he leave Trout like this? But so much depended on what they would find beyond the portal.

Bayard grabbed his arm. "We have to go. Now. Or we never will."

His heart breaking, Sean looked back toward Trout a last time. The Montanan took up most of the light filtering from the entrance, but around him now swirled sinewy, lightning-quick shadows.

"Find a way to live," Bayard said, before moving toward the tunnel.

"Just hold on," Sean added. "We'll be back. Fast. Be here."

Sean and Bayard turned, and as they entered the tunnel, it began to close behind them, they heard Trout's voice raised loud and bouncing from stone to stone.

"Montana!" was the last thing they heard before they were swept away, and the cave disappeared.

The lights of the portal continued to whirl around their heads as they stepped forward. Within a moment, it felt as if their feet were no longer touching earth. They floated along, and their stomachs heaved uneasily. Sean remembered how his time travel had felt, and this was very similar. If he had hoped it would be gentler, he was disappointed.

He reached to his left and found Bayard's shoulder there. He gripped it. Tighter than he'd intended, but the knowledge that Bayard, his friend, powerful Peripheral, was still with him gave him strength. Bayard. The last of their fellowship still here. The others. All scattered.

The lights gave way. Slowly. The spinning wound down. The sun-bright beams dimmed. Slightly, and then then they were gone.

Sean opened his eyes. He risked a glance, and Bayard was still there.

They found themselves in the most beautiful glade of golden grass. Tall silver trees reached into the sky almost as high as they could see and swayed in what was the most comforting breeze Sean had ever felt.

In the distance, a white palace shone perfectly. Crenelated. Bristling with grandeur, and beauty, and an otherworldliness that Sean instinctively knew could never come from mankind.

A river flowed through the glade; golden wading birds strutted through the verdant water rushes on the gently rolling banks.

Bayard's eyes shone. Sean remembered that it had been a long time since he had been home, choosing to spend his time alone. Or now with the Grumbles. Sean gripped his shoulder again. Humming under his breath and hoping some of the strength Sean could conjure would find its way to his friend.

Out of the brilliant glow of the palace, three figures appeared. Silhouettes only at first. But they paced quickly toward where Sean and Bayard had appeared. Two women and a man, that was clear, but only that much.

Sean held the Singing Sword loosely at his side, and he heard the gentle snick of Bayard's blades sliding into his hands.

"Now we find out," Sean said.

"Now we find out," Bayard agreed, his eyes grim.

The three figures approaching paused, and as they reached the shade of the first trees of the glade, Sean cried out and Bayard was forced to stop him from running headlong to them. For the three were none other than Odette, Kallan, and...Breena. Three of their original fellowship Peripherals.

Breena. The one he had thought so much of in the past weeks. The one he loved. The one he doubted. The one he needed.

But something was wrong. Kallan, strong, fearless Kallan, was listing to one side. He seemed barely able to keep up with the others. He shuffled, limping. Bayard gasped when he saw that he was shackled. His hands and feet in chains.

Breena, too, seemed…off. As she drew closer it became clear that she had been traumatized. He beautiful blond hair had been shorn, nearly to her scalp. Her black fighting clothes that she'd adopted after their first battles, were torn and, in places, sliced. Her face was bruised. The gleam in her brilliant blue eyes nearly extinguished.

Odette, however, strode proudly between the other two, lengths of chain in her left hand keeping them close to her. In her right hand, she carried her spear. The spear Kallan had carried when she disappeared, captured by the Dullahan, only to return it to her when she was rescued.

"Sean," Breena said quietly when she saw him. "No, no, no."

Kallan raised his battered face but couldn't speak. Tears streaming from his eyes.

But it was Bayard, not Sean, who stepped forward.

"Odette, my sister," he said. "What have you done?"

CHAPTER 19

In the cave, Trout turned to Dünker.

"Find a crevice somewhere in the rocks, buddy," he said. "Close your eyes and wait until everything is quiet. I never wanted you to get hurt. I never would have brought you if I'd known."

But he knew his words were falling on deaf ears. The troll smiled at him, wiped his nose on his sleeve, and threw an arm around Trout's neck.

"Dünker say he stay with Trout. So Dünker stay. Friends no leave friends."

Trout shook his head. The Wendigos were almost upon them. He hefted his axe, pausing to take in the bear totem that Kelphit had bound to it all those months ago.

"Stay behind me, then, buddy," Trout said.

The Wendigos rounded the corner in front of Trout. There were at least ten of them, pushing each other in their hurry to get to the lone defender where they had expected to find a stouter defense. Their ash-grey skin sagged and looked ready to slide off of them. Their long yellow fangs snapped in anticipation of the flesh they would soon feast upon. Greenish talons swept the air in front of them. Brittle antlers scraped across the stone above them.

Trout knew there was nothing he could do against these numbers. At least Sean and Bayard had made it through. The glow of the portal had flared and then disappeared. He'd done everything he could.

The first Wendigo reached him, and Trout dodged a swipe of the talons and answered with a full-bodied swing of the axe. The axe that deflected off of the leering face. It was useless.

"Not good, not good," he said to himself. He readied himself to swing again, but it would do nothing. He had run out of ideas. And time.

But before the next blow could land, a massive cave-shaking voice came from over his shoulder.

"No touch Trout," it shouted. "Friends no leave friends."

Trout spun around and found himself dwarfed by a figure behind him. While Trout was tall and brushed the top of the cave, this creature was tall *and* broad, filling the entirety of the space. It dwarfed Trout. In every way.

And as Trout gaped at it, the creature gently put the Montanan aside, stared deeply at him, and spoke again.

"Trout called me friend," it said, and smiled. "Dünker never let Trout down. Trolls have secrets. This our secret."

Dünker had somehow morphed, shifted, into the towering figure. The running nose was gone, the flesh a healthier shade of green. But the eyes were the same kind, worried, loyal eyes.

Dünker moved faster than Trout could see and took the first Wendigo in a massive fist and, using it as a battering ram, ran blindly into the crowd, smashing them against stones in every direction, leaving them torn apart and crushed as he barreled toward the entrance and the water beyond. The creatures had no hope against the troll turned giant.

He paused to look back at Trout. "Come, buddy, Trout," Dünker called. "Find Brandy. Find Cinder. Dünker like the wolf. Come."

And Trout followed this new Dünker out of the cave and into the blazing daylight.

"What have I done?" Odette said bitterly to Bayard. "What have *you* done, faithless man. You stay in that other world with your human *friends*? If you spent time with your own kind, you would find no surprises here. What *he* is? If he continues as he is, we will never be able to stop him. He. Must. Die. Spare me your reproach. It means nothing. And you, Sean. What took you so long? We were about to give up on you. Not much of a savior, are you?"

"Breena," Sean whispered. "What have they done to you?"

"I'm sorry, Sean," she answered. "I tried to get to you. I spurned the marriage they'd arranged. But they imprisoned me instead of honoring my feelings. My own family. Once I knew what was happening, I wanted to get word to you. But it was too late. They had me. They're my people. I didn't want to believe they were capable. I was wrong. You shouldn't be here. They will kill you. You have to run. They know everything. They're waiting."

"*They* did that to you?" Sean demanded. "Your family? I knew there had to be a reason. I just knew it. But it took so long...No more. I'm done running. What do *you* want, Breena? I need to hear you say it. Do you want to come with me?"

"Yes, Sean. Yes. I was afraid to admit it. But I couldn't ignore it. I've always wanted that. Since the first time I saw you."

"Then let's go," he said. "We'll figure the rest out later. And we're taking Kallan, too. Odette, get out of the way."

"Oh, Sean," Odette spat back at him, "this is our land now. Your powers are nothing to us when we are here. You've come to die and to cover me and my family in glory."

"Yeah, I don't think so," Sean said. "And I don't have time to deal with you. Trout may be dying right now. And all he's ever done is help me. I'm finishing this with you. Now."

He drew the Singing Sword and lifted it high in the air, crying out in a perfect clear note. The blade seemed to come alive. It writhed and rippled with golden light, flames. Sean swung it in an arc and a blast leaped from it, crashing into Odette, who kept her feet only by thrusting her spear deep into the earth at her feet and clinging to it, as a raging wind arose.

Breena and Kallan, though, were suddenly cocooned in beautiful silver globes of light and lifted gently off the ground. With a flick of his wrist, Sean brought them to him and set them lightly down. The globes expanded, and joined to encircle him, too. Gently, it gathered Bayard into it, as well. But Sean was far from done.

He swung the sword wide, allowing its flames to scorch the earth in every direction. Wherever it touched, the beauty evaporated. The gleaming grass and shining trees fell into the earth. Everywhere was laid low and revealed to be dust. An illusion. There was no beauty. No purity. It was all artifice.

"The ugliness inside you is only matched by the shell of a home you claim to value," Sean shouted. "All you have to do is leave us alone. Leave mankind alone. Leave my friends alone."

As they turned to the palace, it was as if an enormous hand was pulling it backwards. The tunnel from the portal returned, but this time, as they stood still, the landscape slipped relentlessly away. The palace retreated. Retreated. And was gone.

"Now you see?" Odette hissed at Bayard. "What have they done? As they destroy their own miserable lands, they destroy ours, too. Look what this one does with one gesture. One small piece of old magic, a sword, and he does to our land what his kind have been doing to their own for too long. They are killing their earth! Stripping it bare. Killing the creatures that share the space with them! And, though we are in the Otherworld, it affects us. Our beloved home. The longer it goes on, the closer we grow to losing...everything. Do you see what they have done? It is too much. Soon it will be beyond us to stop it. Them. Our only hope is to finish them. Claim it all for ourselves. You soft fool."

As the shining world fell away, three more figures appeared. Moving towards them from where the palace had just stood. One on horseback, a whip carving the air above it. Its head carried in its left hand. The Dullahan. As powerful as ever. The next was one fair of hair and dressed in shining white robes, with brilliant blond hair. His bearing was regal. Haughty. And somehow diminished by the company he kept. And the last, taller than the others. Nearly twenty feet tall. It took paces fit for a giant, and seemed to condescend to wait for its companions, showing annoyance while urging them along.

It was Balor with his golden crown of one eye back upon his head, its red jewel constantly scanning the surroundings, throwing a sickly crimson hue wherever it fell. He was enormous, but strikingly handsome, confident.

"That's quite a sword you have there," Balor said, approaching. "The one time you've actually managed to surprise me. I will need to discover who has helped you. But it will do you no good. We're far beyond that now."

Breena stared at the tall fair man in despair. "Father," she said, tears falling on her cheeks. "Do not do this."

The man stared straight ahead, without even a glance at his daughter.

"He does what he must," Balor replied. "He has no choice. He never did. It begins now."

"What begins?" Sean asked.

"War," Balor replied. "And in war there is no room for indecision. Or divided allegiance."

At a nod from Balor, the Dullahan lifted a blade and ran it through Odette's back. She fell without a sound, surprise in her eyes before they dimmed and went out.

"Why?!" Bayard cried. "She was with you!"

"Was she?" Balor said. "She was not always. She had doubts. That is not acceptable. And her death angers you. That says all I need to know."

Sean shouted. A primal sound he had never known could come from him. The sword sung with him now, leveling all it touched. A duet of pure destruction. The entire landscape became a desolation of sand and decay and death. The Dullahan and Breena's father were swept up and away. Neither made a sound.

But Balor remained where he stood. He grasped Odette's spear, still stuck in the ground. He lifted and, with a bitter smile, made to cast it at Sean, but a flick of Bayard's wrist sent a blade flying, catching the spear flush and knocking it from the Fomorian's hand.

"Ever the good pet, eh, Bayard? Good," Balor hissed. "Easy would be boring. So let it be war."

Balor turned then and despite the howling storm Sean had summoned, he walked slowly into the distance, at the same deliberate pace with which he'd arrived. Quickly, he was gone, and the echo of his laughter was all that remained.

"What now?" Bayard asked.

"We go home," Sean said, placing an arm around Breena. He turned to Bayard. "And take this sword away from me. I should never hold that kind of power again. Not unless the world is ending. And maybe not even then."

He watched as Bayard retrieved Odette's spear, stowed it on his back, and placed an arm under Kallan's shoulder. Sean gently took Breena's hand. With Sean's orb of light still encircling them, they turned, and it lifted them gently off the ground, floating back toward the portal.

"We go home," Sean repeated. "We find the ones who mean us harm. And then we burn them all."

Returning through the portal was easier than opening it and they found themselves back in the cave within minutes. They emerged into it with weapons drawn, still surrounded by the cleansing light, hoping that somehow Trout had managed to stay alive. It was silent. The only sound was the gentle lapping of the incoming tide.

Bayard and Sean exchanged a look. There was no sign of Trout or Dünker. And certainly, no Wendigos. What had happened?

Sean extinguished the orbs, and they started out. Darkness settled over them. Bayard led the way toward the entrance. Breena and Kallan went next, Kallan limping badly. He still hadn't said a word. Sean came last, watching behind them for any sign of trouble. Something was not right.

At the entrance, they paused as the darkness of the cave gave way to the brilliant light of the late morning sun. Bayard stopped suddenly. When the others reached him, they understood why.

Trout was standing, knee deep in water, the tiny troll on his back again. He held his axe, and in the eddying water around him floated the remains of a dozen Wendigos.

"My friend," Bayard said quietly, "that axe is mightier than I imagined. I..."

"Trout!" Sean called. "You did it! You don't know how happy we are to see you!"

He ran to give the Montanan a hug and stopped before he reached him. Something in Trout's expression was off. He shivered in the frigid water. His eyes were wide, he still hadn't spoken.

"Dan," Sean continued, "look! We got Breena and Kallan! Are you okay?"

"Fine," Trout answered. "I'm completely fine." His voice was robotic, stilted.

For his part, Dünker clung to Trout and smiled broadly. His nose leaking onto Trout's shoulder.

"Save Trout," he said. "Help friend. My purpose."

Sean looked to Trout who still seemed stunned and gave a quick shake of his head. *Later.*

"What should we do about the portal?" Sean asked. "Now it's been reopened, I'm afraid someone could use it to attack. Us. Lubec. Anything."

"True," Bayard replied. "To leave it unguarded would be inviting problems."

The now little troll pulled on Trout's sleeve and gestured for him to kneel by him.

"Trout is friend. Love Trout," he said quietly. "But think Dünker will stay here. Keep others safe. Lost my well. But can maybe still do good. A new *kildevand*."

"No way, bud," Trout answered, putting a hand on Dünker's shoulder. "You stay with me. Just like you said."

"Trout. You know this right," he said. "You have Eleanor. You always moving. Go here. Go there. But me troll. I made to stay in one place. This good place. Town is near. I like town. And cave needs guarding. This is me. Guard. Thank you for all. You saved Dünker. Believed when me had no one. Come see me sometimes. Share stories of travel. And be friend."

Trout looked to the others for help but found none. He felt how right the little troll was in making this choice, but his heart suddenly felt heavy. He surprised even himself by reaching out and dragging the little creature into a huge bear hug. He tried and failed to hide his tears from the group.

"I'll always visit," Trout swore. Wiping his running nose on his own sleeve. "Friends forever. And if you ever need me, I'll come. You're the best little buddy ever."

Dünker's face lit up. He laughed and capered in a circle. Eventually, he slowed and stopped. And then he turned to the cave and strode back in. He turned once and gave a small, shy wave.

"Now home," he said. "Friend Trout. Dünker love Trout."

"And Trout loves Dünker," Trout said. "Buddies forever."

The little troll disappeared into the cave.

"Let's get up top and find Brandy," Bayard said, gently. "We have a lot to discuss."

As they began their ascent, and left the troll behind, tears fell freely all around. With some difficulty, they managed to get everyone up the cliff trail. As they arrived, they saw the wreckage of the Red

Caps, strewn everywhere. Panic set in and they searched among the dead for a clue as to what happened. Brandy, however, was not to be found. Neither was Cinder.

More worried glances. Bayard called out for Cinder and very faintly they heard a howl in response, echoing through the forest.

"They're at the truck," Bayard excitedly announced, and started in that direction at a run, leaving the others to follow.

When Sean and the others finally caught up to Bayard at the truck, he was on one knee alternately hugging and ruffling Cinder. Brandy leaned against the Bronco looking exhausted. And...something else.

"What the hell happened up here?" Sean said. "You guys look like you saw ghosts."

Brandy looked at Sean but seemed unable to speak. Trout gave her a looking over but found nothing visibly wrong.

"Tell us later. I'm just glad we're all here," Trout said.

"Jotunn?" Brandy finally managed to say.

"I'll tell you that later, too," Trout said. "He's safe. But his name's not really Jotunn. Come back to visit him. Maybe he'll let you in on the secret."

"You really like that little guy, don't you?" Brandy asked.

"More than I could ever express," Trout answered, with another look back in the direction of Gulliver's Hole. "I owe him. I owe him everything."

They climbed into the truck to head back to Lubec. Once on the road, Sean and Bayard filled the others in on what had happened in the Otherworld. The truck fell silent when they recounted the killing of Odette, and no one spoke again until they pulled up to Cohill's.

The school buses were still parked in front of the inn. Kath and Mal were in the small memorial park across the street, watching the tide come in.

But something had changed. The town felt empty. All of them noticed it. The magic was...different. Diminished.

Brad walked up the street and stopped by the truck as they piled out.

"Glad to see you all made it," he said. "And you have some new friends."

"We found what we needed," Sean replied, his arm protectively around Breena. "Have they all left? Something's different."

"They're gone," Brad said with a nod. "The refugees have all gone inland. To the North. The Guardians are leading them."

"I'm sorry," Sean replied. "I know how much they meant to the town. To you."

"It's more important that they're safe," Brad said, staring at the ground. "That's what matters."

"Before they left," Mal said, "more refugees came in. Trying to escape whatever's happening. I've never seen anything like it. More Little People, but others. Elves. Some not-so-pretty guys in red caps. Even some shape shifters. Like the Wullivers. Some others told me they were River Elves. And Forest Elves. Will-o'-the-wisp. Goblins. Even some spirits from beyond. I guess no one feels safe."

"It was beautiful," Brad said. "So many colors and races. So much of what makes Maine so…Maine. One of the last untouched places. But it was heartbreaking, too. Because they were all fleeing. We failed them."

He wandered back down the street, slowly.

"It's a damn shame," Kath said, stepping to Mal's side. "We wanted to help, but somehow I feel like we made it worse."

Sean turned to the others.

"Well, now is our chance to change that. This story isn't over yet. The song's not done. Shall we head to the rooms?" he asked. "We're all exhausted and we need to get Kallan and Breena patched up. And it looks like we have a war to plan. This time we'll take it to them. For the first and last time."

The End

If you enjoyed this book, please take a moment to visit Amazon and provide a short review. Every reader's voice is important for the continued life and growth of a book or series and vital in helping authors find their audience. I appreciate each and every one.

The World of The Peripherals is expanding.

Look for Book One in the *Brethren of the Coast* series soon, *Shallow Water, Deep Lies*. And, of course, Book Five of The Peripherals.

Pre-order *Shallow Water, Deep Lies* at:
https://a.co/d/i38buk7

Keep up to date on all things Peripherals at

www.markaldrich.net

where you can also sign up for a mailing list. Rest assured it will be used sparingly and only for announcements about the books.

Follow me on social media @marktheginger

GLOSSARY

This glossary includes spoilers, so it is best to finish reading first, if you are so inclined.

PLACES

America's Stonehenge - America's Stonehenge actually exists, although I was completely unaware of it until I was driving back to New York City after a summer of performing in Maine. After seeing the road signs and doing some research, I detoured with my wife and daughter to explore. It is a privately owned attraction and archeological site roughly thirty acres in size. It contains a number of large rocks and stone structures, and sits in the town of Salem, New Hampshire. There are many theories as to its origin, although nothing is definitively known.

It was named Mystery Hill until 1982, when it was renamed. "America's Stonehenge" was first used in a news article from the 1960s. There is evidence of human habitation dating back four-thousand years. Most signs lead to it being of indigenous creation using stone tools, rather than European settlers building it.

Previous owner William Goodwin believed that it was proof that Irish Monks had lived in the area before the time of Columbus. However, there has been no archeological evidence of this discovered.

The arrangement of the stones does reflect a knowledge of the astronomical calendar, and there is a large stone table there that could have been used for anything from sacrifices to pressing cider.

It does, in fact, include an alpaca farm.

<u>Maine State Music Theatre</u> - Founded in 1959, Maine State Music Theatre (originally called Brunswick Music Theatre), is one of the preeminent performing arts organizations in Maine. MSMT produces a summer season of four musicals each year at the Pickard Theater on the campus of Bowdoin College. They also produce a concert series and frequently produce in conjunction with other organizations in the state and beyond.

The theatre continues to thrive, and I have had the pleasure of performing there numerous times. It remains one of my favorite theatres.

<u>Monhegan Island</u> - Monhegan lies roughly twelve nautical miles off the coast of Maine in the Gulf of Maine. In 2020, the year-round population was sixty-four. That number has risen with an influx of visitors and transplants brought on by the shut down and the pandemic. It's accessible by scheduled boat service from New Harbor, Boothbay Harbor, and Port Clyde. Visitors' cars are not allowed.

The name Monhegan is derived from the Abenaki term for "Out-to-sea island."

It has long been considered an artist colony. That reputation began in the mid-nineteenth century and was clearly established by the turn of the twentieth century. William Henry Singer was an early artist in residence. Other notable artists through the years include Edward Hopper. George Bellows, and Jamie Wyeth. Today, it continues to draw artists from around the world, and seeing easels set by the hiking trail is a common sight.

Monhegan Island Light sits on the hill overlooking the village. The museum devoted to the island's history is situated next to it.

Monhegan Island Brewing is a family owned and operated brewery near the village and is open April through November.

Cathedral Woods is a popular hiking area and has been the center of a controversy around the creation and placing of small *faerie houses*, with division as to how and when they are appropriate.

Owls Head Lighthouse - One of my favorite lighthouses in Maine, it is an active navigation aid located at the entrance to Rockland Harbor in the town of Owls Head. It is owned by the U.S. Coast Guard. It was added to the National Register of Historic Places in 1978.

It was constructed of granite and brick in 1825 and sits in a thirteen-acre state park. It is a relatively small thirty feet in height but sits atop a tall cliff.

It is also rumored to be one of the most haunted lighthouses in the state. The most commonly experienced spirits are a young girl, a dog named spot, and a Keeper who regularly is seen completing tasks from his time working there.

Lubec, Maine - is a town in Washington County, Maine. It is the easternmost municipality in the contiguous U.S. The 2020 census reported a population of 1,237. It is situated on a peninsula overlooking a harbor.

On a visit there, I noticed a tree trunk in a yard that had been transformed into a gnome village.

West Quoddy Head Light - is located in Quoddy Head State Park, just outside the town of Lubec. It is the easternmost point in the contiguous U.S. and draws visitors to witness the first rays of sunlight. It was constructed in 1808 to guide ships through the

Quoddy Narrows, and currently bears a distinctive red and white striped pattern. It was added to the National Register of Historic Places in 1980.

The surrounding park is 541 acres and includes hiking trails, forests, two bogs, many rare plants, and some of the most striking views I've found in Maine.

While Gulliver's Hole exists, it is a foaming sea pocket and not a cave. Please do not try to access it.

THE CREATURES

<u>Aziza</u> - The Aziza are benevolent spirits from West African mythology. They live primarily in forests and provide helpful magic to hunters. They are sometimes referred to as simply little people, but the winged image is also mentioned in some accounts.

<u>Balor</u> - In Irish mythology, Balor was the leader of the Fomorians, evil supernatural beings who were the adversaries of the Tuatha De Danann. He is described as a giant with one eye, who causes destruction wherever he passes and is often likened to other mythological creatures such as Cyclops. His strength is sometimes compared to the scorching power of the sun. He was considered the most powerful of his kind.

<u>Dünker (Jotunn)</u> - Jotunn is the singular name of a troll/giant species in Scandinavian mythology, the plural being Jötnar. They are often depicted as ugly, with tusks and sometimes cyclopic eyes. I have chosen to blend various troll traditions for the character Dünker. The name, Dünker, is taken from a troll depicted in a folktale from Fosen.

In some traditions, trolls are linked to a specific place. A cave, or bridge, or body of water. The story of the house troll in Somerville, MA is one that was circulated for some time and had its roots in a house that was believed to be haunted. A medium who was hired to investigate, claimed the haunting was the work of a troll who had been guarding a well, his *kildevand,* in what was now the basement of the house. The medium convinced the homeowners to banish the troll in order to restore peace. That action would have left the troll bereft of purpose and a home. Thus, our Dünker and his refuge in America's Stonehenge.

Shapeshifting trolls are also a school of belief in some folklores. I adopted that, as well.

Dullahan - The Dullahan is a creature from Irish folklore. He is described as a headless rider on a black horse. He carries his own head and is often depicted as carrying a whip made from the spine of some unfortunate creature, sometimes believed to be human. The severed head bears a malicious smile that stretches across its entire face, ear to ear. Its skin is ashen and stretched tight across its skull. It bears a stench often described as moldy cheese.

He sometimes is described as driving a black coach and his coming portends an imminent death.

There are many tales of headless riders that can be traced to the Dullahan tradition, including that of The Legend Of Sleepy Hollow and the Green Knight of Arthurian legend.

Gluskabe - Gluskabe is a legendary figure in the Wabanaki peoples, located in Vermont, New Hampshire, Maine, and the Atlantic Canadian regions. Gluskabe is considered a benevolent and powerful figure, with particular dominion over the waters of the region, and introduced fishing nets and canoes among other things to the natives. He possesses great magic and is as tall as the pine trees of the Atlantic Northeast. His influence on the humans serves to teach a balance between mankind and nature.

He is credited with creating and protecting many islands and waterways, including his favorite, Prince Edward Island.

The scene between Brandy and Gluskabe, where she receives gifts from him after answering his questions honestly, is taken from a Finnish folktale, but is reflected in many other traditions worldwide.

<u>Hide Behinds</u> - The hidebehind is a fearsome nocturnal creature from American folklore. They are said to be able to conceal themselves and if someone does lay eyes on them, they quickly shift to hiding behind any nearby object. They use this ability to stalk their prey, often wanderers in the forest, and drag their targets back to their lair to be consumed.

They are reputed to have a violent aversion to alcohol, which made for the scene at the Dispensing Company.

Despite no one being able to see them, they are described as large, shadowy, animal-like figures.

<u>Pukwudgies</u> - is a small human-like creature in Wampanoag folklore. The name translates to "little wild man of the woods that vanishes". They are found in Delaware, Indiana, Massachusetts, and Prince Edward Island.

Legend has it that they are small (two to three feet tall), with large ears, noses, and fingers and grey skin. They can appear or disappear at will. They look remarkably like a porcupine or hedgehog from behind and half-human, half-troll from the front. They are considered mischievous and were once benevolent toward humans but now are best left alone.

<u>Red Caps</u> - Redcaps (sometimes known as Powries), are evil, often murderous, creatures from the folklore of the Anglo-Scottish border. They are known for soaking their headwear in the blood of their victims and are described as goblin-like, with prominent teeth, long fingers, eyes that glow red, and wearing iron boots while wielding large pikes. They are more normally considered solitary creatures, but for the purposes of the events in Beyond Darkness, I have altered that behavior.

They are sometimes referred to as Red Comb and Bloody Cap.

<u>Wendigo</u> - The Wendigo is a cannibalistic monster from the mythology of the North American Algonquian tribes. They are said to possess humans and crave eating human flesh.

They are reported to be tall, with emaciated features and gray skin. Often, they are depicted as having antlers atop their heads. They have sharp claws and yellowed fangs. Their presence often brings with it a foul stench.

In many traditions, Wendigos are symbolic of insatiable greed.

<u>Woodwose</u> - The Woodwose is often referred to as "the wild man of the woods" and appears as a mythical figure in art and literature of medieval Europe. The Woodwose is a human figure covered entirely in hair or fur. They appear in many artistic depictions, including in Canterbury Cathedral. Tolkien referred to a race of wild men called "Woses" in his writing.

They are frequently compared to satyrs or fauns.

I chose to depict them as benevolent guardians. While they are not comparable to the Sasquatch/Bigfoot/Yeti traditions, I chose to make them in league with each other.

<u>The Wullivers</u> - The shape-shifting family from Scotland is based on one of my favorite folkloric creations. In the Shetland Islands of Scotland, a Wulver is benevolent take on the werewolf legends. Wulvers have human bodies with wolf heads. Sometimes they are described as shapeshifters, sometimes not, but the constant is that they are kind, patient, sedate, and helpful.

TIME TRAVEL

<u>Timestriders</u> - The concept of the Timestriders is purely my own. I researched quite a bit to find time travel folklore to suit my narrative. I was not successful. The first instance where I didn't find the mythology or folklore that filled the role I was looking for. I enjoy the research aspects of my books, but this time came up empty and created my own folklore. I enjoy the idea of very rare time hopping Fae. I hope you do, too.

Chronovisors - Interestingly, the chronovisor *is* an actual device. Whether it worked or not is an entirely different matter. The visor is said to give the wearer the ability to see through time. A book published in 2002 by a Vatican priest, claims that the device was real. It was reportedly developed by a Benedictine monk, a famous physicist, and a former nazi scientist. Supposedly, the team was able to chronicle many significant events of the past. The researchers were active on the project in the 1960's and 1970's, and though the claims are dubious, some of those involved insisted the device was real and functioned.

Conspiracy theories swirl around the chronovisor, including claims that it was deemed dangerous by the Vatican and CIA and hidden to prevent it doing any lasting damage.

ARTIFACTS

The Lorg Mór - The legendary weapon of The Dagda, a powerful Irish god associated with wisdom, the arts, and fertility. The club is known for its dual nature: the ability to both kill and heal.

Tishtrya's Mace - this mace was wielded by the benevolent Persian God Tishtrya and was used to create lightning and tornadoes.

The Singing Sword of Conaire Mór - a legendary Irish sword, the Singing Sword was said to resonate with a magical song, granting the wielder enhanced abilities. It appears in Irish and Scottish folktales and frequently favors use by bards.

Acknowledgments

No author is an island. We plow forward through the help of family and friends, colleagues, and collaborators. The list of those for this book is long, and I am deeply appreciative.

Once again, I begin with my family. My brother, Stephen Aldrich, and sister, Cindy Vollmer, have been sounding boards, cheerleaders, critics, publicists, and, above all, friends. I can't imagine this book, or any of my books, coming to fruition without them. Stephen, in particular, fielded many phone calls and emails about this book and always responded with wise advice.

Thanks, also, to my father. He introduced me to reading very early in life, sharing favorites of his long before I was of an age to appreciate them fully. Somehow, though, I found something in them to inspire me, beginning a lifelong fascination with storytelling. He's not here to see my books being published, but I know he would have been thrilled. Somehow, somewhere, he knows. My very own Peripheral.

Thank you to my mom. I know she *knew* I had a flashlight under the covers to read by long after I should have gone to sleep as a child, but she let me read on. She took me to the store to get the latest comic books and to the bookstore where she would let me roam and discover and dream. Look where it led. Thank you doesn't seem enough. She was always eager to let me imagine. I do so still because of her.

I'm also grateful to the many theatre artists with whom I've collaborated. They inspire and motivate me, and all of them have played a part in bringing me to this point. Theatre is a collaborative art. Writing can be very solitary. But the creativity that surrounds me on stage, inspires me when I sit in front of my computer.

Teachers. They impact us in so many ways and for our entire lives. I renew my thanks to three outstanding teachers who, to this day, inspire and encourage me—Ken Link, Brian Nelson, and Tom Watson. All were ahead of their times, and we students knew and were grateful. The simplest encouragement can give students wings. I remember them giving me mine.

Amy Gillespie has become a vital part of my author process. Thank you for your keen eye and tackling these manuscripts with intelligence, humor, and alacrity. Your willingness to stick with these, and me, is a gift I can never repay.

Profuse thanks to Chris Sorensen for his formatting and his cover design. Once again, he was able to create something that so wonderfully captures the tone of the book. He is a magician. I am grateful.

Gretchen Douglas, proofreader extraordinaire, once again provided invaluable insight both grammatically, logically, and thematically. She is a boon to anyone fortunate enough to work with her.

A heartfelt thank you to my beta readers, who took this latest venture seriously and offered excellent ideas, corrections, suggestions, and encouragement. Stephen Aldrich, Cindy Vollmer, Robin Lee-Thorp, Amy Gillespie, Jennifer Evans. Thank you is not nearly enough.

Once again, I single out two individuals for special thanks, Nick Sullivan, and Chris Sorensen. From practical help to encouragement to ridiculous banter via text or over a nosh and beer, they have been invaluable. Not just helpful, but friends and part of a burgeoning author network. Thank you.

Without doubt, my biggest thanks are reserved for my wife, Jennifer, and our new daughter, Stephania. Jennifer has encouraged me throughout, pushing when needed, handholding just as often. Stephania has opened my eyes to all the possibilities still surrounding us. The gift of being able to watch her grow and discover the world is the most magical journey I've ever taken. She's the sweetest. She's the smartest. She's the Nugget.

Lastly, I thank you, the readers, for taking another journey with me. I've always told stories, whether on a stage, a screen, or a page. None of it would have been possible without people willing to come along. People like you. Thank you for loving stories. Thank you for sharing mine.

About the Author

Mark Aldrich was born in Massachusetts and raised in Virginia. Most of his adult life he has made New York City his home while traveling extensively as an actor and singer. He has appeared in television, film, and theatre, including Broadway and many of the world's most famous stages. However, some of his favorite performances were given in village pubs late at night on the wild West Coast of Ireland.

Mark has written extensively for web publications, periodicals, and industry journals. After helping to tell others' stories on stage, he decided to commit some of his own to the page. *The Peripherals* marks his debut novel and combines his love of history, travel, folklore, music, and his decades-long knowledge of the inner workings of live theatre and the artists working there.

Please feel free to follow and keep in touch at markaldrich.net and @marktheginger on Instagram and Twitter.